D1277172

Shooting Star

3 1705 00233 7159

Shooting Star

RODMAN PHILBRICK

ST. MARTIN'S PRESS
NEW YORK

NORTHWEST BOOKMOBILE CENTER

STATE LIBRARY OF OHIO
SEO Regional Library
Caldwell, Ohio 43724

Copyright © 1982 by Rodman Philbrick
For information, write: St. Martin's Press, 175 Fifth Avenue, New York, N.Y. 10010
Manufactured in the United States of America

Library of Congress Cataloging in Publication Data

Philbrick, Rodman.
  Shooting star.

  I. Title.
PS3566.H474S5   813'.54   81–16710
ISBN 0–312–71757–1   AACR2

(I Can't Get No) Satisfaction
© 1965 ABKCO MUSIC, Inc.
All Rights Reserved
Used by Permission

10 9 8 7 6 5 4 3 2 1
First Edition

82-21230

ACKNOWLEDGEMENT

The author would like to thank Jerry Duberstein, Frank Coffey, Pamela Dorman, and Lynn Harnett for their help in developing this story.

TO LYNN

Shooting Star

Manhattan

She woke up alone. In the dream he had been there, curled against her, his face lost in the dark penumbra of sleep. She stretched languidly, arching her body against satin sheets, wondering idly who he was meant to be.

The dream had aroused her, gathering heat, but she decided to do nothing about it. Better to let it charge and intensify, for tonight she would need the strength.

She put her long, slender legs to the carpet and stood up. At the touch of a luminous switch the drapes began to slide back, drawn floor to ceiling across a wall of tinted glass.

Ronnie Garrik pressed her hands against the cool pane as she gazed out over the city. Already the lights were beginning to blink on like the jewels of some fantastic dragon. Colored lights moved on the Hudson, gliding over the surface of the water.

The view was intoxicating. There was always something new to discover, some shape that had previously escaped her. She even enjoyed the slight vertigo moving like a seductive whisper in the back of her head.

And the whisper said, *Tonight.*

A buzzer rang. She ignored it. Not until the last blush of the sunset had faded and the evening star begun to glimmer did she moved dreamily toward the door.

"I know a thing or two about the weather," said Sergeant Piezer. "And I know a thing or two about mobs. If it happens to rain we could have trouble, am I right?"

On Park Avenue the fog that had drifted in from the harbor thickened into a drizzle. Sergeant Piezer stood in the portico of the Waldorf-Astoria, sipping from a mug of hot coffee and surveying the barricades as he conversed with the bored young patrolman who was assisting him.

"Am I right?" he repeated. The patrolman shrugged.

"It's like this. You've got your crowd, see. Celebrity freaks, autograph hounds, photographers, and then you've got your nut element."

The sergeant gestured with his coffee cup, intent on the stentorian sounds of his own voice. He did not notice when the patrolman rolled his eyes.

"The nut element is what we've got to look out for," he continued. "The rain don't discourage the nuts, it just makes 'em mad. I guess they're thinking, what few of 'em have actual brains, that once they get wet they're damn well going to get close enough to touch one of the *luminaries.*" The sergeant rolled the word around his tongue, as if it had special significance the patrolman could not possibly comprehend. "They simply got to make a dash for the *luminaries,* and that's when we got to smile for those television cameras and pretend what nice guys we are and keep back the nuts without actually breaking their waterlogged heads. Heads can get busted later, in the dark."

"They don't look crazy to me," said the patrolman. The several thousand people encamped behind the barricades looked docile enough. There had been some jostling for space along the rails earlier in the day, but the sergeant had resolved that with a few choice words and the expert placement of his small, lead-weighted billy club.

But that was before the weather broke. Now the sergeant shook his head and frowned. "Plenty of nuts out there. Don't know enough to come in out of the cold and wet. Am I right?"

"Anything you say, Sarge." It was easier to agree. He listened to the drone of the older man's voice, nodded when appropriate, and looked fretfully at the darkening sky.

It began to rain.

Jade Gustave, Ronnie's agent, arrived with flowers. He was accompanied by two strangers. Ronnie knotted the sash of her silk kimono and looked at Jade quizzically.

"They're from Equity," he explained, introducing his companions. "Sammy and Charles. Charles is stage makeup. Sammy is the decal lady I was telling you about."

"Sure. I'd forgotten."

Sammy was a diminutive woman with china doll features. She was dressed bizarrely: stiletto heels, a skintight black jumpsuit with chromed zipper running from crotch to left breast. She wore a decal of a heart upon her cheek. Her androgenous companion, who appeared to be slightly stoned, wore oversize horn-rimmed glasses and carried a bulky makeup kit.

"I'm just up," said Ronnie, leading them into her suite. "No conversation please. Not for a while."

Jade smiled. If she had slept he knew she would be okay. She would be fine. He issued instructions in a low voice, rang for hot coffee, and soon had Ronnie seated at her vanity, bathed in the bare yellow light.

"Gown delivered?"

She nodded. "A knockout, Jade. Glove." she said, knowing he would understand her verbal shorthand.

Ronnie looked into the mirror as the kit was unpacked, but it was hard to focus. The surface of the mirror shifted, and yet she knew it was only sleep, or rather the waking from it, that made her eyes blurry.

One of the dreams fluttered in, the reoccurring one about the empty cabin and the mountain of ice. She wanted to tell Jade about it—he was always interested in her dreams—but the makeup artist was turning her chin gently, a small brush poised, and she lost the sense of it.

The coffee arrived. Jade touched the artist's hand—Charles? Or was it Sammy?—and said, "Let her drink this. We've got plenty of time yet."

"Thanks, darling." She let the aroma steam up, delicious and new.

"All the time in the world," he said.

The steam rose in billows, giving the illusion of moving clouds to the enclosed space. He inhaled and felt the hot moisture pass into his lungs. Too much smoke, he thought, he would have to cut down, once this was over. The hot water circulated with luxurious undulation, easing his tense muscles. It had been a grueling tour and he was glad it was almost done.

One of the twins was soaping his chest.

"Oh, Zach," she sighed." You're just too bee-*oo*-tiful for words."

The other was pearl diving. Or something like pearl diving. He felt her mouth encircle his big toe. Tongue tease. It tickled, but he tried not to squirm.

"Doesn't she ever come up for air?" he asked.

"Nah. She's half mermaid."

He was about to ask which half but decided not to confuse the issue. He'd been introduced to the pair by a concert promoter in San Diego. They were identical twins and billed themselves, in groupie slang, as a bookend act. So far he liked what he'd seen of it. The mermaid was fishing around between his legs and he twisted sideways involuntarily. What was making him so damn ticklish all of a sudden?

He reached blindly behind him and pressed a button. The door opened immediately.

"What can I get you, Zach?"

"All set here, Douglas. What's the word on the fucking headwinds?"

"No problem. We've increased airspeed. ETA is now seven-twenty P.M. That still cuts it tight, so I radioed ahead for an escort. That should get us through traffic. And I know you like the sirens and the flashing lights," he added, grinning.

"Great. Thanks, Doug."

Zachary Curtis sank back into the churning water, content. The hectic pace of the touring life had its compensations. The combination of altitude, hot tub, and bookend act was beginning to get interesting. One of the twins was licking the tender spot under his chin and the other . . . he sighed as the steam rose around him. Yes.

Tonight.

Zach heard a sputtering sound and felt a splash of hot water. The mermaid had come up for air. He reached for her.

"Come a little closer, honey," he said. "And let me show you how the other half lives."

John Lloyd Talbot cradled the telephone and smiled. If what he'd just learned was true, and he was reasonably certain it was, then the cake was iced. As he had promised her it would be.

He touched the intercom. "Send my driver around, please. Security entrance. I'll be ready in thirty minutes."

Time enough for a visit to what he deprecatingly referred to as the "shrine." Actually the old Wurlitzer was his one superstition: No record was released by Liberty without first passing the jukebox test. He unlocked the door to the adjacent room and flipped on the green-shaded overhead light. It illuminated the billiard table where he frequently relaxed by experimenting with impossible cushion shots. To one side the juke glowed dimly on squat legs, lights flickering like some object come down from space, or so he liked to imagine. It was at once his temple and his treasury.

He slipped two bits into the slot, took a deep breath, and punched a three-hit combo. The machine coughed, sighed, sent an arm tracking out to pull a disc and flip it neatly onto the revolving platter. The hiss of the needle. And then, like a first tentative heartbeat, the bass thumped up from below the region of hearing and he began to fingerpop, snapping his fingers neatly, feeling the music pulse.

> *orphan child*
> *don't pit-ty me*
> *sha-hooting star*
> *will set me free*

He sang along with it, bent over the old Wurlitzer so that his face was made golden by the neon light, snapping his fingers and tapping his feet and twisting his shoulders in syncopated time like a boy on the corner, singing his heart out on a Saturday night.

Jade eyed her critically but couldn't keep the smile from his eyes. "You are exquisite," he said, and then paused in a characteristic pose, fingers curled under his chin, hand cupping the opposite elbow. "The pendant?" he asked.

"Do you think I should? You know how Kyle feels about—"

"Never mind that," said Jade firmly. "It was his to give. He gave."

She went back to the dressing rooms barefoot, carrying the heels lightly in one hand. The diamond pendant was in the vanity drawer. She held it first to the light, then laid it gently in the hollow of her neck. The clasp snapped easily. Jade was right, of course. The star, trailing sparks of diamonds, was perfect.

Kyle would be watching. He could make what he liked of it.

In the corner of the vanity mirror she saw the lacquered enamel box, the latest of John Lloyd's splendid gifts. Ronnie picked it up, marveling at the cool touch.

She pried off the lid and looked speculatively at the crystalline white powder. It was tempting, to be sure, but she clicked the lid firmly back in place. Tonight of all nights she wanted to be straight.

"Ronnie? They're waiting, darling."

She hurried back to the salon, Kyle's pendant cool against her throat.

The luminaries, as the sergeant called them, began to arrive shortly after the camera crews finished their meter readings. The crowd surged forward, drawn by the approaching headlights. They pressed up against the barricades as the gleaming limousines glided into the spotlights. Two footmen in livery, keenly aware of the cameras, pulled open each door with a flourish. They were protected from the intermittent rain by an elaborate awning.

The luminous quality of a particular celebrity could be accurately gauged by the reaction of the crowd. A popular game show host, beaming as he exited his limousine on the arm of a rented blonde, got oohs and ahhs and his name rippling through the throngs. A svelte model, known more by face and figure than by name, got wolf whistles and ribald comments. A recording executive, a god in his own domain but unknown to the public, was greeted by silence until, in the hush, the voice of the television announcer carried his name and position and a few cheers went up in recognition.

But when a real luminary appeared the barricades shook and Sergeant Piezer was forced to shout himself hoarse. He was right, of course. The rain made it worse. But the sergeant, wise as he was in the ways of crowd control, was not prepared for the arrival of Ronnie Garrik.

She saw the twin beams of light sweeping across the underside of the clouds. And then, from far down the avenue, she saw the mob.

"I'll be damned," said Jade softly. His eyes widened at the sea of people surging behind the barricades. Ronnie squeezed his hand. She knew this scene by heart—the push, the shove, the frantic cry of hysteria. Jade knew it, too, but he'd never liked it.

"They'll eat that guy alive," he said, with an air of wonder.

Ronnie followed his gaze. Up ahead the mob had swarmed over one end of the barricade and buried a limousine. A lanky figure in a white linen suit was trying to extricate himself from the wave of flesh.

"It's Zach!" cried Ronnie.

"I believe it is," said Jade. "Good lord, I think he's *enjoying* himself."

Zach Curtis was holding both hands high, grinning as the police came to his rescue. He didn't seem particularly displeased by the crush of fans who were trying to get a piece of him. Ronnie and Zach had been lovers, years before. She'd been on the road with her first band and he was on the lounge circuit. Now they were in competition for the Goldie. Friendly competition, or so she hoped.

Now her Rolls was coasting silently to the curb and the liveried attendants were rushing to open her door. The mob, temporarily restrained by the police, took a collective breath. Ronnie stepped out ahead of Jade and ducked under the awning. A light mist was falling and the bright lights made jewels of the dewdrops in her dark hair.

And then the sound came over her like a warm wind. It was her name, distorted by thousands of open mouths, until it lost all connection to its source and became a *thing* that cried out to her.

Rrrrrooooooooonnnnnnnniiiiiieeeeeeee. Like the wind.

The television cameras dollied in and she struck a pose, flashing her brilliant smile. The white gardenia made a striking contrast to her raven hair and the lights illuminated the gold-leaf design on her cheek. A gold star trailing sparks.

"-onnie Garrik! -ooting Star!" The announcer's voice was swallowed by feedback, lost in the roar of the crowd. The barricades trembled.

A gust of wind ruffled her translucent gown and the paparazzi got a clear shot of her long, elegant legs. Backlit, the diaphanous fabric was rendered translucent, and her nipples, barely covered, stood out under the gauze like insistent fingertips.

The crowd roared.

"We'd better run!" Jade hissed in her ear. A moment later the barricades came down, the screams pitched higher in intensity, and a great mass of arms and hands and eager, wild faces converged on them.

"Run!"

A squadron of security guards broke through, pushing back part of the mob, then charged for the door. Her name was being chanted in ritual cadence as she was carried down the carpet, parting the sea of people who, in their ecstasy, longed to touch her. Or maybe, she thought, as two guards lifted her clear off the ground and spun her into the relative safety of the Waldorf, they want to tear me apart. . . .

He was just executing the Windsor knot on his best tie when the door opened. In the nine-year history of Liberty Records no one had ever opened the door to his private suite without first being cleared through the outer offices. But the two men, dressed in similar conservatively cut gray suits, entered without hesitation.

John Lloyd Talbot cleared his throat. It was the only nervous habit he allowed himself. He met the eyes of both men.

"I'm afraid you won't be going out this evening, Mr. Talbot."

"No?" He pressed back his lapels, dusted a speck of lint from the jacket. He knew who they were and why they had come, but he preferred to let them go through the motions.

"We have a certain matter to discuss, sir." There was nothing obsequious about the way the man in the steel gray suit said "sir."

"Yes," said John Lloyd. He placed one hand carefully into his trouser pocket. "Yes, I suppose we do."

When Jade had recovered his composure, keenly aware that Ronnie had never lost hers, they entered the great hall.

"This is it," said Ronnie softly. Her arm was entwined with Jade's and he squeezed her reassuringly.

Cones of multicolored light moved through the shadows, focusing on the stage area with its bright facets of commercial glitter and oversized props. The audience here was a different beast from the mob in the street. Most were discreet enough not to approach Ronnie, but as the usher ran interference for them she heard her name passing from lip to lip, and the words *shooting star* echoing in her wake.

"Smile, darling," Jade whispered. "Smile until it hurts."

All the equipment the media could muster was aimed at them. Monitors caught her from a half-dozen angles, zeroing in for a shot of the blazing gold star on her cheek. She walked down the aisle with the natural elegance of an Egyptian goddess, serene and regal. Most of those in attendance were connected, in one way or another, to the business end of rock 'n' roll and the sense of envy that rippled through the spacious ballroom was nearly palpable.

"You're looking gorgeous, baby," she told Jade. He grinned

back, but he knew whom the eyes were for, and why the cameras were trained on them.

"Hot stuff, Ronnie!" Zach Curtis stood up and kissed her, well aware that the image was being carried to fifty million viewers. The show's director, intent on building suspense with his pan shots, had seated them together.

"Great to see you, baby." Their tongues had touched in the kiss, message received.

Zach had long, fair hair, a dazzling smile, and his pianist's fingers glittered with the Indian jade rings he collected. Close friends like Ronnie knew he had a secret melancholy streak. But tonight he was full of intense energy and his kiss had been electric.

"Beats me where Talbot has gotten to," said Zach, indicating the vacant seat at the table. "The old boy must be backstage goosing the showgirls or something."

"Unlikely, to say the least," said Jade, arching an eyebrow. He and Talbot were roughly the same age and he disliked hearing him referred to as "old boy." "He'll be along presently, I'm sure."

"Don't mind me, Jade, old boy," said Zach. "I'm nervous is all. Here, let's drink up."

The Waldorf had staffed the mezzanine with waiters and a slender man with Valentino looks brought them an iced bottle of Dom Perignon.

Zach clicked his crystal glass to hers. "To a lovely lady." And then he added, "And may the best man win."

Ronnie laughed and the star on her cheek shone like a golden promise. "Not a chance, baby. This one is mine. All mine."

Then the house lights dimmed. On stage the cameras dollied in, red lights blinking. Figures hurried about, as if in a panic, or trying to start one, and the screen monitors began to glow with the flickering, hypnotic light of television.

Staring into the bland eye of the monitor, Ronnie remembered another stage, another night . . .

West Texas

1

The little girl with the midnight black hair and the sea blue eyes frowned in concentration. Everybody was watching her. She liked that, and she knew it made her daddy happy. She gripped the banjo with all her might, looked up at the enormously tall man with the fiddle tucked under his chin. He smiled and she began to pluck the banjo strings.

A moment later he came in with the fiddle and she was swinging to the rhythm, plucking the tune on her banjo, delirious with joy.

Swinging.

In West Texas, in 1956, swing was still the thing. Not the swing of Benny Goodman, or the Dorsey bands, or Ellington, but the lively, countrified swing of Bob Wills and his Texas Playboys. Light, easy music based on the rhythmic folk tunes of the West, it was a jazzy evolution of barn dancing. It was *made* for dancing, for high bliss foot-stomping, and on a hot August night at the Grange Hall in Lubbock, Texas, Larry Garrik and the Palamino Boys were swinging.

And the crowd, swigging booze and beer out of paper cups, was hopping. The Palamino Boys were a bald impersonation of Bob Wills's band, and Larry Garrik made no bones about it.

"Old Bob is busy with radio and TV. He ain't got no time for the little folk no more, and we aim to take up his slack," he would drawl as he solicited engagements at the numerous dance halls in rural Texas.

Garrik was a tall fellow with the rangy build, sun-drenched

3

complexion, and ready smile of a man who was used to rough work and hard play. He worked weekdays for the railroad, inspecting desolate stretches of track, but he meant to carve out a place for himself in the world of country music. He would start out imitating Wills—"taking up his slack"—but after he'd earned a little money he intended to develop a style of his own.

"I got me a hard drivin' sound in the back of my head," he would say. "And one of these days I'm gonna cut loose and let everyone hear it."

Larry Garrik was open and friendly, full of ambition and good intentions, and his band was booked most weekends. Some nights they drove two hundred miles, played until dawn began to crack along the enormous Texas horizon, then packed up and drove home.

And there were those who thought Garrik's imitation was nearly as good as the original. True, Larry Garrik didn't quite have Bob Wills's flair on the fiddle, but he was younger and his lack of experience was supplanted by an excess of energy. It was obvious he played from the heart. And if the Palamino Boys weren't quite up to the Playboy's snuff, well, they surely liked to stomp some, and they kept the beat.

Things were looking pretty good to Larry Garrik in August of 1956. From the stage, where he urged the band on with the rhythmic cadence of his bow, he could look out into the dimly lit Grange Hall. His pretty wife was out there somewhere. Probably dancing—Mae Ann loved to kick up her heels. And there was his little boy, Jackie, still in diapers. It seemed the boy could sleep through anything, even the Palamino Boys at full stomp. He knew exactly where his daughter Ronnie, barely four years old, blessed with the most beautiful pair of big blue eyes he'd ever seen, was —backstage with Alice Chilton, the banjo player's wife, who had taken a shine to the little girl.

"She's got the smile of an angel, Lawrence Garrik. What's a devil like you doing with an angel?" Alice had asked as she bounced his giggling daughter on her broad knees.

Oh, Mae Ann loved her, too, there was no doubt about that,

but Mae Ann hadn't quite grown up herself. Larry was sure she would, eventually. For now, let her kick up her heels and get the wildness out of her system. Later, when he had a better band and maybe a radio show of his own, they'd settle down and make a real family of it. Yes, there was time enough for that.

Without pausing, the band kicked into a jazzed-up version of "Tumbleweed," and as he continued to search the dark corners of the hall for a sign of his wife, Larry reflected on the essential difference between his baby boy and his little girl. Jackie seemed to be sleeping his life away, although in truth his life had barely begun, while Ronnie had been brimfull of energy right from the start. It had been impossible to keep that child in a crib; turn your eyes away for an instant and she had scrambled over the edge with the agility of a monkey. She was delighted by the smallest things, a broken rattle an old Navajo woman had given her by the road-side one day, or that foolish armadillo he had roped to a stake out behind the barn. One day he'd caught her stirring up a nest of red ants, bent over, poking with a stick, her little bottom perked out like an exclamation point. Miraculously, she'd not been bitten. Why, right at that moment she was probably running Alice Chilton ragged, though Alice seemed to enjoy it.

And sure enough, later that evening when the crowd had thinned—there was still no sign of Mae Ann—Ronnie broke away from Alice and came bounding on stage, her long dark curls flying as she made a beeline for her daddy and locked her arms around his knees.

When Larry picked her up and whirled her around the audience cheered. Ronnie grinned with such obvious delight that Larry set her down and brought out the half-sized banjo he'd fashioned for her.

"Listen up, folks. This little gal of mine has learned herself a tune."

The banjo was nearly as big as she was, but Ronnie didn't hesitate as her father began to pick out the melody of the old standard. She bit her lip in concentration, formed her pudgy fingers on the fretboard, and strummed the chords he'd taught her. And when he picked up the tempo and the rest of the Palamino Boys joined in, Ronnie kept pace, instinctively bobbing her head to the beat.

The Yellow Rose of Texas
Is the only gal for me

When it was over Larry picked her up and waltzed her off the stage into the waiting arms of Alice Chilton, amidst the raucous laughter and cheering whistles of the crowd.

"Why, hell, Larry," someone called out. "You got yourself a million-dollar baby!"

The warm touch of hands, the bright smiles, the yellow lights, the soft bosom of Alice Chilton, who rocked her to sleep, these were the only fond memories of her childhood.

2

The static of the radio, the scratch of the fiddle, and the gurgle of whiskey in the jar. It was the same thing each evening. Already, at seven years of age, Ronnie could anticipate her father's moods.

Each afternoon she ran from the school bus to the front porch, where Alice Chilton waited, rocking in the glider, shucking green peas or corn, or whatever fresh thing had come from her garden. The Garriks lived on the outskirts of Lubbock, where it was still possible to farm a little, where the ravenous sprawl of the city had not yet taken over the open landscape.

Soon enough, thought Alice, one eye on the encroaching skyline, soon enough. Now she looked to the girl who bounded up the steps to her, a hopeful smile illuminating her face. For the best part of six months Ronnie's first question had been, "Is my mom home yet?"

To which Alice would reply, in her slow drawl, "No, child, she's not."

Now the question remained unspoken, and Ronnie had come to understand that her mother would never be home again. *Flew the coop* was the phrase she had heard her father use, and she imagined Mae Ann spreading invisible wings and flying off into the hot summer sky, an exotic, iridescent bird of the passing season. With that flight her father's perpetual grin had faded.

Little Jack and Ronnie needed looking after, and Alice Chilton, whose youth and beauty had been squandered by sharecropping, and whose ample bosom and generous heart had mothered half the neighborhood, came by to see them off to school. She returned each afternoon to greet them with a crushing hug. It was her belief that home and heart should be made indistinguishable, especially where children were concerned.

Larry Garrik's kids did not suffer from a lack of attention or compassion, not so long as Mrs. Chilton was around—they got more of it, probably, after their mother left.

It was Larry himself who bore the brunt of the abandonment. He quit the band and went to work full time for the railroad. At night, with his children in bed, he tuned in the old console radio to the live shows broadcast from San Antonio. They came crackling over the ether with an air of vitality he no longer felt. With a look of grim concentration spoiling his once handsome face, he tuned his fiddle and played along, a ghost member of the band.

And he drank.

Ronnie often lay awake, silently watching from the dim corner of the room she shared with her younger brother.

Ronnie knew, watching his face, his chin jutting out to cup the fiddle, that something terrible and mysterious was happening to her father.

He was letting go of his dreams. They had flown on the same wings that carried Mae Ann away. And the letting go left him hollow and defeated.

The static of the radio, the scratch of the fiddle, the gurgle of whiskey in the jar. These sounds would stay with Ronnie all her life. One night she stole from her room—little Jack slept like the dead—and ran to his lap.

"Daddy, don't you ever go to bed?"

The question was asked in innocence. So far as she knew, he never slept. He worked, he drank, he sat up with the radio, and when she woke in the morning he was long gone.

Larry regarded his daughter solemnly. He was feeling morose that evening, more so than usual, and he noticed that the fumes from his breath made Ronnie's eyes water. Deep, watery, and as blue as a cobalt lake he had once seen from the air. Mae Ann's eyes.

He shook his head.

"I got to make some music, child." His words were thick, forced. "The world needs it."

He looked at Ronnie, but he was speaking to himself. He meant that the world might well need music, but it no longer needed Larry Garrik. And the Palamino Boys had long since drifted back to their farms, to the oil rigs, to the gas stations and the road.

He could not tell her of the terrible loneliness he endured each day as he walked the desolate miles of railroad track, clipboard in hand. He carried a gauge to check the cross ties, and a steel tape to check the span, and a flask for company. High overhead the clouds moved by with unfathomable purpose. Sometimes the shapes he saw in them disturbed him. No, he could not speak of these things to his seven-year-old daughter.

But Ronnie saw something of this in his eyes, and she fled back to her bed, and with pillow over her ears to muffle the sound of his melancholy fiddle, she cried herself to sleep.

In her thirteenth year Ronnie began to take a serious interest in her body. It was beginning to do things over which she had no control. Her long legs, previously inordinately skinny, grew suddenly longer still, and at the same time began to fill out, taking shape at her hips.

Ronnie wasn't at all sure she liked her new "padding." Her flat, boyish bottom was now round and full. But she knew it meant she was finally growing up, as well as out, and for that she was grateful. For a long while she had thought it would never happen, that she was doomed to be forever flat-chested and gawky.

One fair September afternoon Ronnie dragged the hamper over to the sink and stood up on it, surveying her progress in the medicine cabinet mirror. The sun streamed in through the bathroom curtains and put an amber halo around her hair. She cupped her hands under her breasts. The soft swell was thus exaggerated and her pink nipples, tingling curiously, poked through her fingers like the inquiring eyes of small, startled birds. Between her legs the wisp of blonde down was beginning to darken.

Like the blond beard of a baby billy goat, she thought. It was this part of her newly developing body that most fascinated Ronnie. She knew that many of the other girls her age had already started having their periods—it was often mysteriously alluded to, as a point of pride. But as for her, not a drop. True, she had experienced some distinct abdominal cramps. A sure sign, so they said. But nothing had come of it.

It was probably indigestion, she thought, disgusted. *They* get their periods and I get indigestion. And the odd hot flashes that sometimes flickered through her loins—what was that all about?

Ronnie was a farm girl. She had been around animals, particularly horses and steer, all of her life, and the mechanical act of breeding was no mystery to her, though it did seem ludicrous. As to the particulars . . .

The September light poured in like honey, bathing the room in its yellow glow as she took a small hand mirror and propped it on the edge of the sink. Then, with her hands pulling at the back of her thighs, she looked down at the juncture of her legs, where the mirror captured the reversed image of her sex, spread like the damp blushed bud of an opening flower.

Intriguing. Secret. And somehow forbidden. The very act of examining her intimate self was exciting and the strange tingling sensations began again. She seemed to be at the mercy of some uncontrollable impulse.

Ronnie looked up, embarrassed, as if she had been caught in the act of doing something naughty. But she was alone, of course. Her father hadn't returned from work yet. Probably he had stopped off at a roadhouse. She sighed and put the mirror away. There was no telling what shape he'd be in when he showed up. Her brother, she knew, was finishing up his chores and soon it would be time for her to start supper.

She adjusted the shower and stepped under the spray of warm water. It made her feel clean again, washing away the embarrassment of her imagination. But she lingered over her nipples as she soaped herself, enjoying the ticklish sensation that produced, and she ran the bar of soap between her legs long after she was squeaky clean. The heat she felt there was more than just the heat of the shower.

Ronnie had begun to lather up her hair when she heard a sound. She turned in the stall and gasped.

"Jack!"

Her younger brother had his head thrust through the half-open window. The gauze curtain was draped over his forehead and his eyes bugged out. He appeared to be trying to speak, but the voluptuous sight of his sister was clearly too much for him. Instead, he gasped like a beached fish, his cheeks puffed out.

"Pig!" she shrieked. Ronnie tried to cover her breasts with one arm, in vain. Then without thinking she grabbed the first thing at hand, her father's shaving mug, and hurled it at the window.

It broke with a splendid crash. Jack whimpered and disappeared. Ronnie wiped the soap from her eyes and approached the window, trembling. After the brief whimper there had been nothing, silence. Had she killed him? A sudden blow on the head . . . she peered cautiously over the sill.

"Jack! Oh, Jackie!"

Her brother looked up, dazed. The barrel he had used to boost himself up to the window lay overturned at his feet. The broken mug had opened a gash on his cheek and the blood poured down his chin. He started to blubber when he saw her horrified look.

"Honest, Sis. I was just gonna give you a scare. I didn't mean nothin' bad—"

Just then her father came around the corner of the house. Ronnie immediately saw the whiskey glaring in his eyes and knew there was going to be trouble.

"What in hell is goin' on here?"

He stood with his thumbs hooked in his belt, surveying the broken evidence of the little drama. He slowly eyed his son, the overturned barrel, his daughter's startled, soapy face, and the broken mug. Neither child answered him. What had happened was self-evident.

Larry Garrik glared at his son as he bent over and picked up the handle of the shattered mug. He looked at it, opened his fingers, dropped it to the ground, and then opened the buckle of his belt.

Little Jack cringed, his voice breaking.

"It weren't me, Daddy. She threw it. Ronnie threw it!"

"Don't tell me what happened, boy. I know *exactly* what happened. Now take off that shirt."

The belt swung free and dangled menacingly. Jack hesitated, looking reproachfully at his sister.

"Get your eyes off her, boy!" Larry's voice was thick with drink and his face had darkened with rage. "Ain't you seen enough of her to satisfy you? Ain't you?"

"But, Daddy, I—"

"Don't 'but Daddy' me. Get that shirt off your back and quit blubbering." He flicked the buckle end of the belt, hurrying up the frightened boy.

"Daddy, please!" cried Ronnie from the open window.

But her father would not look at her. He stared at his son. "You keep out of this, Ronnie. This is between me and Jack. The boy needs to learn some manners."

"But, Daddy, it was me who broke that mug," she said, near tears. Her little brother was sometimes a pest, but she couldn't bear to see him hurt. And it was her fault, doubly so. If she'd had to throw something why couldn't it have been the bar of soap, the bottle of shampoo—anything but that foolish mug?

"Never you mind. I knowed exactly what happened. It's as plain as the goddamn nose on this little sneak's face. Right, Jack? Now turn over and show me your back, boy."

Her father still refused to look at her and Ronnie knew why. The shaving mug had been special to him. It had been a present from Mae Ann, and he'd carefully lathered his face with it each morning for all those years.

There were tears in his eyes as he swung the belt, and as Ronnie saw her little brother cringe under the blows, she wondered just who it was her father meant to punish.

Fifteen was a bad year for Ronnie Garrik.

Something had gone wrong. The great, gnawing hunger she felt for experience had become twisted into an actual physical hunger. And it showed. Her figure had filled out too much— Ronnie was not actually fat, but she felt thick and heavy and awkward. Her body was out of control, it had become a cage she inhabited, a movable, mechanical cage that did not always respond to her commands.

And to make matters worse, her physical awkwardness had been transmitted to her mouth. She never knew what to say. The other girls said clever, witty things, while she could only mutter and stammer, acutely aware of herself.

It was pathetic. Pathetic and *stupid.* She grimaced, thinking about it. But she was about to put all that stupidity behind her, or so she hoped.

Ronnie put an extra dessert on her plate, slid her tray down the chrome rail, and gave the cashier her token. The extra dessert was a reward for her bravery. For the new leaf she was about to turn over. Today she was going to saunter gracefully into the lunchroom and plunk herself down right next to Tom Henry. She was going to be pretty and charming and witty and, well, *attractive.* Tom had smiled at her one day in biology, returning a book she had dropped. And he had, she was certain, smiled fondly. The idea of speaking to him had obsessed her for the last week and now she was going to do something about it.

Ronnie searched for his handsome, aquiline profile and found it across the crowded room. Tom Henry had laughing eyes, a quick smile, and thick, fair hair she longed to brush back from his clear forehead. As she imagined herself doing that she stumbled, nearly upsetting her tray.

"Hey, baby. Watcha step." A boy with bad skin leered at her, his tongue licking his lips.

Ronnie brushed by. I must be graceful, she thought. Think gracefully. His back was toward her. Tom had broad shoulders, a thin, narrow-hipped build, and an unconscious swagger in his walk that made Ronnie breathless when she thought about it. She put her tray down across from his and sat down.

"Hi," she said weakly. The clever greeting she had composed and refined had vanished abruptly.

"Hi there," he responded. He flashed his white smile, then looked back down at his plate.

"Hello, Tom," she said. Then clamped her mouth shut. How could she be so dumb?

He looked up again, sensing her nervousness. "Your name's Ronnie, isn't it?"

She found herself nodding enthusiastically.

"I guess we're in a class together?"

She was still nodding, captivated by his eyes. She ignored his voice and let his eyes speak to her. Ronnie could imagine all sorts of things as she saw herself reflected there. At the same time she was aware that she was, in some subtle way, making a complete fool of herself.

"—I guess you understand all that stuff, but frankly it's way over my head," he was saying.

"Oh, yes!" she said suddenly. "Your head."

He looked at her quizzically. And before she could rescue the conversation, Sheila Banks was there, her arm draped comfortably across his shoulder.

"Tom, darling, won't you come over to our table? I'm just dying to tell you about the party Jean and I are planning."

Sheila Banks was one of those people who move through adolescence with unerring grace. Her honey blond hair was the envy of the school. She turned her pert nose up and smiled deprecatingly at Ronnie.

"You don't mind, do you?"

Ronnie hated her guts, and she did mind, terribly, but she smiled weakly as Sheila walked Tom away, her arm threaded intimately through his. Ronnie followed that pretty blond head with death ray eyes.

She skipped her afternoon class and went directly to the drugstore.

"I don't know, miss," said the elderly druggist behind the

counter. "We stock all sorts of processes, of course. But I'm not certain that—"

"I want to dye my hair blonde," she said defiantly.

"Of course. I understand perfectly," he said, regarding her solemnly from behind his steel-rimmed spectacles. "All I mean to imply is that we don't guarantee the results. Your hair is, well, very dark. Black, I should say. Yes, indeed, quite dark."

He seemed to be musing to himself, gazing curiously at her long dark hair. Ronnie assumed he was toying with her and she flared up.

"I simply *must* be a blonde. I don't care how much your precious dye costs." She slammed her purse down. The druggist was before her, looking a bit startled, but she was seeing Sheila Banks. Hateful Sheila Banks and her condescending smile.

"That's the problem, miss," the druggist was saying gently. He had daughters of his own, long since grown up, and he had an inkling of what her real problem was. Still, he was wise enough to know that the attractive young lady with the spark showing in her eyes was not about to be talked out of her decision by a man old enough to be her grandfather. The young had a will and stubbornness impossible to tamper with.

"That is the problem," he repeated. "It's not simply a matter of dyeing. First you must strip the hair of all its pigment. Which is, quite frankly, damaging to the follicles."

"I don't care about the follicles. It's *my* hair." Ronnie tossed her head disgustedly. Couldn't he understand? Had the whole world gone bad against her? She was on the verge of tears, the frustration welling up.

"Not good for the follicles, miss. And then it must be bleached. Another problem area with hair as dark—and I might say as lovely—as yours. The result may be, how can I put it . . . unusual?"

But she would have none of it and finally he gave up with a sigh. She took the bottles and kits home—she'd no idea it was so complicated—and locked herself into the bathroom.

Two hours later her hair was bright orange.

"Sis, are you okay?"

The querulous voice of her little brother roused her. She turned from the sink and gave the door a kick.

"You get out of here, Jack, and leave me alone."

"But, Sis, you been in there for hours and hours. Are you sick or something?"

"No, I'm not sick. Doesn't a person have the right to be alone? Now leave me alone, *please,* Jackie."

"Sure, Sis," came the muffled voice. "I just wanted to make sure you weren't dead or nothin'."

Dead? She wished she was. Ronnie had waited the correct number of minutes before applying the last rinse, she was certain of that. But when she went to the mirror, expecting to see an improved version of Sheila Banks, she had seen instead a young woman whose hair was the precise color of a Halloween pumpkin.

She thought for a moment that her heart would stop. She beat her fists in rage against the sink and sat down on the edge of the tub to reread, through a blur of tears, the instructions.

Now, hours later, she had applied half a dozen other rinses and bleaches and her once blue-black hair was the color of moldy hay. She decided to stop there, before she ended up with something even more horrid.

"Well, Jackie. What do you think?" Ronnie made a regal exit from the bathroom. She turned, spinning, the terry cloth robe flapping up above her bare knees.

Her younger brother stared. His jaw dropped. It looked to him as if her hair had been exploded by a phosphorous bomb. But he had enough sense to stammer, catching the steely glint in her eye, "Great, Sis. It looks real beautiful."

Ronnie knew better. But she was ready to live with a lie, at least until it grew out.

Billows of steam rolled through the shower room. The moist air was thick with the mingled fragrances of soap, sweat, and heat. Ronnie pirouetted under the needlespray of water. Her muscles ached from the absurd exercises the gym teacher had put them through. And someone had hit her in the chest with a medicine ball, of all things. Her breasts still stung from the blow.

The clouds of steam made it difficult to see the other girls, and Ronnie was never sure whether or not they were aware of her presence. It was something she would think about often, over the next few weeks.

"Hey, Jeannie! What do you get when you cross a rooster with a peanut butter sandwich?"

Ronnie recognized Sheila's voice and grimaced.

"A cock that sticks to the roof of your mouth!"

Gales of high-pitched laughter. Ronnie couldn't help grinning. She peered around the corner and saw the shining, sudsy bodies of Sheila Banks, her best friend Jean, and a couple of hangers-on. As much as she detested Sheila, Ronnie wanted desperately to be part of her crowd. She would have to ask her brother for a joke—he was of the age when he knew hundreds of them—and then she could try it out on them at the next gym class.

"You ever had one stick to your mouth, Sheila?" The question was half-serious, half in jest.

"Don't be uncouth, Jeannie. I never kiss and tell. Hey, did you guys catch the 'Roothead' when I hit her with that medicine ball?"

More laughter. Ronnie shrank back against the tiled wall. She knew instantly that they were talking about her. There was a ringing in her ears and a flutter in her stomach. It was exactly as if she were on an express elevator going down. *Roothead.*

Sheila's voice rose above the others. "What can you expect? Her old man is nothing but a drunk. My dad told me he's always making a nuisance of himself and getting thrown out of bars. It's a wonder he doesn't get arrested. And I guess her mother was a whore or something like that. They say she had Indian blood, and that's worse than being Mexican, my dad says."

The hangers-on giggled helplessly. Ronnie's face was hot. She was frozen against the wall, trying to remain invisible. Or maybe to dissolve under the stream of water and melt away.

Roothead.

"—but what's even more pitiful, Jeannie, is she's got a crush on Tom, of all people. Can you imagine? It's just too precious. . . ."

The voices became hollow, echoing through the clouds of steam, until Ronnie could not distinguish one voice from another. She stayed under the shower until long after the class was dismissed. Until the locker room was empty.

Until the elevator hit bottom.

3

It was like a dream.

Ronnie was lounging in the front seat of the convertible, cruising down the highway under an open sky. Her legs tingled with the steady vibration of the road and the rocking car. The ghost of Buddy Holly's voice came over the radio, singing:

> *Be bop a doo bob, she's my baby*
> *be bob a doo bob, she's my baby*

And Tom Henry was beside her, tapping his fingers on the wheel, his thick hair snapping in the wind.

"My brother Dick knew him," he said, stabbing his thumb at the radio.

"Buddy Holly?" Ronnie turned in her seat, eyes wide. Holly was legendary throughout the country, and had been since his untimely death. His legacy still lived on in Lubbock, where he had grown up. *Lubbock Texas Home of Buddy Holly* read the sign at the city limits, and a full-sized oil portrait of Holly was proudly displayed in the main foyer of the high school. Closing her eyes, Ronnie conjured up his bright, narrow face, the intense eyes, and the trademark horn-rim glasses.

"Yeah. Old Buddy himself. He and my brother were good buddies. Real good. They used to drink together and stuff. And when Buddy and the Crickets broke up my brother backed up his new band. 'Course he wasn't along for the fatal crash," he added solemnly.

"Wow! That's super!"

Everything seemed worthy of exclamation that afternoon. Scarcely an hour before Ronnie had been on the steps of the library, browsing through a paperback mystery. School was out for spring break, her father and brother had taken the pickup to East Texas to buy a steer, and Ronnie was bored.

Then Tom Henry sat down beside her. And before she'd had a chance to tighten up he'd engaged her in conversation. In a few moments she was smiling confidently and laughing as he joked about school, about the basketball tournament, about their deaf biology teacher, Mr. Schnapps.

Tom impersonated Schnapps, holding onto his ear lobe, his nose twitching like a rabbit's as he struggled to hear the words.

"Eh? Eh? Vood you be gut enoof to repeat, please?"

Ronnie clapped her hand, delighted. He had it exactly right. And it was so much easier being with him there on the library steps. The confusion and embarrassment of the cafeteria was like some vague nightmare, and Sheila Banks was the figment of someone else's imagination. Nothing was real but the handsome boy who sat next to her.

He stood up.

"I guess I'll be seeing you around, Ronnie. It was real good shooting the breeze." When he saw her face fall he hastened to add, "I got wheels today and I'm gonna hit the road. I just saw you sittin' here and all . . ."

He explained that he was on his way to Juarez "just for the hell of it." He was going to check out the sights, maybe try some tequila. Watching him, watching the way his blue jeans tightened across his buttocks, Ronnie felt in a hellish mood herself. Before she had time to think about it she had joined him—"riding shotgun" as he put it—and they were heading south in his father's convertible.

He drove easily, one finger hooked through the steering wheel. He put his free hand over hers.

"You know, it's a funny thing, Ronnie. I mean, it's like we've been good buddies for years, and everybody at school says you're stuck up."

"Stuck up! Me?" She took it as a compliment. Ronnie assumed that her classmates thought of her as a dummy, or as someone who was, well, *weird.*

"Yeah. Arrogant. 'Course you're real good-looking and everything, so it's no wonder they think that. I guess it's just that you're kind of shy, right?"

Ronnie nodded and squeezed his hand. He understood. It was like a revelation—someone understood.

"You sure your old man ain't going to light out after us?" he asked. His expression was a sly one, but Ronnie read concern in it.

"Oh, no," she said hastily, as if he might change his mind and run her back home. "He and my brother have gone over to Jasper. They won't be back 'till tomorrow night. Maybe later if he stops along the way."

Tom smiled to himself, his eyes on the visions of heat in the road ahead. "He sure likes to drink, don't he?"

"My dad?" Ronnie tried to shrug casually, as if it were no concern of hers. So Tom knew. Did he also know about Mae Ann?

"Hell. Ain't nothing wrong with that," he said. Then, deepening his voice, "It's a man's business to drink."

They drove for hours. The world turned steadily beneath them, and the dreamy, hypnotic rhythm of the ride inspired fantasy. Ronnie saw herself walking the high school corridors with Tom, their hands linked. Maybe they would exchange class rings —she had previously scorned the practice as dumb, but now it seemed wonderfully symbolic. Sheila Bank's blond hair would turn green with jealousy. Staring through the windshield as the breeze kissed her cheeks, Ronnie imagined the future: engagement, marriage, bliss, all the romantic abstractions she kept buried in her heart now were detailed and complete.

A soothing cadence came over the air:

My girl, I got my girl

Tom bobbed his head to the tune, glancing now and again at Ronnie, who glowed with happiness.

Dusk was beginning to fall as they came into El Paso. Tom pointed out the sights confidently. He was evidently a man of the world, vastly more experienced than she. They drove through the downtown area, dazzled by neon. Idling at a red light, Tom turned to her, flashing his white smile, snapping his fingers.

"El Paso!" he cried. "Ain't it nice to be in a real city?"

She had to agree. Compared to El Paso, Lubbock was a hick town. She felt sorry for the poor folk still in Lubbock, when they might have been in El Paso with Tom Henry. An electrical excitement was stirring within her, a spark ready to jump.

"Far out!" she cried as a car full of teenagers spun by them, shouting into the night.

They crossed the border into Juarez. It was as if they had crossed into another world. The great slum of the border town was fetid, its smell all around them as the convertible cruised slowly over the rutted streets. But at the same time it was exotic. Dirty children ran through the streets, screaming. And women Ronnie assumed to be whores leaned in the open doorways, their cigarettes glowing like red eyes in the dark.

"This is a pretty tough spot," said Tom as he locked up the car. "You stick close to me, hear?"

He needn't have asked. They ambled down a boardwalk, hips bumping. Tom casually slipped his arm around her back and down under her arm, where his fingertips almost touched the swell of her breast.

"I'm parched. How about you? A shot and a beer would be about right."

She followed him into a cantina. They were assaulted by a wave of hot air, the blast of a jukebox, and the dreary gaze of the mustachioed bartender.

"Beer and tequila for the gaucho," he said, pushing the glasses at them. "And beer for the senorita."

It was Ronnie's first beer, and she drank it greedily. The mug was warm and greasy but the beer was cold. It went down easily enough, but left her feeling slightly bloated. She had a tequila after that.

"Let me see your hand, baby." She willingly surrendered her hand to Tom. He licked the back of it—she shivered at the touch of his tongue—and poured salt on the wet spot.

"Now you got to lick that off, see. Then you hold your nose and toss down the shot. It really burns the first time. Then after that you grab ahold of this lemon here and take a little bite of it. That helps kill the taste."

She licked the salt, tipped back the shot glass, and sputtered as the tequila rose in the back of her throat. She grinned, triumphant. The bartender watched with ancient eyes.

In a very few minutes she was drunk.

Ronnie began to lose time and focus, like a movie being run at the wrong speed by an inexpert projectionist. She floated from the cantina to the street.

Cool night air against her face. Warm breath in her ear.

"You okay, Ronnie babe? You're not gonna be sick, are ya?" And he was holding her, one hand cupped over her breast. She didn't mind. It felt nice. "Come on. Let's take us a walk, pardner. That firewater hit you pretty hard."

She saw the blurred faces of ragged children. They looked up at her with enormous dark eyes. Someone was giggling. After a moment she realized it was herself. The thought of disembodied laughter struck her as acutely funny, and she began to laugh even harder. Tom was laughing right along with her, his fingertips kneading her breast.

Later, trying to salvage her memory of the night in Juarez, she could vaguely recall buying something to eat from a cart in the street. Whatever it was tasted hot and vile and she emptied her stomach in the gutter. Tom held her by the hips as she said, over and over,

"Don't be mad, Tommy. Don't be mad."

He made her rinse her mouth out and then hushed her with

a kiss on the forehead. They sat somewhere on a bench, watching fireworks explode in the sky, until her head cleared a little.

"Come on, baby. It's still early."

Tom was swigging from another bottle of beer. Where had that come from, she wondered? Things were appearing as if by magic. She hooked her fingers through his belt and followed him into a dark alleyway.

"Si. Si. I have got. One dollar for each. One dollar for gold."

The shining face of a dark-skinned boy, his forehead hidden by the visor of a baseball cap. Tom was paying him for something. They left the alleyway. Tom was running his hands down over her hips.

"I'm dizzy, Tom."

"Ssssh." He was pressing himself against her. She did not resist. The shadows of the night were whirling. "I'm gonna get you a place to lie down. You take a rest and you'll be okay."

The sound of marimbas, a guitar, and the shouted chorus of a song.

"You wait right here. Don't move."

The light streamed from the window of a cantina. Ronnie pressed her nose against the glass.

Then Tom was helping her up a flight of narrow stairs. She realized they were in the hallway above the cantina. Tom opened a door and carried her into a small, hot room.

"Fuck! It smells like shit in here."

He set her down on the edge of a narrow bed and opened a window. It looked out onto another alleyway, but she could see a patch of sky, the clear white stars, and another rocket exploding.

"It's only two bucks for the night," Tom was saying, "and I'm too drunk to drive yet."

Ronnie noticed he was weaving as he walked toward her. A lamp with a green shade illuminated the room. Tom pulled a string and an overhead fan began to turn, its wide blades whooshing in the air. Ronnie smiled weakly as he sat down beside her on the bed.

"I've never been drunk before, Tom."

"No kidding? Well, you're doing real good." He took something from his shirt pocket. They looked like old cigarettes. Old cigarettes made from yellow paper.

"I'll bet you never smoked a reefer, either," he said. "This here is supposed to be 'gold.' Maybe it is, maybe it ain't. I think that kid cheated me on the price."

Ronnie peered down at the curious cigarettes.

"Only one way to find out," said Tom. He struck a match on his jeans and sucked in the acrid smoke.

"You gotta try and hold it in, is how you do it," he said. The reefer was making a sizzling sound, like the buzz of a bluebottle fly. When Ronnie inhaled the sound increased, expanding from her ears. Then she was choking violently, her lungs burning.

"This is dynamite shit," Tom was saying.

Oddly enough she didn't mind coughing. It made her laugh. He coaxed her into taking a few more hits and then she raised her arms slowly in the air, sighed, and fell backward on the bed.

When Ronnie surfaced from the whirling buzz, her blouse was up over her breasts and her blue jeans were down around one ankle. Tom was huddled next to her, one hand under the elastic waist of her panties.

"Don't be mad, Tommy," she said. Ronnie hardly knew what he was doing, although she could feel his fingers probing her. On one level she knew what was going to happen, but on another it was as if she were watching someone else.

She could still hear the marimbas and the guitar.

"Come on. Lift up your ass."

Tom was working her panties down over her hips. He was talking to her, his voice low and guttural, but she couldn't make out what he was saying. Something hard and wet was pushing into her.

"Tommy, I don't think—" There was a point of pain, the unpleasant sensation of something letting go.

"Damn!" exclaimed the boy. "You're a *virgin!*"

But he didn't stop moving. The room began to fade again and she drifted in dreamy unconsciousness.

Years later, swapping stories with Zach Curtis, she would laughingly recount how she got drunk, stoned, and laid in the space of three hours, all for the first time.

"I lost damn near all my cherries at once," she told him, and they both giggled over it.

It was an intimation of her life in the fast lane, perhaps, but at the time it was mind boggling, and a little scary.

Early that morning she awoke to find herself in the back seat, sick and aching, as Tom drove back to Lubbock. She was confused, but Tom was not in the mood for conversation. Or explanations.

He left her at the door with a curt nod. Ronnie crawled into bed, hungover and miserable, and twenty-four hours later Tom's final gift arrived.

Montezuma's Revenge.

4

"Jeesum, Sis. I hardly know *what* color your hair is gonna be."

Ronnie scowled at her younger brother. Grim concentration had failed to make her hair grow faster. So, with more reason than ever to despise the nickname "Roothead," Ronnie had returned to the elderly druggist, purchased another series of dyes, and made her hair black again. She put down the brush, shook her long curls free, and ignored the inquiring looks of her brother.

Then, just as she was about to turn away from the mirror, Tom's face floated up behind her eyes. She gritted her teeth. Get out of my head, she thought. *Get out of my head.*

For three days she had waited for his call. School was back in session, but Ronnie was home sick with something she told her father was the "grippe." He did not question her, although he was puzzled when she would not let him call the doctor.

"Just leave me be, Daddy. Do you hear?"

She groaned, tossing and turning under the thin sheets. "Just leave me be."

He left her alone, shaking his head. Ronnie was getting wild and unpredictable, just like her mother. First the bleached hair. He hadn't said a word about that—he knew better. And now this mysterious illness she was determined to endure alone.

In between the paroxysms that sent her limping to the bathroom, she lay in her darkened room, waiting for Tom to call. She stared at the telephone as if it were a tiger about to leap. Did he know? Did he care?

She hadn't seen or heard from him since he had dropped her

27

off. That afternoon, when the illness had come suddenly full upon her, feverish and violent, she had looked it up in the dictionary: dys'en-ter'y   a disease attended with inflammation of the large intestine, gripping pains, and a constant desire to evacuate the bowels.

Instead of love, he had given her dysentery. She lay back on the damp pillow, half-wishing she was dead, or at least unconscious. It was her own fault, she supposed. What had she expected?

The fetid room and the green light. The sound of marimbas. And Tom pressing himself against her, hot and anxious. In her fever these images marched by like floats in a nightmare parade.

Why didn't he call?

She returned to school four days later, pale and shaky. Tom was at his locker, joking with his pals as he put his books away. Ronnie stood there, just beyond his circle of friends, clutching her own books as she gazed silently at him. He would not meet her eyes.

"Hello, Tom."

She said this twice before she got his attention. He nodded, his eyes aimed somewhere above her head.

"Hello." Just hello. It was as if he were afraid to speak her name. "I gotta run. I'm late for homeroom."

"Will I see you later, Tommy?"

He hurried on down the hall without a backward glance. Ronnie's lips were trembling. She cursed herself—how could she be so low? She was practically begging him to acknowledge what had happened that night in Juarez. And he was probably terribly ashamed, afraid she would accuse him of taking advantage of her. She longed to chase after him, to throw her arms about his neck and tell him it was okay, that she wanted nothing from him but love.

But that afternoon, looking out from the study hall window, she saw him leaving on the arm of Sheila Banks. He was whispering in her ear and she was giggling. Ronnie knew, as a black cloud of bitterness began to seethe within her heart, that he was saying something intimate and naughty.

Not long after that Ronnie learned the art of sweet revenge. It was, to be sure, a fantasy revenge, but that didn't make it any less pleasurable.

Late one Saturday night she lay on the couch, watching television. Her brother was asleep—Sleepy Jack, she called him, just to get his goat. And her father was out, God knew where. She had turned the sound off and watched the flickering images, lost in her own thoughts.

Tom Henry came into her head again. Get out! she thought, but the command was halfhearted. She let him stay. She even tried to imagine him more clearly. He was wearing a T-shirt, a tight one that accentuated his muscles.

And then Sheila Banks floated up, blond and smiling, her almond eyes were possessive and cruel. Ronnie didn't bother trying to make Sheila leave. Let the bitch stay. It was as if Ronnie extracted a measure of satisfaction from the torment of her imagination.

On the television screen a cowboy in a wide-brimmed hat was talking to a woman in a ruffled dress.

It might have been Tom and Sheila. Yes, she could see them now, folded in each others' arms, conspiring against her. They were whispering intimate promises. Tom took off his shirt. Now they were kissing.

The evening was warm and Ronnie had on a thin cotton sundress. As she lay back on the cushions with her knees up, one hand began unconsciously kneading the delicate flesh on the inside of her thighs. With her other hand she idly massaged her breasts, letting her fingers just stray across her nipples. Her eyes were closed and her lips were parted.

Tom and Sheila were kissing passionately now, but she didn't intend to let that go on. She made herself draw closer to the picture in her mind.

Sheila looked up over Tom's shoulder, her lips wet. Tom followed her gaze and saw Ronnie. He smiled, his teeth gleaming like pearls. He didn't want Sheila, he wanted Ronnie.

In her fantasy Ronnie had been transformed. She was no longer an awkward, ugly adolescent, she was Ronnie Garrik, a grown-up. And she was radiantly beautiful and famous. Yes, that was why Tom wanted her so—she was world-famous. Glamorous. She was something like a movie star or a model. And Tom was coming toward her, his jeans whispering provocatively.

Imagining this scene, Ronnie squirmed, pushing her buttocks back into the cushions. Her fingertips grazed the satin strip at the crotch of her panties. She was wet. She felt the moist heat spreading like a thick syrup through her loins.

Ronnie had often touched herself there and enjoyed a mild tingling sensation. But she'd never made herself wet before, except once, when she had woken up from a dream she could not, try as she might, remember. She let her fingers stroke the damp patch as, in her mind's eye, Tom came to her.

I've loved you always, he was saying.

Ronnie began to rock her hips slowly, instinctively, as her fingertips slipped back and forth. She found one spot that tingled with particular intensity and she let the ball of her thumb rotate around it.

Sheila was trying to clutch at Tom, she wanted him back, but Tom pushed her roughly away. Tom wanted Ronnie. He wanted her beauty and her fame. He touched her hand to his lips . . .

Ronnie's hips were pushing out a little faster now, and the dampness was spreading over her thighs.

Sheila was trying to get between them, but she backed away, intimidated by Ronnie's superiority. You're just another nobody, Ronnie said to her, you're nobody and I'm Ronnie Garrik. Sheila was cowering, her hands covering her face. Then she began to melt, her body dissolving into a molten puddle, exactly like the Wicked Witch of the East after Dorothy threw the bucket of water on her.

Sheila shrieked I'm melting! I'm melting!

And now Tom was on the couch with her. His hands ran tenderly up the inside of her thighs. I love you like this, he was saying, so slippery and hot. She reached out to unzip his pants . . .

Ronnie was using both hands. With one hand she worked her panties into her vaginal crack, thrusting her hips against the friction of the tight satin. With the other hand she churned three fingers against her clitoris. Tom's hot tongue was licking her neck and she felt the head of his *thing* slipping into her. Oh God, he was saying, it's going to happen going to happen—and he was pumping furiously into her. Suddenly she was over the edge. Her face, her hands, her swollen sex, everything wet and burning and her legs were suddenly twitching spasmodically, out of control, and her back was arching up against the intensity of the surprise.

Moments later she heard a car door slam. It was her father, and she knew without seeing him that he was drunk. Ronnie jumped up from the couch, switched off the television, and went hurriedly to her room, her thighs still dripping from her first climax and her sweat-drenched sundress plastered up against the small of her back.

She slept as if she had been purged of all animosity, dreamless and complete.

Ronnie looked forward to Sunday dinners. It was the one time slot her father reserved for sobriety. By noon he had sweated out the previous evening's aftereffects, consumed the better part of a pot of black coffee, and was in reasonably good spirits, his bitterness pushed aside for a few hours.

Alice Chilton, a widow now, came by to help Ronnie prepare dinner. She always arrived promptly at twelve-thirty, a basket of sweet breads under her arm. She was a lonely woman, although still indomitable in spirit, and it was Ronnie who kept her company and cheered her up, their old roles reversed.

This was steer country, and beef was plentiful and cheap, so the main dish was usually an outsized roast or, if the weather was fair, ribs barbecued in a pit dug out and lined with stone.

Alice Chilton's eyes were beginning to fog over with the cataracts that would eventually make her blind. She refused to be operated on and Ronnie knew she no longer saw things clearly, except in her memory, but she shucked the corn, peeled the potatoes, and prepared the gravy with an unerring touch. As she worked she was inclined to whistle. Even after all these years, Ronnie was still delighted by the cheerful, birdlike tone of Mrs. Chilton's whistling.

"You're getting to be a full-sized woman," observed Alice. The kitchen was hot and Ronnie had just opened a window. "I trust you lookin' out for the boys?"

Ronnie was careful to consider her reply. Did the old woman know? Had some sixth sense of hers revealed what Ronnie had spoken of to no one?

"Oh, I'm lookin' out all right. You don't have to worry about me."

Alice chuckled, her dark face beaming. "Ain't worried about you. Worried about the poor boys in these parts. You'll be breakin' hearts right and left."

Ronnie flushed. The only heart she had broken was her own. The old woman must have seen something of this in the young girl's eyes, for she clucked softly and said, "Now child, there's plenty of time for loving and the raising of a family. Don't be rushin' it. Boys your age don't know whether they're coming or going, but it's a fact they know what they want. Don't you blush now, you know what I'm talkin' at. But you listen up to your old Mama Chilton, hear?"

Ronnie nodded, staring down at her work. For some reason she felt a lump rising in her throat.

"If you have a need for somebody, go and get yourself a man. These boys ain't nothin' but trouble. They'll mess you up and then leave you like you was an empty bottle, or yesterday's leavings. You need somebody—and Lord don't we all—get yourself a man. A *real* man, hear? I cain't tell you what a real man is, but you'll know him when you find him. . . ."

Then, abruptly, she was whistling again, and they continued to prepare the meal, working side by side.

After dinner they retired to the front porch, as was their custom. An afternoon shower had invigorated the air, and its fresh smell rose from the damp grass. The low storm clouds were rolling off toward the horizon and the landscape was infused with clear light.

Alice Chilton took her seat on the glider, her broad hands folded in her ample lap. Larry Garrik, his smile beatific and satisfied from the repast, dragged out his favorite chair, his pipe, and his fiddle. Ronnie mixed up a pitcher of iced tea, sweetened it with honey, and joined Alice on the glider. Jack, as usual, had bolted down his dinner and run off to play baseball with his friends.

"Mighty fine fixin's we had," said Larry, pulling on his pipe. "Real fine. You two do something wonderful to a poor old roast of beef."

Alice nodded contentedly. Larry's praise was a ritual she thoroughly enjoyed. Her children were grown and moved away, "scattered like jacks" as she put it, and since Joe died she depended more and more on the Garriks as her substitute family.

"That box of yours still have strings on it, Ronnie?" Her father eyed her slyly, then winked. The question was also part of the Sunday afternoon ritual.

Ronnie returned with the battered case and carefully took out the guitar. She kept it wrapped in a piece of soft felt. It was a beautiful old Martin, a D–7 model her father had bartered for.

Alice Chilton tapped her fingers on her knees as they tuned up. Larry still played a decent fiddle, and Ronnie, although her repertoire was limited, was a competent accompanist on the guitar. Her long fingers easily found the chords and she played unconsciously, her eyes glued to the fiddle's fingerboard so that she could correctly anticipate the changes.

Her father stroked the fiddle with his eyes closed, imagining an unseen audience, as Ronnie sang:

> *Dream of easy living*
> *Sleeping under the sun*

It was an easy, lilting folksong, a favorite of Larry's when he was in a relaxed, full-bellied mood, and Ronnie sang as easily as she breathed, her voice carrying like church bells in the still evening air.

This could be the one
The day my heart will fly

Alice Chilton clapped her hands together. "That sure is pretty, child. Your voice has filled itself out. I can hear it."

"It's more than just pretty. It's quite splendid."

Ronnie looked up, startled. It was Mr. Jacobsen, one of her father's friends. He was coming up the walkway, dressed in his Sunday best: a dark suit, black spit-polished shoes, and a brushed derby carried in one hand. He had a gimpy leg and used a cane. Jacobsen was in his mid-fifties, and in Lubbock was considered a natty dresser, but Ronnie, with the wisdom of her seventeen years, considered him elderly.

"Just happened to be in the neighborhood, Larry, and thought I'd drop in." He braced himself against the cane and stumped up the steps to the porch.

"It's a pleasure, Jake. A genuine pleasure."

Larry brought another chair out as Alice poured the visitor a glass of iced tea. Mr. Jacobsen sat down and balanced the derby on his knee. He thanked Alice for her kindness, cleared his throat, and then looked directly at Ronnie.

"Young lady, I must confess I came here under false pretenses. Your father and I were talking and I—"

"Jake!"

"Now, Larry. Let me do this my way. I've just come from church and I can't bring myself to tell a fib. I realized that as soon as I sat down." He massaged his lame knee as he talked. "Ronnie, your father has been bragging to me about you for some time. According to him, you sing like an angel."

"Daddy. Did you really—" But she didn't finish. Ronnie felt a blush spreading over her cheeks.

"And he also warned me that you were dreadfully shy about it. Determined, apparently, to keep your light under a basket. Now, now, don't protest. Modesty is indeed a virtue, particularly in those who can't sing on pitch. In your case, undue modesty is a sin, or something like a sin. But I'm getting ahead of myself."

Ronnie looked at Alice Chilton. She was smiling to herself, her head nodding gently as if she knew a secret Ronnie did not. The object of Mr. Jacobsen's little talk, which had obviously been carefully prepared and perhaps rehearsed, shifted nervously in her seat.

"I'd had enough of your father's bragging, you see. It was really quite shameless. Voice like an angel indeed! Yes, that's what I said to myself—we shall *see*. 'If that's the case, my good fellow, won't you bring her round?' I said. You may or may not know, young lady, that I direct the choir at Saint Theresa's Chapel. The Methodists in these parts can sing nigh as well as the Baptists, though I'm certain Mrs. Chilton here would disagree." He tapped his derby on his knee to accent his point. Ronnie watched him, fascinated.

"But I digress. Suffice to say your father was convinced that you had an absurdly low opinion of your singing abilities and that you would therefore refuse outright to demonstrate for me. Or possibly—and it happens sometimes to the best—your throat would close from sheer funk. There. Have I made my point?"

Jacobsen smiled cheerfuly, raising his shaggy eyebrows as he begged an answer. Alice Chilton tittered. Larry tapped his pipe on the railing and said, rather gruffly, "You're running off to the high-falutin' end of your tongue, Jake." He turned to his daughter. "What this gentleman is trying to say, Ronnie, is that he made it his business to be visiting with the Carters at about this time Sunday last. And he cracked a window so he could hear you singing along with your daddy."

The Carters were their next-door neighbors. The idea that someone like Mr. Jacobsen, practically a stranger to her, had gone to such lengths merely to hear her sing a silly folk tune was embarrassing. It was also exciting. Her father was always going on about her singing ability, but she had paid him little heed, assuming that his compliments were intended to ensure her being there on Sunday evenings.

"Exactly," Jacobsen was saying. "That's exactly how it was. I often wish I had your manner, Larry. Hard bitten and blunt. Right to the point. And let me get right to the point, Ronnie. Last Sunday I heard, to my surprise and delight, one of the clearest and most perfectly pitched voices I have ever, in a career which has not been undistinguished in a modest sort of way, had the pleasure to hear. The fact that it is completely untrained, 'au naturel' as it were, is at once astonishing and challenging. In other words, young lady, you do indeed have the voice of an angel." The derby tapped three times as he enunciated the "of an angel." Then he sat back in his chair and sighed. He fanned himself with the hat and beamed at his audience, as if he had just delivered a soliloquy from the classics and expected to be applauded for his efforts.

"By Christ, Jake," said Larry, chortling. "You really ought to run for office. That's the damnedest speech I ever heard. Right on the old target, at least when you got down to the end. But what Mr. Jacobsen here forgot to add on, Ronnie, is that he wants you to sing in his choir, and that's quite an honor in these parts."

The angel in question, her cheeks burning, did not dare protest.

The sky was beginning to dim as Mr. Jacobsen took his leave, shaking hands all round like a politician come to a fund raiser.

"Yes indeed, young lady," he said, his eyes twinkling. "A pleasure *indeed.*"

He stumped back down the steps, placed the derby firmly atop his head, and left Ronnie to her thoughts.

5

Years later, when asked to supply material for a glossy, gratuitous biography being prepared by a public relations firm, Ronnie sat down with pen in hand to take a mental inventory of her past. The biographer, a copywriter who specialized in "as told to" stories, wanted to know when it had all started. Could she pin it down to an actual day, or an incident?

The request came at a time in her life when she did not relish dredging up old memories, but she dutifully scratched a few lines. *The choir. Daddy's pass. My song. Dropping out. The band.*

Staring at the words, written in her peculiar, slanted hand, she recalled the spring of her seventeenth year. The sense of tremendous promise, of hope. And then other, crueler emotions began to rise, old ghosts of bitterness and regret, and she crumpled up the paper and threw it away.

When the biographer came round again she dismissed him stiffly.

"Use your imagination," she told him. "Invent a nice little story. That's what you're getting paid for, isn't it?"

The robe made her feel clean again. It was white and pure. Unlike herself. The trace of Indian blood was evident in her skin, and as for purity, although she hadn't let herself be touched by a boy since Tom Henry had humiliated her, she was certainly not pure in the Methodist sense.

She arranged the folds of the robe and waited attentively for Mr. Jacobsen to begin.

"Let's try that again," he said. The other choir members stirred, rustling their programs. "And this time more *profundo* in the bass. Sopranos, sing like bells, if you please."

If you please. That was Jacobsen's polite way of command. He struck the piano top with the flat of his hand, setting the beat.

> *Sister Mary had-a but one child*
> *born in Beth-le-hem*
> *and ev-er-y time a the ba-by cried*
> *She'd a rocked Him in the wea-ry land*
>
> *Rocked Him in the wea-ry land*
> *rocked Him in the wea-ry land*

Ronnie had never paid any particular attention to gospel music, and she never thought she would enjoy singing with Mr. Jacobsen's choir. At first she went to please her father, who insisted that Jacobsen was a musical genius. Later she went to please herself. Mr. Jacobsen treated her with respect, and the other sopranos, most of them much older than she, deferred to her almost immediately.

It was a new world for Ronnie. She had never before experienced respect and deference.

"You have a special talent, Ronnie," Jacobsen told her after the first choir practice. "I have a very good ear, if I do say so myself, and what I hear from you is this: perfect pitch. That might be expected in someone who has had years of voice training, but for a raw beginner it is something special. Something to be cherished."

To be cherished, to be special. If Mr. Jacobsen had been a little younger, a little less gray, she would have had a crush on him. As it was she drank in his praise and banked it against her sorrows. Tom Henry, despite his good looks, despite the way his blue jeans tightened across his buttocks, was not special. And Sheila Banks, her hair the color of golden honey, was not cherished.

With her heart open, Ronnie sang with all the strength of her newly discovered pride, her shoulders swaying with the unrepressed rhythm of the spiritual:

> *Oh Lord, she rocked Him in a wea-ry land*
> *rocked Him in a wea-ry land!*

Ronnie searched for the latch, found it, and opened the door as quietly as possible. She stepped over the threshold and into the darkened house.

Ronnie hadn't meant to be out so late. She had gone to the movies to see an old print of Elvis Presley's *Jail House Rock*. Ronnie loved it. She loved it so much she stayed to see it again. Alone in the near empty theater, she bathed in the suffused light of the flickering film and watched the undisputed 'King of Rock 'n' Roll.' He swaggered and strutted, his hips writhing, his voice husky with sex. She loved the beat that dominated each song, a pervasive beat that quivered in the very shape of his tender, expressive lips. Ronnie loved the movie, she loved each and every rocking song, and she loved Elvis. She loved him so much she wanted to *be* him.

Now she stood just inside the doorway, her eyes adjusting to the darkness. Her father's pickup was in the yard and since the lights were out she assumed he was asleep—or passed out.

When she saw his shadowed figure in the big easy chair, she took it for granted he was unconscious, and she began to tiptoe across the floor toward her bedroom.

But the figure moaned and stood up. He began walking toward her. Ronnie caught her breath. As he passed out of a shadow she saw a strange expression illuminating his face. The years had dropped away from him. There was a brightness about him, a light in his eyes, as if he were looking through her into an imagined past.

"Mae Ann," he whispered. "Mae Ann, you come back to me. You finally come back."

   And then his arms were around her and he was smothering her face with kisses. He reeked of whiskey and the stubble on his chin scratched her. She gasped, pushing at him.

   "Daddy! Daddy! It's me—it's Ronnie."

   But he was in another world. Mae Ann had returned at last. His hands encircled her waist—why was she struggling against him?—and now he was carressing her buttocks. It had been so long.

   "You come back. You finally come back." And then he was trying to push the front of her blouse open, his powerful hands mauling her breasts. It had been so damned long.

   "Mae Ann. Mae Ann, I—" Ronnie felt his hardness pressing against her.

   "Daddy!" she screamed.

   The scream went through him. He shook his head, as if just waking up. He looked at his daughter, at her terrified expression, at her disheveled clothes. Then he looked down at his own hands, as if it were they who had betrayed him. Finally he dropped to his knees, buried his face in his hands, and began to sob.

   Ronnie stood over him. The man who had been the giant in her life lay crumpled at her feet, his body convulsed with despair.

   "Daddy?" She touched him on the shoulder. He wanted to run away from her, from himself, from his shame, but he was too drunk to move.

   "Daddy," she said, trying to soothe him. "Daddy, it was only a dream. Only a dream."

   She continued to talk to him, her voice even and mellow and soothing. It was as if she were the parent and he the child. Gradually the sobbing stopped. His breath shuddered and then he sighed. The sigh was big enough and sad enough to fill the room. After a few minutes his breath became low and regular and Ronnie knew he was asleep.

   She closed the bedroom door softly behind her. It was only a dream, she told herself. Suddenly she knew she had to get out. She had to find some way to escape from the suffocating closeness of her hometown, from small-minded people like Sheila Banks, from heartless fools like Tom Henry. From her father, who was beyond her help, lost forever in a nightmare.

She had to get out of the dream. She had to wake up.

Everyone was there and Ronnie was paralyzed with fear. Cold sweat broke out on her forehead and her underarms were clammy. Her heart raced. It would never work; she'd been a fool to think it would. Now they were all staring at her, waiting for her to fail.

It was his fault. Gordon Thatcher, the principal of the high school, approached her after the church services one Sunday. He shook her hand vigorously, working her arm up and down as if it were an old pump handle.

"That was positively inspirational," he said. He glanced over at Mr. Jacobsen, who beamed appreciatively. "Jake here tells me you've only been singing gospel for a few months, Ronnie. It's hard to believe."

She didn't know what to say as she to extricated her hand from his. Mr. Thatcher wasn't the first to praise her singing—the whole congregation seemed to be enthusiastic—but she always found herself at a loss for words.

"Yes! Positively inspirational. As a matter of fact, hearing you sing out on "Go Down Moses" I felt a shiver go down my spine and I was kind of inspired myself."

And then he had asked her if she would be willing to lead the opening service at the student assembly. Usually the high school glee club did something like "God Bless America," or, when they felt up to it, "The Star-Spangled Banner." But Mr. Thatcher thought it would be particularly effective if Ronnie would do a solo, unaccompanied.

"Just one clear voice, Ronnie. That would do the trick, I think. And I know you'd do a fine job of it," he said. Jacobsen was in the background, nodding his approval. "And the kids will be mighty impressed," Thatcher added.

That was what decided her. Here was a chance to get even.

Her chance to show all those who'd ignored her that she possessed a unique talent. That she wasn't just another gawky, lonely girl.

She had imagined revenge and triumph, but she had never imagined it would be like this. The auditorium was full, nearly two thousand students. Two thousand potentially hostile faces, all looking at her. They waited, fidgeting, through the traditional moment of silence, and now they were standing, waiting for her to sing. Waiting for her to make a fool of herself.

Mr. Thatcher was smiling at her, making little motions with his hands. It was time. Too late to back out now. She took a deep breath and began: *Amer-ica* . . .

As soon as the first word was out she knew it would be okay. Her voice wasn't going to crack. And as she continued to sing, her voice rising to fill the auditorium, she knew it was going to be more than just "okay." Her voice picked up strength as her confidence increased.

My song, she thought. It may have been written for somebody else, but it's my song now.

America, the beautiful
God shed His grace on thee

Ronnie swayed, belting out the song with all her heart. She had meant to sing it note for note, as it was written. But now, caught up in the surge of emotion, she began to embellish it. The changes were subtle, but evocative. The air quivered with her strong young voice, and beneath the standard melody was the textured rhythmn of a gospel song.

It was an old tune, done so frequently that it had become a cliché, but the way Ronnie sang it was brand-new. The audience began to sway with her, as if hypnotized, and when the last note pealed out, reverberating to the rafters, they continued to sway in the silence, unified in the desire to soak up every last faint echo of her voice.

And then Mr. Thatcher was on his feet, applauding wildly,

and the assembly dissolved into a thunderous cacophony of cheers. In that moment, in that single moment just before it began, Ronnie *knew.*

She left by the side door while the applause was still strong. In the hallway she was alone with her thoughts. She walked toward the exit in a daze. The sound of the applause was fading, but the electrical sensation that was coursing through her body had not. Ronnie looked up at the portrait of Buddy Holly. He seemed to be smiling down at her, his eyes full of secrets. And she knew, finally and completely, what she was going to do and who she was going to be.

Ronnie pushed open the door, walked out into the street, and never looked back.

On the Road

1

The air-conditioned tour bus stops there now, on the corner of State and Seventh, and the passengers look out through smoked glass windows while the guide makes his speech about the humble origins of the famous and the fortunate.

In those days it was just another vacant warehouse in the stockyard district of Amarillo. It was humble, just as the guide said, and ugly as well. But it was not entirely vacant on that hot day in June when the girl in the flowered hat came to town. One of the lower bays had been let on a weekly basis to a young guitarist named Paul Stokey.

It was Stokey's band to begin with. What happened later could not have been foreseen. Not the rocket ride to glory, or the price paid—and not the sordid death of one of their number. In those days they were Paul Stokey's Roughriders, right down to the last coil of speaker wire. Amps, lights, mikes, the long-body Chevy van with the rebuilt engine—even the tambourine belonged to Paul.

He was wearing tight, low-hipped jeans and an undersized black T-shirt in imitation of Frank Zappa, the Los Angeles rocker he admired. He'd have worn a chin beard like Zappa's if he'd had the stuff to grow it. As it was his bare and boyish face, framed by a mop of rust-colored hair, was spoiled by an intractable scowl. Stokey's arrogance and his chameleonlike talent would eventually earn him the sobriquet "The Mean Machine," but on that particular afternoon his foul mood had been sparked by the audition of an inept vocalist.

47

It was a disaster. A farce. The would-be singer, a cowboy more familiar with Gene Autry than Mick Jagger, had departed under a hail of the guitarist's insults.

"The hopeless fuck oughta be out calling *hawgs!*" Stokey swigged the last gulp of Lone Star beer and hurled the bottle out the open door. He hated losers. "Fuckin' shitkicker!"

"I thought he was kind of the Rod Stewart type," said Kenny. He sucked on a joint, tapping the rim of his snare drum because he knew it irritated Paul.

Ray and Eddie Okie, the two brothers who played a variety of electric and acoustic instruments, busied themselves with the amplifiers. Paul had hired them at a grange hall where they had been playing square dances and the brothers, both introverts, knew when Stokey was in one of his moods, when to cool it.

Not Kenny though. Kenny was a natural clown and liked to rile Paul whenever he got the chance. He was the youngest of the Riders and a fine drummer. Paul pulled him right out of a high school marching band, bought him a new kit of Ludwigs, and put him on the road, where he'd begun to acquire bad habits with the cheerful abandon of a boy swapping baseball cards.

"Yeah," he repeated, "just like good old Rod Stewart."

"He sounded like Rod Stewart's *asshole,*" growled Stokey.

But Kenny was spinning on his stool, bare feet tucked up under his legs, and grinning. He knew that would irritate the hell out of Stokey.

"Get serious, man!" Stokey strummed his Fender Stratocaster with nervous, upward strokes. The amp was off and the strings buzzed like angry flies. "I mean you want to play roadhouses all your life?"

But Kenny was watching the hat float in the door. It was an enormous black hat, the floppy rim weighed down with faded paper flowers. The girl beneath it wore a satin blouse with the crucial button missing, and worn velvet pants tucked into high Spanish boots.

Cute. Outfitted in a wetback thrift shop, maybe, but definitely cute. Stokey turned and saw her and forgot all about being mad at Kenny.

"What's happening, baby?"

When she moved into the light he could see she was trembling with fear.

Money.

That's what it came down to. You had to have it to do anything, even leave home. You had to get a job or something and save it up, and that took *forever.* You could get old and wrinkled before you saved up enough, and then it was too late and you were already married and had a couple of brats and you were trapped forever.

There had to be a better way. A way to make it just happen, like magic or something.

Magic.

Ronnie had been holed up in her room for the better part of a week. She stopped eating. Too busy thinking to be hungry. Lying belly down on her bed, her thick black hair fanned out over her shoulders, she leafed through piles of glossy magazines, looking for clues. Looking for a way out of Lubbock, Texas.

Redford, Fonda, Hepburn, Streisand. On page after page the handsome and the beautiful looked out to her, frozen in the spectacular light of flashbulbs. These were the people who knew how to do it. The men grinned with perfect teeth, their eyes bright with promise. And the starlets, leggy and sensual in their daring gowns, seemed to gasp like exotic goldfish under the incandescent strobes.

She stared at the pictures, dreaming.

"Ronnie."

Her father stood in the doorway. Ronnie scanned him for the telltale signs of drunkenness. Evidently he was sober and composed, save for a slight trembling of the hands. She looked at him expectantly and a little rebelliously, for he knew better than to violate the sanctity of her room.

He drew a breath and spoke quietly. "I hear you ain't been in school."

Ronnie was about to protest, or lie maybe, when something

in his voice made her hesitate. For once he wasn't accusing her. He was merely stating a fact.

She nodded. It was true.

"Can you tell your old dad why?" He sat down, his bony fiddler's hands clasped over his knees, waiting for an answer.

Ronnie shrugged. She lay on her back with her hands behind her head, resting on a pillow of magazines. How could she explain it? Something had happened that afternoon in the auditorium. Something had changed forever. To go back would ruin it.

"Did something bad happen?" he asked simply.

"No, Daddy. Nothing bad."

"You ain't left your room only to go down the drugstore and buy them magazines."

How did he know that? Ronnie sat up angrily. It had to be Alice Chilton. Alice was the only person in the world who knew.

"But she *promised,*" cried Ronnie, her voice breaking.

Larry nodded. He had indeed spoken to Alice. And he tapped his fingertips against his knees, as if in rhythm to a song only he could hear.

"There's secrets that need telling, child. We had our troubles, I know that. But once in a while I do something right. Making you and your brother come into this world was a right thing. So is this."

He took an envelope from his breast pocket and placed it on the edge of her bed.

"This here is a going away present, Ronnie. Comes a time to leave. And you can't go by jumping into one of those pictures you been mooning over. You got to do it for real."

"Oh, Daddy." Ronnie was on the verge of tears. Alice had told him everything. *Everything.*

"Never mind that, honey. I heard a lot of crooners in my day, let me tell you. Some real fine ones, too. And I never heard one half so good as you. I saw what you did to them folks at the school. They didn't know to laugh or cry. All they knew was the feelin' you gave 'em."

"Oh, Daddy, it felt *right!*" Ronnie jumped up. Now that her father knew, she wanted to tell him all about it. "I wasn't nervous or anything, not once I started."

Larry Garrik sat back and smiled, despite the sad weight he felt tugging at his heart. The last time he'd seen such exuberant joy in his daughter's eyes was the night she stole the show at the barn dance, and she couldn't have been more than four years old. He'd known then that she had the heart for it, but as for the talent and the guts, that had been a waiting game.

"There's three hundred dollars here," he said, indicating the envelope. "It ain't much, when it comes down to it, but it will get you to Nashville. . . .

"And there'll be none of this crying nonsense, hear me?" He stood up, a frown masking his face. "I aim to get drunk tonight. Roaring, godawful drunk. And I don't want to see you here when I sober up, get me?"

He strode out the door. And, as it happened, out of her life.

On the bus she opened her purse and for the hundredth time checked to make sure the ragged piece of newsprint was still there. "Working band needs hard-rocking vocalist with big voice. Now or never, wherever you are."

Now or never. It was as if the ad, buried in the classified section of the Amarillo *Ledger,* was meant for her alone. They were holding auditions that afternoon. Rocking in her seat, trying to hurry the bus along, she held the clipping as if it were a sacrament. Her father had Nashville in mind when he gave her the money, but when she saw the ad she knew it was right.

It was like a power you switched on, a kind of magic power that made things happen. Just yesterday she had despaired of ever saving up enough to get out of Lubbock, and then, presto, it had appeared. Or rather her father had made it appear. Not that it mattered now, so long as it happened.

Shielding her eyes from the glare of the asphalt, she thought again of her father, worn down before his time and as proud, in his way, as the aristocratic old Mexican who sat across from her. He'd gotten lost somewhere along the way, pulled under by the

sheer mass of it all: family, job, booze, poverty. But once upon a
time he'd known about the magic, Ronnie was sure of that.

All you had to do, if you wanted something bad enough, was
want it with all your heart and soul and you could make it real.

The low diesel hum came up through her bones with drowsy
insistence, and the bus shuddered with a blast of the hot June
wind that came charging across the plains. Ronnie, really alone
for the first time in her life, closed her eyes and slipped into
daydream: She saw herself transformed, perfected, her song flung
clear across the planet, the world at her feet. Supplying the details
of this fantasy, she smiled dreamily.

Amarillo, thought Ronnie, rolling the word in her head. It
was as good a place as any to cast a spell.

Later Ronnie Garrik's belief in magic would be shattered by
lies and deception, but it worked for a while.

It worked for just long enough.

She stood rooted to the spot, unable to turn away. Kenny was
right about the thrift shop. The flowered hat, the blouse, and the
pants, which clung to her thighs provocatively, had been gotten
for pennies at a storefront thrift shop on the way to the bus
station. But the boots . . .

"Cat got your tongue, honey?"

Yes, the knee-high doeskin boots that seemed to be gluing
her feet to the warehouse floor—the boots belonged to her
mother. Mae Ann had flown the coop like some splendid bird,
and her daughter could do no less.

"I'm here to audition," said Ronnie, defiantly.

The boy at the drums was smiling, but the guy with the
guitar was giving her the once over with eyes like cold fire.

"Singing?" Stokey was dubious. What he saw under the
flamboyant hat was a skinny kid with big eyes. She had a nice
build, and dark, sensual looks, but he couldn't see her standing
up to a crowd of rednecks in a smoky beer joint. They'd eat her
alive, those boys.

"He's looking for a Rod Stewart type," said Kenny, jerking
his thumb at Stokey, who glared back.

It was as much in defiance of Kenny as anything else that Stokey decided to try out the kid in the velvet pants. And if she didn't work out, maybe she'd be good for a quickie in the back of the van.

He ran down the repertoire, trying to find something she was familiar with, but as he rattled off the old standards she kept shaking her head.

Finally, exasperated, he growled. "What the fuck *do* you know?"

" 'Stand by Your Man.' "

Kenny giggled, tossing his drumsticks, and Stokey shook the neck of his Fender like it was a chicken wanted wringing.

" 'Stand by Your Man'? Shit, that's Tammy Wynette. That's fucking *country* shit."

But Ronnie shook her head. She took a deep breath, which served to press her breasts tight against the fabric of her satin blouse, and said, "Not the way *I* do it."

Stokey stared at her for a moment, taken aback by the husky conviction in her voice, then shrugged—what the hell, a dizzy little broad—and clued the band to chord changes.

Kenny tripped in with a standard rock beat, while Stokey opened with an insolent guitar lead, bending the strings as if daring her to prove him wrong.

Ronnie closed her eyes, put one hand on her hip as she picked up the rhythm, and began to sing.

Kenny was grinning before she'd gotten through the first verse. Maybe it was because he'd seen her first, slinking into the barren warehouse as if it were a dragon's lair and she the thief of Bagdad. But whatever the reason, he picked up the beat, heard her follow without hesitation, and the next moment the Rough-riders were rocking.

Even Paul smiled, taking his cue from the twitch of her hips, those slender hips that tick-tocked with the irresistible beat of a natural-born blues belter. And it wasn't so much the blues, the way she sang it, for there was something joyous and new in the old standard. Tammy Wynette had been going to the bank with it for years, but this kid sang it like it was the first time, like it had just been written for her.

It was clear she loved to sing. She had her eyes at half-mast, sneaking up on the microphone, her whole body moving with the pleasure of the song. And where had a young girl picked up that sexy, throaty growl? Hell, that voice made promises she couldn't possibly be prepared to keep.

Kenny slammed down his sticks and cried, "We got it!" and in his exuberance tipped backward off the stool, cymbals crashing.

Paul Stokey was, in his cool way, impressed. But he had reservations. "Listen, honey. We play the Southwest circuit. That means a lot of zoos. I mean these dives are chock-full of animals. You got great stuff, but I don't think you could stand the heat, if you know what I mean."

She didn't. Trembling with the adrenaline that coursed through her and the trickle of sweat between her breasts, she thought, what the hell was he talking about? Zoos? Animals? Wasn't it enough that she could belt out a song?

Kenny came up behind her. "What he means is, what happens when some drunk redneck does this?"

He reached around her with both hands, grabbed her tits, and squeezed tight.

Stokey was amazed. Not at Kenny—nothing that wildman did was unexpected—but by what happened next. Ronnie, moving with the fury of a pent-up lightning bolt, wrenched herself free of his hands, screamed, "You *fuck!*" and then delivered a vicious, wild horse kick to his, as the Mexicans say, *cojones*.

"Keep your mitts off me!" she bellowed, looking a bit startled at her own audacity; convinced she had blown the job and not caring.

Kenny lay writhing on the floor, hands between his legs, trying to decided whether to laugh or cry. Paul surveyed him dispassionately and turned to Ronnie.

"You're hired."

2

The Cactus Club is situated directly opposite the single road that passes through Cuervo, New Mexico. Cuervo is somewhere between Santa Rosa and Tucumcari—a long, long way from nowhere.

The Cactus started out as a roundhouse for a spur railroad, long since defunct. A succession of owners expanded by tacking on sheds and enclosures of various shapes and sizes, and the club grew into an organic mess of low peaked roofs and blacked-out windows. All the roofs were tin. When it rained the sound was nearly as deafening as the band.

The two lane blacktop that passes by was laid out with geometric precision. It is absolutely straight and absolutely flat. Stand in the middle and look both ways and you'll swear it goes on forever, unwavering and infinite.

Saturday evening. It is deathly quiet. The silence is like a breath being taken, and then a white speck appears where the road vanishes. The blur becomes a dusty Chevy van, tires hot and soft from a three-hundred-mile run, and the windscreen is a graveyard of insects.

The van pulls into the patch of desert that serves as the Cactus's parking lot. It skids up to the back entrance, spraying gravel and steam. A girl with long dark hair jumps out of the passenger seat and stretches her legs.

She looks up.

They say Montana has a big sky, but there is no place on earth that compares with New Mexico on a clear night. The stars come down like beacons out of time, the moon is rung with halos, and the edge of the night washes down way off at the end of the world with the translucent blue of some impossible watercolor.

In absurd contrast to the sky, the ugly, rambleshack Cactus squatted on the desert floor.

"It looks like a goddamn armadillo factory," she remarked as she helped Ray and Eddie unpack the van.

That cracked Kenny up and it was armadillo this and armadillo that as they set up the equipment, and "please pass the armadillo" as they shoveled down chili in the cafe. Until Paul Stokey told him to cut the armadillo crap or he'd turn him into one, tail and all, and if Kenny didn't think it possible he ought to give it a fucking try. Stokey used "fucking" like it was essential punctuation.

"This is a fucking *chicken* club," he told them. "Don't forget it."

At certain clubs in the Southwest, where drunken brawls have been known to erupt into small-scale wars complete with pistol fire and battle tactics, the stage is separated from the audience by a chickenwire screen. This is to protect the band from thrown objects, such as beer bottles, boots, and molotov cocktails.

The Cactus was just such a club. It was the only place for a hundred miles in either direction where you could buy a drink or two on Saturday night. Sometimes it got pretty wild.

"Class joint," said Ronnie as she surveyed the dressing room. Kenny had likened it to a "hole in a hole in the wall," but at least she had it to herself.

Ronnie put down her traveling case, smirked at herself in the grimy mirror, and lit up a cigarette. The place was a dump, thick with fetid odors, but she'd learned not to complain.

The door rattled and Kenny poked his head in, grinning from ear to ear. His eyes were rabbit pink and he was definitely high on something.

"Sound check in twenty minutes, sugar. We're going to knock the fucking walls down, such as they are." He added, in a stage whisper, "Damn place is *crawling* with armadillos!"

Ronnie gave him the high sign. When he left she turned back to the mirror.

The young woman reflected there was, in many ways, a vastly different person from the kid who left Lubbock by Greyhound bus. She had grown some in that year, or at least she felt taller. The *dare me* glint in her eyes had intensified and her features had jelled. Her adolescent puffiness was gone; there was still a little girl in there somewhere, but the face the world saw was womanly and sensual. Her smile turned up on one side and you could see where someday a line might work its way into her cheek. A funny kind of smile; hard to tell whether she was going to kiss you or spit in your eye.

Ten months on the road with the Roughriders had honed her reflexes to an adrenaline edge. That worked out to forty thousand miles of one- and two-night stands, give or take a few. A good weekend was three nights under one roof, and then it was back to the routine. Knock down, pack up, and drive into the bloodshot sunrise looking for someplace like Caballo, New Mexico, or Weed, Texas, of all places.

"Get your ass out here, Ronnie!" someone called from the main room.

"Gimme a minute, facrisake!"

The Roughriders were booked by a guy named Tex Rankans. Ronnie had never seen him, but to hear the other guys tell it, Rankans was a cross between P. T. Barnum and Will Rogers, with maybe a little Slim Pickins thrown in for good measure. He'd been in business for about twice as long as Ronnie had been on earth, and he booked bands all over the Southwest. Not all of them were rock bands; there was a different circuit that hired country acts, and Tex even booked folkies if they had enough draw. But the mainstay of his business were the hard-driving, hard-rocking bands like the Roughriders, who could be placed sight unseen in some godforsaken watering hole, knowing they could stand up to a rowdy crowd and deliver a solid mixture of Top Forty cover hits. There wasn't a lot of money to be had once Tex Rankans got his cut, but there was enough to cover expenses, fuel the van, and maybe cop enough pot to keep them sane.

"Ronnie! Shake it *down,* baby!"

The roadhouse pace was one stop down from full-blown frantic, and the only time she had to herself was taking a pee (and not always then), but it didn't matter. . . .

Now, stealing a couple more minutes in the so-called dressing room, Ronnie puffed on her Lucky Strike (made her look tougher, she thought) and giggled to herself. No, nothing mattered—not the stink or the dirt or the endless hours on the road.

She loved it. She loved every minute of it.

Even after the routine had been drilled into her until she could have done a set standing on her head, there was still something incredible about it. Because she knew she was going to make it. The fear that made her knees liquid every night before the first set, that delicious fear she had learned to love, dissolved with the first shimmer of Kenny's cymbals.

"Hey! Hey, Ronnie!"

Ronnie flicked her cigarette into the sink and wandered out to the main room.

Psychedelic drugs had just come into vogue and the wagon-wheel decor of the Cactus had been spruced up with glowing acid posters and black lights. A couple of cute little numbers in black miniskirts and spangled silver stockings were setting up the tables. Several longhairs were ranged along the bar, tipping back near-lethal doses of rotgut tequila. The bartender had a burned-out peyote look about him and kept a twenty-eight-inch Louisville slugger under the bar as a peacekeeper.

Ronnie sauntered up to the stage, practicing her grand entrance. Someday it might come in handy; as it was nobody noticed.

The brothers were setting up their instruments. Paul Stokey was absorbed in perfecting the balance of the sound system. Kenny was out back somewhere, getting ripped, or maybe negotiating a a quickie with one of the teenyboppers, Ronnie thought ruefully.

She'd gotten it on with Kenny for a while. For about a week, actually, although it seemed longer. It had been sudden and it had a lot to do with being out there, all alone for the first time in her life. Not that traveling with the band was *alone*, but it was lonesome and she was a long way from home. And she didn't know half the things she pretended to.

It was Kenny who clued her on to the Pill. He'd just about flipped when he discovered she didn't "take precautions" (he didn't know and she didn't tell him that she had made love exactly once, if you could call it that, before joining the band). It was definitely not cool not to think ahead.

"Now listen here, baby. A foxy chick like you has got to look out for herself, man. Some slippery character is going to talk his way into your pants some night—"

"Like you?" Ronnie lay beside him, running fingertips down the inside of his legs. He sighed.

"Yeah, like me. Only unlike me, 'cause at heart I'm a wonderful person and all that. I mean this cat is going to pretend everything is cool and it'll be dark and you'll be drunk and horny and you'll let it go and pretty soon you'll be knocked up and we'll be auditioning a new singer."

He was right, of course. She stopped at a clinic in Albuquerque and got fixed up. Sometimes she slept with somebody and sometimes she didn't, although after Kenny she didn't sleep with anyone else in the band. Often sex was just too damn much trouble, as Kenny turned out to be, but whatever happened she was covered.

Babies? The very idea made her shudder. Ronnie would be singing a different tune a little further down the road, but in those days the idea of motherhood put a shiver down her spine.

Not me, baby.

When Stokey was satisfied with the sound levels, Ronnie lit another cigarette and went out the back door, where a bit of cool air was beginning to glide in off the desert.

She could hear Kenny in the van, getting it on with some girl. Jailbait, probably. He'd never learn.

The band was like a family to her now. They played together
and fought together and, less frequently, loved together. But they
were tighter than the family she'd left behind, and although she
sometimes thought of her father and brother and Alice, they
became, in recollection, almost dreamlike.

Ronnie leaned against the building, blowing up rings of
smoke and waiting for the night to begin. She could hear Paul
ranting about something or other. He was so intense about everything. He charted the songs, got them to practice when it was the
last thing they wanted to do; he spent hours on the phone hassling
with the Rankans organization, and he knew how to handle the
club owners when it came to the crucial moment: getting paid.
He made it happen, as far as the band was concerned.

But it was evident right from the beginning that he and
Ronnie were not destined to be friends. He was so damned
changeable. One moment he would be charming and sweet,
showing her how to ride a tune for all it was worth, and the next
moment he would be ridiculing her.

"You dumb fucking cunt!" he said one night. "Whatya
know about it? I been setting up bands since I was twelve years
old. I played every high school gym in the world. I been sweating
every fucking lick for ten years, spending my last dime on fake
books, playing till my fingers bleed!" He held up his hand, shaking
his calloused fingers at her.

"I can lift a cover tune from the radio as fast as I hear it.
And play it better than the fuck who cut it. And *you.* You waltz
right off the fucking farm whistling a goddamn sap tune like
'Stand by Your Man' and you're telling *me?*"

He paused for breath, his face red with indignation. They
were crashed, all five of them, in an eight-dollar motel room. Just
sitting around, passing a couple of joints to help smooth the
wrinkles out of a rough night. Ronnie had been telling Ray how
she thought they ought to do one of the songs when Stokey blew
up.

"You want to be a Roughrider lady, remember this. It's *my*
fucking gig. You just shake your little fanny and sing the fucking
songs and I do the rest. Get it?"

She got it.

Stokey cooled off as quickly as he blew up—he knew how much she meant to the band—but it went against Ronnie's grain to take shit from anybody, especially about music.

Just once she wanted to do it her way. Just once she wanted to sing a song that hadn't been sung by anybody else.

Outside the Cactus, Ronnie kicked at the gravel and drummed the heels of her fists against her thighs, psyching herself up for a hot night.

"Hey, watch the zipper, honey!"

It was Kenny, tumbling out of the van. His jeans were down around his knees and he was groping for them. A little bit of blond fluff in short-shorts was trying to help him. She couldn't have been a day over fourteen, despite the eye shadow she had caked on.

"Hey, babe," he said to Ronnie, his eyes glazed with whatever it was he'd been snorting. "Like you to meet my, ah, friend."

Hell, he didn't even know her name. Ronnie just shrugged. A few months back she would have been pissed, but it was no use getting mad at Kenny. He was like a little boy at a sweetshop window, and the candy kept jumping into his pockets.

"Come on, you old billy goat," she said." It's showtime."

She was eighteen. He was nineteen. They'd been around for centuries.

Midway through the second set Ronnie knew it was going to be one of those nights. The Cactus was getting ready to rock out of control. She could feel the electric tension gathering in the room. It was hot and sultry and the acrid dope smoke came up off the floor like something from a fog machine.

The Roughriders were into their Stones medley. Ronnie, her hands flapped back against her hipbones like Jagger, was pulling the tune from the deepest part of her throat. Making it cream on the way up.

Out on the floor the bodies were moving and weaving to the sound, sweating and tight and bumping as they danced. A few of the dancers stripped off their tops. Mostly it was guys, but Ronnie could see a couple of pairs of bare breasts shaking out there. Her own blouse, damp with sweat, cupped her breasts and made her nipples stand out like little brown thumbs.

Hot flesh, hot music, and hot tempers. One fistfight had already erupted and been instantly cooled by the bouncers, but the tension hovered. It was like a scream waiting to happen.

Without missing a beat or interrupting the pulse of his fuzz tone, Stokey cut into the opening riff to "Satisfaction." It was mean.

I can't get no

To the crowd in the Cactus it was an anthem. They knew it by heart because they lived by it, and as they jumped and turned the dancers began to chant the chorus.

Sat-is-FAC-tion

It was breaking in waves over the mob and Ronnie couldn't help herself. She pointed the microphone up like she was taking aim with a pistol and shook her tits. It felt good. She didn't care what anyone thought. *It felt good.* She clung to the mike, bumping out the words with a thrust of her pelvis. She curled her lips up in a sexy make-believe grimace like Mick Jagger and she knew damn well it was time to take a break and let the excitement drain, let the crowd cool off. But fuck, it felt so good. Like she was the heartbeat that pumped the adrenaline into the crowd.

Fuck. Yeah, it was like some kind of hot, urgent fuck you woke up to, waking up from a dream in the dark to the arms of a faceless lover. Giving yourself up to the need. Moving into the sensation, your nerve ends raw with desire.

She picked up the tambourine and crashed it against her hips as the crowd clapped time, eating her with their eyes, their bodies jerking to the beat. Her combination of naïveté and talk dirty naughtiness turned the crowd on, and they moved for her. They were puppets tied to her voice. They were *hers,* mind and body. When she said "go" they went. And when she said "come," they *came.*

Sat-tis-fac-tion

Ronnie could see the club manager trying to fight his way through the mob. His eyes were in a panic. He waved. Ronnie waved back. He made a face. What is it, little man? You want us to stop? Forget it. This is too *good* to stop.

Then she heard a roaring sound. At first Ronnie thought it was Paul, trying out some new kind of feedback. Then the mob surged and parted and she saw the motorcycle.

A big old Harley, looking like a giant metallic bug, was gunning into the room. Leaning over so the pegs were grazing the dance floor. The four-cylinder engine roared and sputtered and the Roughriders, never a band to back down from a challenge, cranked the volume up another notch.

Can't get no
no no no no

Kenny, his long blond hair smeared against his naked back, his face bathed in sweat, had become a machine. His arms were a blur, his eyes were closed, and his lips were pulled back into an ecstatic grin.

Even the usually placid brothers were into it. Ray was bouncing at his Vox, squeezing every last note out of the organ, and Eddie, on his six-string bass, was making little jumps like a lesser version of Townshend, dueling it out with Stokey's lead.

SAT-TIS-FAC-TION

Ronnie was wailing, letting her voice go wherever it wanted. She felt like a goddess, a goddess of heat and light and sound.

The freak on the Harley was out of it. He was wearing mirrored sunglasses and he was blind drunk to boot. Tables were tipping over, chairs flying. One of the bare-chested girls was clinging to the rear of the bike, her eyes wild and her mouth open in a little red O. She started rocking her hips like she wanted to fuck the bike. Guys were trying to grab her as she went flying by. She didn't care.

NO NO NO NO

Ronnie heard a loud bang. A gunshot. Some lunatic was firing a pistol into the roof, making little holes for the stars. At the same time one of the bouncers managed to pull the driver off the Harley. But the bike had a mind of its own. The throttle kicked down and the bike took off, leaped over a table, and went airborne through the ladies' room door.

It made an awful noise. A girl came running out, yanking her dress down, and suddenly the bathroom went up in an orange ball of fire.

That was it for Saturday night.

The Cactus emptied out and the crowd melted into the night as the band ground to a reluctant halt. Kenny, who was bent over his kit in a trance, finally relinquished his sweaty sticks. Ray got hold of a fire extinguisher and helped douse the flames as Stokey stood by, giving his free advice.

"Looney tunes in a chicken club," he said. "Story of my life."

The club manager was sitting in the middle of the rubble, his head in his hands. His Stetson lay crushed under an overturned table. Someone had ripped his shirtsleeves and his pants were soaked with beer.

"Never again," he said. "Never."

But the money was good. Tomorrow they'd sweep up the broken furniture and hire a few more bouncers and next week, when the word got round, there would be more customers than ever. And the fuckers would be paying a cover, you bet.

Rock and roll was loud, it was a headache, and it was a risk —but it paid off.

You had to take your chances.

What Ronnie had no way of knowing was how much, in the end, she would have to gamble.

3

Ronnie Garrik fell in love for the first time at two in the morning at the Mile High in Denver, Colorado. Maybe it was the hour, or the mixture of booze and altitude, but it happened very suddenly. Like a switch clicking on, opening her to endless possibilities.

The Mile High had all the atmosphere of an airport lounge. Carpeting that crept up the walls, abstract blotches of sterile pastel room dividers, cove lighting illuminating a small jungle of plastic ferns, and lots and lots of blond formica. The bar dispensed drinks automatically, in premeasured portions, and the cloned cocktail waitresses marched like robots from table to table with cybernetic efficiency.

It was a wretched spot, but Ronnie couldn't have cared less. Her whole being was focused on the baby grand and the man playing it.

He had thick blond hair, dark green eyes, and a slender, narrow-hipped body that made her ache, thinking about it. She knew there were others who ached in a similar way, for the stools around the piano were occupied exclusively by women. Ronnie watched them from the bar, her eyes narrowed speculatively, sizing up the competition. They ranged in age from the very young to the not so very, but they had this in common: They were beautiful, every last one of them, from the nubile teenager in the plunging Quiana gown to the regal, high-coiffed woman of fifty or so, who could have passed for a diva.

Ronnie had had just time enough to pull on a fresh leotard

and a pair of well-worn jeans. She could feel a sheen of sweat cooling under the leotard, evidence of an exhausting last set at a club across the way. A lock of hair stuck to her forehead. There were nights when she'd looked better.

She stirred the Rob Roy idly and immersed herself in his voice, in the pictures he made with his songs.

> *satin sheets my lady,*
> *and champagne from a shoe . . .*

The young man with the beguiling voice was born Zachary Brigham Curtis, of devout, and very wealthy, Mormon parents.

His father, a dark man with the foreboding looks of an Old Testament prophet, had parlayed a modest inheritance into a substantial fortune by shrewd manipulations of industrial real estate. At the time of his son's birth he owned a controlling interest in the largest bank in Salt Lake City, as well as a block in the heart of the business district.

Jacob Curtis, despite his stern visage and the intensity with which he administered his financial empire, was a gentle man, although he sometimes confused a investment of love with fiscal endowments.

"My son's fortune is assured," he told a business associate after establishing a trust fund in the infant's name. "He will not be troubled by uncertainty."

In an odd way Jacob was right, although a time would come when he would curse the sacred memory of Brigham Young for giving him such a son.

Zachary's mother, a plump, birdlike woman who conceived late in life, believed explicitly in the existence of angels. She firmly believed that Zachary's conception, while not immaculate, was somehow divine.

One of the boy's earliest memories was of waking up to find her kneeling at his bedside, deep in prayer.

"The archangel Moroni spoke to me in a dream," she told

the infant. "He said you are to be a holy man, a prophet. You will carry his word to the unbelievers. You will tithe your fortunes to a choir of angels and sing the praises of God Almighty."

Zachary was but four years old, but right then, looking into his mother's wild eyes, he knew there had been a mistake: Somebody up in heaven had messed up. He had been born into the wrong family.

He soon discovered that his life had been laid out like a finely detailed map. After primary schooling he would attend a military academy and later Brigham Young University. After taking a master's degree in business administration he would be rewarded with a modest position in one of the Curtis establishments, rise through the ranks on his own merits, and eventually assume a position of importance in the Mormon hierarchy.

His parents envisioned all of this long before he was born.

Zachary began to deviate from the grand scheme in his eighth year, when he stole a Case jackknife from a hardware store. At the council that convened to hear his crime, Zachary had the audacity to question the wisdom of the Elders.

"He is young, and so tempted by waywardness. Therefore, in our mercy, we suggest that he be confined to the house for a year. Do you accept this wisdom, Zachary, and humble yourself before the judgment of God?"

"No." said the boy. "I don't think God worries about jackknives."

It was scandalous. His mother retreated into her religious texts, looking for guidance in what was plainly a trial given unto her by God. His father, wishing to avoid further embarrassment, purchased the hardware store. It proved to be an excellent investment, but it did not prevent Zachary from further insolence.

He played hooky from school. He read forbidden books with the aid of a flashlight. He defied his classical piano teacher by playing rude boogie woogie music. And on his seventeenth birthday he undressed the girl next door in a strip poker game he initiated.

The deck was marked.

"You are halfway down the road to Hell," his mother said.

She retired more or less permanently to her room, where she prayed that her only son be delivered of the devils that possessed him.

But Zachary was not interested in halfway measures. It was all or nothing. Liquor, according to his father, poisoned the soul and addled the mind, opening the body to the forbidden risk of sensuality.

It sounded intriguing, and shortly after the incident with the girl next door, he got drunk for the first time. Blind, roaring drunk. It started in a Salt Lake cellar club with 3.2 beer, escalated to solo boilermakers in the A&P parking lot, and ended the next morning in Wastach National Park, where Zachary woke up in possession of a milk truck he had evidently borrowed for a joyride.

Under the circumstances, he thought it best to quit the state of Utah. He puked three times, drank deeply from a mountain stream (for some reason it made him feel drunk again) hid the milk truck in a grove of alpine spruce trees, and went to stand by the road with his thumb out, an innocent, hung-over-for-the-first-time grin on his whiskerless face.

A red convertible stopped for him.

"Next stop Los Angel-ees," said the driver. "City of Angels."

Years later, when he could look back on his troubled child-hood with a measure of equanimity, he would say that his mother's angels followed him there. But that morning, his close-cropped hair ruffled by the breeze, he felt wonderfully alone. He shed his past like a snake sheds its skin and already, in his imagina-tion, he was weaving the fabric of his own, self-made legend.

> *Fire from the Mormon waters*
> *a taste of living too high*
> *gonna put on a firebird suit*
> *and fly, Daddy, fly*

The driver was a drug dealer. Zachary, to be polite, shared a joint with him. It was his first. It was hot and sweet and smelled of the desert. He liked it. He felt as if he had been cut loose from

a great weight. The dead flat length of Route 15 seemed to be
an incline descending from a great height, and the convertible
was a Hovercraft moving at the speed of sound.

The driver sniffed at a spoon of white powder, put his foot
to the floor, and powered by Philco rock 'n' roll and methedrine,
they blew through Las Vegas as if it were nothing more than a
neon mirage.

It was night when they came to Los Angeles, and the city
lights looked like stars come down from heaven. The driver left
him off on Sunset with a bit of advice.

"Have a blast, kid. But keep off the needle." He added, "You
got sweet looks. Let the girls take care of you."

> *walk in the mist*
> *see what I see*
> *and let the girls*
> *take care of me*

It would become his life's anthem.

That first night he roamed the Strip, marveling at the crowds
of flower children, acid freaks, scrawny junkies. He had five dollars
and spent it on pinball machines and tacos. He had no place to
sleep and no desire to. He was afraid he might miss something.

Zachary did not see the desperate part of the Strip that
night. The seedy pimps with their teenage tinsel whores, the
gimped-up Holy Rollers, the honey-tongued thieves. He saw only
the incandescent lights, the bright eyes, and especially the lovely,
swaying hips of the sloe-eyed girls who dressed like storybook
gypsies, all silk and chamois and bangle-braceleted.

He walked on, smoking a reefer the driver gave him, listening to the music that ran through his head. The city was alive.
It had the pulse of song, the clashing rhythms of an acid vision.
From the record shop windows, open to the night, came that
year's theme song: "purple haze, across the sky." The woolly,

breathless voice of Jimi Hendrix who, loosening his shackles with flames and the hell noises he made from the hip, was not long for this earth.

By noon the next day Zachary had come down enough to know he had to find a job. He wandered the length of Alameda Street, unaware that he was about to be in the right place at the right time.

The place, celebrated in one of his early ballads, was Mister J's, a music store catering, oddly enough, to musicians—oddly because so few of the musicians had money and Mister J's could ill afford their trade. All that would change, of course, and Mr. J. himself would be moving from Mission Street to Laurel Canyon soon enough, but on that afternoon the ballad was in embryonic stage, just teasing at the edge of Zachary's mind.

He stood gazing through smudged plate glass at the display of axes, the Fenders, Les Pauls, Gibsons, and of course, at center, like an operatic mother surrounded by bebop chicks, the Grand Wurlitzer organ with the Lesley speakers.

Sign in the window say "white boy wanted"
live in a shack where the blues men haunted

Mr. Willy Jarvis, ex-tenor sax man, who once sided with Eric Dolphy at the Vanguard, was as black as a barge of Newcastle coal. It amused him to have a white boy step and fetchit in his store. Preferably a short-haired, fresh-scrubbed boy who could be trusted not to rip off the day's receipts. Zachary, with that Boy Scout grin of his, managed to look fresh scrubbed despite his twelve-hour sleigh ride in an open convertible and the sixteen unwashed hours on the dirtiest strip in the civilized world.

"What you get is a four-beat sawbuck and a sack in the shack," explained Mr. J., by which he meant the clerk was paid forty dollars a week and got a bunk in the storage "shack," actually a small, air-conditioned warehouse. "The main thing is to keep the marbles peeled for pocket men."

Zachary tumbled to Mr. J.'s argot immediately. It was the clerk's responsibility to see that no one walked off with a set of twenty-dollar guitar strings, or a box of reeds, or any of the thousands of small items Willy stocked.

He and Willy hit it off. The old jazzman let the boy have free run of the shop. Zach was gregarious and cheerful and, most importantly, honest. This rubbed off on the sometimes light fingered musicians who traded there, the long-haired, brightly clothed rockers and street buskers with whom Zach quickly identified. They were homeless gypsies who lived in their heads, just as he did. To be a musician was obviously as far from Mormon as you could get without actually leaving the planet.

At Mr. J's he had access to a wide range of instruments, and when it was slow, Willy encouraged him to doodle around on the Hammond or any of the new line of electric keyboards. Some of the busier musicians began to give Zach "slough-off" work at the smaller lounges, where he was expected to make what Willy sarcastically referred to as "underwater modulatories," or cocktail music.

Zach didn't care what they called it. He liked making up little snatches of melody and working them into the soft standards he was expected to trickle out at the lounges. In his head he was happily writing his own songs. On Tuesday nights he went to the hoot at the Troubadour, where the LA scene was happening, and where more than a few unknowns made their breaks.

Zach was never actually discovered at the Troub, but he became a fixture there, slowly working himself into the mainstream of Los Angeles entertainment. There was no real transition point, no time when he could say "*now* I am," but eventually his gigs began to take him out of town for days at a time (by then he was playing a mix of his own tunes and old bar-happy standards like "As Time Goes By") and he had to leave Mr. J's.

Cut loose from his sack in the shack, he drifted from girl to girl, crashing for weeks at a time, but never committing himself.

"Zach hangs loose, baby," he told them. "He stays in tune, dig?"

By the time he got to Denver the only heart he hadn't broken was his own.

It happened suddenly. Ronnie was deciding on how to make her move, how to get past the possessive women hovering around the piano without making an absolute fool of herself, when Zach ended the set with a final, unexpected chord and left his piano.

The teenybopper, her lips parted in surprise, looked stricken. The diva, contriving disdain, sipped her Campari and watched his back through lidded eyes as he headed directly for the disheveled, dark-haired girl at the bar.

"You're Ronnie Garrik," he said. "I've been dying to meet you."

Ronnie managed to summon up her best cool. She tried out a smile she'd seen Lauren Bacall use in *Key Largo* and gestured to the empty stool beside her.

"Can't be done," he said. He eyed the little fan club around the piano with a mixture of fear and loathing. "We'd better split for my dressing room. There's a bolt on the door."

It proved to be useful. Zach had just time enough to pour a couple of drinks when someone began pounding on the door.

"Oh, Zach. You promised!" The voice matched that of the scantily clad teenager. Zach whispered something through the crack in the door and returned.

"Not what you think," he said. "Just a bopper I made the mistake of being nice to. The old broad with the lacquered hairdo is her mother. Trying to sic the kid on me, believe it or not. . . ."

He paced the tiny room, gesturing with the untouched drink, never taking his eyes from hers. "I skipped over to the Grove between sets last night and caught you and your boys. Blew me *away,* phew!" He mopped his brow theatrically and grinned. "You got hot stuff. A great set of pipes. Why not ditch those cowboys and hitch up with me?"

She thought he was kidding. Twenty-four hours later it was no joke. Anticipating more knocks and pleas, they fled to his motel room. At "home" Zach began to slowly unwind, striding the boundaries of the room, his hands making signals and images like some crazed perpetual motion machine. Ronnie kicked off her boots and watched him. She could smell his vitality, and in those first few hours she learned to anticipate his soaring moods, his elaborate, instant fantasies.

"Look out there," he said. He indicated the picture window, which framed a postcard scene of the distant mountains. The light was just beginning to break along the jagged horizon. "There's a song in everything, it's buried way up there at the peak, like gold in a treasure chest!"

And then he would be off on another tangent, describing a club he'd gigged in, a rodeo he'd been to, inventing pretty lies about the future. He took it for granted that he was going to hit it big someday soon, that Ronnie (whom he'd known for all of ninety minutes) was going to "rock the goddamn planet right out of orbit." He spun a web of fantastic colors, surging with energy, and Ronnie, responding, could feel the excitement building, the anticipation gathering like a static charge ready to spark.

They drank themselves silly on warm champagne and in lieu of satin sheets they jumped between serviceable percale. Both of them thought it was all in fun; a strangers-in-the-night game to soothe the nerves bruised by too many days on the road, too many knocks on the dressing room door.

They moved together for a while, straining against each other for release. But for the slip and slide of flesh, nothing happened. The spark wouldn't jump. Zach stopped, swung his long legs over the side of the bed, and lit a cigarette. Lying there, her knees tucked up under her chin, Ronnie felt like crying.

She watched his naked back, the plume of smoke rising over his mass of blond hair, and she wanted to bawl. Why couldn't this have happened a couple of years before? Then they might have been sweethearts, stumbling through innocence. As it was they were two raw nerves in a dingy motel room, sweaty and desperate.

"Okay," said Zach. He put out the cigarette and stroked his fingertips across her forehead, tousling her bangs. His eyes were wet. "Let's make it real, okay?"

Slowly, with infinite gentleness, with a touch as light as a warm breeze, he began to make love to her. The tightness inside came undone as she shuddered, as his lips, humming a warm, low melody, traced up the insides of her thighs. She wove her fingers into his mop of hair, urging him up. They came together quickly.

It was as if time were slowly unwinding, as if the clock, hesitating between moments, waited for them. Zach sighed. Ronnie laughed. They both cried.

Stokey found them early the next morning. They had been in bed, with brief respites for room service and hot showers, for sixteen hours. It was as if they had been joined together by a suction of lust, a rude vacuum that swept them back together at intervals of not longer than twenty minutes.

"Must be the bopper," mumbled Zach when the first knock detonated against the door.

"No." said Ronnie. She knew the sound of Paul Stokey's fist. She wrapped herself up in a damp sheet, stumbled to the door, clipped on the chain, and opened it.

"We had a rehearsal at five." He hissed through the crack. The one eye she could see was furious. "Now it's eight at fucking night. We go on in an hour."

"Go away."

"I want you backstage in twenty minutes, get it?"

"Stokey, you're a jerk. Please go away."

"*I'm* a jerk!" He kicked the door, rattling the chain. "Listen, you little slut. If you miss this gig tonight you miss *all* of them. Do I make myself clear?"

Ronnie made a show of slamming the door. She tried to feel mad at Paul, but all she felt was sorry for him. The poor bastard wasn't in love.

Zach put the phone back in the cradle as she dropped the sheet and danced back into bed.

"I just canceled," he said. "I'm very ill. Food poisoning from that garbage they call room service. I won't sue if they'll scratch my last three nights."

"Zach!" His hand came up where she hadn't expected it.

"Let's go to the mountains," he said. "I'll be Nelson Eddy and you can be Jeanette McDonald."

"Do we get to yodel, Zach?" Ronnie managed to wriggle out of his grasp. She straddled his chest, her thighs brushing his cheeks. He grinned at her, licking his lips.

"We'll yodel all day long," he said. "And all night."

4

It lasted four days. They hiked the last mile up the trail, fought through a landscape of wind-stunted undergrowth, and stepped into an extraordinary vista. The sky had that quality of vast distance, of a breath just taken, of light breaking through clouds like a signal from heaven.

The cabin, high up the west face of Shadow Peak, overlooked the desolate Sunveil Wilderness. Fifty miles away the jagged, mountainous terrain faded off into a mist at the edge of the world. Ronnie held her breath, her teeth indenting her lower lip. It was too much to take in all at once.

"The Cheyenne say the gods live here," said Zach. He hooked his fingers in the back pocket of her cutoff denims, pulling her closer. "I believe it. You'll see, Ronnie. It's like getting your batteries recharged."

Coming upon this extraordinary perspective just as she entered her first love, Ronnie was certain that something absolute was about to change. With each step higher up the mountain the Roughriders receded deeper into the past. Leaving the smoky, beer-drenched confines of the Alpine Grove (indistinguishable from hundreds of other clubs she'd gigged) for the crystal clarity at ten thousand feet was like passing from one world into the next.

"You can feel the power here," he said. Ronnie saw the sparkle in his eyes and was again amazed at the sudden leap he had made into her heart. "It's like water bubbling up from a spring."

"I can feel it, Zach. I swear I can."

She had never had the slightest inclination toward religion, but here on the mountaintop she sensed the secret machinations of time, felt the majestic spin of the planet. Her new discovery, love, with all of the intensity and surprise, seemed part of a greater scheme.

The cabin belonged to one of Zach's musician friends, who lent it free of charge. A massive stone fireplace dominated the single room. Oversized, rough-hewn timbers gave it a solid, comfortable air that reminded Ronnie of the little frame house in Lubbock.

They were miles from the power lines, relying on kerosene lanterns for light. The "frigidaire," as Zach called it, was a mountain stream a few yards from the back door.

"So who needs food?" He picked up Ronnie and waltzed her across the smooth, worn pine boards. "We'll eat the scenery."

"And each other." She giggled. Ronnie tossed back her head, letting her mane of hair shake free. Zach nibbled at the underside of her throat and ran his hands inside the waistband of her shorts.

"Time for the christening," he whispered, his voice husky and urgent.

They made love on the hardwood floor. He entered her easily but as she luxuriated in the slow, deep movements, a bittersweet memory snuck in: The squeak squeak squeak of her father pacing the pine boards in the parlor, lonesome and worried and drunk again.

Ronnie closed her eyes, banished the memory from her head, and gripped Zach's back with iron hands, urging him deeper. Her orgasm was intense and exhausting, curling up from her toes, releasing with it a deep longing: to be forever as happy and satisfied, never to be alone again.

Afterward they dragged a couple of canvas chairs out to the meadow and sat there bare-assed, sharing a Colombian number as they watched the sun drop over the Rockies. Zach picked idly at his guitar, using a glass pill bottle to cross the strings, which made little crying noises as he played.

"On a clear day I can almost see home from here," he said, nodding toward the distant mountains. "It's as close as I care to be."

Ronnie had heard him sing it that night at the Mile High, but now, knowing him, she understood.

> *There ain't no lake*
> *in Salt Lake City*
> *It's dry dry dry*
>
> *Can't go home*
> *can't go on living a lie*

The song drifted off. He'd lost the sense of it, staring at Ronnie. She passed him the number, her hands trembling slightly.

"Zach," she said, "I love you."

He exhaled and smiled, his green eyes luminescent. "The feeling," he said, "is mutual."

It ended with a song.

On the third night she lay awake next to him, aware of each place where her body touched his, a sweet ache in her loins. Listening contentedly to Zach's measured breathing, Ronnie began to reshape her fantasies. It was as if she had gained the power to control her dreams.

She saw their lives entwined: the two of them bathed in the spectral, stroboscopic lights of the magazines that dazzled her as a girl. She and Zach were lovers in the grand tradition of Bogart and Bacall, Lombard and Gable. There would be children, of course, beautiful, perfect children, and a circle of important and gracious friends.

The fantasy went on, one image spinning into another. Ronnie curled up next to him and slept content. In the morning she woke up to an empty bed and panicked.

Zach was out on the front stoop, hunched over his guitar, scribbling on a pad of paper.

"Getting a tune down before I lose it," he said, biting the words. He shrugged when she pressed her lips to the back of his neck. "Just leave me be."

She went into the tiny, railroad-style kitchen, made a show of rattling the coffeepot as she put it on the fire, and sat down and cried for a while. An hour or so later Zach wandered in, lured by the smell of coffee.

"You got hay fever or something?" he asked when he saw her red-rimmed eyes. His own were distant—he was a million miles away, writing a tune in his head.

He was genuinely surprised when she put her head in her arms and sobbed.

"Hey, what's wrong?"

"I had this dream last night." She didn't mean to, but it came out as a wail of anguish.

"A bad dream?" Zach sat down, looked at her curiously.

"No, it was a good dream. Till I woke up." But there was no way to explain, and she sensed he didn't really want to know.

Zach poured a mug of coffee and lit them both cigarettes. "I gotta get back, Ronnie. Got a gig in Tucson opens tomorrow."

She nodded, the tears freezing inside her. Suddenly she did not want him to ever see her cry again.

"I have this great little tune," he said. It was as if he spoke to her over a yawning gulf, an unbreachable distance. "I can't wait to try it out on my baby grand."

Ronnie listened, her heart pounding itself to death against her ribs. It was a kind of nonsense tune, snatch phrases woven through a bright melody, but she got the message.

Meadow below
blue sky above
airstream baby
in love with love

gonna fly

gonna fly
away

Ronnie imagined that the smile he gave her was the one he reserved for the fan club that gathered around his piano.

"Zach," she said. "How often do you bring girls up here?"

"Every couple of months," he said. He made a show of blowing smoke rings in a halfhearted attempt to amuse her. "I get some great tunes out of it, Ronnie. Now "Airstream Baby," that's kind of *your* tune, if you know what I mean."

"I think I do," she said, her heart falling. "I think I know exactly what you mean."

The Greyhound rolled through the desert, through the sudden twilight on the other side of the Rockies. How many miles had she logged in smelly, rumbling buses and low-rent vans? He was headed for Tucson, headed for clean sheets and someone to put between them—easily accomplished, given his circle of squirming admirers. And Ronnie was chasing after Paul Stokey's Roughriders. It was a rough ride indeed, with fragile memories behind and a shouting match, at the very least, ahead of her.

"Don't be a bastard, Stokey," she whispered to herself. "Just this once don't be a bastard."

The ride down from Shadow had been a nightmare. Zach chatted amiably, evidently unaware of how deftly he'd crushed her. At the bus station he gave her a long, lingering kiss, his palms stroking the backs of her flanks.

At that moment she wanted to stay in his arms forever. Then she wanted to break his neck. The four days they'd shared together ran through her head like a videotape on endless loop. With her eyes closed and her forehead leaning against the black night of the bus window, she kept trying to stop the action. She wanted to know why. How had she managed to convince herself that Zach loved her, or that she loved him, for that matter? Diving headfirst into the vision in his eyes and not knowing how to swim.

Airstream baby in love with love.

I don't even know what love really is, she thought. The tears were ready to well up again and she fought them, building a dam, brick by brick. No, she didn't know what love was, but she sure as hell knew what it *wasn't.*

The other thing she knew—a kind of relief came to her as she thought of it—was that she would never again put a man ahead of her. *She* would come first.

Her voice. Her talent. Her song.

Love could wait. Maybe when she'd made it into the spotlit world she imagined, maybe when she had arrived—maybe, just maybe she'd take the time to find out about love. Until then, fuck all the dreamy cowboys with their promises and lies, their four-day love affairs. Fuck Zachary Curtis.

And oh, oh how she wanted to.

5

Ronnie caught them in Reno. At the dirty little bus station, feeling pretty damn dirty and little herself, she splurged the last of her money and hired a cab. One last indulgence: She was going to need all her strength to deal with Paul Stokey.

"What's the name of this place, lady?" The cab driver appraised her through dark glasses, his fingers drumming the wheel.

"I forget," she said. "Drive past every club in town."

"Anything you say, lady," he said, veering out into the traffic. "Some like to gamble, some like to get taken for a ride."

"And some do both," she muttered, settling into the hollow of the back seat. A pair of dice hung from the mirror, a talisman of luck. Ronnie needed some. Her fingernails were bitten to the quick. Her stomach was sour. She wanted a drink but figured the last thing she needed was an oiled tongue spitting out things she would later regret.

"First time in Reno, lady?"

Ronnie, peering anxiously out the window, ignored him. Her bus ride resolution had vaporized in the light of day: The thought of being broke and alone in a strange city terrified her. By the time she spotted the beat-up Chevy van at the curb of the Linda Lido Lounge, she was ready. Ready to swallow her pride. Ready to beg for her job back, on her knees if necessary.

"Fifteen bucks, lady."

"Keep the change." Being absolutely flat would make it easier to be humble.

At four in the afternoon the Lido was a gloomy forest of

chrome chairs tipped up on tabletops. Someone with no more substance than a shadow was pushing a broom across the linoleum floor and missing most of it. In the dimness by the stage Ronnie discerned several figures.

The Okie brothers were playing cards, content unto themselves, as usual. Kenny stood with his hands in his pockets, bemusedly watching Paul, who was talking with a large man Ronnie had never seen before. The stranger was built like a pork barrel, with a thick, short chest. He wore a white Stetson, a string tie, and his sharply creased trousers were tucked into a pair of tooled leather boots.

An argument was in progress—she heard Paul's high, strident voice—and Ronnie assumed the stranger was the club owner, or maybe a liquor commissioner looking to get fixed.

"Ronnie!" Kenny hailed her, obviously delighted. As the rest of the group turned she saw a pocket watch in the stranger's hand. Kenny gave her a bear hug and whispered, "Be cool, baby. This is the big honcho."

"Speaking of the devil," said Paul Stokey, wearing a deadly grin. "Here's the little gal now. Right on time."

The stranger grunted, snapped his watch case shut, and proceeded to look her up and down.

"How's your daddy, girl?" he asked.

Stokey was giving off waves and she read the signal in his glittering eyes: Don't fuck this up, bitch. Play it as it lays.

"He's better," she said hesitantly. Stokey nodded. "*Much* better," she said, emboldened.

"Glad to hear it," said the stranger. As his face shifted in the light she saw the knot of tobacco nestled in his cheek. It gave him a curious slur as he spoke, adding to his porcine aura. "This here is a ten-week tour, girl, and we can't be running off to nurse invalids."

"Ah, Ronnie, this is Mr. Rankans," interjected Stokey. He put his arm around her waist. So far as the stranger knew, they were the best of friends. "He's the guy that's been booking us all these months."

"Just Tex. This 'mister' stuff is for shitheels and sheriffs." He moved in closer to survey her, his eyes as cold as an Arkansas blizzard. "Gonna need an alteration or two. No big deal."

Ronnie shivered. Tex Rankans looked capable of altering her limb from limb.

"Just the suit, honey." He chuckled from deep inside his barrel chest. "Just a little old cowboy suit I brung along for ya. That ragamuffin look is okay for piss joints, but not for aud-it-or-iums."

He pronounced it like several words, all of them valuable. "Auditoriums?"

Rankans nodded, jowls puffing. He smiled with all the charm of a gila monster on a rock in the noonday sun. "Right. I just stumbled onto a good thang, honey, and I'm passin' it round. You gonna be travelin' with some good ol' boys from Macon, Georgia. Name of the Laker Brothers."

Ronnie stared at him, unaware that her mouth hung slack. With his fat, hooded eyes and a drawl that had to be partly for effect, he looked like a creature from another world; a cunning creature to be sure. She'd never heard of the Laker Brothers—not many had—but Rankans seemed to be promising something special. What her part was in this was not yet clear, but since Paul was obviously enthusiastic and had ignored his best chance to humiliate her in front of the band, it had to involve money or recognition, which amounted to the same thing.

"Let's get us all some red meat," said Tex, indicating his ample waistline. "Then I'll spill the beans."

He sported them to a meal at The Longhorn, one of Reno's better restaurants, and over numerous courses and gallons of Don Equus beer, Ronnie came to understand what was coming down.

The waiter responded to Tex's soft-spoken requests as if a whip cracked over him, setting out plates of chili peppers, large black olives, salted scallions, and pan-fried shrimp, reeking of garlic and fresh butter.

"First we warm up the boiler," chuckled the big man. With that he chomped into a whole chili pepper, his eyes watering happily. "Then we stoke up with this fine Mex beer and just a wee snort of this here poison I brung along."

He uncorked a bottle of something that looked suspiciously like contraband mescal, and placed a shot glass of it next to each beer. "Raise 'em up, children," he ordered. "A toast to Capricorn."

Kenny, sitting close enough to bump her knees lasciviously under the table, filled her in. What Tex Rankans had "stumbled" into (actually he had been negotiating for months, but it amused him to play it down) was a contract to book the promotional tour for a new, soon-to-be-hot band. Capricorn was releasing what was touted to be the album that would put the Laker Brothers on the map. The purpose of the tour was to flog the LP city by city, right through the Sunbelt and then up to New York for a closeout at Fillmore East.

"This boy Alvin is hot," explained Tex, as he rubbed his hands gleefully over a platter of steaming, pit-barbecued corn. "Finger-lickin' hot."

The Okie brothers nodded sagely. They'd heard of Alvin Laker and his extraordinary, steel-crying solos. But Ronnie was more interested in watching Tex Rankans as he consumed ear after ear of buttered corn with the smooth, clicking efficiency of an electric typewriter, pausing frequently to regale them with anecdotes, all the while urging them to gorge themselves.

At first he impressed her as gross and monstrous, cut from the coarse cloth of the rural south (he was from Alabama, not Texas), but the more she listened the more she began to respect his geniality, his expansive, if cold-blooded view of the music world. The old boy had been around. Nashville, Memphis, Kansas City. Hell, he'd booked Buddy Holly and the Big Bopper, once upon a time. He'd sat up into the wee hours, boozing with Patsy Cline. He'd even had a few run-ins with the Colonel when Elvis was first starting to happen.

"Y'all listen to old Tex, hear?" he told them, spearing another beef rib from one of the platters that seemed to be arriving perpetually. "I string bullshit out like sausage links, but it's Prime

Number One bull, lemme tell y'all. And the prime purpose of this here business—which is show business and don't ever think different or you'll be back at the pickle factory—is money. M-O-N-E-Y, just like the Kingsmen sing it. . . ." He wiped a platter clean with a hot corn tortilla, folded it up like a handkerchief, and injected it into his throat. "I aim to get a hunk of the action and there's droppings for us all. That's where you folks come in. Like this: Old Tex books the main act, 'n he had to negotiate his balls off, hair and all—pardon me, honey—for a might slim cut. So I make it up on the second fiddle, which is, if you ain't guessed, *you.* " He glanced round, making eye contact with each of them. "Yessiree, the good ol' Roughriders, bless their larcenous little hearts." He reached across the table and touched Ronnie's hand. "That's on account of you, honey. Capricorn wants a backup band with a girl singer so as not to cramp Al Laker's style, and the clubheads—" in Tex's vernacular, the club owners or managers "—tell me you're the hottest thang to hit my circuit since Janis split for Cal-if-horn-aye-ay. Frankly, if you hadn't showed when you did I was goin' with another band entirely. And I loved that tall tale about your sick daddy, so don't let these boys run roughshod on you, ha ha." Seeing Paul glare, he chuckled good-naturedly. "Hell, looky that fire there! I *like* to promote a little friction, it gives y'all sparks, hear?"

Ronnie ignored the heat in Stokey's eyes. The beer and the mescal were starting to go off in her head with that familiar sense of temporary well-being. And she liked Tex better the more he talked, particularly if his subject was Ronnie Garrik.

Praise from the club owners was news to her. She knew the 'Riders were drawing better than they ever had; SRO had become the rule, rather than the exception, even on weeknights. But that it might be *her* doing, or that the management people were aware of *her* drawing power, rather than the 'Riders as a whole, was a subject she'd never dared raise, not with Paul in command. He did the arranging, selected most of the tunes, and he sure as hell ran the band. The dynamic tensions that had alternately drawn the two of them together and pushed them apart were all wrapped up with egos, she knew, hers and Stokey's, with Kenny bouncing from one to the other like a pinball clown. But that some of Paul Stokey's resentment might be plain jealousy had never seemed plausible (he had plenty of talent of his own, didn't he?) until Tex made a point of mentioning it.

"Works out like this," the booking agent was saying. He continued to use the soft tortillas like napkins, polishing platters, daubing sauce from his chin, then inhaling the unleavened dough like a puff of yellow smoke. "Capricorn is financing the tour. The whole thing is to sell the record, 'n' they'll be lucky to break even on the tour itself, seein' as how Alvin and his boys demolish an expense account. So they budget fifteen hundred a week for the warm-up act—I'm puttin' this right on the table, folks, so we all know where we stand." He spread his hands out, and from his pudgy fingers came a glitter of rhinestone light. "Because your old pal Tex here is taking exactly one half of that, namely seven hundred and fifty bucks, and the good ol' Roughriders are takin' the other half and not bitching about it, see?"

"I don't get it, Tex." The glaze in Paul's eyes was fading, and his fist clenched a beer bottle, knuckle white.

"Looky here, boy," said Tex, bearing down. "Seven and a half is better than you're makin' right now. And it's really a hell of a lot better, 'cause you'll be eatin' and sleepin' with the Laker band." He glanced Ronnie's way and chuckled slyly. "And in mighty fine style, too. So you can bank your salary, or waste it on goofballs, or whatever. All you gotta do, boy, is say the wrong word and I'll find me another band."

"But that's a *rip-off!*" cried Paul, tense with indignation.

Kenny took a blank ear of corn and poked Stokey in the chest. "Belay that, you asshole! We're in, all of us. Aren't we?" Kenny, grinning mischieviously, looked from the Okie brothers to Ronnie, and back to Paul, who was rubbing the spot right over his heart.

"Right," said the guitarist. "Forget what I said, Mr. Rankans. It's a deal."

Tex remained in Reno for another ten days, alternately eating prodigiously, working with the band, and taking brief respites in the casinos, where he fed an endless supply of silver dollars into the one-armed bandits.

"Gotta lose a little before you win," he intoned, jerking the arm down, watching the totems flick by. He made it sound like a mysterious litany of success.

Tex's boisterous enthusiasm contributed to Ronnie's growing sense of excitement. They were due to join the Laker Brothers in Baton Rouge in a matter of days, and she tried to imagine what it would be like, traveling with a band that had made it, or was about to. She would soon discover it was not so very different, just more of everything: more people, more shows, more drugs, more sex, and more, much more, of the road.

But in Reno, rebounding with a vengeance from Zach Curtis, she basked in the attention Tex Rankans focused on her (later she would understand just what he'd been up to) and soaked up his expertise.

He rented a rehearsal hall convenient to the Longhorn, and the Roughriders began to pare their numbers down, refining the best fifty minutes they could come up with. Tex left the music to Paul. What he concentrated on was the presentation.

"You got to do more than play the songs," he said. "Sounds obvious, but there it is." He ruminated, chewing his cud of Redman chaw like an old range bull. "This is an act, no different than juggling oranges or spinning plates or riding one of them you-ner-cycles. So you got to *act*, see? Got to strut your stuff." This was directed toward Ronnie, who had trouble getting "up" for a mere rehearsal. "I don't claim to love this kind of music, folks, surely I don't. Gimme a sweet country fiddle and a five-string banjo anyday, but I make a mighty fine livin' selling this stuff and I know what it's about. Rock 'n' roll is just loud sex, pure and simple. So you got to give 'em a taste of it, get their blood hot."

The loud sex Tex had in mind was made specific in the white cowgirl suit. It was a bone of contention between Ronnie and him.

"Looky here, girl," he said, fixing a stone grin on his enormous face, "we ain't talking clubs now. This act needs costumes. And this here is *your* costume, get it?"

Ronnie took the suit into the back room. It took her twenty minutes to wriggle into the white satin pants. The crotch seam was cut so high they were, in her estimation, obscene. The seat molded her buttocks, revealing all of her considerable curves. And at Tex's direction the little rhinestone-studded over-vest was altered so that her bosom, already puffed up with perfectly ridiculous ruffles on the sheer blouse, was made to jut out like a pair of Cadillac head lamps.

"I feel like Dale Evans in a porno flick," she complained. "Or somebody's creepy wet dream."

Tex guffawed. Kenny broke up at the sight of her, made a show of getting down on all fours and panting like a dog. She treated him to a sharp prod from her new, extra fancy cowgirl boots.

Tex looked solemn when he presented her with a flat, velvet-lined box. In it were two chromed pistols with carved ivory handles.

"These are for the finale," he explained. "They fire smoke-charged blanks, just so you don't get carried away and shoot somebody with real bullets, honey."

She slung the pistols into her tooled holster. The pistols were just corny enough to appeal to her, but the pants were embarrassing.

"I *can't* wear these," she wailed. "I look like a two-bit whore."

"Trust me," said Tex. "A year from now you won't need a prop like this, but right now the point is to get noticed. They may not remember the name, but they'll sure as hell recall them pants and the shiny pistols."

"But *Tex*—"

"Wear 'em, damn it."

She wore them. And she let him bring in a makeup artist from one of the girlie shows who taught her how to accent her eyes in the broad, heavy-handed manner that worked best under bright stage lights. At first she was miserable, caking on layers of crude paint, but after a while she got into it. Garish makeup was definitely out that year, and it amused her to be different, to emphasize her dark blood, to try out a new, outrageous personality.

"You're a natural-born ham," Tex told her. "Take advantage of it. Save up your crazy and use it on stage."

The tunes got tighter and tighter, choreographed and perfected. Kenny sketched out a lighting plan, later to be implemented by the tour producer. Ray Okie, normally a reticent vocalist, worked on harmonizing with his brother until, sweet and high-pitched, they could doo-wop with the best of them for an a cappella version of "Ain't Misbehavin'," the Fats Waller classic.

"Only thing missing is some original mat-er-ial," said Tex, pronouncing it the way he did auditorium, as if it implied money.

It was the opportunity Ronnie had been waiting for. Using Tex as a front for the idea she introduced three of Zach's songs, including "Airstream Baby." Weeks later she would still be singing it with a mysterious vengeance that left her trembling and the audience incredulous.

She made it her song in a way Zach never envisioned, and she was never sure if it was hate or love that made it work for her.

In the air of excitement and anticipation Paul Stokey's mania for perfection peaked. Kenny responded, and in the sessions, where he usually goofed off, he became, to everyone's amazement, a tight-lipped, tight-assed, ultra-tight trap player.

Stokey's moods, always changeable, became euphoric.

"We'll blow them away," he bragged after taking "Back Door Man" apart and putting it back together in a new, fast chop version. "After they get a load of us those fucking Georgia boys will be like *nothing.*"

That got a belly laugh from Tex Rankans. "Dream on, sonny," he said. "I like what you got, but nobody is gone blow away Alvin Laker. No siree." He kept chuckling until Paul was dark with fury.

That evening he practiced until his well-calloused fingers

began to bleed. He played on, working like a frantic pistoned engine, until the strings were slimy with blood. Rankan's goad had worked.

The best part of Reno for Ronnie was rediscovering her voice. She had been using and abusing it for months, taking it for granted. Now, with Stokey concentrating on the small details of each tune, she began experimenting, using her voice like an instrument. She discovered that slight shadings conveyed a whole range of emotions, that she could project feelings that could only be expressed in musical phrases. She learned to use her own sorrows and joys as a conduit: To conjure up a sense of desperation for "You're Not There" she had only to think of Zach and she had a real catch in her throat; she recalled the home she'd taken too much for granted when she sang "I'm So Lonesome I Could Cry"; she reexperienced the frantic, fast-lane pace of road life for Carole King's "Loco Motion."

"I don't know what it is you're doin', honey," Tex told her, weighing her down with a heavy arm after a late session. "But it sounds fine. Real fine."

"She's got the Hook," said Kenny.

"How's that?"

"The Hook. Ronnie just reaches out and grabs you in. No use resisting when she's got her Hook going."

The Hook. She loved it. And she began to think of it that way, as a physical thing she used on an audience, a bridge built by her voice, drawing them to her. There would be times when she would regret having that ability, when all she wanted to do was build an impregnable shelter around herself.

But in Reno, burning off barbecue food in happy, eighteen-hour workouts, she wanted it all. The arms reaching up to her from the dancing mob. Her name on their lips, and her song beating like a new heart to pump the adrenal flows of rock 'n' roll.

Tex handed Paul a yellow clasp envelope.

"Tickets, vouchers. First week's pay. You'll meet with the main act in Baton Rouge for sound checks. From here on in you take your orders from their road manager. Be good, hear?" He gazed at them with cold, dispassionate eyes. Then he swaggered to the back door and let loose a stream of brown tobacco juice.

"You're on your own now," he drawled. It was late in the day and the Alabama was showing through his Texas veneer. "All on your lonesome . . ."

They were ready.

6

The cocaine was seventy percent pure and it cut through her veil of exhaustion like a bolt of ice-white lightening. The hum of the air conditioners and the muffled vibrato of the diesel began to work into an imaginary duet. In the back, in the dark, someone plucked a banjo to the click click rhythm.

Song of the tarmac. Dueling diesels.

"Cop another line, angel?" His eyes were shining with a false, chemical light. His name was Nick, no last name offered, and he'd brought a head of long, sun-bleached hair from Santa Cruz, his point of origin. At the moment he was employed as a gaffer on the light and sound crew, although his real function seemed to be to procure and dispense drugs.

"This is good buzz dust," he told her. "Straight from Bogata by way of San Jose."

Ronnie didn't care where it came from. She just needed something to cut the edge. It was day thirty of the tour, and it might have been year thirty, the way time dragged. The early morning hung over her like a slavering wolf with electric eyes, ready to pounce and drag her into an exhausted, unpleasant unconsciousness, full of muscle twitches and bad dreams.

"You're a doll, Nick. Just what the doctor ordered."

As she did the line, bending down over the mirror he held, she became physically aware of his lean thigh as it pressed against hers. He was as cute a surfer boy as ever she had seen. He seemed to be less vulgar than the other roadies, and it was one of those "any port in a storm" nights.

He put his hand on her knee and began to massage it. She saw his white smile in the darkness.

The first two weeks had been one long, continual rush. Now, although the actual performance never failed to stimulate her, the grimy task of waiting for breakdown, waiting for the roadies to pack up, waiting to get to the next city—all the minor irritations of a traveling entourage were starting to get major. The sense of late night tension came and went as Ronnie adjusted to the alternating rhythms of the tour, but that night, with Nick's smooth hands sculpting her upper legs, it was particularly strong.

She needed release.

Ronnie took a deep breath and let the coke wash over her. The bus was one of three employed in their migration. Leased from a custom service catering to tour shows, it had been converted into a lush playpen on wheels. Due to limitations in size it reminded her of a submarine. A soft, luxurious submarine, to be sure, with all the hard edges foamed and covered, with private nooks, an undersized waterbed, a stainless steel kitchenette, mostly unused, and a stereo with display dials that made it look like the command bridge of a sci-fi spaceship.

But in the end there was nothing that could save it from being a bus.

"Can you feel it, baby?" Nick whispered, his breath cool and minty. He was referring to the cocaine, which was at that moment making little stars appear behind her eyes. His hands touched her breasts, tracing the shapes of her nipples, and she didn't bother to resist.

"Lemme make you feel good, huh?" whispered Nick, his tongue like a feather at her ear.

In that moving edge of darkness, far from the dreamless sleep she craved, it was easy to let him have his way. Nick unsnapped her jeans, shrugged them down far enough so he could slip a hand between her legs and work deft fingers into her underpants. After a while she gave herself up to the fingers, burying her face against his warm neck and letting the tension go like a breath being exhaled. The wetness came as he flicked in and out of her. She began to rock her hips slowly, unconsciously picking up the rhythm of the bus.

Thoughts drifted in, cocaine images. The hot, fetid room in Juarez where, with the prop of an old fan stirring the syrupy air, she had first been laid. What was his name? Tom? Strange to have forgotten. And those motel nights with Kenny (now sleeping platonically two buses behind her), that hot urgency, akin to his drums, the beat beat beat as he stroked into her.

Nick's voice soothed her as his fingers worked, as her hips twitched and her breath came faster, remembering the best part of Zach Curtis, the wild romance.

"Oh, yes," she whispered. Fingertips thick with her honey, encircling the nub where sparkles of pleasure rose in measures toward crescendo. "Yes." His tongue probing the secret thrill spot under her chin. "Yes." And the hot, electric tightness curling up from her toes. *"Yes, oh!"* And the flush of heat radiating, hot behind her eyes, building, tightening her body like the single string of an instrument. "Nick!" Riding those marvelous quick fingers up over the last peak as it came flooding, pouring out of her, all the forgotten sighs like a blast of steam in her blood and the lust to keep driving his fingers into her, letting it keep coming, milking every last twinge of pleasure.

"Okay. It's okay, angel," he said. He could feel her tears, the cold sheen of sweat on her forehead.

Ronnie reciprocated by going down on him, hoping the shadows would conceal them. He was ready, had been on the verge of it, untouched, and was done in a few moments. One hot gush, warm and salty. It doesn't taste like anything, really, she thought as she drew back. He's a nice guy and we both need the sleep. . . .

Daylight broke, mean and low, as she stumbled out of the bus. They waited at the curb of yet another Holiday Inn while the road manager got his shit together, dealing with the desk clerk.

What a sorry sight we are, she thought. A group of pale boys, some not old enough to vote, and their camp followers, little chirpy girls with madras handkerchiefs covering small, proud breasts. Hard to imagine that in twelve hours they would transform themselves into a high-driving, heavy rocking band capable of blowing away a mob of eight thousand demanding fans.

Nick slung his arm around her waist. Ronnie didn't mind, but thought: I hope he knows I'm going to my room alone. That mild dilemma was resolved in the next moment, when Alvin Laker trailed out of the bus, carrying two guitars.

"Hey Vinny, baby!" cried Nick, strutting up to Alvin. The roadie made sure everyone could hear him say: "You owe me a ten spot, buddy. Not only does the cowgirl give great head, she *swallows!*"

The laughter began. Ronnie remembered the endless mortifications of high school, when "Roothead" had been the butt of similar jibes. The sensation of returning to that nightmare was intolerable, like something hot bursting inside.

The next thing she was aware of was Nick falling, the resounding crack of her furious, full swing slap contorting his face as he headed ass backward to the pavement.

She stood over him, fists clenched. "I don't care what bus you ride in, surfer boy, so long as it ain't mine. Got it?"

He nodded, the shape of her hand a red blotch on his cheek, and the laughter swung round to him, to the frightened willingness of his sudden reversal.

Rule number one, she thought, picking up her bags and marching toward the front desk, don't fuck the roadies.

The legend began at the Palladium, in Memphis. There the planets moved into line, or the auspices were favorable, or perhaps time and place collided to the beat of a five-piece band.

A relic from another era, the once grand Palladium was originally a showcase for light opera and for the surviving white aristocracy, or those who aspired to it. A pantheon of gilded cherubs still leered from the proscenium arch, as if seeking an aerial glimpse of the fashionable gentry who had once inhabited the private boxes to each side of the orchestra.

Those days were gone. As the interest in opera faded a new, black aristocracy blossomed, and under the aegis of W. C. Handy syncopated music seduced all of Memphis, inundating not only the Palladium but every theater in town.

A native son named Elvis Presley eventually shattered the color barriers; later Mr. Presley would have a boulevard named for him, and his final rest made into a shrine, but that evening the Boss and his music were still alive and well, and the old Palladium was undergoing its final evolution as a showcase for "name" rock bands.

The Laker Brothers, nearing the end of the tour, had begun to attract international attention. Their album was dominating the airways, and T-shirts with their logo were sell-out items on every corner of the city. But the legend born in Memphis did not belong to the boys from Savannah, Georgia. It belonged to an unknown vocalist from Lubbock, Texas.

It belonged to Ronnie Garrik.

Watch out for the cowgirl.
The rumor moved through the crowd as it waited for the box office to open. The night, warm and sultry as only a night in Memphis can be, with the musk of the great Mississippi drifting in across the Chicksaw Bluffs toward the heart of the city, was a night made for getting high, for confiding secrets, for being one of the chosen.

The little girl with the long black hair, they whispered, swapping illicit reefers, sipping illegal beers, look out for that one, she's been shooting up the crowds, I shit you not.

They came to see the Laker Brothers, of course, to hear the songs that now dominated the airways, to catch a glimpse of Alvin himself. But still the rumor passed from ear to ear.

Ronnie Garrik, they told one another, is as hot as a gun slinger's pistol.

It was intoxicating to be part of the underground, to know what was coming down. So it began, a ready-made, mob-woven myth about a half-breed, badass blues belter from the plains of West Texas.

Like most myths, it was not far from the truth.

"My boots! Where in hell are those damn shitkickers?"

Ronnie, barefoot and anxious, was having her regular pre-show heebie-jeebies. Sometimes, in moments of inner clarity, she knew she brought it upon herself, as a way of focusing her energy for the ordeal to come. But at the moment all she could think of was the boots.

"Don't look at me, kid. I ain't got 'em," drawled Gene Laker. He was occupied with the horde of groupies who had lately descended on the tour like a plaque of horny locusts. One girl, encased in a pair of extraordinarily tight hot pants, was gazing at Gene with undisguised rapture. Ronnie thought she looked like a dime store goldfish in a dollar bowl, and just about as sexy.

"Boots?" The groupie tittered, reaching out to touch Gene's forearm, as if stealing touches from a forbidden shrine.

Ronnie stomped out, disgusted. Damn the boppers, they were getting to be like a pack of simpering puppy dogs thick underfoot, all gooey with ready sex and idolatry. Maybe one of the light-fingered little bitches had stolen her boots.

"Try the green room," Paul told her. He and Ray Okie were going over the charts, making yet another refinement in the Stones medley. "And be ready in ten, sweetheart," he added, not without malevolence. "I want to run through the light cues again."

Ronnie bit her tongue and headed for the green room, where the buffet had been laid out earlier in the afternoon. The boots were there, of course, exactly where she'd kicked them off. She jacked her feet in, gave her eyes a final touch-up, and leaned back against the wall.

She began to breathe deeply and quickly, forcing the oxygen, pumping herself up.

They kicked off with "I Fought The Law," an old standard resurrected in a new, hard-driving version. Paul leaned into a series of quick chops, tripping down scales as Kenny walked through his Zildjian cymbals like a demented witch doctor, flashing his patented grin. The Okie brothers stepped in, driving a wall of sound out into the auditorium with the accomplished ease of professional sound chauffeurs.

Ronnie waited, crouched behind Paul's bank of amplifiers, her heart trip-hammering against her ribs. This is what I live for, she thought.

And then she leapt over the amplifiers, one hand on her hat. Under stage lights the cowgirl suit was a sparkling, rhinestone vision in white. Ronnie did a high heel strut up to the microphone, thumbs hooked in her holster.

As she drew the pistols Ronnie heard the cheering start, way up in the third balcony, and a chill went up the back of her neck.

I fought the law

And then six quick shots straight up in the air, six explosions of blank shot smoke, synchronized with six explosions of sound from the band. In the sudden silence, as the crowd drew breath for a roaring response, came Ronnie's clear, defiant voice.

and the law won!

The Palladium broke loose. For the first time the security forces had to link arms and protect the warm-up act as the mob surged forward, clapping time, chanting the chorus, and dancing, leaping straight up in the air, leaning toward Ronnie like flowers toward the sun. She could feel it pouring over her. They always got the crowd going, that was what they'd been hired to do, but it usually took fifteen or twenty minutes to get them there, rocking in rhythm. Tonight they'd been ready, waiting for her. The chemistry was there and she was the catalyst.

As Ronnie poured herself into the microphone she could feel it coming back at her, an animal response of heat and motion.

Instant love.

The best kind, she thought, the only kind.

When the knock came she was alone in the dressing room, naked under an oversized bathrobe, holding a ice-cold beer to her hot forehead.

"Go away. I'm busy being sick."

After a show she felt like she'd run a ten-mile road race. Her stomach, knotted by nerves of excitement, needed an hour or so to unwind. She'd locked the door, thank God.

"Some guy to see you, Ronnie." The voice was Ray Okie's. And he knew better than to disturb her.

"There's no fucking guy I want to see, Ray. Now go away, please?"

"Ronnie, I think you'd better open the door."

Ray was holding onto a bouquet of yellow roses with both hands, it was that big.

"So where's the guy?" She took the bouquet and buried her nose in the delicious perfume of the golden blossoms.

Ray gave her the accompanying envelope.

"There's a car outside, waiting," he said. And then he did a thing which was, for Ray, absolutely unexpected. He leaned over the flowers and kissed her on the cheek. "Good luck." He left, embarrassed at his own audacity.

The face of the card was engraved with a sketch of a Southern mansion. Inside, in a large childish scrawl, she read:

Loved your version of "Jail House Rock"! There's a cold pitcher of mint juleps here, why not come over and cool off?

Elvis.

When she put the roses on the dressing room table her hands were trembling.

7

The Cadillac idled at the curb, taillights glowing with the cold light of distant rockets. Subtle refinements to the chassis and coach caused it to look improbably long, though not disproportionately so. The convertible top was down and neatly booted, and in the argon blush of the street lamps the paint job looked like solid gold.

Maybe it was.

The chauffeur, a pleasant-looking boy in chinos and a flowered shirt, vaulted out of the driver's seat at her tentative approach.

"Nah, he wasn't at the show," he explained as he opened the rear door. "Caught it on the radio. Local broadcast. Man, the Boss went wild when he heard you."

Ronnie was too startled by the implausibility of it all to reply. Was she appropriately dressed, she wondered? She had changed hurriedly, lest the note and the flowers vanish in a puff of smoke. Her offstage wardrobe was usually limited to jeans and tank tops and weird things from rag shops, but she had managed to scrounge up a gauzy, burnt-orange wrap-around skirt with a matching halter top. Selecting three of the finest roses, she placed them carefully in her hair.

She needn't have worried. Out of sheer desperation she had arrived at the simple mode of attire that suited her best. The burnt orange complimented her dark complexion, adding brilliance to her smile and a flash to her eyes, while the thin fabric of the halter gently molded her breasts, accenting her figure. The

102

yellow roses in her black hair were an asterisk, proclaiming unreasonable beauty.

Leaning back as the limousine pulled away, she noticed that the upholstery was of an incredibly soft substance. It seemed almost alive.

"Is this what I think it is?"

"Sable," said the chauffeur. "The Boss don't mess around."

Ronnie wanted to take off her clothes and roll around in it, right there in the back seat, as the Caddy glided down the boulevard, under a canopy of juniper trees, as if on a cushion of air.

She put her head back into the sable and laughed.

"Don't mind me," she told the boy. "I just don't want to wake up. Not yet."

The security guard, who looked as if he might have been the chauffeur's brother, waved them on, and the Caddy sailed through the gate like some great yacht, homeward bound with exotic cargo. The soft, fat tires hissed over the gravel drive, making a sound not unlike an advancing wave on a deserted beach.

The young woman in the back seat was giddy and, by the time they'd docked at the portico, a little frightened. The driver set the brake and opened the door, but Ronnie did not stir.

He was waiting there. A giant magnolia tree made shadows across the face of the mansion, but he spoke from the darkness and she recognized his voice. It occurred to her, as he stepped from the shadows into a thin swathe of starlight, that she didn't really know what he looked like. She had seen pictures, of course, hundreds of them, over the years. But in each he looked slightly different, like an actor altering himself for a new role.

Reverting to an instinct reinforced by the observation of Bette Davis in matinee melodramas, she let him kiss her hand.

"I knew it," he said, leading her through the portico and into the cool interior of the mansion. "I knew you'd be a knockout. I could tell by the way you sing." His voice was soft, compelling, a slow drawl. He took care shaping his words and Ronnie found herself staring at the beautifully formed lips she had admired in so many photographic manifestations. "I should have gone down to the Palladium, maybe," he said, apologizing. "But when I'm home, I kinda *stay* home, is how it is."

They were traversing a burgundy hallway, fantastically appointed. If Ronnie had been ruined by sophistication she might have thought it garish, that lavish, Spanish motif he favored. As it was she thought she had been transported into a dream made real; not her own, but his, and the transfiguration of fantasy was close enough to her heart to make her feel dizzy, almost euphoric.

"The pitcher's full, just like I promised," he chuckled, then laughed in a rich baritone. He was dressed entirely in black, wearing spit-polished boots that looked as deep as ebony. "I almost asked you to come up and see my etchings—I actually have a collection, see—but I thought you might get the wrong idea."

He laughed again, putting her at ease as he poured drinks from a tall iced pitcher.

"Need anything, Boss?" A young man hurried in from a glassed-in porch. He clicked his heels and made a mock bow as Elvis introduced her.

"Want a bite to eat, Ronnie? Not sure? Just in case, Rick, bring in a bowl of that creole shrimp." Speaking, he gestured with hands that were slightly plump, masterfully expressive, and glittering with jewels that would have tempted the Forty Thieves. On another man the rings might have looked ostentatious. On Elvis they were just right.

They sat in opposite chairs and made small talk, sipping their drinks. To start the conversation was a chore for Ronnie. She would have preferred to sit silently, watching him. Immediately she sensed a strong current, almost an undertow of attraction. Oddly, she couldn't interpret it as a sexual attraction, but she did know that he was a man of radiant masculinity, which he had learned to focus at will.

Together they polished off the highly spiced, delicately textured shrimp and most of a pitcher of mint juleps, their tartness an odd but pleasant contrast to the shrimp.

"You've got the raw sound I like," Elvis told her. He seemed more at ease flattering her than talking about himself, no matter how hard she tried to steer the conversation in that direction. "Don't let 'em mess you up with lessons. Keep learnin' by listenin', that's the true method."

He implied, by constant reference to her "career," that she was on the verge of busting out, making it big. It was a perfect compliment to her fantasies. After blowing out the Palladium and attracting the attention of the man who had started it all, it seemed not only possible, but immediate. Tomorrow the contracts would come rolling in, records would be made, tours arranged, and she would soon inhabit the glossy photographs she'd mooned over back in Lubbock.

All of it was to happen. None of it happened the way she imagined.

"Once you get there, well, that's a different kettle of fish." Elvis was pacing the room, suddenly agitated, as if disturbed by all this talk of stardom. He constantly readjusted the pink-tinted glasses he wore. "All the little things are different. But the big stuff stays the same." He knocked back the last of the drink, his eyes gone distant, secret. "The big stuff surely stays the same. You just have to keep busy. Keep takin' care of business. I had 'em put that on the tail of my airplane: Takin' Care of Business."

Over the course of the next few hours Ronnie was to notice these periodic distractions or abrupt mood swings. He would be seemingly content, almost intoxicated with a sense of music, or yarn-swapping, or wherever the conversation strayed, and then suddenly the fire would die in his eyes and he would lapse into silence.

It was not something he cared to refer to, although he made certain oblique references to the cause of his melancholy.

"Listen to that boy wail! Damn, but he sounds fine," he clapped his hands together, delighted by Alvin Laker's long, bottleneck solo. He had switched on the radio via a remote terminal (the "boogie box," he called it) and the tail end of the Palladium concert filled the room. "Boy's on his way up now. Get it while the gettin's good, if he's got a brain in his head. Hell of a lot better

lookin' forward than back." He searched her eyes, trying to impart
—what? A sense of loss, of loneliness? But before she could push
it any further he was on his feet, his body radiating energy,
happily guiding her toward the rumpus room, where he kept a
record library, his collection of musical instruments, a glass case
jammed with martial arts memorabilia, and enough recording
equipment to rival the most advanced studios.

"If it's worth hearing, I got it," he said proudly as she stared
in awe at the catalogued library. Thousands, upon thousands of
albums, forty-five's, and even the old seventy-eight's, arranged by
artist, category, and occasionally by whim alone. "You got a
couple of good old Oklahoma boys in your band, I believe. Get
a load of *this* Okie."

He touched a switch and Leon Russell's gravelly southern
voice drifted in, raspy and real.

> *I got a right to love*
> *under the stars above*

The reproduction was so good that Ronnie had to resist the
temptation to look behind the partition and see if old Leon was
there, spoofing on her. Elvis paced the room, his face wide open,
delighted with himself as he strummed an invisible guitar to the
song.

He began cueing up albums like a reefer-mad disc jockey,
exhorting her to listen, to hear this, to marvel at the incredible
range of creative talent he could summon to his fingertips, song
after song.

"Whole lot of good people out there, all of 'em singin' their
hearts out. And Ronnie," he pivoted on a boot heel, leveling an
extended arm at her, "you are as good as any one of them. *Believe*
it!"

He sounded like an evangelist, summoning her faith. She
had given up denying his compliments. He wouldn't stand for it.
From time to time one of his entourage—the Memphis Mafia,

as he called them—checked in to see if the Boss wanted anything; food, drink, companionship, but he waved them away.

"Got my hands full, Dave. Got the 'Yellow Rose of Texas' here, and I want her all to myself." He chuckled lasciviously for the boy's benefit, but when they were alone he made no attempt to seduce her. They were both too excited by their sudden intimacy to risk the complication of sex.

Elvis played gracious host in the grand manner, making her forget all about her original nervousness. Ronnie felt as if they had laid the foundation of a new and complex friendship by the time dawn began to streak in.

"Ain't ready for morning yet," said Elvis, his voice suddenly tight. He readjusted the venetian blinds. "No way."

"I should get going," Ronnie offered. The intensity of their conversation had begun to exhaust her. "We have another show tonight."

"No!" For a moment his face was contorted, but he softened as soon as he knew she did not intend to pick up and go right that minute. "I'm not ready to have you leave yet, Ronnie."

There was a strange, foreign note of pleading in his voice. She was incredulous when he told her he didn't want to be left alone, not right then.

"Alone?" she asked. The mansion was chockfull of companions, servants, members of his extended family.

"Come on. Got to show you something."

He took her out to the stables, where he kept his collection of motor vehicles. A slant of eerie light partially illuminated the warehouse, which was large and opulent enough to rival a museum. Row upon row of Cadillacs, Lincolns, and deep lacquered Rolls glittered there, tuned and polished and ready to go.

His motorcycles were stored in the room beyond. They gleamed like black, demonic bugs, their headlamps like unblinking eyes. Harleys, Nortons, a pair of custom BMW's with sidecars, and a rare old Indian, fully restored.

More love and time had been invested here, she sensed, than in all the rooms of the mansion.

"These are my babies," he explained. "Sometimes it gets lonesome no matter how many people I pay to hang around. That's when I come out here . . . been back from a Vegas swing for two weeks, and I'm goin' stir crazy already."

For the first time she pinpointed the peculiar lilt of his voice, the focus of his inflection: He was talking to himself. And yet it was not a selfish act. It was something beyond his control.

"Things are mighty fast out there in Vegas," he said dreamily. "Real fast. I like the speed." His hand brushed the saddle of one of the big, squat bikes. He swung a leg over, seating himself, but made no effort to actually start up the machine. "Sometimes, late at night, I climb on one of these old Harleys and just let her rip."

Ronnie wanted to go to him, to hold him, but there was a barrier, a wall of his own construction, and she knew he could not be touched, not in a real way.

"Just shiftin' up through the gears, clicking 'em in nice and smooth. Purring. On that stretch of Fifty-one, headin' south. You got to hang on with both hands." He gripped the bar, clenching his powerful forearms. "Get her flyin' up around a hundred and sixty, real easy. Lock the throttle back and *fly.*" He laughed without a vestige of mirth. "Lord, don't the wind feel good."

Ronnie stood stock still, afraid to move, afraid to disturb the morbid drift of his thoughts.

"I guess that's what I like best, driving flat out. There's something there, inside the wind. You keep tryin' to get *inside* it, see? Don't ask me for what, or what's there. I don't know what. But it must be something you can only have the one time . . ." Abruptly he swung off the machine. "Damn, what am I sayin'?"

He put an arm around her shoulders as they walked back up the drive toward Graceland. Little fingers of mist drifted up from the vast lawn.

The chauffeur who drove her back was the same freckled boy, but the limo was a chocolate brown Rolls. Under different circumstances she would have loved it, cruising in that immaculate conveyance, watching the sun glance off the winged ornament, so quiet and cool she might have been in a Swiss bank vault.

As it was she was too drained, emotionally depleted, to appreciate it. After a quick, hot shower she crawled into bed. The blankness in her mind spread like a blot of ink as she slept the profound sleep of mental exhaustion.

By the end of the next day, as the tour moved on to the next engagement, she had given up trying to explain why she hadn't slept with him.

The state of grace came to an end in Savannah, Georgia when, one afternoon, they found the stage door bolted shut.

"Can you believe this shit?" Paul Stokey scuffed the toe of his boot against the door. "I mean, what the fuck is going on here?"

They walked around to the front of the Coliseum and discovered the box office padlocked from the outside.

"I don't like this," said Kenny. He shivered in the murky afternoon heat. "I got a real bad feeling."

They drove back to the motel through the sleepy streets of Savannah. It was late fall and the air had the hangdog smoke of Indian summer. The rented limo swung off a wide, near empty avenue onto Montgomery Street, where the median strip was bright with late blooming flowers.

Ronnie watched them blur by like chips in a kaleidoscope.

They heard it coming from the lobby before they entered: the high keening sound of women mourning.

Alvin Laker was dead at twenty-five, run down by a truck, and the tour disintegrated. The 'Riders were out of it again, and nobody knew it better than Ronnie.

"It's not fair," she said, fighting the panic inside. "We were so *close.*"

The cruelest twist had been the tease of Memphis, where they had first connected, first had intimations of what it would be like to headline. The Palladium had fired them up, made them expectant and eager. Now they were expelled into a stark, unemployed reality.

While Ronnie lay supine in her locked motel room, sipping bourbon and fighting off the depression that hovered all around her, Paul Stokey called Tex Rankans. He shoveled quarters into a pay phone, fending off insistent reporters waiting to file Alvin's obituary.

"I'm real sorry to hear it, son. A tragedy, I sincerely mean that. But I can't do nothin' for y'all now. Truth is, my calendar is full, boy. Ah figured the 'Riders would be bookin' on another tour, or maybe gettin' a tour of your own. I can't dump another band now to make room for you boys, it ain't done that way."

Paul felt so low he didn't bother to slam the receiver down.

Over the next few days Ronnie gained a new respect for her lead guitar player. While the rest of them wallowed in depression, Paul put on a clean shirt, polished his boots, and went to work. He leased a van with their last paycheck and went from club to roadhouse to café, cassette player in hand, hustling gigs.

110

"We've got to dust ourselves off and climb back up on the horse," he told Ronnie. "We finally got some momentum and we can't let it go."

He was right, of course. Later, when things got tangled and mean between them, she remembered. You can't let it stop. You get slapped in the face, doused with cold water, a scathing review, an album that flops. Whatever.

You don't stop.

Stopping is the end.

They gigged at places like The Pink Flamingo, The Buttercup, J & Dee's Bar-B-Q. Weaving a crooked, last call path across rural Georgia, playing in run-down factory towns, in grange halls, in brick cities built around bankrupt cotton mills, working their way toward Atlanta.

And they *worked.*

Working each and every song, working for the attention and eventually the admiration of the sullen, boozy patrons. Bearing down, number after number, developing reserves of finesse and sheer guts Ronnie never knew she had. Those backwater months became the crucible in which her professional aplomb was forged and tempered; where she learned the art of looking into the audience, finding the few who resisted, and reaching out to them, drawing them in like reluctant trout after an iridescent lure.

Ronnie didn't allow herself to worry about why they had stalled after the Laker Brothers' tour, why no one was breaking down the door to sign them. It would happen. It *had* to happen, and for now she made the best of it, working the grueling circuit again, night after night.

When Tex Rankans finally put a call through to them at a club in Eastman, where they had been playing to a packed house for a week, Paul was able to tell him politely but firmly that the Roughriders were booked for the foreseeable future, thank you.

Rankans' response was hearty and genuine, as if he had been expecting as much. "Yeah, ah heard through the grapevine y'all been cutting through Georgia like Sherman to the sea," he chuckled. "Wish y'all the best of luck, 'n' if it all falls through, gimme a few weeks' notice and ah'll put you back on top in the Southwest."

"Mr. Rankans, sir," said Paul in his coolest voice, "I don't care if we never see Weed, Texas again."

"Can't blame you for that, son, but don't go burnin' no bridges till y'all crossed the river, hear?"

They heard him, and they continued to burn their way across Georgia, county by county, until, on the outskirts of Atlanta, in the month of December, they found a home at Dugals.

Irene Dugal, a widower, managed her roadhouse with an attention to detail that extended to her patrons, whom she treated as part of the family—to the degree that she administered motherly scoldings to those who screwed up. A proud, broad-hipped woman with the mien and humor of an Eve Arden, she was unaware that she was about to become a small part of a very large legend.

She did know what was good for her club, and after three nights, each bringing in a bigger take than the previous, she asked the 'Riders to be her house band.

"Honey," she told Ronnie, "this place ain't sold so much booze since Lester Maddox rode by on his bicycle, backward. Stay as long as you please. You keep the cover charge, I'll keep what I make from the bar."

Mrs. Dugal hovered over Ronnie like a mother hen, bringing her fresh towels after each sweaty set, offering homilies, advice, and, several times, protection.

"You got to save yourself, honey," said Mrs. Dugal after chasing off one of Ronnie's more forward, and inebriated, admirers. "It's like a priest saving himself for the Mass, see? Tease 'em, but don't let 'em touch you."

By the end of the show Ronnie was usually too tired to consider bedding down any of the young studs who hung around, ready to buy her drinks, or drugs, or the moon, if that's what it took to get into her pants. It was easier to let Irene show them the door.

"Git yer redneck backsides out of my sight, boys! Keep your grimy paws off my Ronnie, hear?" All this with many gestures of mock anger, after which she would lock up and fuss over her little star, bringing her beakers of iced herb tea and small, pan-fried delicacies from the kitchen.

Ronnie loved it. Dugals experienced a popularity it had never before achieved and Miss Ronnie Garrik became a local celebrity, courted by other lounge owners who wanted to steal her away and by the regional press, eager to cover a local—not to mention sexy—phenomenon. An article in the Sunday paper featured photographs exclusively of Ronnie, galling Paul Stokey and putting attendance up another notch.

The mainsprings were winding. It had to happen soon, of this Ronnie was certain, and when Hank Grossbeck turned up she believed him. Grossbeck had thick, matted hair he wore long in back. His Western-style shirt was open to the third button, showing off a well-developed chest and a small gold medallion he claimed was given him by Sinatra for "services rendered." He knew his part and played it well. That he managed to charm his way past Mrs. Dugal was indicative of his smooth delivery.

He took a surprised Ronnie by the shoulders and kissed her like a long lost lover.

"You and I have business to discuss, darling." He flashed a white, perfect smile, a shark's profile. "How much do you want and when do you want it?"

Her first impression was that his lips had a mean twist, but he personified all the stories she'd heard about fast-talking agents, and he won her over, initially, by entering wholeheartedly into her fantasy of incipient fame and fortune.

"I'm an independent talent scout. Capital, MGM, A&M, I work with all of them. The game is numbers, Ronnie, and names. I know who they are and how to get their greedy little ears on the phone. And believe me, they know who I am. They may hate my guts, but that doesn't stop them from dealing with Hank Grossbeck. They can't afford not to."

Oh, she believed him. She wanted to, and he had the story

down pat, spiced with details. He dropped names with the dexterity of a shell game artist working a pitch at the county fair.

Later she discovered that the closest Hank Grossbeck had gotten to Frank Sinatra was reading about him in *Billboard*. But in the smoky twilight of Dugals he sounded like a real, if sleazy, McCoy.

While the rest of the 'Riders departed, either skeptical of the sleek stranger or not wanting to spook the deal, Grossbeck hoisted up an expensive, gaudily monogrammed attaché case.

"This is neither the time nor the place," he said, eyeing Mrs. Dugal, who watched surreptitiously as she wiped down the bar. "But what I have in mind is an MGM development contract. Just an option to start, then when we hit I'll go for the big money."

It all seemed a bit forward and vulgar, but she assumed that was how it had to be. She knew from the start that Grossbeck expected her to sleep with him. That was a given. If he had been entirely repulsive she might have chucked him out on his ear, connections or no; as it was he had a kind of sensual, animal appeal. The eyes were cold and the lips cruel, but he had a powerful build and a physical confidence that made part of her curious, if not exactly enthusiastic.

"Look, this dump is shutting down," he said, squeezing her knee under the table. "We'll go back to my suite and talk business."

No option was offered. Even the implacable Mrs. Dugal was intimidated, although she did manage to pull Ronnie aside as she left.

"Keep your legs crossed, honey. This one is a real snake."

He was a snake, all right, and he kept his tongue flicking hypnotically, drawing her in.

"You've got it, baby. I knew the minute I saw you. Foxy, dynamite voice, the works. It was fortunate for both of us I was passing through. But let's get something real straight." They were tooling along in his Buick sports coupe, heading for the hotel where he was, he said, "putting together a package" for a group of "local bigwigs." "There is talent under every fucking rock,

Ronnie, I mean it. You think you got the only great set of pipes in the country? For*get* it. What matters is the connection. You want all the goodies, your pictures in the fanzines, your songs on the air, your pinup jacked off to by every horny kid in America? *Sure* you do. So you got to cooperate with me."

Ronnie nodded. That was how it was. They were just passing the motor court where she had been staying for the past few weeks, and she felt a sudden pang for her own, solitary bed. But opportunity was knocking in the form of Hank Grossbeck, hustler and putter-together of packages, and she had to swallow her pride and be realistic.

"You want to get something, you give something," he was saying. "A year from now, maybe you can tell *me* to piss off, but now I'm the one calling the shots. I'll put the right kind of demo together and get the right people to hear it. Trust me on that, baby."

His suite, as it turned out, was just a single room with an ominous king-sized bed. He explained his less than magnificent accommodations by blaming the "idiots" who ran the hotel. "Fucking ignorant crackers," he raged, gesturing with a bottle of cheap champagne. "I'll get you out of this rube city, baby. New York, New York. LA. Man, I *know* LA like the back of my hand. I'm a close personal friend of Roman Polanski. Hell, I used to date Sharon Tate before *he* did."

There were no chairs in the room. Ronnie sat on the edge of the bed, gulping champagne to steady her nerves.

"You know what you really got, baby?" he asked. She was fool enough to shake her head. "You got a truly great set of tits."

He took off his shirt and sat down beside her.

Months later, when she was in a position to find out, Ronnie made inquiries. Henry Grossbeck was not and never had been an agent, nor had he ever represented anyone of importance or talent. He was a jobber for an industrial vinyl manufacturer, which gave him limited access to the purchasing departments of record producers. From there he elbowed his way in to see public relations people, ostensibly to pick up PR handouts; but really to overhear tidbits of gossip that made his invented importance more believable.

Separated by a little time and distance Ronnie could laugh at the report, but that night, caught up in the audacity of his lies, he convinced her. And probably himself as well. He took a small vial from the nightstand.

"Keith Richards laid this on me," he said. He prepared a pipe of kief. The brown powder was real enough, and in about three puffs Ronnie was flying. The kief was of hallucinatory strength, and made what was to follow seem worse even than it was.

For a moment she was giddy, taken up by the tingling rush of the drug. The garish colors of the room softened and the smoky air turned a delightful translucent blue. But then her lungs started to tighten and the kief came down hard, making her feel paralyzed as Grossbeck brushed back her hair and kissed her on the nape of the neck.

He bit her.

Not hard enough to draw blood, but hard enough to leave the mark of his teeth. He had one arm locked around her, crushing her breasts, and she could feel his strength.

"I'm going to fuck you," he said. "Like you've never been fucked before."

The kief bounced off the champagne and made his voice distort, reverberating inside her head like a hollow laugh from a funhouse tunnel.

Ronnie looked down to her ripped-open blouse and saw that her nipples, responding to something she couldn't feel, had stiffened. His large hands wrenched her jeans open and then she was falling back, bouncing into the soft, clinging mattress as he worked her pants partway down her hips.

"Wait a fuckin' minute!"

Ronnie looked around for the shouting voice, realized it was her own just as his hand caught her cheek. She felt nothing, but the sound of it cracked like a gunshot inside her head.

His eyes are pink, she realized, rabbit pink, and his tongue, flicking at his lips as he struggled with her, was a darker shade of the same color. But while her eyes were intrigued with the shifting, abstract hues, her body was tossing, resisting. It was as if there were two Ronnies: one a disinterested observer, the other fighting with all the guts she could muster.

"You're hot, you little bitch!" he panted, crushing her with his weight as he uncoiled one of her arms and pushed it back. "There!"

A cold bracelet on her wrist. She pulled, tried to shake loose, saw the loop of a handcuff locking her to a slat in the headboard. She sat up as he crawled to the other side of the bed. Her head spun; she wrenched at the wrist he'd manacled.

"Lemme go or I'll scream." Her voice broke and she heard herself sobbing.

The hand floated through the blue air, and she was unable to duck as it clamped over her mouth. He began to work her other arm across the bed to where he had another handcuff, waiting.

The bastard had planned the whole thing.

Ronnie bit down on the soft palm of his hand, hard, as hard as she could. Even as he bellowed she tasted the salty blood. He let go, and as she rolled out from under him, his Sinatra medallion broke free and clattered to the floor. That enraged Grossbeck more than the bite on the hand.

"I'm going to beat the shit out of you," he said in a guttural dog growl, and she knew that was exactly what he wanted to do. As he raised a fist, curling lips up over the white shark teeth that had already marked her, Ronnie jerked her arm with all her might.

The pine slat snapped and she was loose, the manacle dangling from her wrist. Panting, she stumbled backward, trying to pull her pants up, her knees hobbled.

Grossbeck put down his head and charged, his massive arms flung wide. Ronnie tripped, and as she went down she swung the manacle.

It caught him full in the face.

"Jesus, my nose!" He was on his knees, hands covering his face. She saw blood pouring between his fingers and heard again, as if delayed between ear and brain, the sickening crunch as the manacle broke the bridge of his nose. "Jesus, you bitch—I just got it fixed!" He was sobbing, the words made mushy by the gushing blood and tears. "I'll kill you, fucking hear me?"

But Ronnie was clutching the torn blouse to cover her breasts and wrenching open the door—he'd slipped the bolt, the bold bastard—and he made no attempt to follow her.

It was about a mile to the motor court. Ronnie walked parallel to the road, off to the side to avoid oncoming lights, and as she walked the shaking gradually stopped and her breath began to come in regular wheezes. She managed to work her wrist free of the cuffs and hurled them into a viaduct.

Fuck it. She was ready to gig at Dugals for the rest of her life. The next sonofabitch who talked big time with her was going to get a mouthful of broken teeth.

Not to mention his balls in a sling.

9

So it was that Jade Gustave, approaching Ronnie after the last set not two days after the Grossbeck incident, was received less than enthusiastically.

"Fuck off!" she told him, point blank. "You and the white horse you rode in on."

Jade, wearing a tropical-weight suit, a raw silk shirt the color of pale lime sherbert, and beige espadrilles, was not the sort of gentleman often spoken to in that tone of voice.

"There must be some mistake," he said, in the even, mellifluous tone he'd once made famous. "I arrived by limousine, not horse."

The joke went flat. It was indicative of his vast experience with stars of varying incandescence that Gustave instantly deduced that someone had gotten to Ronnie before he had, and had blown it. He kept a discreet distance—one of the band members was looming in, ready for a physical confrontation, of all things —and said politely, "Please reserve your judgment until you've heard me out, Miss Garrik. I am here at the behest of John Lloyd Talbot, president of Liberty Records. I have credentials," he said, handing her his card.

Ronnie tossed it over her shoulder. It spun down like a pale leaf.

"Any jerk can have one of those printed up, mister," she said. The drummer had initiated a staring contest, coupled with a malicious grin. "Ten bucks and you're in business," continued Ronnie. "Any fucking business."

Jade Gustave nodded, holding his soft brimmed panama deferentially. "I sympathize, Miss Garrik. There are a number of vile characters in the recording arts, or on the periphery of it. However, I'm here with specific instructions to sign you, come hell or high water."

Ronnie tittered. Who was he kidding with his hundred-dollar haircut and his James Mason voice?

"If some other party has already signed you," he added, "and I gather they haven't, I've been empowered to use unlimited financial clout to bring you over to Liberty. Mr. Talbot takes Mr. Presley's recommendations very seriously. I think—"

"Who?"

"Elvis Presley."

"Mister, lemme clue you, I happen to *know* Elvis."

"I'm aware of that, Miss Garrik." Bone-tired after an exhausting exploration of most of the bars of Atlanta (John Lloyd had dispatched him with but the vaguest idea as to her whereabouts), he would dearly have loved to sit down and drink something tall and cool. But the object of his search wasn't in a hospitable mood, and so he continued to stand. "Mr. Presley was highly impressed with you," he said. "He sends his regards."

Ronnie's expression altered slightly. She was convinced that the stranger, exquisite attire or no, was an impostor of some sort, but his approach was so gentlemanly—there was no sense of name-dropping when he mentioned Elvis—that she was taken aback.

"Mister, if this is a con, I swear I'll get somebody to break both your legs."

"That won't be necessary, I shouldn't think," he said. The drummer looked rather the physical type, but not a limb-breaker by choice, and Jade sensed that Ronnie was about ready to come round. "Perhaps I should apologize," he said. "I assumed, apparently in error, that you knew that Mr. Presley called John Lloyd Talbot and told him he'd be a damn fool not to sign you immediately. I've had the devil's own time tracking you down, or we'd have been in touch sooner."

Ronnie looked at him speculatively, lit a cigarette, and retrieved his card from the floor. "This says 'Talent.' Is that what you are?" she asked.

He shrugged. "Once upon a time, perhaps. Now it is what I do. Here." He extracted a brushed silver stylus from his breast pocket and applied a small, neat script to the card. "This is Mr. Presley's latest number. If you ring him up, I'm certain he'll vouch for me."

Ronnie took the card back, snapped it as if testing for veracity. She was trying to be tough, blowing smoke out of the side of her mouth. How young she looks, he thought, and how ingenuous, despite the worldly pose.

"Sit down," she told him.

There was nothing ingenuous in her command. Jade took a seat as she marched to the pay phone. He tried to ignore the drummer, who was making aggressive, rhythmic fingertaps upon the scarred Formica tabletop.

They waited.

In the spring of 1940 a son, Jacob, was born to Yevgeny Gustovitz, a tailor at Gimbels, and Maria Rossali, a stock clerk in the same store.

Yev was thirty-two, Maria twenty-one. Their courtship, in the way of very shy, inexperienced lovers, was short and intense, so all-encompassing that neither of them anticipated the severity of their families' reactions.

The day Yev was married the Gustovitz clan held a *shiva*, a mock funeral mourning the loss of a son to the Gentiles.

"You are dead to us, Yevgeny Gustovitz," his father told him. "You are lost to your tribe. Unless you should smarten up and renounce this little whore who has tricked you."

Yevgeny, rising to a flush of pride, puckered up and spat in his father's face. His Maria was no whore, and far from being tricked, he rejoiced in her fruition.

The Rossalis were no less outraged at Maria's malfeasance.

"Not only have you married a Jew, a descendant of those

who betrayed Our Saviour," said her mother venomously, "but you have married a *poor* Jew, which makes you doubly a fool. Leave him, Maria. I will see your Uncle Paoli who has connections and have this crude joke annulled. And then," she said, eyeing her daughter's belly. "we will put your bastard in a special place for the unwanted offspring of the unclean."

Maria tried to do as her Yevgeny had done, but fury made the spittle dry in her mouth. Instead she slapped her mother's face, dislodging a gold cap and causing her father, who had been excluded from the confrontation on account of his vile temper, to inebriate himself and later lay hands upon young Anthony, who sided with his sister as a matter of principle.

Ostracized, Maria and Yev made a small, private world for themselves. But they never forgot, never completely forgave, even after the initial eruption had cooled into a long-term antipathy.

"It is a great burden to be a Jew," Yevgeny told his son. "Thank God you are only half polluted with Jewishness."

His mother made similar declarations. "Thank the Lord you are not entirely fouled with Sicilian blood," she told him. "To be a man and to be Sicilian is to be an ape with an earring."

When he was a little older Jake would wonder why his parents were always thanking their respective gods for the inequities visited upon them. Deprived of familial assistance, Yev and Maria were condemned to a borderline poverty that their only son grew to despise with all his heart.

There was always enough to eat, but *just* enough. They always had clothes to wear, but always from Gimbels. Theirs was a small, clean flat—in a large, dirty building. And so on, down an endless list of small but irritating deprivations.

His parents, who had the refuge of a good, loving marriage, accepted their lot in life with a gentle resignation that disgusted Jacob by the time he was an adolescent. How did they stand the constant budgeting, the endless drudgery, the lack of even one small possession of real quality?

Jake got his ideas of what "possessions of quality" were from *The New Yorker* magazine and from staring, entranced, at the display windows at Bonwit Teller. Of solitary disposition, he found solace in his imagination, where he could own the breathtakingly beautiful glass figurines he saw at Steuben. Where he could imagine how it would feel to be helped into a perfectly cut houndstooth blazer in the fitting rooms of J. Press.

Jake wanted to own things not for their material value, or even for their status, but because he had a need for that which was beautiful, a passion to touch the cool surface of a Tiffany crystal.

He sat happily for hours in the Metropolitan, intoxicated by the perfection of color and form he saw there, the mere proximity of which seemed to make his thoughts clear and cool, untroubled by the reality of the gritty subway back to Brooklyn that awaited him.

The adulation of beauty became, at an early age, an addiction for Jacob Gustovitz, son of Yevgeny the tailor. But the boy was wise enough to know that the dream he dreamt at the Bonwit Teller window would eventually shatter, leaving him destitute of mind as well as money. He had to make it real. He had to find a way to vault from the uneasy poverty of Flatbush Avenue into the penthouses of the upper East Side.

The traditional way, he knew, was to exploit a talent. Yet he had no talent, he was convinced, beyond an inborn sense of good taste. He couldn't sing. His voice, in the bass register since fifteen, was limited to less than an octave. His grace deserted him on the dance floor—Astaire was out—and the thought of appearing on stage was terrifying. There was nothing he could take to the bank, and he began to despair that he would ever escape.

It came to him one evening, a gift from "The Firestone Hour." The radio drama was Shaw's *Pygmalion,* and it spoke to Jacob as no play had ever done. He listened attentively, chin in cupped hands, a dreamy look in his eyes, as a Cockney girl was transformed into a lady of society through the magic of changing her manner of speech.

It was a truth so absolute that its beauty transported him. Yev, with his adenoidal, Yiddish patois; Maria with her nasal

"Brooglun" tongue—his parents were consigned to poverty by the indelible mark of their speech. But Jacob, their son, with the flexibility of youth and a deep reserve of determination, could undergo a self-induced metamorphosis and emerge as beautiful and rich as one of Whistler's butterflies.

At about the time he discovered his speaking voice, Jake found that his passion for beauty extended to the human body, male or female. The gender was unimportant so long as the skin was flawless, the eyes clear and deep, the form impeccably proportioned.

This revelation, nearly as important to him as the secret of speech, came to him in the form of twins, brother and sister. Both studied at the New York Public Library on Forty-second Street, where Jacob sought books on elocution, and over the course of that year Jacob came to know them intimately, if only from a distance. The girl, with her lithe body and long, plaited hair, might have been lifted from the frieze of an ancient temple; her brother, lips parted unconsciously as he studied, had the look of an Alexandrian chamberlain, seductive and innocent at once.

Jake lacked the courage to approach them directly—his sexual experiences had been limited to a few rooftop gropes with neighborhood girls—but they became active participants in his imagination. He daydreamed, trying out combinations of bodies, choreographing his erotic fantasies.

He wanted them both, but he knew such luxuries had to be in some way purchased, just as you had to pay to acquire Picasso's lithographs or Brancusi's sculptures. He busied himself in his studies with a new fervor and purpose.

Someday, somehow, he would have them.

Shortly after his eighteenth birthday, after dozens of discouraging auditions, WBNB saw fit to hire him. A fifty-watt all-classical station with office and studio in one partitioned basement, the announcer's on-air responsibility was limited to imparting precise information at the conclusion of each selection.

"Fugue Number 6," he would read into the mike, taking

care that his voice was properly modulated, that the gain was not picking up the noonday traffic on Eighty-third Street. "Composed by Johann Sebastian Bach, an Odyssey recording by pianist Charles Rosen."

That was all. By station policy he was not allowed to comment on the music, or mention his own name, or in anyway establish himself as a personality. Perhaps this was to ensure he would never become popular enough to move on or rise above his thirty-eight-dollar-a-week salary.

After six months of robotlike oration the thrill was completely gone and Jake was casting about for a real job, sending his demo tapes around in the forlorn hope that someone, somewhere, needed an announcer with a definite sense of *duenna,* that indefinable sense of class first intuited by jazz critic George Frazier, whom Jake idolized. But the prospects were grim. New York positively seethed with aspiring radio personalities and Jake was lucky to have a job, period, let alone a better one.

He almost didn't have that. WBNB, then supported by listener subscription, had never been in a strong financial position, and Jake was not surprised when it was acquired by a chain of mid-wattage stations. He was, however, naive enough to believe the initial rumor that things would remain as they had been.

The following Monday morning the new station manager arrived. It was, he explained, his sad duty to fire the entire staff.

"WBNB is going all rock," he announced. "Roll over Beethoven and make room for Buddy Holly."

Jake was cleaning out his desk when the manager tapped him on the shoulder.

"How old are you, son?"

"Eighteen."

The manager nodded, digesting that information. "And what kind of music do you prefer, Mr., ah, Gustovitz?"

"Rock music," he lied. "I'm wild about it."

"And your favorite singer?"

Jake searched his head for an article he'd scanned in the current issue of *Billboard.* "Elvis has the pelvis," he said, quoting verbatim, "but Jerry Lee is the man for me."

The manager's smile was cynical—he'd read the same article. "I like your attitude, son," he said. "I'll keep you on for a few days. We'll see what happens."

At the manager's insistence Jacob came up with an on-the-air pseudonym; a shortening of the surname, and for the given, his favorite gem stone.

Jade Gustave.

His rise was as sudden and irresistible as the raw, rhythmic sound that established itself as the song of his generation—and the next to come, for that matter.

While the rest of the New York disc jockeys competed in outlandish impersonations of Alan Freed and Wolfman Jack, Jade retained the strong, quiet inflection he'd developed for classical introductions. He was almost immediately pegged as the "cultured" voice of rock music. Profiles of the new rock personality invariably mentioned his penchant for elegant dress, his seemingly effortless grasp of the complexities of successful broadcasting, and his quiet wit.

Under his guidance WBNB became the premier showcase for the hottest acts in rock 'n' roll. Chuck Berry popped in, pushing "Maybeline" and "Johnny B. Good." Screaming Jay Hawkins dropped by for a midnight special. Fats Domino warbled "Chantilly Lace" and chatted amiably into the wee hours, charmed into loquaciousness by the boy wonder, Jade Gustave.

At Jade's suggestion WBNB arranged a live act hookup and their star jock, became a familiar sight at concerts, dressed to the nines as always, in startling contrast to the shaggy musicians he introduced.

In the fall of 1961 his show "Top of the Rock" was syndicated and a few months later, at the age of twenty-one, a televised version was an instant success. The suave young man appealed to the mothers of the bobby soxers as well as to the girls themselves, and Jade experienced the sudden, massive rush of popularity only television can generate. There was much talk of a film career, and endless gossip columns linking him to this starlet or that heiress, some of whom he actually dated.

And he was able, in the midst of that fervor, to indulge all of his appetites, sexual and otherwise. The upper East Side opened like a randy oyster, disgorging the specimens of physical perfection he had long desired. The smooth sculpted bodies were there, discreetly tasted like fine champagne or Iranian caviar. There was no longer a reason to be denied, or, more pointedly, to deny himself the feast of kings.

He had it made.

And then, at the height of his celebrity, at the peak of "Top of the Rock" popularity, the payola scandals broke wide open. Jade, unlike so many of his colleagues, had never accepted a penny to favor certain records. The network, eager to protect their new find, hired investigators who pronounced him clean.

It seemed he would be untouched by the scandals until a rival DJ, passed over in favor of Jade for the network show, made certain accusations. A new flurry of investigation took place, and it was determined that Jade's ice-blue Mercedes coupe was the gift of John Lloyd Talbot, promotional director of Sunburst Records. That the coupe was presented after Jade sent one of Sunburst's releases to the top, rather than before, was deemed a moot point, and the networks immediately canceled.

Jade's fall from grace was of classic concinnity. The press, sensing the odor of disgrace, moved in on him. They slunk outside the doors to his building, hid in the back seat of the famous coupe before it was returned to Talbot, pawed through his trash bin looking for incriminating—or titillating—evidence, blinded him with powerful strobes because the snapshots thus produced made him look gaunt, fearful. He received bundles of letters denouncing him as a charlatan, a traitor, a communist.

The suddenness of it all left him numb and ruined. Finally, unable to comport himself with the dignity the situation demanded, he fled for Europe.

He lived well enough in Sainte Maxine, just across the peninsula from Saint Tropez, where he was one more young expatriate, vaguely notorious. Even the notoriety faded after a year or two, and he existed in a sort of pleasant limbo, unable to erase his past ignominy or imagine a future in which he participated. He lost himself in sun-drenched debaucheries, tried absinthe, smoked a pipe or two of opium, danced with sailors in Marseille, and tried to forget.

Time drifted by, unmarked, for the most part, until the money began to run out. He was forced to auction off a Ming vase he'd acquired in the first flush of success. He knew it was a dreadful thing to do, letting the vase go, that it was a downward turning point, but he was unable even to care. He had never actually contemplated suicide—too messy and self-indulgent— but if someone had professed a desire to kill him he wouldn't have protested.

He was drinking a rum-laced lime rickey at his favorite café, when the waiter brought the telephone out, indicating, with a shrug, that the caller was not only unknown, but not even French.

"Jade, old boy," said the voice, distorted by five thousand miles of transatlantic cable. "John here. How are the girls in Nice this time of year?"

"The girls are fine. So are the boys, for that matter. John who?" He stirred the lime rickey as his chest tightened.

"John Lloyd Talbot. The guy who ruined you, remember?" said the voice, attempting levity.

"Yes, I remember." The sun was pouring into the veranda, intensifying the already bright equatorial colors, but he shivered, suddenly cold.

"Jade, I've just left Sunburst. I'm starting a new label. I've got heavy money behind me and I need help spending it."

"What do you want with me?" The shape of the fear subsided, but he was no less tense. Talbot, with his damned Mercedes, could never have foreseen what would happen—but still, he had been the catalyst.

"I want you, Gustave. I want your eye for quality. I want your ear for the real thing. I want to know the people you know, and I'm willing to pay for the privilege."

The last thing he did before leaving Sainte Maxine for New York was buy back the Ming vase. He held it in his lap as the jet streaked westward, convinced that it was a talisman of fortune. Whether good or bad he could not then say.

The business relationship Jade Gustave and John Lloyd Talbot developed had, over the course of a decade, made both men abundantly wealthy. Gustave's multiple functions came under one title: *Talent.* He found it, nurtured it, oversaw its fruition in the form of record albums, supervised the talent cumulatively and individually, and made Liberty the most lucrative label in the business.

On the night he entered Dugals in search of a girl from Lubbock, Texas, he had two current platinum LPs, and he wanted to close negotiations with the new young singer as quickly and tactfully as possible so that he could return to Manhattan in time for a Sotheby auction he had been eagerly awaiting.

It might be supposed that for a man of Gustave's esoteric tastes, being made to wait in a beery roadhouse by an unknown vocalist—and a pointedly insolent one at that—would be an exasperating imposition. But it was his life's work to coddle fragile egos, to encourage egocentric behavior. Without his "talents" he would not be seriously considering the acquisition of an exquisite bronze ballerina that Parke-Bernet was representing for the Degas estate. Yes, for that ballerina he could easily endure the hard chair, the smoky, sweat-charged air, and the callous aggressions of the drummer who was, as a matter of fact, not bad looking, not bad at all.

The girl returned. Her face had gone pale, setting off her dark, lustrous hair.

"It's true," said Ronnie. She gripped Kenny's shoulders with more strength than she knew. "All of it is true."

Jade smiled. Oh, Presley was right. She was not only one hell of a singer, but she had the indefinable "it" that projected beyond mere beauty, the aura that had to emanate before he could begin to work with her. His instincts, honed by years of experience, told him that Ronnie Garrik could, with his guidance and a modicum of luck, go all the way.

He could almost see the copy she would inspire, the copy he

would surreptitiously supply to the harried editors who covered his talents. Copy that would hang on her look, the look that was hard and soft all at once, as fragile as a tea rose, and with just as many thorns.

"Please be seated, Miss Garrik." It was time to take charge of the situation. The drummer, he noticed, had already assumed a suitable pose of deference. As he spoke he thought of the ballerina, the other thing of beauty he was about to acquire. "Let me explain what it is we're offering you . . ."

Making It

1

The jet seemed to be whispering as it left the detonation of its massive engines miles behind. Ronnie, new to the experience, gazed out the porthole at the cotton bunting clouds passing far below.

She and the 'Riders had begun whooping it up right after Jade made his presentation, partying through the night and into the morning, when they wearily boarded an eight A.M. flight for Kennedy. The boys were nodded out now, scattered throughout the sparsely booked first class section, but Ronnie kept her eyes locked against sleep, watching the world turn beneath her.

Three seats ahead of her Jade Gustave (how foolish she was not to have recognized him, although he *had* been out of the public eye for years) was flipping through a portfolio, his attaché case open on the seat beside him. She liked watching the way he unbuttoned his french cuffs, rolled them neatly up over his narrow forearms, and settled in to catch up on his book work.

The stewardess brought Ronnie a cup of orange juice. Sipping it, she continued to study Gustave, catching, now and again, a glimpse of his aquiline profile as he worked. Deprived of his television makeup, and with the years leaving a few more lines here and there, his features weren't as symmetrical and perfect as she remembered. He was now more attractive, more real than the vaguely plastic video face that had made him, once upon a time, an instant hit.

For all his courtliness of manner he maintained an elegant reserve that guarded his privacy like a plexiglass shield. Ronnie assumed, rather wistfully, that he would always be a stranger to her.

She was wrong.

Perhaps Ronnie Garrik fell in love with New York because she never had to ride the subways. Certainly her introduction to the city was auspicious enough. Gustave had begun to orchestrate the star treatment he believed essential to the development of his talents. A limousine transferred the party to John Lloyd's Sikorsky, and as the helicopter rose, kicking up a puff of the snow that dusted the runway, he was pleased to note the flush of excitement in Ronnie's cheeks. Over the course of the next few hours he monitored her reactions closely, for never again, he knew, would she be so open to new experience, to the sheer thrill of making it.

And the helicopter flight, bearing down on the skyscrapers of winter Manhattan, also served to intimidate Paul Stokey, whom Jade judged the only troublesome one of the lot. Gustave determined at the outset that it would be necessary to sign all of the Roughriders, although Ronnie was the only truly outstanding talent, because she would require, initially, the company and encouragement of those she knew well, especially in the studio. Later the band could be eased out of the picture if conflicting egos threatened her.

Already he had begun to focus his creative attentions upon her alone. For whole moments he forgot the little ballerina waiting under the gavel at Parke-Bernet. Much of his success, the core of his ability to pick winners, was based on an uncanny sense of timing. And his instincts told him that the time was right for the girl he'd carefully belted into the seat beside him.

She was ready. And so, for that matter, was he.

There was a time, before he became infatuated with its alchemical properties, when John Lloyd Talbot loathed the music. It seemed to him a rude cacophony of grunts and pelvic thrusts, a noisy fad that must, like zoot suits and hoola hoops, pass quickly into obscurity.

His attitude changed abruptly. One glance at the balance sheets transfixed him: The music was turning cheap plastic into gold, and it had all the delicious risk of a forty-five r.p.m. roulette wheel.

He had always been a gambler. In the spring of 1954 he organized a gambling pool while he was studying law as a scholarship student at Fordham. He was subsequently expelled after one of the undergraduates issued a complaint, and it was only his talent for creative story telling that enabled him to keep the news from his family.

The Talbots had a grand name in Boston, but absolutely no money. His father had died a retired schoolmaster and his mother, for all her connections to the Gardners and Cabots, had married without dowry, the Lloyd fortunes having evaporated shortly after the Civil War.

John Lloyd refused to let his ruined law career, on which his mother had been pinning all her hopes, force him back to Boston. There was nothing for him there but a lot of snobbish schoolboy friends, most of whom had money they weren't about to share with him, no matter how beautifully he talked.

Although the thought of laboring over figures like a wimp from a Dickens story was repugnant, he took the first job he could find, as a "floating" bookkeeper for Wexler & Rabinowitz, Accountants.

Most of the accounts he serviced were garment manufacturers. For the first few months he trooped through the district, balancing books in the grimy little sweatboxes. So many dollars for bolts of cloth, so much (and not much) for labor, so much for commissions to the brother-in-law, and so on, ad infinitum. He found his only consolation in the balance sheets themselves. They, like the racing forms he'd mastered as a boy, told a tale, and since the story concerned the accumulation of money, it was of interest to John Lloyd Talbot, who had none of his own.

One day he was detoured from his usual assignments and instructed to brief a new client on West Fifty-third Street. The client was Leonard J. Pearle, doing business as Shaky Rattle Music, Inc. John Lloyd smiled at the whimsical name (an hour later he learned, to his chagrin, that it referred to a song that grossed $46,876 for Mr. Pearle), and proceeded to set up a book-keeping system for the company that, being new and prosperous, was a chaos of receipts, deposits, and monies in escrow.

Over the course of the afternoon John Lloyd smoked more than a pack of cigarettes in order to calm himself and maintain his cool, accountant's demeanor as he studied Lenny Pearle's balance sheets with increasing excitement.

A scant eight months before Pearle had been employed by MGM Records, where he promoted new releases. After developing what he told Talbot was a "feel" for the music called rhythm and blues, or lately rock and roll, he left MGM and, with an investment of seven thousand dollars (borrowed, inevitably, from the brother-in-law) had produced thirty records by thirty different artists.

"Called, in the biznish, a 'shotgun release,' " he told the curious John Lloyd, who was obviously a gentleman of refinements. "You gotta blast 'em out and see what hits, see?"

One of Pearle's releases, "Shaky Rattle Stomp," a ripoff of Bill Haley's "Shake Rattle and Roll," had netted the aforementioned forty grand. Another, "Lover Man," by something called The Shifters, had netted more than one hundred thousand dollars, or one tenth of a million, a goodly sum in 1954.

John Lloyd felt the sweat of excitement in Lenny Pearle's office, the same kind of sweat that came to him just before the cards were dealt, and he continued to examine the books as if they were the Dead Sea scrolls. With an effort, he maintained his composure and quietly pumped Pearle for information.

"It's like playing numbers, this biznish. Ya gotta have luck, you know? But it's also more than just luck. The stuff has to be good—ya gotta learn to listen, see? But the big secret every guy in the biznish knows is you gotta get the record *played.* Get the big-shot disc jockeys to play the fucking thing, see? Just between the two of us, and because I got to fix it on the books somehow, I risked another ten grand in payoffs. A C-note here, a grand there. You got to pay to play, see? Everyone does. Way it is."

So for an investment of $17,000 total, Leonard J. Pearle had, in eight months, realized a profit of $146,000, according to John Lloyd's calculations.

"I think you're on to a good thing, Mr. Pearle." Talbot finished his last cigarette. "A very good thing indeed."

The next day he called in sick. He put on what he considered to be a loud sports jacket (actually a conservative madras) doffed the mandatory straw hat of the season, and strolled into the Seventh Avenue offices of American Radio Device, Recording Division.

"My name is John Lloyd Talbot," he told them. "I've considerable experience managing dramatic artists and I want a job in your promotional department." When no one seemed interested in the story he'd concocted he quickly added, "I'll work for straight commission."

They hired him.

Later he would readily admit that it was a case of being in the right place at the right time. He was an instant beneficiary of the crest of interest in rock music, which made the promotion of merchandise seem virtually effortless. He merely followed Pearle's advice and showered disc jockeys and program directors with gifts, taking care never to actually conceal that fact on his books. He was one of the first to recognize the national possibilities of young Jade Gustave, whom he favored with the famous Mercedes coupe.

The huge commissions he earned enabled him to send checks home to his mother, who assumed he was a corporate lawyer rather than a hotdogging promo man.

And when the payola scandals broke, John Lloyd was covered.

Being bounced from Fordham had not prevented his comprehension of certain legalities, and since his gifts were meticulously accounted for under the heading "Payments for Services Rendered," American Radio Device was not culpable. This foresight on Talbot's part was not overlooked by the directors of the corporation, who awarded him a substantial bonus.

It was the opportunity—and the capital—he had been waiting for. He took the money and ran. Not far, just across town to a suite at the Brill building, where he activated the incorporation papers for his dream company, Liberty Records.

The first thing he did was sign away one of ARD's major acts, taking advantage of a loophole he himself had created in their original contract. This instantly put Liberty in the black.

The second thing he did was hire Jade Gustave.

Two years later, shortly after Dun & Bradstreet listed his assets at better than one million dollars, Fordham awarded him an honorary degree. That they were honoring a career born of cordial graft and courteous piracy was not an issue.

Talbot had made it. That was what mattered.

Gustave separated the boys from the girl.

That the separation should be painless was an essential part of his strategy. Four of Liberty's celebrity escorts greeted them as they disembarked the helicopter. Selected according to Talbot's rigid standards of corporate glamour, all four women were blue-eyed, honeyed blondes wearing minimal makeup, beige satin blouses with the Liberty emblem above the left breast, and well-cut trousers tucked into knee-high Charles Jourdan boots.

"I died and went to heaven," sighed Kenny, putting his arm around the nearest waist. "Take me to the promised land, sugar."

The other 'Riders responded no less enthusiastically to the escorts. They went off for a tour of the corporate headquarters while Gustave took Ronnie in to meet John Lloyd himself.

"Don't be nervous," he told her. "Remember that you're doing *him* a favor by signing, not the reverse."

Ronnie stared at Jade curiously. "Whom do you work for?" she asked. "Him or me?"

He smiled, making a slight shrug. "From now on I work for you. It is understood. John Lloyd believes it is the only way to proceed. What is best for you will be, in the long run, best for Liberty. It's the method that has given this company the highest profit margin in the industry."

He did not bother to add that the method also produced the most flamboyant—and vulnerable—of stars.

Gliding down the corridor, Ronnie wondered what they put in the air. Her head was full of helium, or something very like it, and it was all she could do to keep her toes touching the carpet.

Gustave's technique of cutting her away from the herd had not gone unnoticed. She knew it would lead to trouble with Paul Stokey, but at the moment she didn't give a damn. Jade Gustave wanted *her*, not the band, that much was obvious.

She liked the idea. And when the doors began to open she liked it even more.

The executive structure of Liberty had been designed to accommodate the notoriously large egos of rock stars. One small function of that design was the door plan. Each of the assistants of each office, forewarned, contrived to sweep open suite doors just as the star arrived, creating the illusion that the whole of Liberty's efforts were devoted to ennobling the particular luminary being entertained that day.

It was heady stuff. The psychological pampering helped Liberty's artists sparkle, attracting media attention. And the Liberty treatment drew other artists from less imaginative labels, contributing to Talbot's reputation for gracious but cold-blooded piracy.

Ronnie stopped by a water fountain to adjust her bangs and apply a trace of gloss to her lips. She saw Jade watching her in the mirror.

"You look magnificent," he said. It was no exaggeration. The red eye flight from Atlanta had not touched her. She was radiant.

"Funny thing," she told him, "but I'm not nervous at all."

It was a good sign. A very good sign.

As they approached Talbot's lair the outer offices became more imposing, the doors larger. When the last of them had been swung open by willing hands Ronnie entered a large, high-vaulted room.

Angelo Dongia, with a carte blanche commission from Talbot, had transformed two floors on the east face of 101 Central Park West into a lush, creamy white cavern. The high arched ceiling, finished in a white lacquer, opened on a wall entirely of glass. Through the drifting snowflakes Ronnie saw, thirty stories below, Central Park transformed into a winter wonderland. It looked as clean and new as a toy village under a Christmas tree.

"So you found me the mythical princess, Jade. Marvelous!"

He bounced up out of a swivel chair, where he had been monitoring a recording session through headphones, and greeted her with a light kiss on the cheek.

Ronnie had been expecting a steel blue suit behind an intimidating, glass-topped desk. But there was not a desk, as such, to be seen, and John Lloyd Talbot was wearing Ruffini slacks, a crew-neck cashmere sweater, and a pair of scruffy Topsiders with bare ankles showing.

"Jade is my knight errant," he said affectionately. "He always manages to slay the dragon and return with the Holy Grail, so to speak." Until that day, he had never even heard her voice, but he knew Gustave wouldn't have brought Ronnie back unless she had the potential. And the idea of signing an unknown quantity appealed to his gambler's instincts.

"What's the word, Jade?" he asked casually.

"Go," said Gustave. "With a capital G."

It was all he needed to know. Ronnie Garrik was in. At Jade's signal he was prepared to throw the full weight of Liberty Records behind her.

As Talbot arranged for a light lunch and hot cocoa to be brought in, Ronnie gave him a surreptitious appraisal and decided she liked what she saw.

His close-cropped, curly hair was the color of brushed chrome; no one would dare call it gray. A large, boney nose—a feature that might, on another man, have spoiled his looks—served to magnify the deep structure of his eyes, a few shades darker than his hair. He had inherited the small, molded chin of the Lloyds, and it gave him the aristocratic look of a Hamilton polo player, or the slightly rakish relation of David Niven. Indeed,

Ronnie expected him to speak with an English accent, rather than with the nasal, blue-blooded isogloss of his native Boston.

As Ronnie took her seat, bathed in the winter light reflected off the park, she knew it was going to work. She was passing from the realm of secret dreams into the place where reality happened.

"I want Kyle in on this," Talbot was saying. "That means LA. I'll put the *'Belle* at your disposal." He turned to Ronnie. "I'm sure you have your own ideas about clothes and what looks good on you, Miss Garrik. But I'm going to ask you to trust Jade's sense of style for right now. He'll take you down to Bergdorf Goodman and swathe you in something appropriate." He chuckled. "And expensive. Gustave loves to spend my money. And the Kingsley salon is holding a chair open for you. After than there's a cosmetics specialist who can make those terrific eyes of yours look even *more* beguiling, believe it or not. . . ."

Now it was her turn for the once over, as John Lloyd examined her face, her carriage, her hair, conferring with Gustave, making suggestions for a photographic session. She didn't mind. As long as she could keep her voice, her song, they could do what they liked with the rest of her.

"One last question, Jade," said Talbot. "Does she sing as good as she looks?"

"Better."

"Marvelous," said Talbot. He kissed her again on the cheek. "Now," he said, "the fun begins."

2

Jade gave them very loud Hawaiian shirts, and the boys gamboled through the aircraft, high on more than altitude, looking like stoned refugees from the Don Ho Orchestra.

John Lloyd used the *Liberty Belle* to transport his top bands, and it had been altered accordingly. The all suede upholstery was offset by a crimson field Oriental runner, focusing the eye to the center aisle entertainment center. The custom Betamax was stocked with a wide variety of first run and collector's item videotapes, including the unexpurgated *Emmanuelle*, *Behind the Green Door*, *Klit*, and other erotic classics. Two of Talbot's blond escorts, similarly customized in what Yves Saint Laurent thought a stewardess ought to look like, served as hostesses. Both women had the *frisson* necessary to gracefully fend off the boys and still leave them charmed.

A butler in black tie and tails dispensed drinks and delicacies from an oiled teakwood bar. He managed to contain the 'Riders with an Arthur Treacher-like aplomb developed from intimate contact with all sorts of "difficult" people.

Ronnie watched bemusedly as he showed Kenny how properly to trim and ignite a Havana cigar she was certain the drummer would never finish. She and Jade were seated at a worktable, selecting publicity stills from the studio photographs shot the day before.

"Isn't this putting the cart before the horse?" she asked. "I mean, we haven't even starting recording yet."

"Not at all," said Jade, dismissing her reservations. "The

142

machinery must be set in motion now. We want to create curiosity, anticipation. The mere fact that Liberty has signed an unknown and alloted a substantial budget for her publicity will create a certain amount of interest."

One picture captivated her. In it she was looking back, a silver fox stole draped over her bare shoulders. The shot had been cropped to suggest nakedness, and had the effect of creating a kind of dare-me sensuousness. She looked delicious.

If I ever get turned on to women, she thought impishly, I'll take me to bed.

Oh, she loved the pictures. Philip Kingsley had brought her hair back to life, and the wardrobe Jade selected was absolutely right. There was only one thing missing.

"Jade," she said cautiously, "who is this Kyle person you keep mentioning?"

Gustave gave her a pointed look; she got the distinct impression he'd read her thoughts.

"Kyle is a genius," he said. "More than that I cannot say."

The aircraft flew on, a silver glint in the sun, its vapor trail an arrow piercing the stratosphere, pointing west.

"Zach!"

Ronnie had just strolled in to studio B, where Jade suggested she wander about, getting a feel for the Sunset West recording facilities. There was no doubt about it—the guy in the absurd purple T-shirt and UCLA track shorts was Zachary Curtis himself, looking as tanned and fit as ever.

"Hey, babe!" He put down the guitar he'd been toying with and took her in his arms. They did not kiss. It was going to be, she knew instinctively, a brother and sister act. "Ya don't have to tell me what's been happening," he said. "Baby, I *know.*"

"Zach, what are you *doing* here?" Ronnie knew she ought to be angry with him, but six months seemed like an eternity, and although, touching his lean body, she felt the stirrings of physical desire, she knew it was no more than that. Mere chemistry.

"I was gigging at the Troubadour night before last. This cat from Liberty tugs my cuff after the show and breaks the news. Hot new torch for Liberty wants to cut two of my tunes on her debut album, he says. Yeah? That's me saying yeah, 'cause I hear this kind of shit all the time and it never seems to happen. But this cat insists the thing is going to be cut like *tomorrow*, so I start acting polite and then he drops the bomb." Zach paused to draw breath and made his eyes wide, mocking his own surprise.

"What bomb?"

"You! This new torch is none other than Ronnie Garrik. Hell, you could have knocked me over with a feather."

It was amazing. She'd casually dropped a name to Jade Gustave and two days later the name materialized, wearing a sexy pair of gym shorts. Gustave had been discussing categories of songs and the concept for her album. The mysterious Kyle Hersch, whom Jade was reluctant to discuss, would be doing the producing and possibly writing a cover tune, but they were still looking for material. Ronnie suggested Zach's "Airstream Baby," and when she told him the singer/songwriter was prolific in areas other than seducing young ladies from Texas, Jade expressed an interest in hearing his material.

And now, incredibly, he was there in the flesh, flashing more than a bit of it, full of himself.

"I had a kind of half-assed publishing contract with a no-where label out here, but this guy Talbot bought me out. Imagine, just like a poor little slave—me! Right now it's kind of an option thing, but if I come up with some right stuff they'll let me cut an album."

"Zach, this is fabulous. It's happening so fast," she said wistfully. It was as if she had been an idling engine for all of her twenty-two years until Jade and John Lloyd conspired to let out her clutch. Now she was moving onward and upward at lightning speed, a little dizzy with the suddenness of it all.

"I got here first thing this morning," Zach was saying. "Hell, I ain't been up this early since we got cabin fever up there in the Sunveil Wilderness."

She quickly put a big sister smile on and kept the pang of regret to herself.

"I mean, Ronnie baby, do you know what is coming down here?"

"Sure. Me and the 'Riders are going to cut an album."

"Ronnie." He gripped her by the arms and looked directly into her eyes, consumed with his own sense of drama. "Liberty just took this fucking place over. Do you get it? There was a band all set to record here, they had a contract for the time and the engineering and all the bullshit it takes to get a record going, and Liberty just waltzed in and picked up the cost of moving them to another studio. Just because Talbot wants you to have the Sunset Sound, for christsake. And Ronnie, they've got *Kyle Hersch* producing you."

Zach looked like a surfer boy who'd just sighted the perfect wave curling up over the horizon. "Kyle Hersch," he sighed.

"Whoa. Replay that one for me, Zach. What is the Sunset Sound," she asked, wriggling out of his grasp, "and who is this Hersch character everybody is so impressed with?"

"You mean you really don't know?" Zach looked at her like she had marbles pouring out her ears. "You're a fucking virgin, Ronnie. The Sunset Sound is *the* sound, on account of this studio has the best stuff, the best studio musicians, the best . . . well, they don't cut nothing but hot records here. And Kyle Hersch. I mean, Ronnie, if there is a man alive who can make Beethoven roll over, Kyle is it. I've been wandering around here hoping to bump into him. I mean, dig this, *I* want his fucking autograph."

"Oh, come on, Zach. Be serious."

"I'm serious, really. The guy is some kind of recluse. He was a prodigy, a whiz kid, but something bad happened—I forget what—and now he hides out in Big Sur with a bunch of body-guards." Zach took a deep, shuddering breath, trying to get a handle on his energy. "Come with me, babe. They have an absolutely gorgeous Steinway here, 'n' I got a new tune I want you to hear."

They headed for the next studio, Ronnie trying to ignore the fact that they were holding hands.

At twenty years of age Kyle Hersch was the wunderkind of Broadway. Two of his shows opened successfully in one season, and a third, *Caper,* celebrated a birthday, the first of many yet to come, at the Shubert.

Kyle embraced the *vie de célèbre* occasioned by his fantastic, near sudden success with the fervor of a boy bedding his first mistress. With his thick, shoulder-length hair swept back like a maestro, he was a striking and soon familiar figure in tux, and if ever he saw daylight after sunrise, he kept it to himself.

Much of his careless gaiety was illusory. He approached composition the way Astaire choreographed dance. In each "easy" step, hour upon hour of grueling exercise was fluidly disguised. Kyle sweated out each verse, discarding dozens of drafts as he perfected the score of whatever musical was then entering production.

He kept the sweat to himself; it amused him to cultivate the notion that his music sprang to life full blown. He lived with the sense of high style and grace that permeated all his works and made him, for one splendid season, Manhattan's most eligible male.

Hersch leapt directly from the Juilliard School of Music to the Shubert Theatre on the wings of a zany operetta studded with sixteen of the finest show tunes heard under one roof since Oscar Hammerstein and Richard Rodgers ceased collaborating.

It started as a gag, a revue written for classmates who wanted to spoof the melodramatic genre of the staged musical. But Kyle got carried away, and before he knew it had thrown out the revue numbers and replaced them with songs of his own. His classmates decided to play it straight, and they buckled down and put their hearts into it.

The show was rough opening night. The lighting hadn't been worked out, the acoustics were less than adequate, and the student orchestra kept blowing cues. But it didn't matter. From the first bar of the first song it worked. The book was not particularly original and as whimsical as most musicals, but the *songs* stayed with you, burning images into your heart, leaving a melody dancing between your ears.

Five months later, revamped and, much to the disappointment of Kyle's classmates, recast, *Caper* opened at the Shubert.

It stayed at the Shubert.

Hersch's musicals lived and breathed. And prospered. Oh, how they prospered. Hersch moved out of his aunt's walk-up in Queens and into a suite at the Plaza. From there he was a short walk from the several theaters and rehearsal halls where his shows were either running or entering production.

It was a good life. He assumed it would last forever.

Kyle met Natalya Stavrogin at a backstage party at the Lincoln, where she was principal dancer in the City Ballet production of *Coppelia.* The columnists had them married almost before they actually fell in love. Not quite, only because it happened between them with blinding speed.

Theirs was not a theatrical romance. Neither of them played it as a role, although, in the end, it was staged with all the elements of tragedy.

Natalya had defected from the Moscow troupe not for political reasons but because she wanted to dance for Meilotz, whom she considered the greatest choreographer in the world. It was a case of mutual admiration, since Rudi Meilotz considered her the *ne plus ultra* of the young ballerinas.

In the beginning he tried to discourage her romance with Kyle Hersch.

"If you must sleep with a genius, sleep with me," he begged her. When Natalya laughed he looked at her reproachfully. "This man Hersch will have you tap dancing in one of his vulgar musicals and you will forget your beautiful *en pointe,* Natalya."

Meilotz was only half serious. He knew Kyle was a fine young man, and what he saw in Natalya's eyes convinced him that his advice would be as unheeded as his attempts to seduce her had been.

"Don't be silly, 'Lotzy. I am a Stavrogin, and we dance and love, how do you say, simultaneously. I will *never* leave Rudi Meilotz, just as I will marry Kyle Hersch," she insisted. Her face, with its clear, translucent beauty, was alive with love.

She was only right about the latter, for she did leave Meilotz. Rather he granted her a leave of absence shortly after their marriage so that she might have a child and still maintain the hope of returning to the corps, although both knew she would probably be beyond her prime.

Natalya, who had never even considered getting pregnant before it actually happened, became positively radiant with joy. She astonished Kyle with her eagerness.

"Just think, my darling. What a symphony of a child we create! What talent, what beauty! Ah, she will have the Stavrogin eyes. And the Hersch ear, of course, never doubt that." Her enthusiasm for the child forming within her inspired Kyle. He began to work on a musical version of *As You Like It*, to be produced in the grand manner.

He had a sizable chunk of the score roughed out when the butterfly appeared.

"What is this?" he said, touching the mark on her cheek.

"A rash," said Natalya evasively. "It is less than nothing."

But it was not nothing. The redness deepened, marring her faultless complexion. When she began to have severe pains in her lower legs Kyle insisted she return to the clinic.

"But it is not time," she said. Her eyes closed in a spasm of pain. "Not for two more weeks do I go back."

"We'll go right *now*, Natalya." The thought of his wife enduring pain was more than Kyle could stand. His stomach began to knot into bundles of nerves.

"Then take me not to the clinic, but to Dr. Nick, please."

He was startled by her request, but complied without comment. Natalya maintained close contact with many of the other Russian expatriates in New York. Each Wednesday afternoon she attended a tea at a brownstone on Eighty-sixth Street. There Russian was spoken and the cult of the samovar preserved with the sort of unaffected pomp only Russians of a certain class can carry off. The brownstone was owned by Dr. Nikolai Kirilov, whose family was from Natalya's native Minsk, and so it was natural that he should be her personal physician.

Alerted by Kyle's urgent call he greeted them at the office he maintained a few doors down from the brownstone. When he saw the mark on Natalya's cheek he threw up his hands.

"Ah!" he cried. "The wolf returns."

They spoke earnestly in Russian, and although Kyle knew a few words nothing they said was intelligible to him. Finally he broke in.

"Tell me, Doctor. What is this 'wolf' business?"

Kirilov looked at Natalya, his lips pursed. When she nodded he turned to Kyle and spoke quietly.

"It is the mark of a kind of sickness, my friend. A romantic term invented by Natalya which she thought more dramatic than systemic lupus, which has come and gone from her over the last ten years. In that way, stealing in to ravage her for a few months, than disappearing for a year or two—in this case two—lupus is much like the wolf for which it is named."

Kyle sat down heavily. Natalya held out her hand, squeezing strength into her husband as if it were his illness Kirilov went on to describe, not her own.

Kyle had never heard of lupus and was surprised to learn it afflicted nearly a million young women in the United States alone. The cause, and cure, was unknown. Kirilov smiled when he said that; the same firm, enduring smile which he used when describing the slaughter of his countrymen at Leningrad. It was a smile of ice and fury, tempered with an Old World acceptance of fate. The smile chilled Kyle to the bone. His wife smiled the same smile, squeezing his hand tighter.

"Our Natalya has a classic case, of course. Nothing less for a woman who dances with such perfection!" Kirilov reached out and touched her gently on the cheek, tracing the butterfly-shaped rash. "Just as this is the classic mark of our little wolf."

It dawned on Kyle that Natalya's aching legs were not from strenuous dance, but from the lupus. He cursed himself for being insensitive to the symptoms that now seemed so obvious.

At one point Dr. Nick spoke to her in Russian, quickly, as if he didn't want Kyle to overhear even one word. Natalya's reaction was violent. She exploded from her chair, shouting one furious word again and again.

"No!" and again, "No! No! No!"

Kyle had never seen her so pale. Or so defiant.

"As you wish," said Kirilov. "It is, of course, your decision."

Natalya was stroking the slight swell of her small, firm belly. "She will dance like an angel," she told Kyle. "We will name her Louise for your mother's sister who was good to me, and she will dance like an angel."

When Kyle took her away from the office he imagined the sky above was an unbroken gray membrane, and he no longer felt the urge to complete *As You Like It*, or to do anything but be with Natalya, who did not discourage his renewed attentions, but who refused to acknowledge or speak of her illness.

"Let us talk about Louise," she said firmly. "Perhaps she will hear us and come early."

The birth, though three weeks premature, was uncomplicated. Natalya bore down and delivered her daughter after a short, intense labor.

Kyle was jubilant. In the last two months Natalya had rallied. The rash and the pain vanished and he managed to put it out of his mind, a nightmare from which they had both awoken. He was surprised by his wife's decision not to nurse her daughter.

"Dr. Nick has found me a good woman," she told him. "Louise will have a wet nurse, just like a little czarina. And I will keep my figure and dance again."

In a very short time he learned the real reason for the wet nurse, and for the pale glow that emanated from Natalya's cheeks. The wolf was back, this time in a more virulent form. Natalya began to have violent headaches, spasms of viselike pain that left her weeping. She ran a constant low-grade temperature that made her always weak, and at times delirious.

Kyle, with his vivid imagination, was haunted by his vision of the beast that gnawed her from the inside. At times his helplessness verged on hysteria, accentuated by Dr. Kirilov's refusal to give a definite prognosis.

"My dear fellow, you ask the impossible. No one on earth can say, not even Natalya, who knows her little wolf as well as she knows you. Be strong, Hersch!"

But Kyle did not find his strength until he knew that Natalya was dying and that nothing could save her. Louise was seven months old, a delightful, vivacious baby, and he knew he had to make the transition, in his heart, from what surely must end to what had just begun.

Kirilov lived with them in those last few weeks as Natalya drifted in and out of her final coma. One evening, while the silence, interupted only by the quiet hiss of the oxygen that helped her breathe, lay like a pall over the sick room, he spoke to Kyle.

"Hersch," he said. "Do you believe in God?"

"No."

"Ah." Kirilov sighed. "That is bad for you. God will help you, as he is about to help Natalya. You should believe in something, Hersch."

"I believe in Louise."

"A sweet child. She has the look of a Stavrogin. But a baby is not God, Hersch."

"You are wrong," said Kyle. "Louise is *everything.*"

The doctor, seeing the flash in Kyle's eyes, did not press the point. That night Natalya drifted away, dying so quietly it took several minutes with the stethoscope before her passing could be marked.

And all night long Kyle held Louise to his breast, rocking as the child slept, writing, in his mind, the score of a future with all the immortality it was in his power to give her.

Shortly after the funeral he left New York forever. He took Louise and Mrs. Manilov, the wet nurse, to California.

Using an assumed name, for he had decided that only in anonymity would Louise be safe, he purchased a secluded estate in Big Sur. He chose it not for its prestigious location, or because he wished to be part of the artistic community there, but because it could be fortified.

Frank Lloyd Wright had designed and built it for the Hearsts, who called it Aubade. Kyle saw no reason to change the name. He did make certain modifications. A modern nursery was installed in one wing. It included cleverly disguised emergency room facilities and apartments for Mrs. Manilov and whatever pediatrician was in residence. Most stayed for a six-month tour; Hersch's fee went a long way toward paying off medical school debts. From the nursery there was direct access to the earthquake-proof shelter, ingeniously secured to the basalt by a series of sixty-foot pins. If the San Andreas fault shifted in a big way Aubade might slide down the mountain into the sea, but the shelter was immovable.

The driveway, winding up a mile or so from Route 1, entered the estate over a steel-girded bridge spanning a deep gorge. Kyle hired an engineering consultant and had it converted, medieval fashion, into a drawbridge. The ninety-foot gorge served as an admirable moat, and tended to discourage the journalists who set out to find and interview the suddenly mysterious Mr. Hersch. Those ambitious reporters who tried roping themselves down a cliff bordering the far side of Aubade found themselves under the siege of a Doberman patrol, slavering hysterically on the other side of an electrical fence.

Interests in the whys and wherefores of Hersch's seclusion gradually collapsed. He cut himself off from his theater friends because they reminded him of Natalya and because they didn't seem to understand his consuming fear that Louise might be similarly taken from him if he didn't retire from the world.

The gods had been tempted; he would not tempt again.

Life at the estate settled into routine. Louise was a normal, healthy child and the pediatrician never had to prescribe anything stronger than St. Joseph's aspirin. Mrs. Manilov, freed of other domestic duties, served admirably as a surrogate mother, battling, with her Russian pride, whenever Kyle tried to spoil his daughter with too much attention.

The only problem was money. Kyle had made a bundle, but spent most of it buying and maintaining Aubade. *Caper* was still playing at the Shubert and seemed likely to be there when the millenium turned, grossing him a steady $50,000 a year in royalties. With regional productions of his other two musicals and ASCAP quarterlies it came to about $75,000, which, after taxes, left him with the original gross from the Shubert.

It helped oil the machinery, but it wasn't nearly enough. The security service alone cost almost that much. He needed another source of income. The theater was out. He would have to enter the mainstream again to make a musical work, and there was no way he was going to do that. He made a few discreet inquiries.

One of them appeared at the gate one evening.

"Mistah Hersch. Gentleman named Talbot just telephoned from the other side of the gorge."

It took a moment for the name to sink in, and then Kyle remembered that Liberty had released his original soundtrack albums. He'd met Talbot once, briefly, at an opening. Or it might have been a fund raiser—who the hell could remember what had really happened in the fog memory of New York? And who wanted to?

"Tell Mr. Talbot he must have the wrong estate. Send him along to the Brownells. The Who are there this weekend, so the gardener tells me."

The guard returned a few minutes later. He read from a notebook.

"Mr. Talbot says to tell you he wants to make an offer you can't refuse. He says he's not the Godfather but he has almost as much money. He says you won't have to go to New York to get it."

Kyle spoke to him over the telephone at the guard booth. Then he signaled the bridge down and John Lloyd drove his convertible Lamborghini, a West Coast model identical in every respect to his New York vehicle, over the gorge and into Kyle Hersch's life.

"Mr. Hersch, I heard through the grapevine you are looking for a quiet way to supplement your income."

"That depends on how you define quiet, Mr. Talbot. You've

had a long drive, can I get you something to drink?" They were sitting on the veranda outside the guard shack, overlooking the magnificent arroyo. In the distance was a wedge of the blue Pacific and high cirrus clouds rolling in from the Orient.

"Iced tea, thank you. Tall, no lemon."

Kyle buzzed the kitchen. The beverage was delivered in a frosted glass.

"What I have in mind, Mr. Hersch," said John Lloyd, clinking the ice, "is a mutually profitable arrangement. You're not aware of this, I'm sure, but in my youth I staged musicals. Not Broadway, of course, but I'm familiar with your career and your accomplishments. . . ."

Kyle smiled his best wolf smile. "Let's hear it, Talbot. What have you got?"

"What I have is a new division opening up in Los Angeles. The move is toward this coast, for the moment, and some of out major talents want to record here. What I propose is that you produce three albums for us per annum. Any studio you like, take your pick."

Kyle was scratching doodles in the dirt with the end of a twig. He was surprised to see, in the dust, a crescendo of rising notes. "I've never produced a record, Talbot. You must know that."

"A minor point. If I weren't sure you could do it I wouldn't be here. You would have total control, of course, from scoring the charts to contributing as much original material as you wish."

"I haven't worked for two years. I'm out of touch."

"Some people are gifted with that timeless quality, Mr. Hersch. You're one of them. Dionne Warwick is looking for classy numbers not unlike the songs from your shows, and believe me she isn't the only one. I could mention a lady named Barbra Streisand, but I won't because she's contracted elsewhere at the moment but give me a chance and I'll—"

"I'm not interested in helping you promote records. I won't be photographed. I won't go on talk shows. I won't go to shopping malls."

John Lloyd smiled. Hersch, he knew, had taken the bait. That was a given when the bridge came down. Now it was a matter of reeling him in, as delicately as a speckled trout on a two-pound test line.

"I'll do the promoting," he said. "That's what I'm good at. You just make the records—in the privacy of the studio, I might add. In the credits it will say 'A Kyle Hersch Production.' That's all I need. To be truthful, you will lend us invaluable prestige, and that is almost as important to us as your musical abilities. Almost."

Kyle scuffed out the doodle and started another. Notes flew from the twig end, impregnating the dust. "How much are we talking?"

"For the aforementioned three LPs I will pay you three hundred thousand per year. Anything you make on royalties for original material is of course extra. I would suggest an open-ended contract, meaning either party can back out at the end of any given year if it goes sour." He paused. The hook was set. "A deal?"

"I'm thinking." What he was doing, as a matter of fact, was composing, trying to get an idea solidly in mind before it dissolved back into his subconscious.

"Hersch, I would get down on my knees and do my Al Jolson routine for you, if I thought it would help."

"That won't be necessary, Mr. Talbot."

Over the years the arrangement had been, to put it mildly, mutually profitable. Of any three records Kyle touched, two invariably shipped platinum, giving him by far the best track record of any producer of twelve-inch vinyl discs in the world. His "thing" with Liberty kept the expensive mechanism called Aubade ticking as smoothly and unobtrusively as a fine Swiss watch.

He had no way of knowing, when he started work on the Garrik album, that the alarm was about to go off.

3

"I can't do it! I just *can't!*"

Ronnie threw off the headphones, tears bursting hot in her eyes. How could this be happening to her? In a rage she kicked the loathsome phones against the soundproofed wall.

"I hate this shit!"

Blinded by tears, she stumbled out of the studio. She tried to slam the door but was foiled by the airtight seal. Kenny followed her out and found her slumped in the hall, her face buried in her arms.

"Ronnie?"

"I feel like such a jackass, you know?" Salt caught in the back of her throat and she sniffed. "All this buildup, and the pictures and now I can't even carry a *tune.* It's so fucking embarrassing."

"It's new, that's all, baby." The drummer knelt down and tried to stroke her shoulders, but she was rigid with anger and self-loathing. "You'll make it, don't worry."

"I wish, Kenny. But I can't hit the right fucking n-n-note." And this was worse than blowing her first recording session, this blubbering, making a total fool of herself. But it just wouldn't stop.

Kyle Hersch had suggested—from the invisible command post of the control room—that since none of them had recording experience the first number they worked on should be a familiar one. After glancing over their repertoire he decided on "She's Not There," an old Zombies tune that Ronnie had done at least two thousand times.

It *had* to be easy, and Ronnie, giggling with anticipation and cocky as a barnyard rooster, had positively strutted into the sound room. First Kyle had the boys lay down the drum, bass, and lead tracks (a sax chorus would be added later) as Ronnie swigged Cokes and flipped through magazines until they were ready for the important part, namely her.

That's when it started to go sour. She put on the padded headphones, which made the room eerily silent, and stepped up to the microphone alone. Kyle's instructions were crisp and perfunctory. On a stand at eye level was a chart with the vocal line indicated in red. It couldn't be simpler. All she had to do was watch the green light for a cue and sing the goddamn song.

When she opened her mouth a stranger's voice came out. It was the headphones, or maybe the infinitesimal delay of the sixteen-track master tape, but whatever it was she couldn't hit the right notes. It was like being underwater in a bad dream, with her voice coming out in glistening bubbles, and it freaked hell out of her.

"That was flat, Miss Garrik. Let's run it again, please."

Ronnie held her breath as her stomach sank to China, but when the cue came round she was off again, sharp this time, and it had never happened to her like that before. She had *perfect fucking pitch,* now where the hell was it?

"Again, please."

And they had gone on and on, with Ronnie tightening up until her voice was practically squeaking. *I sound like Porky fucking pig,* she thought. She couldn't stand another second of it and tore out of the room.

Zach Curtis, who had been sitting in on piano, found her in the hallway.

"Come on, kid. It happens to everybody." He chuckled, making light of her tantrum.

"Not to *me.*" She glared at him. Him and his know-it-all looks. "Not to me it doesn't."

"No use acting like a spoiled brat, Ronnie. You gotta climb back on the horse and try again, that's all." Zach sighed and put his hands on his hips. Didn't she know it cost money, screwing up like this? "Hey! Where are you going?"

"Never mind."

Ronnie hurried through the maze of corridors until she found an exit, bumped the panic bar, and launched herself into the muggy heat of a Los Angeles afternoon. A shaft of sunlight poured in off Sunset. She followed it out of the alley and onto the Strip itself.

Immediately she was almost run down by a samba line of Hare Krishnas, staring at her blank-eyed and bald, chanting their little atonal song.

Krishna, krishna krishna
Hare hare, Hare krishna

But it was good to be out in the real world, strange as it was on the Strip, where the weirdness was palpable. Anything was an improvement on the silent, mechanical maw of the studio, where the making of music was so tight, so controlled, that it choked her.

"Got some psylosybin here," a furry, bearded beast was whispered in her ear, out of nowhere. "That is positively A number-one *silly*. Technicolor, body rush, auditory hallucination, and assorted visual delights."

"No, thanks." Ronnie managed to ditch him, but it was good, feeling like she was part of the street scene. Not some nervous kid from Lubbock, screwing up the biggest deal of her life.

She dodged to the left as a platoon of Moonies came by, trying to hawk stale candy for a buck a throw. She bumped into a Salvation Army Santa Claus ringing a bell and looking, in the heat, like he was about to chuck the dog's last breakfast.

"Don't look at me that way, lady," he said earnestly. "I'm not a wacko like the others. I really *am* Santa Claus."

It broke over her suddenly, the need to laugh, and as she

leaned back and let it out, roaring like the rest of the Strip lunatics, she knew what was wrong and how to fix it.

"Oh, my God!"

Jade couldn't believe it. Ronnie had opened the doors and was inviting in the riffraff from the Strip. It was as if an invasion was underway. Furry-looking humanoids swathed in dirty leather and cheap jewelry, street urchins in miniskirts, antiquated beatniks, and an emaciated elderly man with a white beard and staff who seemed to be looking for a lost herd of sheep.

It was too awful. The idea of being in the same city with these creatures was bad enough, and now Ronnie, flipping out from a case of first-time nerves, had actually opened the front door and was leading in the whole scruffy lot of them.

"Jade, isn't it marvelous?"

"Ronnie," he said in a furious whisper—he could actually *smell* some of them—"what on earth is going on?"

"Me," she said. "Me is going on stage just as soon as we can set it up and then me, AKA Ronnie Garrik, The Uptight Recording Artist, is going to do a *live set* so I can show these studio cats I can *fucking well sing like bloody hell.* That's what's going on, Jade. Don't be mean about it, please?"

There was no use arguing with her. It was a *fait accompli.* He had them open up D, the studio used for big band and symphonic recordings. Ronnie directed the operation like it was her coming out party, yukking it up with the crowd she had collared, and Jade could see that she was working herself up into a regular showtime frenzy. Maybe she had the right idea.

But rather than rub shoulders with the rough beasts—already he detected the pungent odor of marijuana—he went into the control room with Kyle and the engineers. And locked the door behind him.

One never knew.

When Kyle first started producing for Liberty he had serious reservations about rock music. He thought it a limited genre, lacking the challenge of his previous work. He soon found out just how dead wrong he was. Once you eased through the noisy membrane of Top Forty hits and actually started to explore, the variations of sound and quality and rhythm were infinite. You could be as bad or as good as you chose to be. Both extremes could be successful, but to be good you had to be *very very* good. Anything less would be quickly lost in the limbo of the thousands of released LPs that never got airplay.

The gamut ran from show bands like Kiss, where technical skill was less important than the degenerate decibel level, to Steely Dan, whose complex, jazz-oriented sound was entirely created by consummate studio musicians.

Kyle's approach tended more toward the Steely Dan end, where, as arranger and producer, he maintained total control over the creation of a particular album. He preferred to have each piece firmly in his head before the amps were turned on, before the musicians were rehearsed.

The situation in D was an aberration he didn't like one bit. Studio West hadn't seen such a motley assortment of human beings since Zappa recorded Wild Man Fisher with a freak filled cheering section. He had half a mind to not even tape the session. Let the screwy girl work out her problems. Let her show off for the groupies and later they'd all get down to the exacting business of making a record. He flipped the monitor switch.

I thought I'd never feel the same

Kyle wasn't the first and he wouldn't be the last to be captivated by Ronnie Garrik. But few men reacted as intensely to her as he did. Her voice struck a responsive harmonic somewhere deep inside.

I know I'll never love again

Hersch was famous for his moderate language. In an environment where "fuck" was used as punctuation, Kyle's idea of cursing was "darn," or if he was really worked up, "nuts." So when Jade saw him leap from his seat and hover over the monitors as he exclaimed, "Jesus Christ, what a sensational goddamn voice!" he knew something was up.

"You like?" he asked with feigned casualness.

Ronnie was warming up with the old ballad Lenny Welch made famous, "Since I Fell For You." She was stroking the tune, drawing the heart out of it, using the embellishments and range that had impressed Presley and started the whole ball rolling.

"I like," said Kyle. "Sonofabitch, I *love.*"

Jade stared at the composer. Hersch was one of the coolest, most controlled personalities with whom he'd ever worked. The man did not show excitement, no matter what happened, no matter how hot the session got. And now he was responding to Ronnie like he was a kid in the front row, cheering her on.

It was highly unusual. Gustave just hoped it wouldn't interfere with the recording process.

The Regent is a quiet, mannerly hotel. It is not of a size to cater to conventions, or of a grandeur to attract film stars and rock musicians, with their troublesome, demanding entourages. Perhaps because of this it has not suffered the ravages of annual redecoration and has, therefore, a sense of time and place and old world elegance—a rare thing in Los Angeles.

Ronnie was in residence there for the five weeks it took to record *Shooting Star.* She learned how to survive the wearing sessions, with the continual and seemingly endless reruns, and after twelve or fourteen hours she looked forward to the hushed hallways of the Regent. Learning to relax there became a ritual.

First she unplugged the telephone. Then she drew a long, hot bath and slipped into it. Silence, lovely silence. After the ritual of water and steam she was content to lie at the edge of sleep in her air-conditioned room, letting it all unwind.

One Sunday she woke up at noon and remembered, with a pleasant start, that Gustave had arranged a two-day hiatus and that she had no responsibilities or duties to fulfill, was not expected anywhere.

I shall linger over breakfast until long past dinner, she thought, and then wander down to the kiosk in my slippers, at a snail's pace, admiring the Oriental tapestries and marble wainscotings. At the kiosk I will select a paperback novel, quiet in tone, the kind with a happy ending. Then I shall order a bottle of California white wine—Provence, which Jade likes, ruin it with ice and spritzer, and sip it until I've finished the story and am ready to crawl back into bed, delightfully alone.

Not exactly an exciting way to spend the day, but that was how she wanted it. The knock on the door, then, was not particularly welcome.

Kyle Hersch blinked at her, smiling uncertainly. He was wearing white duck trousers, an Armani shirt and, implausibly, a pair of rubber thongs that must have set him back eighty-nine cents. He had his hands behind his back. "I was just in the neighborhood," he said.

"And you just happened to have a few dozen of my favorite roses."

"I'd have called, but . . ."

"But my phone is unplugged. Well, come on in." Ronnie swung the door wide, and with her free hand adjusted the neck of the brushed satin camisole she'd acquired in the first splurge of shopping. She'd given up being curious about Hersch, so reserved and distant had he been, and decided he was an eccentric, albeit a talented one. He was the last man in the world she would have expected to show up, flowers in hand and obviously, from his nervousness, in the role of gentleman caller.

"To what do I owe the honor?"

"Nothing special," he said. She saw him staring at the upholstered chair—damn, she'd left her underwear out—as if he thought he might have to fight for the right to sit there. He turned and met her eyes for the first time. "I was hoping you'd be up for a Sunday ride. We could go up the coast, see the sights. You know."

"Sure." She'd meant she knew what he meant, not that she was agreeing to it, but a light switched on in his face and from then on she couldn't say no without making it awkward. Kyle was doing great things for her album, everybody told her so, and she didn't want to make an enemy of him.

Besides, once she got used to the idea a breezy ride in a snappy convertible might be fun. But it wasn't a convertible and it wasn't snappy, not at all.

"Hey, what is this, anyway?" asked Ronnie. She settled into the shotgun position and looked around, trying to pin down what was familiar about the dowdy, oversized vehicle.

"It's a Checker," said Kyle proudly. He pressed a floor starter, set the choke, and backed carefully out onto the boulevard.

"You mean like a taxicab?"

"Exactly. Safest car on the road." He rapped his knuckles on the walnut dashboard. "Would you buckle your seat belt, please?"

"You gotta be kidding."

He slowed, pulling the car over to the side. "Please, Ronnie. I can't drive properly if I have to worry about you going through the windshield."

"You're serious, aren't you?"

He nodded glumly. "It's a problem of mine, being serious."

"So okay, I'm buckled in, safe as churches. Now step on it and let's get out of the Yellow Peril, shall we?" The smog had settled in and she could feel it like a hand inside her throat.

Given his seat-belt fetish, she expected him to be a fussy driver, but once on the freeway he cruised skillfully, weaving the big car in and out of the traffic stream, jockeying for position. She knew without asking that he trusted no one else in the world to drive as he did.

Ronnie was watching the sky, mesmerized by the motion of the road, when Kyle spoke abruptly.

"Have you got something going with Zach Curtis, Ronnie?"

She looked at him, surprised. From the tone of his voice she knew he'd been waiting to pop that since the beginning.

"Zach and I are pals. It wasn't always that way, but it is now."

"I don't mean to be impolite. I just wanted to know how things were with you."

"I'm on the loose, if that's what you mean."

He laughed and she saw, for a flash, how handsome he could be when something amused him. His thick hair was still worn shoulder length and brushed back, but it was now streaked with veins of silver, in contrast to his still boyish looks. He had strong features and striking, thick eyebrows like an artist's stroke across his brow. She looked curiously at his lips, which were somewhat feminine in shape, and at the cleft that might have been printed by a hot fingertip. Hersch was an indifferent pianist, but his hands, with long, sensual fingers, would have been the envy of an aspiring Van Cliburn.

"This may sound weird, Kyle, but up until about an hour ago I could have sworn you didn't like me. I mean you never speak to me in the studio, except to cue songs or tell me I've messed up. And you never say boo about what it sounds like, or if it's good or bad."

"My apologies, Ronnie." He smiled her way. "I'm pretty tightlipped when I'm working, but I happen to think you're the best. I told Jade that the very first day."

"Yeah?"

"Yeah." He laughed again, amused at his own ability to project exactly the wrong image. "I've produced a lot of albums over the last few years. This one excites me more than any of the others. So do you, for that matter."

"I'd never have guessed," said Ronnie.

"The guy in the glass booth, that's not me, Ronnie. It's someone I have to be to get the job done. What I really—"

"Hey, where are we?" He was coming on too fast, too strong, and she wanted to lighten it up. They were coming up on a shimmering blueness that had to be the Pacific; convenient scenery to deflect the conversation. Kyle picked up on her mood and began to point out landmarks and chat amiably.

"To your right is the Los Padres Wilderness. To your left, at the foot of that cliff, the rest of the world begins."

Far below the waves curled in, looking small and delicate as they threw up spumes that must have been forty feet high. The Checker cruised on up Route 1, running along a line dividing land from sea, locked in at seventy miles per hour, just as solid as a Sherman tank. Ronnie put the windows down, leaning her head into the breeze, feeling the luxurious thrill of the wind teasing her hair.

Kyle slowly relaxed as he drove, his tensions fading the farther they got from Los Angeles. Ronnie was wearing a gauzy sundress, caught with a small red bow that drew the fabric against her breasts, completely contradicting the schoolgirl suggestion of the dress itself. She allowed him his stolen glances and caught herself, for no reason she was conscious of, posing. Holding herself at the prettiest angle, chin up, breasts high, her hair flung back.

"Do you have a destination in mind, Kyle, or is this a magic bus ride?"

"I'd like to show you where I live."

"Is it far?"

"It's a ways," he said vaguely.

As a matter of fact it was three hundred miles, but the signs began to trip by, lovely musical names like Santa Barbara, Santa Maria, Arroyo, and when at last they came to Big Sur Ronnie was scarcely aware of the time lost between the dotted white lines.

"An *aubade,*" he explained, "is a piece of music sung at dawn to celebrate the rising sun."

Ronnie knew Kyle was wealthy and that a big spread was de rigueur in this neck of the woods, but she was not prepared for Aubade. It was a gem, flawlessly set into a mountainside, with the myriad windowpanes catching light like diamond facets.

She thought the bridge a clever prank, but when she saw the guardhouse and fortifications, it came to her like a cold, wet chill: He was afraid of something. Kyle, reading the expression in her eyes, tried to make light of it.

"I've a thing about privacy," he said. "Fortunately, I can afford to indulge it."

He opened her door, his hands warm upon her bare arms. One of the uniformed guards waited to take the Checker away. Ronnie noticed the gleaming black holster on his hip.

"Strictly for looks," said Kyle. "We've never had a shot fired, not since I've been here. Come on, you must be famished. I'll show you around after we've eaten."

A small, delicately featured girl waited inside the foyer. Kyle picked her up, squeezing his arms around her as she pressed her face against his, swathing him with a headful of taffy-colored hair.

"I missed you, Daddy."

"I missed you, too, darling." He turned to Ronnie, the child in his arms, and once more she saw the radiant smile. "This is my daughter, Louise. This is Ronnie Garrik."

The little girl held her arms out with obvious delight, and Ronnie, taken aback by this sudden display of affection, let herself be kissed wetly upon the cheek.

"Daddy talks about you all the time."

"Now, Louise."

"It's *true*, Daddy. She's the one who sings so nice."

Watching him, Ronnie knew she had never seen anyone really blush before, not like Kyle did, with the red climbing up like a thermometer, turning the bottoms of his ears bright crimson. He dispatched the child to the playroom with a promise that he would see her after dinner.

The way he looked after her, eyes helplessly drawn to the small retreating figure, Ronnie knew who it was Kyle Hersch was guarding.

Sleeping with him was absolutely out of the question until it happened.

They dined splendidly in one of the smaller rooms. Brook trout right out of the brook, poached in butter, lemon juice, and diced shallots. Ronnie had eaten well enough at the Regent, but it did not compare with the delicately spiced wild rice from the Aubade kitchens, or the crisp endive salad, or the fresh mountain strawberries sprinkled with brown sugar, or the iced mocha concoction that tasted exactly the way fresh ground coffee smelled.

After dinner Kyle escorted her to one of the open decks that faced toward the incandescent, blood red sunset. Aubade, created at the beginning of the "modern" era, when architecture still aspired to be not only innovative but grand, had been conceived as an exterior habitat: an inner space open to the outside. Working from this central theme, virtually all of the rooms opened onto decks, or balconies, or enclosed glass porches.

Constructed without regard to cost at a time when real money could still buy real substance, mere wealth could not now have replicated the estate.

"This way," said Kyle, with the aplomb of Livingston showing Stanley into the heart of the wilderness. And indeed, it was as if the cultivated gardens below had come up into the cantilevered deck. Exotic giant cacti rose up through openings in the redwood planking, as did a blue-budded wisteria, branches flung skyward. In the gardens below, which verged on being jungle, a care and expertise had been purposely disguised to make a kind of wild Babylon of vegetation.

When a liqueur had been served, a wonderful licorice-tasting thing, Kyle excused himself to put his daughter to bed.

Sipping the drink as she gazed down through the lush gardens toward the edge of the mountain and far out into an endless, open sky toward the sea, Ronnie was captivated by the audacious and unlikely beauty of the place. If you had to retreat from the world, this was the place for it. With a full belly and a slight buzz from the potent drink, she was in a mood to forgive her host some of his eccentricities.

He lived under siege, perhaps, but he lived well.

"Are you ready for this, Ronnie?" He dropped into the chair at her side. His voice was soft, but with a hardness underneath that made her know it was not a casual question.

"I'm not sure what you mean, Kyle. Ready for what?"

"For what will happen once *Shooting Star* is released."

"I've been waiting all my life to find out," she said, emptying the glass and setting it firmly on the table between them. "You're not going to rain on my parade, are you?"

He shook his head, smoothing back a lock of curly hair. "I want the record to be fabulous, Ronnie." He gestured toward the edge of the deck, toward the perimeter, where shadows were lengthening. "That's how I keep all of this from melting away. But I have seen terrible things happen. Kids with big hearts who hit it quote overnight unquote. Ugly things can happen . . ." He let it hang for a moment, not looking at her.

"Do me a favor, Kyle. Don't worry about me, okay? I'm not looking to be the latest reincarnation of Judy Garland, or Janis Joplin, or whoever it is you have in mind. I've worked my— pardon me—*ass* off for this, and I'm not going to have a neurotic genius who has a private goddamned *army* protecting him from the bogey man or whatever . . . I just don't want you trying to spook me, okay?"

She was astonished at her trembling voice. Where the hell had that outburst come from? It was like having a stranger speak from within her. And just what was this son of a bitch doing, wining and dining her and then coming on with this "success equals misery" stuff?

"I'm sorry," he said.

He kissed her lightly, touching lips, and she hardly knew how it happened, or how he'd managed to move into her arms, or why she was still trembling.

They made love for the first time about an hour later, there on the deck, standing. They'd had another round of drinks, had not discussed the kiss or her outburst, but somehow they'd moved together again. Ronnie didn't draw away when she felt him growing hard against her, although she knew that screwing Kyle would make things unbearably complicated between them, she did not draw away because she thought it still in her power to deny him, and she liked being kissed and held and knowing he wanted her. In a very few moments her legs began to betray her, tingling with a sudden heat and damn it she was beginning to flow, getting wet as he pressed himself to her, his long pianist's hands moving under her sundress. He began stroking her flanks, tracing the jut of her buttocks and drawing heat into the middle of her body so that she could not help but move, her hips cocking. He knew enough not to speak.

Ronnie shifted, parting her thighs as she clung for balance, as Kyle slid into her in one motion, full length, driving tight up against her, and it was not as if they were making love, it was sudden, upright fornication.

He began to throb inside her, rocking, pirouetting their equilibrium as her trembling doubled and trembled and tightened into spasms.

The orgasm came as quickly and painfully as a hot, sudden cramp.

They ended up sprawled on the deck. Ronnie tried to push the dress below her waist, covering her ruined, soggy underpants, but her hands were tingling with weakness, and besides Kyle looked even worse, with his white ducks hobbling his knees.

"Oh Kyle, darling," she sighed, using a stage voice. "You're *so* romantic."

And then they were both laughing, drawing huge gulps of air and laughing uproariously and hysterically as they struggled to adjust clothing.

By then there was no point in not sleeping with him. When their strength returned they went to his rooms, using the bed, the floor, and once, just once, they tried it standing up again, with Ronnie braced against the bathroom sink, but it didn't work for some reason and they kept slipping apart. Eventually they fell into an exhausted sleep from which they woke feeling embarrassed and strange.

It was too quick and too intense and they both knew it.

The return down the curving spine of Route 1, heading back into the smoke, was a long one, filled with uncomfortable silences. Ronnie was reminded of the ride with Zach, that awful trip down from the mountaintop with her heart devastated. But this was different. She was not in love with Kyle. She would never, she thought, be in love with Kyle.

But he was exhibiting all the anxious signs of a man in the

act of falling for her. He didn't say so in so many words, but she could feel it like an icy weight in the pit of her stomach.

After an uneasy breakfast she had gone with him to say good-bye to Louise. As they approached the conservatory one of Satie's études drifted toward them. Ronnie assumed it was a recording, but the piece stopped as they entered. Louise, dwarfed by a pale blue Steinway, jumped down from her practice bench and ran to embrace her father.

"I can play it right to the end now, Daddy." She chattered excitedly. "Mr. Ellsworth says I can play even better than he does!"

"I'm sure you do, darling. But I want you to promise me you won't forget what I said about playtime. If you get too over-wrought about this Mr. Ellsworth won't come to give you lessons anymore."

"Oh, Daddy, you wouldn't do that." Louise pouted, still excited about her musical progress. "When you come back I'll play 'Gymnopédies' for you, and I won't make any mistakes, not one."

"Louise, darling," he sighed. "I don't mind mistakes. It's only natural to make mistakes, lots of them. Remember what I said, now. I want you out in the sunshine, getting just as brown as a little walnut, remember?"

"Yes, Daddy, I promise."

Their parting was a ritual Louise was used to, and she seemed less affected by it than Kyle. As they left that wing of the house the études pursued them, as light and airy as chirping birds.

"She's a prodigy, isn't she?" asked Ronnie.

It was the wrong thing to say. He went stiff, and now it was he who was trembling, and not with physical passion.

"That word is not permitted in this house. Louise is a per-fectly bright little girl of seven years. She has a talent for the piano, and I am allowing her to have lessons because it would be cruel not to. But she is not, repeat, *not* a 'prodigy,' and she will not be treated like one, or pushed like one, or—"

"Kyle."

"I'm sorry. But you couldn't possibly know how much this worries me. I want Louise to be like other children. Do you know what happens to prodigies?"

It was so obvious, and that was why it angered and disturbed her: He was talking about himself. She terminated his explanation with a shrug. They left, not angry with each other, but uneasy.

They stopped in Los Padres for a picnic lunch. Kyle seemed on edge as he unpacked the wicker hamper. With great care he unfurled a linen tablecloth, set out tableware for two, and arranged a virtual delicatessen sampler; prosciutto, kishka, herring in cream sauce, the pickled hearts of prime artichokes. The roadside table overlooked a steep drop to the beach, and the air was charged with salt and the roar of breaking waves.

"Kyle, this is incredible." Ronnie slipped on her "just friends" facade, and decided to be purposefully gay and light. "Is this stuff really caviar?"

"Do you like it?"

"I'll find out." She shoveled some on a thin cracker. It tasted like the congealed spray of an edible ocean, and she began to dip fingers into it, smearing it across her lips. "I was born for this stuff, Kyle, don't you think?"

"Yes." He nodded gravely. "Try this."

He indicated a pewter serving dish. She removed the cover. Six oysters on crushed ice, each covered with an enamel shell. Ronnie had never eaten oysters and Kyle showed her how to dip the tender little bellies in hot, pungent sauce, then place it at the back of her tongue, drinking it in rather than swallowing.

She found the pendant under the third shell. A star, the points of diamonds trailing like sparks, and at the heart a luminous pearl.

"It's a shooting star," he said. "Whenever you wear it, I'll make a wish."

His hands trembled as he placed it around her neck. Ronnie wanted to tell him right then that it wasn't fair, that the star—God, how beautiful it was, the radiant light charged from the inside like tiny laser beams gone mad—was too much too soon, that it would *always* be too soon.

But all she managed to say was, "It's lovely, Kyle. Lovely." Because she could see it in his eyes, that quiet desperation, and she knew that from the moment he appeared at the Regent laden with roses he had, in his heart, already given her the star.

And wished upon it, too.

They saw the haze from miles away, as they veered in from the crisp sea air toward the sprawling city. A siren went by, wailing its wee-waw cry, startling Kyle Hersch out of his reverie. The daydream had been as abstract and disconnected as a John Cage composition, but it kept returning to her like the theme of a haunting melody.

He glanced at the clock on the dash. Not a moment too soon. He switched on the radio and punched the button for KTIZ, the fifty thousand watt powerhouse of the LA rock scene.

. . . hang tight and ten guys and dolls. Da Wolf Man whistles, ooh-ee, and now, just like he promised ya, a secret sneak ultra-tip-top-on-the-supreme-sly-side preview from the cats over at Sunset West. Here's the cue from me to you, kiddies, now lay back and let this little lady blow you *all* the way down, Jack!"

"Kyle, could you turn that—"
"Sssssh. *Listen.*"
And then it came through, the opening riff they'd done and redone until she could hardly stand it. But now, snapping and crackling over the ether, it sounded new and sharp, and began to trip up the back of her spine like icy fingertips.

"Kyle, that's *me*," she said. "I mean us. I mean . . ."
It was such a dumb thing, really, just one cut played on one station, big deal—but it was a thrill that swelled and broke inside her, a peak that would never quite be touched again, no matter how hard she tried, not even on the night when the whispers

followed her down the aisle at the Waldorf. She tried to hold onto it by drinking in each detail, by engraving the moment in her mind, but the wind was watering her eyes and the song itself seemed too bright and good to last.

4

Anthony Trendau came in at noon, loping through the Los Angeles bureau of *Rock Steady,* a familiar sight with his thinning hair tied back in a ponytail (a stubborn holdover from the Sixties) and the reflecting shades he wore inside or out, light or dark.

Trendau was somewhat of an enigma to his colleagues. On any given day he could be charming, and there were those who suspected he had a deep streak of shyness that he masked with cynical, rapid repartee. The cynicism was hardly intolerable to the staff of reporters, but on any given night Trendau, after an infusion of sour mash bourbon whiskey, underwent what might kindly be described as a personality change.

He was an ill-mannered, ill-tempered drunk. Not clever, as when sober, and never charming. Simply ugly. An underlying stubbornness, or perhaps fear, prevented him from admitting the problem, but alcohol affected him like venom and anyone who knew him avoided him in those circumstances if at all possible.

And until the Garrik incident his drinking habits hadn't affected his on-the-job performance. He was the best working editor of the lot. He always met his deadlines, turned in excellent copy—he was one of the most influential critics in the business —and the son of a bitch was *always* right.

On the day that proved the exception he scanned his call sheet, threw all but one of the messages in the round file, and leisurely sucked down the first of one hundred cigarettes before returning Jade Gustave's call.

"Trendau here, Jade. What gives?"

"Tony! I wasn't at all sure I got through that Lily Tomlin operator of yours. As a matter of fact there's a bandwagon leaving tonight at the Troubadour, and I thought you might want to be there."

"Come on, Jade. Don't play *me* this way."

"Tony, I'm giving this to you straight. There is about to be a phenomenon, and her name is Ronnie Garrik. You better get used to hearing a lot about that name, by the way."

"Jade, come off it."

"Seeing is believing, Tony. Kyle Hersch just finished the final mix on *Shooting Star*—he wrote the cover tune, by the way —and we're showcasing her at the Troub to kick off the tour."

"News to me, pal." Trendau glared at the phone. He was accustomed to creating bandwagons, not joining them. "I'm beginning to think even the great Gustave has succumbed to hype."

"I don't hype, Tony. You know that better than anyone. We believe in this kid. And she's happening fast. KTIZ played one cut—on Monday afternoon, their weakest density slot, mind you —and they logged five hundred calls."

That piqued Trendau's curiosity, but he wasn't about to let Gustave know it.

"I'll check my calendar, Jade. If I happen to be free this evening I'll try to stop in for a few minutes. By the way, where's the promo?"

"On your desk. I sent it over by messenger this morning."

"Right. So it is. Bye bye."

He turned the promotional copy over and glanced at the mock-up of the cover. Nice tits, he thought, I wonder who she fucked to get this kind of action?

"*Il fait chaud,*" said Zach Curtis, wiping beads of sweat from his brow. "Or like we say in the real world, it's some fucking *hot,* sweetheart!"

Indeed it was. The ventilation system at the Troubadour was kaput, the air-conditioning had browned out, and backstage it was as hot and heavy and wet as the Okeefenokee swamp in August.

Even the ever dapper Jade Gustave had doffed his jacket and rolled up his sleeves.

"Maybe we ought to cancel," he said. He held a cold compress to his neck and looked at Ronnie with concern. "This is inhuman. Probably dangerous as well."

Ronnie had her cheek against the coldest object she could lay her hands on, a bottle of Black Horse Ale, and although drenched in sweat she managed to give Jade a look that would have frosted a three-horned devil.

"I was born in West Texas, remember? This is nothin'. Just a tad warm around the edges." Her head was swimming, but Ronnie was not about to pack it in. She and the band had been rehearsing the new material for three days straight, with breaks for Chinese, beer, and enough "crossroads" to keep them moving.

It was essential that they not lose their momentum.

"Gimme salt tablets," growled Stokey. For once he agreed with Ronnie. They had the stuff ready and it was time to play. Moreover, he knew the room was jammed with media freaks, reps from other studios, the Beverly Hills contingent and the other etceteras who made up the LA rock scene. They would definitely be pissed off if, after enduring the sweltering heat for an hour and a half, the Roughriders failed to show.

"Where the fuck is Kenny off to? Where's that halfwit drummer boy?"

When he finally wandered in he was the only one not heat drenched, and from the glazed look in his eyes and the way he kept licking his lips, Ronnie knew why. They were going to have to do something about Kenny. He'd jumped head first into the local drug scene, and although it hadn't yet affected his music it seemed to be changing his personality. He didn't play it for laughs anymore. His round boyish face was getting drawn and pinched, like a fist clenching.

"I'm right here witcha," he muttered. "Everything's cool."

"Sure, Kenny," said Ronnie. She chugged the ale, knowing it would evaporate out her pores before it hit her belly. "Let's go do it, shall we?"

Gustave was not, as he had insisted earlier that day, the hype type. When he put the word out that something was about to happen, people listened. They came in droves; the hardest kind of crowd to please, the ones who had seen it all, or thought they had. The Troubadour was a launch pad for some of the hottest acts in the business and its patrons were not easily swayed by flash or puffery. So they waited, hot and pissed off and ready to tear this new bitch to pieces if she didn't deliver.

Ronnie stalked out to center stage and grabbed the mike without introduction. "Okay. If you were expecting that cool-looking chick you saw in the picture they got tacked up outside, *forget* it. I feel just as mean and ugly as a bobcat ducked in a hot spring. Me and my boys been buzzed out for days, trying to get this right, and the only thing left is to just let it rip and *kick ass!*"

Before the crowd had a chance to react Paul power chorded into the riff to "Shooting Star Tonight," Kyle's title cut. There would be no teasing, they were just going to drop right into it. Ronnie went down in a crouch, ready to rise up with the heat of that first opening wail.

"Ah-oooooo," she sang, starting low, letting her voice trip way up, showing off all of her incredible range. "Ah-eeeeeeeeeeeeee!"

Orphan child
don't pit-ty me
sha-hooting star
will set me free

Zach Curtis, sitting in on his baby grand, gave thumbs up to his friends in the audience. They howled back, as hot and as mean as this demon-possessed woman who pranced so arrogantly, holding nothing back, demanding and getting their absolute and undivided attention.

when I'm born

and when I die
sha-hooting star
will light the sky

It wasn't until she reared back and kicked that Paul Stokey noticed. She was wearing the same battered, knee-high doeskin boots she'd worn that first day when they'd auditioned her in Amarillo. Her mother's boots, although he didn't know that.

And Paul didn't have time to ponder the significance of what she had on her feet because what Ronnie had in both hands was the audience. He began to work, furious with sweat, to keep up with her.

Anthony Trendau watched from the back of the packed room. He squinted into the haze of smoke, inundated by the sound. She was good. She was damned good. And it pissed him off that half the bozos in LA were right there with him, hearing it just as soon as he did.

He began to drink, sucking down straight shooters of J.W. Dant. The heat poured into his chest and by the end of the single, supercharged ninety-minute set he had reached that special clarity where his rapier tongue became animate.

The bitch had the right stuff, but she was going to have to pay homage like the rest, preferably a homage of the flesh.

"I see you made it after all, Tony."

Gustave, in that silent way of his, had appeared out of nowhere. The critic surveyed him, his mouth twisted in a boozy smirk. Jade knew him well enough to anticipate the inevitable eruption. He had decided to make himself vulnerable by coming into range because he wanted to steer Trendau clear of Ronnie who, along with the 'Riders and a growing entourage, had decamped to nearby *Jason*'s immediately after the last song.

"You've got yourself quite the little star," he sneered, his cigarette glowing like a hot red eye. Gustave steadied him as he staggered, as the bourbon began calling in the bets. "What I want to know, Jade baby, is who is getting her action, huh?"

He was leading the agent down the block, toward the unmistakable sound of a party in progress.

"Now, Tony, I think it would be better if—"

But Trendau grabbed Jade by the elbow, squeezing the older man until he had to pull away.

"I know the score, baby," said the critic. "You're keepin' her under wraps."

The pain in his arm incensed Jade more than the insults, but he fought, for Ronnie's sake, to keep his temper buried. "Ease up, Tony. This is big. Too big for you to fuck up. Or screw, for that matter."

They were under the canopy at *Jason's*. Trendau swayed, hands on his hips as he taunted, "Don't tell me who I can or can't screw, faggot. I know about the precious little boys and girls you buy, don't think I don't."

"Tony, you're making a big mistake."

But Trendau flicked his cigarette in a high, spark-strewn arc, just missing Jade, and backed into *Jason's*, twisting open the double doors with his narrow shoulders.

The tumultuous celebration in progress teetered on the brink of pandemonium, which the advancing presence of Anthony Trendau did not at first affect. But slowly, as one by one the partyers recognized him and saw from his hostile posture that trouble was brewing, the sound level came down, decibel by decibel.

One of Kenny's teenyboppers had somehow got her miniskirt caught up around her waist, but she was too busy pouring champagne over the delirious drummer to notice. When Trendau appeared, his shades leveled like guns, she looked up, bewildered by the sudden silence.

"Whatsa matta?" she said.

"Hi Tony," someone murmured. "Want to join us?"

It was a less than enthusiastic invitation. Ronnie, who had been laughing uproariously moments before, looked around as if something essential had been misplaced.

Tony Trendau stood there like a gaunt, mad bug, his mirror eyes gleaming.

"I came to see the big star," he said.

"Jade, darling," asked Ronnie. "Who is this man?"

"Never mind your pansy agent. The name is Trendau," he said, his words slurring. "And if you're real lucky I might give you an exclusive."

Ronnie, who was so high she was almost clairvoyant, tumbled to the situation immediately. She ignored Jade's signals and stood up with her arms out, as if to embrace the critic.

"Tony Trendau," she said gaily. "I've been *dying* to meet you. Come sit over here by me and I'll dispose of these other people *immediately.*"

It was not the response he'd expected. Anthony stared at her, insolent and confused, and then made a very large mistake. He moved toward her.

"Tony, darling, this is too good to be true." She snaked an arm around his hips and pulled him close.

It happened so quickly he couldn't quite put it together in his head. Ronnie deftly nipped open the top of his jeans, and before he could move his pants were down around his thighs and Ronnie was pressing him against the table, pinning his nakedness in full view.

"Tony!" she exclaimed in mock horror. "Is that a war wound? Why, I've never seen anything quite so small."

She ducked out of the way as he swung at her, driven by the shrill laughter as with one hand he hiked up his pants and tripped backward, upsetting one of the tables.

Two burly waiters came to heave him out, but he was already limping hurriedly away, the shades askew on his deathly pale face, when the cheering began.

"Mandrel speaking."

"Bo! Great to hear your voice, old boy. John Lloyd here. I'm afraid we have a bit of a problem. It's your man Trendau.

"Ah! Anthony is not the endearing type, I know. But he is my best writer."

"Yes. Talented boy. However, he's taken a rather violent personal dislike to someone we think a lot of here. Mr. Trendau is using your magazine to put the boots to her, as it were."

"I give my people free rein, John. If he thinks your act is lousy and he calls it that way it's out of my hands."

"Of course. Wouldn't dream of trying to bend the rules, or threaten to withdraw advertising or anything like that, old boy. We go strictly on merit here, as you may know. Which is precisely what I'm talking about. Let me quote Trendau to you: 'the latest hype promotion from the usually reputable Liberty stable goes by the name of Ronnie Garrik'—her real name, by the way, Bo. I suppose dear Tony is having a jab there—'Your Obedient Servant strongly advises that you ignore, repeat, ignore this tasteless bit of drivel. Garrik sings with the style and grace of a ruptured groundhog, and despite producer Kyle Hersch's vain attempt to cover her inept and rather pathetic mistakes, the album is an utter failure' . . . that's the gist of it, Bo."

"If Tony says she stinks it's out of my hands."

"Bo, what I'm trying to say is, this could be embarrassing for you. Ronnie Garrik has our full and complete backing. More than that she is a *sensation. Shooting Star* was released out your way two days ago and already we have forty thousand copies placed in *two days,* Bo. I don't need to tell you how unusual that is for an unknown. Ronnie won't be unknown for long, either. Three cuts have already been picked up for saturation play by that AM syndicate out there. Not one but *three.* So you see I—"

"Tell you what, Talbot. I'll listen to the record, okay?"

"That's good enough for me, Bo. Cheerio."

An astute observer at San Francisco's Cow Palace, which was SRO for the Ronnie Garrik stage show, would have been treated to a curious sight.

Sitting side by side in third row center were Bo Mandrel, owner and publisher of *Rock Steady,* and Anthony Trendau, his well-known rock critic. Neither looked happy. The critic smoked incessantly, hiding under a fog bank of nicotine vapors as the Roughriders took to the stage and began what was to be, in the annals of pop music, a legendary performance.

Those who knew Mandrel wondered what on earth he was doing front and center in the eye of the mob when he could have been backstage. But he wanted to hear it exactly as the crowd heard it. He leapt up now and then, fist raised, cheering on the inspired, explosive little lady with the great big voice. Bo Mandrel loved good rock and the band was peaking that night, sky high for their first engagement.

There was nothing contrived or hyped about it. The stage was mobbed time and again, not violently, but as an act of love.

It was too loud for conversation, but Mr. Mandrel's glances toward Mr. Trendau spoke volumes. When, at the conclusion of the ballad "Since I Fell For You" (added to the repertoire at Kyle's insistence), the publisher reached over, carefully removed the critic's reflecting sunglasses, and snapped them perfunctorily in two, no one who knew Bo Mandrel would have been surprised.

Mandrel was angry. And Trendau was fired.

Richard Avedon flew in to take the pictures. Ronnie vamped it up with a royal purple boa. Avedon, who had assumed the session would be a snooze, got into it. He caught her in the air, heels up, suspended at the zenith of a joyous leap into fame as the boa streamed like a lion's mane. Other photographers try shots like that. Only Avedon can make it work.

It was just the look Mandrel wanted.

He'd already pulled that week's scheduled cover, stalled the feature, and written a thirty-five-hundred-word rave entitled "THE GARRIK PHENOMENON."

Having written it and named it, Mandrel helped make it happen. *Time* and *Newsweek* trampled each other in their haste to climb on the bandwagon. They picked up Mandrel's catch phrase "the future sex of rock and roll," and while *Time* played up the Buddy Holly angle, *Newsweek* interviewed a rather startled Mr. Jacobsen of the Lubbock Methodist choir. Both magazines used a grainy snapshot of little Ronnie at her father's knee, clutching the half-sized banjo, implying that she had been performing from the moment of birth, if not conception.

Gustave's office was swamped with demands for interviews, endorsements, picture sessions, and the Hollywood fandango began in earnest.

Overnight sensation.

It never happens overnight, but it can be made to look that way. And to Ronnie, upon whom all the resultant hysteria was focused, if felt that way for a while.

For just long enough.

5

"Wake up, Ronnie. They want you, honey."

She came up kicking through syrupy waves, floating up into the light to see, through squinting eyes, that the blinds had been opened and the cold gray sky of Chicago was there, waiting.

"Times it?"

"Ten in the morning, Ronnie."

"What!" She sat up, a dizzy whirl coming into her head. "But I didn't get in till six. Why are you *doing* this to me?"

Ronnie, always a cranky waker, took a swing at the breakfast tray, purposefully missing. She could smell the thick fragrance of the Hilton's coffee, the scent of fresh strawberry jam and butter-crisp croissants.

"Sorry, honey." Didi Hayes, the dresser Jade had hired to oversee costume changes and public appearance wardrobes for the duration of the tour, had, in addition to making herself instantly irreplaceable, developed a soothing tone that worked best for rousing Ronnie in the mornings.

"Who wants me?" She had genuinely forgotten, although Jade's meticulous schedule was there on the bureau in an embossed folder.

"Radio. Three stations, one of 'em network. Network is last so you'll be ready by then. And you've got record stores to do, too, honey. No autographs, just a whirl through. Want me to send up Mr. Ricky?"

The name didn't register for a moment and then she remembered that Ricardo something or other was the resident hair-dresser, and that he was good. Also quiet.

Ronnie nodded. "Give me twenty, Dee. You're a doll." She dipped a croissant directly into the jam pot, licking the flakes from her fingertips. Didi had been a real find. She had enough spare energy for the both of them and when Ronnie was too spaced out to put on a matching pair of socks Didi could make her look like she was going to tea with Garbo.

The concerts themselves had gotten to be the easy part. It was Liberty's "big push" that was eating her alive. If the promotional department could have created a couple of Ronnie Garrik clones, they would have. As it was she had to do it all herself. Of course the incredible split-second-timing network of tour attendants, chauffeurs, dressers, and advancers made the impossible possible until, by virtue of taped interviews and shows, she was often in more than two places at once.

Schizo time. But it was worth it. She had to keep reminding herself of that. This was what she'd dreamed about for all those years, and if her dreams had not included the dreary little details of itemized days and blown-out nights—well, it was *still* worth it.

Didi returned with a list of messages. How she managed to look bouncy and cheerful was a minor miracle, considering how she'd squandered the night before.

"I took care of all these," she told Ronnie. "Except for Mr. Hersch. He said it was personal."

"Oh." The guilt twanged like a bowstring, an internal wince she'd experienced a lot lately. Kyle had been leaving messages each night since the tour began and she had yet to return one of his calls. She kept telling herself that she was too busy, but it was more than that. She tried to feel righteous about it: If Kyle wanted to see her he could damn well fly out and *see* her, and stop playing heavy with her heart over the telephone. But he stayed holed up in Aubade like some kind of feudal lord, disdaining the modern world, save for the few weeks out of the year he deigned to visit Los Angeles.

If Kyle Hersch wanted her he would damn well have to come and get her. In the meantime it was easier to conceal what she felt for him, to pretend it had never happened.

"Didi? Get room service and have them deliver a basket of

eggs to Zach in room two thirty-eight. Nice speckled brown eggs. No, I'm not going bughouse, Didi, it's a joke. Just do it."

Yes, meantime she was back sleeping with Zach Curtis. Well, not sleeping with him exactly. Fucking. That's what it was, nothing fancy about it. Just plain rude, sudden couplings that left them both breathless and physically sated. It had gone from a brother and sister act to make-believe incest, no romance, thank you. No emotional entanglements. Just good old healthy fornication.

Last night in his suite (which, as a result of the partying earlier, looked like it had been hit by a bomb), after their third orgasm, Zach sat up groaning.

"You're wearing me out, Ronnie. I need sex food or something." He took a mock bite out of her naked haunch. He'd lately grown a thick blond beard, the curls of which tickled her. "The poor little devil has gone limp again." He sighed. "Got to eat me some raw eggs, I guess."

They both laughed uproariously. It was exactly what she needed. No heavy commitments, no tremors of the heart. Purely physical. Something that Kyle wouldn't understand, although it was not for that reason that she and Zach kept it under wraps. Zachary had gotten himself married and had a wife in Tucson who would not have been amused.

Curiously enough she did not feel the least bit guilty about *that.* Ronnie had been on the periphery all that time on the road, not bound by the conventions of polite society. But now, in one sudden leap, she was light-years beyond even that. She was free to do anything, or so it seemed. No one would dare criticize her, or find fault in her behavior; she was quite certain she could, if she wanted, engage in the most wild and obscene debauchments and Didi would still be there come morning, smiling, ready to wait on her.

If there was a price for such freedom Ronnie had yet to see it itemized.

That would come later.

They all knew that Kenny had a problem, but no one suspected just how acute it was until the moment had passed.

From Chicago the tour swung into the Midwest, playing to medium-sized halls in places like Dayton, Bloomington, Duluth. Sometimes two shows in one day, hopping from one Farm Belt city to the next in John Lloyd's Sikorsky. Jade had requested the helicopter as an absolute necessity for making quick getaways from the mobs that had become a fixed part of the tour.

The media blitz descended with a vengeance. The first thing Gustave did upon touching down in each city was see that the press kits were distributed to the locals. Immediately after deplaning, Ronnie held a conference, which inevitably degenerated into her posing, cutting up, making up preposterous lies about her past as she charmed and seduced the press. After the conference Ronnie settled into her rooms and prepared for the main assault of the evening, the concert.

The original tour had been scheduled for thirty-two engagements in twenty-six cities. As the Garrik craze intensified, however, promoters began deluging Liberty with cables and calls, demanding part of the action. Jade was reluctant to authorize additional dates. Ronnie was 126 pounds of dynamite, but she could explode in just so many directions. Gustave knew an overwrought, overworked star could blow the whole tour in one bad night, and he clamped the lid on extra gigs. Enough was enough.

When Ronnie got wind of it she was on him in an instant. "Jade, honey. You are looking at Miss One Night Stand, do you follow? I've been singing eight days a week all my life. Or it seems like it anyway."

"Ronnie, we're not talking clubs here. I don't need to tell you how exhausting each date is. Why in Cincinnati we had to—"

"Never mind about Cincinnati. Just look at me."

"Ronnie, I—"

"Look at me!"

She stood before him, blazing, her eyes clear (how was that possible, when his own were red-rimmed with jet lag?) looking as fit and vigorous as a prize Bantam rooster after a noontime nap. Clearly Ronnie Garrik was unaffected by the ordinary limits of human endurance.

"You look great," he admitted. "I don't know how you do it, but—"

"But nothing, Jade darling. We're doing those gigs. Haven't you been telling me how I have to get it while the getting's good? How I have to grab the ring the first time it goes by, because maybe it won't again?"

"I was waxing philosophical, Ronnie. A fault of mine. But I also know that it can be overdone, that you can burn out. I've seen it happen time and again, Ronnie. All you have to do is blink and you're gone."

Ronnie made a play of holding her eyes open, joking him into it. "I'm not blinking, handsome. Let's go."

So they went.

New York had the fever. A second show was added after the Garden sold out the first. The second also sold out. John Lloyd Talbot's biggest headache became the shipping department, which was swamped with reorders for *Shooting Star,* certified platinum four weeks after release. And there had been no slackening of retail interest.

When the tour company arrived for the Garden dates Talbot managed to book them into the Waldorf-Astoria, a feat of diplomacy since that staid and grand hotel had a policy of refusing tour companies of any sort, especially those associated with raucous music. John Lloyd posted a bond, of course, but the deciding factor was the night manager, who had a full-length poster of Ronnie under glass in his suite, and who demanded and got a pair of backstage passes.

Bill Graham fulfilled an old fantasy of Ronnie's when he had the entire backstage area strewn with rose petals.

"You're in good hands with Bill," Jade told her. "He's the classiest promoter in the country and we're lucky to have him."

"I never met the guy," she said, skipping through the blossoms in her bare feet. "But already I love him."

A banquet was laid out in the dressing room, and all those lucky enough to have passes crowded in, cracking open magnums of champagne. When the first platters of food emptied more was brought in and even the usually moody Stokey got into the spirit of the party, grinning widely and embracing Ronnie as the flash-bulbs detonated.

Ten minutes before show time Kenny turned up missing.

"Son of a bitch!" Paul Stokey shook himself free of two adoring groupies. "We're going to have to find us a new drummer, that's all there is to it."

"Kenny will show," Ronnie assured him. "Wait and see."

But he didn't show, and after a thirty-minute delay the crowd began to rampage. Jade put through an emergency request to the musicians' union and a studio drummer arrived, looked disheveled and not a little frightened.

It was an act of courage on his part to sit in without a moment's rehearsal. The crowd didn't notice, or care. Stokey was hot. He soared on solo, meeting Ronnie's scat singing note for note. That first set went so well that all of them secretly hoped Kenny would stay lost. It was this sentiment that doubled back on them after the second show.

They tumbled off the stage, ecstatic with the Garden's vibrant energy, to find Jade Gustave and John Lloyd Talbot waiting. Jade was pale and trembling. John Lloyd broke the news.

"Kenny's gone," he said, his voice husky and strained. "Chivas and reds . . ."

They'd found him slumped in his chair in his suite at the Waldorf. Alone, stinking of the scotch he'd spilled, an empty bottle of barbituates in his shirt pocket. He was twenty-two, but death made an old man of him. The discovery threw Gustave into a funk nearly as deep as the one he'd been in during his self-imposed exile.

"He was just a boy," said Jade, his eyes brimming with tears. "We should have taken better care of him."

He and Ronnie held each other, swaying a slow waltz of sorrow.

There was no shaking it off. A pall hung over the remainder of the tour. For Ronnie it was sleepless lethargy (it was she who insisted they continue, that work was the only solution) intensified by the diet pills she began to gobble, those black beauties that animated her public appearances, turning her into a slack-eyed chatterbox.

Jade knew what she was on to, and because of Kenny's drug-induced death he became positively frantic, pleading with her to stop.

"Amphetamines are not barbituates, Jade darling," insisted Ronnie. Her mouth was dry, caked with a speed jag. "Besides, it keeps me skinny. Now go bother the Okie brothers. Did you know Ray has started taking girls up to his room? Can you imagine? Straight little Ray? I mean what is the world coming to?"

But her attempts at levity rang false, and Jade was seriously considering canceling the last few gigs when the matter was decided for him at the Orpheum in Boston.

Whatever was wrong with her that night was not manifest in her voice. It rang out as true and as clear as ever. But the sea of faces blurred and broke, glittering in a strange cadence before her eyes. It was like being under water. With part of her head Ronnie could hear the 'Riders cueing her to Zach's "Astral Jive," a tune that was just then breaking in Boston, but the idea of actually singing it seemed ludicrous. Ronnie was much more interested in watching the glitter rise from the diamond eyes of the pendant Kyle had given her. There was something about Kyle she was trying to decide in her head, but it was confused, clouded. She kept trying to touch it and ended up touching the pendant instead. She stood fingering it, her mouth open, unaware that she was hyperventilating, unaware that the band had stopped, unaware that the crowd was buzzing, and strangely uncaring as her body stiffened and the stage tipped up and drew her into the darkness.

The room at Mass General was cordoned off, but one of the guards recognized Kyle Hersch and let him pass. The hallway was jammed with the flowers she'd ordered removed from her sight and he had to pick his way through a knee-high flood of blossoms.

"I got here as soon as I could," he told her. "Talbot loaned me the *Liberty Belle.*"

Ronnie didn't bother to lift her head from the pillow. Kyle tried not to notice her lackluster hair or the dark circles under her eyes.

"You really flew?" As she looked away, speaking to the wall, her voice changed. "So the great Kyle Hersch actually flew in an *airplane.* Jesus, what an honor."

He stood by the bed, ready to take her hand. She didn't offer.

"Kyle, I wish you'd . . ." Her voice trailed off. She didn't know precisely what it was she wanted. Maybe just to sleep, to pull the dark cloud up over her eyes again.

"Louise sent you this." He put a bright card on the blanket. On it was a heart drawn in a child's hand, the sentiment expressed in multicolored crayon. When Ronnie pointedly ignored it, he said, "It wasn't your fault, Ronnie. Kenny was a wild kid. It happens. You can't let it eat you up. You shouldn't feel guilty."

"I don't feel guilty!" she screamed. A male nurse hurried into the room. He kept a discreet distance when he saw Hersch already there. "*I* didn't make him take those pills. *I* didn't make him drink two-thirds of a fifth of fucking Chivas Regal. *I* didn't—"

"Ronnie!" Kyle touched her cheek with the flat of his hand. It was too gentle to be a slap, but Ronnie reacted as if it were. "Baby," he said, "I'm sorry."

"Don't be." Her voice came from a hollow place, jagged and mean. "Kyle, do me one favor."

He stiffened, as if he knew what she was about to say.

"You and your precious daughter get out of my life. Do you understand? Can you get it through that thick, genius skull of yours? I don't love you. I don't love *anybody.*"

When he was gone she turned her face to the wall, convulsed with despair. The nurse watched from the corner, silently.

6

The sea broke clean under an azure sky. She watched it for hours. The waves were like white drumming fingertips, rising up until the light broke through, splitting into foam with a sigh. In the evenings the air was laden with salt spray, and it made her lungs feel wonderfully clean, as if each breath she took was charged with vitamins.

"I want you to do nothing but soak up the rays for a month, two months." Jade told her when she was installed in the Malibu "cottage." "As long as it takes. I want to see you brown as a raisin."

She had clung to his arm as he led her over the sand-blown path toward the bleached redwood edifice. "Jade, you ought to be somebody's father," she said in a small voice.

He squeezed her hand and chuckled. "Not in this lifetime. But look, you mustn't worry about a thing. Stokey wants to leave? Fine. Let him. Ray and Eddie already have more studio work lined up then they know what to do with. So you just worry about yourself. Kyle and Zach and I will start collecting material for your next album. No rush. *Star* is still holding its own, quite magnificently, I might add. Here—" He pushed open the door. In the main salon, which overlooked three distinct views of the beach, a late afternoon fire had been lit in the hearth. "Isn't it, dare I say it, *pacific?*" He laughed again and the warm sound of it got her smiling. "Now the important part is you, Ronnie. The trick of surviving in this crazy business is to give it all out—and you've done that perfectly—and then lay back and soak it in again.

You've got to collect your 'juice,' do you follow me, darling?"

She kissed him, felt mischievous enough to give him one quick touch of the tongue, and then laughed at his embarrassment. "Some day, Jade . . . someday we'll get over this thing you have about not sleeping with your talents."

"I'm afraid it's an inviolate rule, darling. Besides, you'd be the death of me. Don't let this boyish face of mine fool you. I'm getting old."

"Forty-three is a long ways from old, baby. But never mind. You're staying for dinner, right?" A trace of anxiety returned to her voice and he nodded assent.

"That's Didi out there." He pointed through one of the glass partitions toward a small figure casting a rod into the surf. "With any luck we'll be dining on fresh striper. I wouldn't miss it for the world."

The dividing line of sea and surf fluttered hypnotically, and as she watched her heart slowed until it began to thump with symbiotic, stately rhythm. It was going to be all right, as Jade had promised.

All she needed was time.

The light scattered through the arches of the white walls, illuminating the high vaulted ceilings and making the manacle on the slender brown wrist glitter like an Inca bracelet. The diplomat caressed it thoughtfully, his eyes expectant. With his free hand he patted his brow with a linen handkerchief. The sweat beaded there was only partly from nerves. Outside Talbot's cool Central Park West sanctuary the August heat was raging.

"Any trouble?"

"There is never any trouble," smiled the diplomat. He waited while John Lloyd slipped the bolt to his office door, a precaution not nearly as casual as he made it seem.

The manacle securing the attaché case to the diplomat's wrist would remain there until he returned to his embassy. But from his waistcoat pocket he extracted a most forbidden key, one which fitted the attaché case itself, possession of which, if discovered, would effectively and instantly end his career.

"Allow me," said Talbot, not bothering to conceal his eager-ness. He took the key from the diplomat, placed it in the lock, and manipulated the intricate release mechanism. The case sprung open.

As the diplomat watched impassively Talbot gently put aside the sealed communiqués—of no interest to him—and removed a rectangular plasticene package.

"Very nice," he said, hefting it. There was no need to verify that the package weighed precisely two thousand grams, or just under four and a half pounds.

The diplomat smiled again as he methodically repacked and relocked the case. When he glanced at the deposit slip John Lloyd placed on the desk the smile became real, moving into his eyes. It indicated that five hundred thousand dollars had been depos-ited in a small Cuban bank in Miami, an account more secure from prying eyes than a Swiss deposit could ever be because the diplomat, through a series of corporate blinds, owned a control-ling share of the bank itself.

John Lloyd, dressed in his summer uniform of Egyptian linen and a pair of trusty old sandals bought for a few drachs in the Plaka of Athens, poured two generous shots of iced aquavit, a liquor favored by the diplomat, who loathed the tequila native to his own country.

"To you and yours," he said, touching the diplomat's glass.

"And yours," said the diplomat, nodding in the direction of the wall safe, where Talbot had stashed the two kilos of cocaine. "Tell me, my friend, what will you do with it? This?" The diplo-mat chuckled, making a gesture with two fingers touching his nostrils.

"No," said Talbot, taking a small sip of the aquavit. "As far as that goes, the stuff is overrated. I don't use it as a drug. I use it as currency."

"Ah," said the diplomat, feigning surprise. His arrangement with Talbot was of long standing. "And what do you buy with so much dust?

John Lloyd Talbot laced his fingers together, the amusement slowly draining from his expression.

"People," he said quietly. "A number of people."

Didi became a creature of the sun and sand, her hair streaked with gold. She spent whole afternoons on the Windsurfer, her lean body braced against the tangerine sail as she tacked through the advancing waves, sometimes capsizing with a delighted shriek.

Ronnie watched languidly from the strand, stretched out in a canvas chair, her body lathered with coconut oils. She was determined to get as brown as a pair of Gucci loafers. For the first time in her life she experienced the delight of baring her breasts to the sun, of feeling her nipples stiffen asexually in the shimmering heat. She found a small secluded dune where she could peel off her bikini bottoms and after a few days her dark pubic curls lightened to a shade of wisped auburn.

She was grateful for the trace of Native American in her ancestry: to bake forever into a copper sheen and never burn. There were those, she knew, who would be willing to kill for her complexion.

One day Didi joined her there, striping off her salt-encrusted two-piece to lay next to Ronnie, bare hip to bare hip. Slowly, with infinite gentleness, she spread the tanning oil across Ronnie's flat belly, tracing fingertips along her thighs, making sure that every square millimeter of exposed flesh was covered.

Feeling lazy and strangely elevated Ronnie did the same for her, smoothing the warm oils over the smaller woman's body. After a while it seemed the most natural thing in the world to touch lips and kiss, oh, so delicately. Ronnie had never before touched another woman's breasts and it was with more curiosity than passion that she cupped Didi's in the palms of her hands. And when she parted her own thighs for the feathery bird of Didi's hand it was with a dreamy indifference that slowly melted as they moved into each other, soft to soft, and made very lazy love in the hot sand.

It happened only once, and neither of them spoke of it, but the gentle interlude provided Ronnie with a physical relief she hadn't known she'd needed and left her, for a while, completely at peace with herself.

Her father answered on the second ring.

"No, honey. I was wide awake. Real quiet here tonight and I guess I was listening to that. The quiet part I mean."

"Did you get the truck, Daddy?"

"Truck? Oh, hell yes. It's a real beauty, Ronnie. Settin' right out there by the shed. I can see it from here, matter of fact. I been lettin' your brother drive it, of course."

"Sure, Dad, that's fine. How about the ranch?"

"Oh, that real estate man came by—he got your letter, I guess. But the truth is, child, I like it right here. I got all my memories kind of tied up in this place, you know, and maybe I'm scared to move." He paused and Ronnie heard the sound of glass against glass, the chink of ice. "Real nice of you to offer, though."

"Are you okay, Dad?"

She heard the glass clink again. Her father's voice was whiskey soft. "I'm fine, honey. Been real quiet here since Alice passed on. I guess you knew about that?"

"You told me."

"Right. Well, your brother got the stereo you sent him set up right in the living room here, and we just about played your record to death, let me tell y'all. And Jack is making out fine with all the girls on account of you're his sister. Kind of funny the way that happens."

"Sometimes I feel pretty homesick, Dad."

"Forget it, honey. Ain't no one here but us chickens now. When I give you that money I meant it to last a good long time." She heard the thick sound of him swallowing. "A good long time. That homesick stuff is just 'cause it's late at night, Ronnie."

"Okay, Dad. Why don't you call me the next time?" she asked, trying to keep the little girl out of her voice. "It's not fair it's always me."

"Sure, honey."

"Anytime, Daddy. Anytime at all."

Outside the floodlights made the tide race into the shadows, into the pool of the night. She put another log on the fire.

"Didi? Who *are* those people out there?" Ronnie peered through the "boggles," the 7×50 Fujinon field glasses Jade had given her. "They look like, I don't know, thugs or something."

Didi laughed. She sat up on the deck, holding her top in place while she tied the strings. "Those 'thugs' are probably Secret Service guys. The senator has a place just down the beach, you know."

"Senator who?"

"Are you nuts? Jimmy Conrad, who else?"

Ronnie shrugged, following the party's progress as they ambled through the edge of the surf. Or rather one man, wearing rolled-up chinos and a straw hat, tripped through the water. He was followed at a discreet distance by four men wearing dark suits and unfashionably short haircuts. None of the men bothered to take their shoes off.

"Didi, I think they're coming this way."

"I wouldn't be surprised." Didi giggled as she opened her sack purse and extracted a compact and mirror. "I bumped into him, sort of. Well, kind of on purpose, see. He's a terrific hunk, Ronnie. And so I told him you'd love to see him. Only after he asked, of course."

"You what?" Ronnie wasn't in the mood for visitors. She stared at Didi incredulously.

"Well, I couldn't tell him you *didn't* want to see him, could I?"

"Didi, this is embarrassing!"

"So put your top on, dummy."

Ronnie looked down, gasped when she discovered she was still bare-breasted, and hurried inside for a halter top. When she returned the man in the straw hat was negotiating the long series of steps that cut up through the dunes. He took off the hat and waved it.

The Secret Service boys fanned out over the crest of sand,

somberly slugging toward the front deck. Didi finished daubing her lips, kissed the mirror for luck, and winked at Ronnie, who was doing a slow burn.

The senator took the last three steps without visible effort and stopped at the landing. "Permission to board, ladies?" he asked. And Didi was right there "helping" him onto the deck, which apparently necessitated pressing her breasts against his upper arm.

"I came over to borrow a cup of sugar," he said to Ronnie. "But I forgot the cup."

"Please have a seat." Ronnie masked her irritation with a gracious smile. "Something to drink?"

"A cold beer would be mighty fine."

Ronnie managed to direct Didi with one cold, stern glance, and she reluctantly disengaged herself from the senator and went inside to fetch the rolling bar.

"I had no idea we were neighbors, Senator, until about two minutes ago." Ronnie tried to ignore the agents, but dark blue pinstripe suits with rep ties were not exactly common on Malibu Beach, and their efforts to blend into the landscape were doomed.

"Sorry if I surprised you," said the senator, smiling. "I thought your blond friend had warned you."

Jameson Conrad, Jr., was the son of J. R. Conrad the actor, and he retained some of his late father's craggy looks. He kept his hair close-cropped, but the famous Conrad widow's peak was still in evidence, as were the flat gray eyes and the deeply cleft chin. Ronnie had seen him often enough on the tube, but the video lense didn't do him justice. She could now see why he had the reputation of being Washington's playboy senator. He had been linked to a number of celebrities, and it was his "star fucker" reputation that initially put Ronnie off. She had no desire to be another of his conquests.

The sentiment must have shown, because he quickly made it clear that his was strictly a polite social visit.

"As a matter of fact," he told her, "I'd just as soon the gossip columnists never knew I dropped by. They'll have us engaged to be married before we've even been properly introduced." He paused to take a puff on a small corncob pipe he'd been thought-fully packing. Not exactly the accoutrement of a sex symbol. And he seemed eager to explain the media distortion of his lady killer reputation. "You know, I escorted Princess Caroline to a charity function once. In company with her mother, as a matter of fact. Next thing I know I was supposed to be the reason she was separating from her husband. I swear to you, Ronnie," he put his hand solemnly over his heart, "that the princess doesn't kiss on the first date. And there never was a second."

Ronnie smiled. He was a charming fellow, no denying that. Didi was starting into her gaga routine again, and as penance Ronnie sent her back to the kitchen to prepare a light supper.

They chatted, he sitting on the deck rail, she with her legs crossed on the lounge, a floppy sun bonnet shielding her eyes. After a while she forgot her guest was a celebrated rake (according to *The Enquirer,* at least) and relaxed. Jimmy, as he was known publicly, had an Irish gift of speech, part of which was to listen attentively whenever Ronnie put in her oar. Although she knew it was a politician's trick, she found herself entering into it whole-heartedly. She began enthusiastically taking sides on issues to which she'd rarely given a thought. Conrad inspired that sort of passionate response. In a very short time she'd gotten beyond his image and discovered she genuinely liked the man.

"I inherited the cottage from my father," he told her. "He never used it, but I often pop down for a working vacation. When I heard you were staying practically next door I had to stop by and see if you looked as good in person as you do in that poster I see everywhere."

"Well?" Ronnie doffed the bonnet, assumed the Avedon profile. She could hardly keep a straight face.

Jimmy Conrad laughed, dredging up his rich baritone. "I didn't know what Bo Mandrel meant by the future sex of rock and roll, Ronnie, but I'm beginning to get the idea."

Just then a buzzer went off. It was a signal from an electronic device one of the agents was monitoring. Conrad was suddenly all business.

"It's been a pleasure, Miss Garrik." He shook her hand

firmly, startling her. "I'd been trying to work up my courage to ask you if you'd like to go for a cruise in my yacht? Tomorrow at ten? Splendid!"

And then he was off, back up the beach at a quick march. The pinstripes dogged his tracks, their trouser cuffs loaded with sand. Ronnie heard a squeal of dismay and turned to find Didi holding a tray loaded with canapés and savories.

"Ronnie, what will we do with all these cherrystones? And the Gulf shrimp? And my very best extra-special guacamole?"

"We'll manage," she said, plucking a shrimp from the iced bucket. "By the way, Dee. Do you have a pair of Topsiders I could borrow?"

She was dressed (at ten minutes of the hour, no less) in what she hoped was proper yachting attire. A soft brushed cotton top with a wide collar, cream white trousers that verged on translucent, well-worn Topsiders and, for a lark, a long-billed fisherman's cap with a false gold braid.

"J. P. Morgan would be proud," said Didi. "As a matter of fact if the old fossil was still alive he'd be trying to get into those so-called pants of yours. Good thing you don't have a pimple on your ass, baby, 'cause it would show."

Ronnie was expecting one of those dark green, bullet-proof limos, complete with the Secret Service treatment, so when the whistle came from the beach she ignored it at first.

"Ron-eee." Just barely audible, drowned in the hiss of surf.

"J. P. Morgan it ain't," said Didi, returning from the deck. She was trying to keep a straight face and not succeeding. "But Jimmy Conrad it is. You better change, honey."

Senator Conrad's "yacht" was, in fact, a Sailfish. A bare board that sails partly submerged most of the time, and the rest upside down. He was rigging the lanteen sail when Ronnie arrived at the water's edge, her eye shadow hastily erased, clad in one of her more microscopic bikinis. She was sun-ripened to perfection and ready to show it off.

"I must say, Jameson, that I had something grander in mind."

"Here, better strap this on." He helped her into a lifebelt that buckled snugly around her waist. "If the wind picks up, things could get wet."

They pushed the little boat out beyond the breakers, got drenched in the process, and managed to get on board without capsizing. Before Ronnie even knew what was happening the sail filled with a pop! and they were skimming over the water. She clutched the aluminum mast with both hands, but it was evident that Jimmy knew what he was doing and that, from the grin on his face, he loved doing it.

"I had a Nautor Fifty!" he shouted. "Pain in the ass! Maintenance! Crew! Crowded mooring! Bah!"

Now he had the sheet in his teeth, trimming for speed. The tiny Sailfish was Conrad's idea of yachting at its finest.

"You like?" he asked.

Ronnie was still getting over the adrenal rush of their sudden acceleration, but she managed to nod her head vigorously. Once she got over the initial terror of being capsized she got off on the speed. The board was vibrating under her, responding to puffs of wind as Jimmy worked the tiller. He slid up next to her to balance the board and trim for increased speed.

"Next stop Hawaii!"

Their bodies pressed together out of necessity and Ronnie briefly wondered if that wasn't the whole premise behind the activity. But a moment later they were rudely capsized by an errant puff and she went into the water with a shriek.

"Sorry!" he sputtered, one arm draped over the board, the other clutching her slim waist.

She was too astonished to complain when he hauled her back up by her bikini bottoms. A moment later they were flying again as if nothing had happened.

The dunking soaked them both afresh and without really meaning to, she found herself checking out Jimmy's nylon briefs, his strong, sun-bronzed thighs. He was a great bear of a man and he handled the boat with consummate ease, tuned to the motions of the brisk green water. Their physical intimacy might have been contrived at first, but after he tacked back, bringing them full into the sun to let it and the wind dry them off, Ronnie didn't mind. She began to wonder what sort of lover he was, if his reputation was justly deserved. And as her mood swung abruptly upward she began to have a keen desire to be outrageous, to indulge herself as she hadn't since the tour ended.

They swept in close to the beach, humming over the wave crests, sending up high sparkles of fume. A change of wind slapped at the sail again and this time they were thrown closer together. On impulse, not bothering with pretense, Ronnie decided to snuggle up to him.

"You know," she said, as Jimmy smiled at her, "the fan magazines are going to have us sleeping together before the week is out. So we might as well go ahead and *do* it, huh?"

The senator was startled by her audacity, but recovered quickly as she dropped her hands to the front of his trunks.

"Your position," he said in his most dignified voice, "is highly tenable."

He flipped the blinds shut, dousing the room in cool shadows.

"Come here," he said.

With her cards on the table Ronnie saw no point in feigning reticence. She undid the knots and flipped the bikini pieces over her shoulder as Conrad hastily peeled off his swim trunks.

For once I'm going to be what the public imagines me to be, she thought. A sex machine. I'm going to get my rocks off first and worry about his later. If ever.

Conrad had the same idea. What they engaged in was not making love, or even sexual intercourse. It was slam bang fornication.

Ronnie gave herself up to it. The muscle tension began to build as he entered her, and it moved like a static charge across soft flesh.

"Never mind the cute stuff," she told him, her voice thickening. "Just a straight fast fuck."

The veneer of indulgence was cracked, briefly, when he

cupped his strong hands under the small of her back, urging her against him. It was a gesture Kyle had used and the intimate signal flashed like a point of pain. But in the next moment her breath was coming in short gasps and the rude wet smack of love erased Kyle from her thoughts.

Physically spent, she fell asleep thinking that the only love she wanted was the kind that need not be returned.

7

John Lloyd Talbot brought the two gifts personally, so that there could be no misunderstanding what they implied.

The first gift was contained in a fired enamel canister that Von Ranke received wordlessly before placing it nonchalantly on a low, smoked-glass table.

The second was contained in the person of one Rory Bender, an urchin-faced boy wearing a purposely tattered leather jacket. He wore skintight chamois pants, the crotch of which bulged over a figured Elizabethan codpiece he was bringing back into fashion in the bizarre underground of rock 'n' roll. His slender chest was bare under the leather jacket, as hairless and smooth as a baby's bottom. Rory plopped himself into one of Von Ranke's sleek patio chairs and proceeded to examine his fingernails, which could have used manicuring or, for that matter, a little soap.

Steffen Von Ranke eyed the boy with frank interest and grinned wryly at Talbot, who he'd been vaguely competing with for years. Steffen was of dark, sinewy build, not handsome, but aggressively attractive. He was involved in a number of projects and pending deals at that moment, not the least of which was the production of records for one of Talbot's rivals.

"Quality goods," he said softly to John Lloyd, who had perched on the arm of a chair opposite the boy. He did not intend to stay long.

He knew Von Ranke was one of Laurel Canyon's leading hedonists—a world-class cocksman with little regard for the rules of society, or law, for that matter. He had once been indicted for the statutory rape of a fourteen-year-old model whose mother had approached Von Ranke quite openly, obsessed with making her daughter a rock star. The girl was more than willing, but as it happened couldn't sing a note despite her eager young throat. Steffen, after an interesting weekend making love to the two of them, had had to break it to the mother that a musical career for the girl was out of the question. Enraged, she brought suit and sold the story to the tabloids. Von Ranke managed to extricate himself by making a generous donation to an intermediary, and curiously enough the incident enhanced his reputation in Los Angeles. He remained a top producer of records as well as movie sound tracks and retained his place on the Golden Disc nominations committee, a position of influence that interested John Lloyd Talbot not a little.

Von Ranke was notorious for the intensity of his sexual obsessions and had, after exhausting the ranks of the Canyon starlets, developed a recent interest in boys, preferably punk rockers, of which Rory Bender was not only the newest, but probably the "punkest ever," to quote Anthony Trendau.

"I think you'll find these in order," said Talbot, handing Steffen an envelope containing Rory's Liberty contract, which John Lloyd had just optioned to Von Ranke's organization.

Steffen grinned as he fingered the gold stud in his left ear. "Johnny boy," he said. "You get my vote for Machiavelli of the year."

Talbot glanced at Rory Bender, whom he was frankly glad to be rid of. The boy was insufferable, ill-mannered beyond belief, and destined, Talbot was sure, to a short if spectacular career.

"That's not the vote I'm interested in," he said, and waited until Von Ranke nodded slowly.

As John Lloyd strode from the room a few moments later Steffen and Rory were already on their knees before the smoked glass table, preparing long, wild lines which shone, in the California sun, like icy white hieroglyphics.

It quickly became a ritual. He never spent the night—somehow that seemed forbidden to both of them—but each morning he came for coffee. He flirted with Didi, quietly cheerful, while Ronnie swam up through the muddy waters of sleep, her mood slowly brightening. When she was altogether human they raced from the front deck to the surf, splashing into the brisk water.

The morning dive became a baptism. Afterward they ate breakfast, played like children in the sand, took the Sailfish into the teeth of the wind, made love with the shades down, and in other ways set about extracting all the pleasure they could from an affair both knew would be brief.

That it would end was mutually agreed upon. But neither foresaw just how bizarre that ending would be.

The invitations to Mick Jagger's birthday party were non-negotiable. The electronically engraved cards could not be transferred or blackmarketed to a lesser celebrity because Bruno Natasy had vast experience hosting extravaganzas and he had arranged for the use of a Polaroid Identi-System. Nothing short of plastic surgery would get a non-invitee through the gates of Natasy's Beverly Hills spread.

The mansion, unlike almost all of the others in those few square miles that so many film people inhabited, had never been "previously occupied." Zsa Zsa had never done the master bedroom in champagne pink and Bogart never soiled the floor with his cigarette butts because Natasy, abundantly wealthy even be-

206

fore his directorial success, had built it new on the last available plot in Hollywood. No pun intended, as he liked to say.

Designed with entertaining in mind, and with the director's penchant for water sports a calculated factor, it resembled nothing so much as a series of oversized cabanas joined around seven landscaped pools. All of the pools were lined with Mexican fire tiles at fabulous expense, as Bruno was quick to point out. One studio wag dubbed Natasy "The Quick Dip" and his current wife "The Old Swimming Hole." It was an envious cruelty because, ostentatious or not, the Natasy mansion had become the focal point to which all Hollywood gravitated.

That evening the winding walkway had been strung with gaslights, real ones, and the amplified strains of the Stones "Some Girls" floated up from external, shrub-mounted speakers.

It was to be Ronnie's first 'public' appearance since her hospitalization in Boston and she clutched Jimmy's arm nervously as they approached the sculptured shrub entrance.

Jagger, who had starred in Natasy's latest film, wasn't due until after midnight. His calculated entrance was unwittingly overshadowed by the arrival of Ronnie Garrik and Senator Jameson Conrad.

Jade, working with his usual aplomb behind the scenes, had flown Halston out for a fitting and Ronnie's simple gown of dark crimson silk fit like a luminous second skin. Seeing her the crowd paused as one, drinking her in.

"This is so *weird*," whispered Ronnie. She had wanted to be stunning, but the silence was unnerving.

"What did you expect?" chuckled Jimmy softly. "Smile. You look like you're about to cry."

Maybe she was. But someone broke the eerie silence with a wolf whistle and suddenly these supposedly callous, cynical Hollywood professionals were applauding, cheering her, as Jimmy guided her deftly toward the waiting Bruno Natasy.

"Splendid!" gushed the director. Behind tinted glasses his small eyes bugged. Natasy had never met her, but at a celebrity bash everyone is intimate and so he kissed her full on the mouth.

He lingered over long and when he turned to Conrad said, "Keep it up, Senator. The good work I mean, ha ha."

Jimmy smiled wolfishly—he despised Natasy—and by signaling two of his agents was able to quickly negotiate through the pressing crowd of guests out to a more or less secluded patio.

"Was I okay?"

The whole thing—the entrance, the introduction, the being whisked away—had taken all of two or three minutes, and Ronnie was still recovering from that first panic-stricken moment when all those knowing eyes turned upon her.

"You're a hit, darling." The senator scooped two champagne goblets off a passing tray and handed her one. "Why, Bruno almost wet his pants. Don't be surprised if he offers to star you in his next picture. He'll be lying, of course."

But Ronnie wasn't really listening to Conrad. The words floated by like the mass of day-glow orange balloons being released by one of the swimming pools. They rose like wobbling moons into the hazy darkness of the night.

Something significant had just happened to her. Stepping over that threshold, carrying herself with as much regal disdain as she could muster, she had been confronted by the three dimensional reality of what it was like to be a celebrity. Everything had been happening so fast—the tour was but a blur of ceaseless motion—she hadn't had time to appreciate or understand her transformation. Tonight she had emerged like a lustrous dark butterfly, and she was determined to make the most of it.

"Let's go back inside, Jimmy." She tossed off her champagne, clinking her goblet to his.

"Whatever for?"

"Because that's where the party is. I want to be there. I want to meet all those people. I want to meet Jagger, too."

"Jagger? Hell, he probably won't even show. This is Natasy's party. Jagger is just the appetizer."

"But I want—"

"*Listen.*" He gripped her elbow with more force than he intended, hurting her. "That's not how it's done, sweetheart. You want to get pawed by all those people, those phonies?"

"Jimmy, what's wrong with you?"

"Listen to me, Ronnie. Don't you understand? *They* want you. Not just that prick Natasy, but all of them. They want to eat you alive. Devour you. You're up *there.*" He gestured skyward. She had never seen his handsome face so clouded with conflicting emotions. "You're peaking now. You're the star of the season, damn it, and they want some of your action."

"What's wrong with that?" She looked anxiously toward the party, toward the sea of familiar faces she'd once mooned over in cheap magazines. "What is all this shit, Jimmy? Why did we come if we can't enjoy it?"

"We came because we're who we are." His voice softened. "Believe me, darling. The worst thing to do is mix with those people. They'll drag you down. That's what they long for, whether they know it or not. They want to pluck you right out of the sky. They want to eat you alive, like one of Bruno's goddamn oysters."

Ronnie stared at him incredulously. "I think you're jealous, Senator. You're used to being the star, not the escort, and you don't like it."

His amused, denying laugh infuriated her.

"Why is it nobody can *enjoy* being famous?" she demanded, jutting the empty goblet against his chest. Once more she thought of Kyle, whose unopened letters lay on her desk. "What are we supposed to be afraid of?"

His smile stiffened and his eyes cooled as he said, "Of not being famous anymore. That's what we're all afraid of, Ronnie. And you should be, too."

She didn't know him, that's what it boiled down to. Their Malibu fling was just that, a calculated dalliance lacking any real intimacy. Ronnie knew every inch of his body but nothing of the man who inhabited it. And now she was paying for her ignorance.

Something had to be done. As the decision clicked in her head she hurled the goblet down, smashing it jubilantly.

"You can sulk here if you like," she told him. "I'm going inside and raise bloody hell."

"Ronnie! You don't know what—"

"I know what I *want*, Senator. And if they eat me alive, well—bon appetit!"

Her spike heels clacked on the slate patio, and she was about to sweep through the open French doors and into the party when Conrad caught up with her.

"No, you don't," he hissed. "We came together and we *stay* together."

He squeezed her elbow again, hurting her, and she reacted by bracing against the door and pushing him away with all her strength. She really hadn't noticed the wading pool and she certainly didn't mean to tip him backwards into it, arms flailing, for all the world to see.

Two of his agents immediately jumped in and retrieved the soggy senator, who was gasping like a beached fish.

"Jimmy, I'm sorry. Really I am." But she couldn't help the laughter that rose in her, immediately echoed by the crowd gathering at the open doors.

Seeing an audience, and a potentially hostile one at that, Jameson Conrad was suddenly all smiles.

"All in fun, folks!" He waved gaily to the crowd, the water gurgling off him as he struggled to climb out of the pool. "All in fun!"

But when he left in company with his silent men the look he gave her was decidedly unfunny.

There would be hell to pay tomorrow, when the scandal sheets got hold of it, but somehow she didn't care. She turned regally, still suppressing mirth, and entered alone, aware of the eyes boring into her. She knew many of the guests despised her on principal but that didn't faze her either. What she did feel was curiously elevated, as if pushing Jimmy Conrad into the pool had put her back in control of her life.

Bruno Natasy had forbidden the paparazzi, but Ronnie heard the click and whir of a Nikon motor drive operated by one of the privileged guests, and she was thankful that someone was there to immortalize her splendid gown. She never expected to look so good again in her life.

"Well done, darling," said a voice emerging from the crowd. "Jimmy can be rather a bore, I know."

"John Lloyd!"

He handed her a drink. She embraced him, more fervently than he expected, perhaps, but she suddenly considered him, in this mob, an old friend.

"Ronnie, dear, you look positively royal. I wasn't going to horn in on your senator, but here we are. And how are you? Has the sun been good to you?" John Lloyd Talbot was being uncharacteristically voluble. Something besides liquor was illuminating his slate gray eyes. "I heard the most interesting rumor," he told her, sotto voce. "Concerning a certain prestigious award . . ."

It was the hour of the wolf. Four in the morning, under a sky as black as the bottom of a hollow well. It was also the hour when the after-party guilts hit her full force.

Jimmy Conrad might be a selfish bastard, but he hadn't deserved public humiliation. After returning to Malibu Ronnie fortified herself with a large cognac, changed into dark pants and a pullover, and began the short sandy trek to the senator's cottage.

Jagger hadn't shown after all. Not that it mattered by then. The party was in full swing and she moved with the rhythm of it, drinking in each moment. And John Lloyd's tale of behind the scene machinations for the Goldie nominations intrigued her so much that even Bruno Natasy, who kept flinging his arm low around her waist, assuring himself that she wore nothing under the gown, had failed to ruin her high.

What mattered, suddenly, was winning the Goldie.

Now, in the early morning, she was getting spooked by the dunes. The eel grass moved in the breeze like bony fingers. The tide lapped in like some great sea beast at the shore. Even the muted lights of Conrad's cottage seemed an alien illumination.

She'd forgotten about the agents until one of them came out of the darkness, startling her.

"It's you," was all he said. He motioned for her to go on. The shadows made it impossible to read the secret smirk she was sure he wore.

The sand drifted under her bare feet and Ronnie looked forward to Conrad's warm hearth, maybe his warm arms, and another cognac. Then they would laugh, the two of them, over the absurd incident at poolside.

The door was unlocked. Ronnie pushed in quietly, intending to surprise him. The lights were so low it took her a few moments to realize that the living room was empty. The banked remains of a fire glowed in the grate. And then she heard a moan from the partly open door of his bedroom.

A plaintive, throaty moan she'd never heard him use before. Evidently the senator had found someone to console him. Curiously she felt not the least bit jealous. She deserved as much, she supposed, and in a way it summed up their relationship. But a twinge of what killed the cat made her take a few quiet steps to the left to see, from the vantage of darkness, part of the bed where she herself had lain not too long ago.

Jameson Conrad was moving there, pumping slowly into Didi's eagerly spread legs. Her eyelids were fluttering with rapture, counterpoint to the high keening moan Jameson made as he pressed his hips to hers.

After a few moments Ronnie left, containing her outraged laughter. She knew then why the Secret Service agent had been smirking. But by the time she trudged back to her cottage it wasn't so damn funny.

Ronnie poured herself another cognac, a stiff one. She took it to bed and sat there fully clothed, propped against the pillows. An hour or so later she heard Didi enter stealthy, probably afraid to wake her. She continued to sip and replenish her drink until she could hear Didi snoring lightly, as innocently as a child.

The image of a sleeping child brought it down. As it happened she realized the darkness had been hovering over her all the while, waiting like a wave to break and drown her. She felt herself falling, as if riding a bottomless elevator shaft with the bowels of the world opening under her, dragging her down.

She had everything she'd ever dreamed of wanting and it was all turning sour. Everything had closed inward until she was blind blind to love, to joy, to everything that mattered.

She had ignored Kenny in his need, as he dosed himself into oblivion. Her father had chosen his own form of self-destruction, and she continued to keep her distance, unwilling to go to him. She was blind even to Didi, whom she had treated like an indentured servant, and who had now extracted an ancient revenge.

As she drank, searching for dreamless sleep, her feelings for Kyle became hopelessly confused. Rendered almost breathless by the continued sensation of falling, she knew she had to do something.

She had to get out.

Shooting Star

1

If he relaxed his eyes in a certain way he could make the garden grow. Spiny tendrils stirred the evening air as he blurred his vision, making the cacti change shape. The hangdog smoke from the west looked like the dream exhalations of an opium pipe, drifting in from the sea.

Kyle Hersch lay on the shoreside deck, looking out at the world through half-closed eyes, utterly lethargic. Except for a few hours here and there going through the motions of supervising his daughter, he had been horizontal on a deck chair for the best part of a fortnight. Never sleeping, exactly, and never really awake.

He knew what the matter was. He also knew there was nothing, not a thing, he could do about it. And that was the core of the problem.

Cyclical depression, they called it, "they" being the psychiatrists he could never bring himself to consult. It was like the proverbial leaky roof: When the sun shone it didn't need patching, and when it rained it was too damn wet to fix. But he'd read the textbooks and knew enough to give it a name.

It happened once or twice a year, like the flu, or hayfever. But it had never been as bad as this. This was a black tunnel into which he peered, an endless labyrinth with no exit. Part of him knew the only cure was time, that eventually he would rise from the bottomless pit of depression and be human again.

Meanwhile he was reduced to the idle game of playing tricks with his eyes, something he had done as a boy. Kyle lay on his back, squinting at the garden, not caring a damn for anything or anyone.

217

"Ten minutes before the hour, Mr. Hersch."

In what seemed like a supreme struggle of will, he managed to extricate himself from the deck chair and walk through the double sliders into his study, where the Advent screen had been set up as he requested. The sound was off, but the images were already there, moving in lush, orchestrated colors.

"Will there be anything else, Mr. Hersch?"

He shook his head. For the next hour or two nothing would exist but the images on the screen. He raised the volume for a moment, heard the announcer babbling about the significance of the Golden Disc Awards, turned it back down. The voice bothered him like a dentist's drill.

He drew up a chair, and when he raised his eyes to the screen she was suddenly there, walking resolutely through a mushroom forest of white tabletops as the camera tracked her. She held her head high, the lights catching a glimmer of the gold star découpaged upon her cheek.

And yes, about her neck was the diamond pendant.

It flooded into him, as if he were there again, nervous as a boy on his first date, fastening the clasp at the nape of her neck, aware of her dark hair brushing his fingertips.

Whenever you wear it I'll make a wish. What a fool he'd made of himself that day.

Kyle leaned forward. The volume had crept up, seemingly of its own accord, but he paid no heed to the breathless announcer as he described the riot Ronnie Garrik's arrival had precipitated. No, all of Kyle Hersch was focused on the face that now turned, unknowing, to look directly at him. He stared into her twice life-size blue eyes. Cobalt blue.

It was a mere trick of light, just television, the coarsest medium of them all. So by what magic did it wrench his heart from the still abeyance of lethargy and set it beating to the rhythm of a song he had not dreamed was there?

Oddly enough he was not particularly surprised when the moment came. He'd been aware of the risk, but the grandeur of the idea was intoxicating and having committed himself he found it impossible to withdraw. He had hoped, in his optimistic fashion, to brazen it out.

But now the game had been called and the two men were as toneless and self-contained, seemingly unaware of the power he had, until that moment, possessed. Deciding that the situation demanded grave courtesy, he offered them drinks. Both declined, but allowed him to pour one for himself from his office bar.

John Lloyd drank it off more quickly then he'd intended as the two agents waited impassively. Foremost in his thoughts was the desire to leave the building—*his* building—under his own power. It would not do to be seen with his hands cuffed, dragged through his own lobby like a common criminal, especially not on this of all nights.

Surely they would grant him that one courtesy.

"Could be," said one of the laconic agents. "Depends," said the other.

They presented him with a search warrant and asked that he open his wall safe. It was obvious that if he didn't cooperate they would simply have the safe ripped from the wall and opened forcibly.

"That won't be necessary," he assured them. The thought of his office being ravaged made him feel distinctly nauseated. He pressed the combination on the push-button matrix, opened the vault, and removed what was left of the diplomat's plasticene package.

"I assume this is what you've come for?"

"That and you," said one of the agents, smiling for the first time.

One last time he pressed back the lapels of his black formal jacket, fluffed the black silk tie, and shrugged on his favorite cashmere overcoat. Then he walked through the empty rooms of his building and his life, closely escorted by two men in cheap gray suits.

It caught her by surprise.

After they'd been nearly torn apart at the Park Avenue entrance, Jade, who knew the Waldorf intimately, led her to a quiet lobby. One had to enter an event of this magnitude calmly, he explained, with elegance. Not as if you'd been chased in by a rabid dog.

A moment of composure was necessary.

"I've been in this game for twenty years," he said, adjusting his slightly disheveled hair in one of the marbled mirrors. "And at times it still scares the pants off me."

But Ronnie had already forgotten the mob outside and was eager to proceed. "How do I look?" she asked him. Reversed in the mirror the gown shimmered under the chandeliers.

"Like a million bucks," he chuckled. "Actually, like about three million, give or take."

He took her arm. They entered.

That year's Goldie producers had contrived to make the Waldorf's great hall into an Edwardian orchestral garden, complete with myriad round tables, lush floral arrangements, and sleek, white-aproned waiters with dark mustaches. When Ronnie entered on Jade Gustave's arm, cones of multicolored lights tick-tocked though the shadows, focusing on center stage, where Robin Williams, master of ceremonies, was receiving last-minute cues from the stage director.

A sort of aisle had been left open between the tables, and Ronnie had to pass within a few feet of most of the other nominees. The gauntlet of sharklike smiles disturbed her, but Zach Curtis was waiting at the end of it, holding down the Liberty table, and he leaped up to embrace her.

"Great to see you, baby!" And then, in an undertone, "If looks could kill, kid, you'd be ten times dead. The envy in this joint is knee high and rising rapidly."

John Lloyd's chair was empty, but before they could determine where he was the house lights dimmed and the monitors clicked over to the green signal. Ronnie smiled brightly, fingering the diamond pendant, aware that the cameras were on her.

The edge of excitement dulled for an hour or so, taken up with minor awards, commendations, and some rather poorly executed dance numbers that, Ronnie supposed, probably looked a hell of a lot better on the screen than in the flesh. She and Zach set about polishing off most of the champagne, ignoring Jade's advice to take it easy, and so when it happened she was drifting off, daydreaming, lulled by the flawless monotony of the floor show.

"This is the *beeeg* moment, folks." Robin Williams held his hands far apart to indicate just how big it was, but he managed to look serious when he took the envelope from the platter. His mobile, impish face registered surprise as he unfolded the slip of paper and read the contents. He looked up, eyes wide.

"Ladies and gentlemen, it is my pleasure to make an announcement unique in the annals of these awards." He paused, cleared his throat, looked into the eye of the camera. "In racing they call it the Triple Crown. I don't know what they call it at the Goldies and neither do *they,* because it's never happened before."

"Get ready," whispered Jade, nudging her.

"But one person," the comedian continued, "one very special person has just won Best Album, Best Hit Single, and Best Vocalist. Her name is *Ronnie Garrik!*"

What happened next was never clear in her mind. There was a lot of noise and everyone was standing, cheering apparently, although she wasn't aware of it as Jade attempted to weave her through the tables and up to the stage where Robin was waiting with his arms out. And then she was at the podium and of course she was expected to say something, preferably something gracious and witty.

She looked over at Jade, who was standing just out of camera range. He had his fist clenched and raised, silently rooting for her, as he had from the very beginning. She saw his eyes glisten and that was when she lost it.

Ronnie Garrik stood there in front of the world, looking like every penny of three million, give or take, and bawled like a baby.

They went to Georgio's. After the uproar at the Waldorf it was really the only place to go that they could be assured of a table to themselves. Georgio knew how to keep the media hounds at bay, by physical assault if necessary, and his upper East Side patrons would sooner eat canned spinach than acknowledge a celebrity.

"I feel like such an idiot," Ronnie was saying. She guzzled the ice water, trying to wash away the dry, salty taste that had choked her.

"But you were perfect, darling," Jade assured her. He covered her trembling hand with his. Zach was in the anteroom, placing a call to his pregnant wife; his Best Songwriter award had been anticlimactic to everyone but him. And, curiously, John Lloyd still had not shown up, neither for the ceremony nor the after-hours celebration.

While Jade ordered for the three of them, Ronnie tried to focus on the small dining room. She tried to concentrate on the frost-white table cloths, on the animated conversation around her. But she was still distracted, and the sensation was vaguely unpleasant. The dreamlike interval of the awards ceremony was superimposed over the present like one of those Chinese scrims alive with fantastic dragons and impossible landscapes.

Something about it frightened her. Or maybe it was the dream that had come to her more frequently of late. The dream in which she was suspended, as if in ice, unable to move, but fully conscious that something bad was about to happen.

"You okay?" Jade asked her. "Here, knock back a drop of this." He put a shot glass of schnapps to her lips but she barely tasted it.

"Where is Talbot?" she asked suddenly, as if startling herself awake. "Where the hell is John Lloyd Talbot when we really need him?"

After quitting Malibu she'd flown back east with John Lloyd in the *Belle*. The aircraft exuded a different aura when not transporting raucous touring bands like the Roughriders. The long, luxurious interior was eerily silent and just a shade too ostentatious, although she had never noticed that before.

Talbot had pleaded exhaustion and retired to his stateroom

alone, leaving Ronnie in company with the two flight attendants and Arthur, the butler cum bartender who'd so impressed her on her first flight and who now looked tired, wan and a trifle dull.

Flying through the night from west to east, defying, in a way, the spin of the planet, it seemed she was making a significant change. Or, more accurately, that she was waiting for it to happen. *Something* was about to happen, she sensed it instinctively, as some people can sense the approach of a summer storm hours before it begins.

And it was more than the upcoming Goldies, although the prospect of winning one was intriguing. John Lloyd dropped several hints about using his influence, but he had a habit of being maddeningly mysterious and Ronnie knew she couldn't jog the facts from him until he was damn well ready.

All in good time, he said, she would just have to wait.

She knew all about waiting, but still there was the uncomfortable sense of a breath being taken and not yet exhaled, and the overpowering certainty that time wasted was time stolen.

And there was only so much of it to lose before it ran out.

"Ronnie," said Jade gently, drawing her out of her thoughts. "You're supposed to be laughing at a time like this. Whooping it up. Getting silly."

She smiled into his kind face. "It's not what I expected somehow," she said, not knowing why she said it, or even what exactly she meant.

"It never is," he sighed. "Where the hell has Zachary gotten to? Everyone keeps disappearing at the last minute."

But Zach was coming across the crowded dining room and Ronnie felt her spirits lift—Zach would *make* her have a good time, he was great at that—until he got close enough for her to see his deathly pale face.

"I just heard it in the lobby," he said. "John Lloyd has been busted. They've taken him to jail."

2

They emerged from the static yellow light of the Lincoln Tunnel into a sky just breaking along the steel horizon of the Jersey Turnpike. Jade eased the Mercedes into cruising gear. The coupe glided effortlessly over the bumpy tarmac, as if locked into frictionless rails.

"The flask is in the glove," he said. "Help yourself."

There was an argon haze over the city of Elizabeth. Ronnie thought it made the urban sprawl look almost beautiful, but in a few moments the sun would rise through the acrid air, destroying that tenuous illusion.

Ronnie pressed the lock to the glove compartment. The flask was sheathed in blue-gray suede, matching the coupe's upholstery —one of the many details of custom styling suggested by Gustave. She poured into the sterling tumbler cap, took an experimental sip of the cognac, and offered the tumbler to Jade while she drank directly from the flask.

"Easy now," he suggested. "Drain every drop if you like, but take it slow."

"Yes, Daddy," she said. But she drank until her eyes watered and her throat was as hot as the fist in her heart. Off to the left was the distant industrial illumination of Perth Amboy, moving by as if in a dreamscape. "By the way," she said airily, trying to make light of it, "are we going any place special?"

"Yes," he said. "Very special."

Ronnie nodded, wanting to believe him, and took another pull from the cool flask. She ignored the blur of motion blipping by out of the corners of her eyes and let the cognac melt her into the seat. It seemed to her as if she had always been moving this way, like a fish who must keep swimming into the teeth of the current for fear of shapes lurking behind, waiting to snap with mighty jaws.

Leaving Georgio's had been nightmarish, But on recollection it was mild compared to what awaited them at the Sherry Netherland.

"They got us covered," Zach had announced, slumping into his chair. "I swear I've never seen so many reporters. And every damn one of them looks, you know, kind of *eager.*"

Jade shuddered. He borrowed one of Ronnie's Luckys, tapped it against the back of his hand, and pursed his lips in contemplation. "Did they say what John Lloyd was charged with?"

Zach had just knocked back a scotch and his voice was tight. "I think they caught the son of a bitch with drugs. I assume cocaine. And there was something about a valise of laundered money. It was all very garbled."

"Good Lord." Jade eyed Ronnie, who had been dazed by the sudden turn of events. "I hate to spoil the party, darling, but I think we'd better get you out of here."

"That's not going to be easy," said Zach, who seemed to perversely relish the crisis. "The limo is buried under the mob, with no sign of the driver. The poor guy must be shell-shocked —it's like a blitzkrieg out there. Georgio has his bouncers blocking the front door, but I don't know how long they'll hold out. As a matter of fact I saw a couple of wise guy reporters waving money under their noses."

"What do they want?" Ronnie asked. The bottom dropped out of her voice. Jade stroked the tops of her hands, attempting to calm her.

"They want you, darling." he said quietly. "They've got John Lloyd and now they want you."

"But why, Jade? I don't understand."

But he avoided meeting her eyes. They left via the steamy

back kitchen, under the eyes of the astonished cooks, as Georgio guided them toward a rarely used pantry exit. "Brando beat it this way once," he told them with evident pride. "Keep left through the alley. You'll find an entrance to the trains just beyond that. Duck in there and hoof it over to Lexington. They'll never think to look for you in that filthy subway, believe me."

They alley was black, reeking of garbage, stray cats, and urine. Zach tripped over an empty wine bottle, whispered a hoarse curse, and managed to regain his balance. Ronnie followed blindly, clutching Jade's sleeve, only just beginning to understand why they were fleeing from the very people she had been courting all of her adult life.

She was too frazzled and confused by the suddenness of it all to appreciate the irony: She who had been escorted by liveried footmen scant hours before was now stumbling through refuse on spike heels meant to traverse marble halls.

"So far so good," Zach whispered. He and Jade took Ronnie by the arms and helped her down the subway steps. "I feel like Clark Gable in *It Happened One Night*, you know?"

Georgio was right about the subway. It was deserted but for a few derelicts huddled by the mouth of the concrete tunnel. They watched silently as the elegantly attired trio floated by like something out of a panhandler's daydream, too unreal to bother accosting.

"Left!" said Zach urgently. "Let's not get lost now. Not tonight."

They came up the Eighty-sixth Street exit. A taxi was idling at the curb. At that crucial moment, when Ronnie didn't think she could walk another step on her ruined heels, it looked like the manifestation of a minor miracle. Jade opened the rear door and spoke to the driver.

Once inside Ronnie slipped off the heels and examined the tattered hem of her gown. Ten thousand dollars and it hadn't lasted the night. As the taxi accelerated she caught a glimpse of her face in the rearview mirror. The starry decal on her cheek was blurred, her underarms were clammy, and she wanted badly to take a hot shower.

"Will somebody please tell me what's going on?" she asked. But both Zachary and Jade ignored the question, either unwilling or unable to answer.

The cake is iced. Ronnie remembered John Lloyd telling her that, alluding to the upcoming awards. And yet what had that to do with his being busted for coke?

Conversation in the taxi was leaden. Jade, assuming that the press would be staking out Ronnie's suite at the St. Regis, suggested they return to the Sherry, where Zach had rooms reserved.

"We'll hole up there for a few hours," he said, trying his best to sound jovial. "I'll get on the phone and see if I can determine exactly what has happened." On impulse he leaned forward and brushed his lips to Ronnie's cheek. "Then we can arrange a press conference on *your* terms, darling."

Unspoken was the assumption that the press already knew a hell of a lot more about the Talbot affair than they did. Gustave, knowing John Lloyd's propensity for dispensing drugs to intimates, was afraid there might be a warrant out for Ronnie on some spurious charge. This fear he kept to himself, for she was obviously highly distressed already. He could see it in her eyes, could smell it in the sweat of anxiety the three of them were secreting.

The hotel was ghostly quiet at that hour of the morning. Zach picked up his key at the main desk. As they waited for the elevator Ronnie smoked a Lucky into oblivion, the paper glowing rosy red with the force of her anxious lungs. The nicotine did nothing to calm her.

The lobby that had once impressed her as unerringly elegant now looked garish and contrived. The elevator doors opened at last. "I feel kind of sick, Jade," she whispered as they entered. A knot of tension pulsed in her stomach, and her mouth had a metallic bitterness not wholly accounted for by too many cigarettes. "Do you think everything will be okay?"

"Don't worry," he assured her. "We've got it under control."

But when the doors slid open on the seventh floor everything was not under control. One of the waiting mob of reporters clamped the gate shut, ruining their chance of retreat. The television crew moved in, backing them further into the elevator compartment.

It was the first time Ronnie had ever been genuinely frightened by the press. A sense of overpowering physical exhaustion made her eyes blurry, but she could clearly see Anthony Trendau grinning at her. His once long hair was now reduced to a mod clip and he was wearing a blue blazer with a gold WABZ logo on the breast pocket, but he was still the same old Trendau, arrogant and cocksure.

He pointed a microphone at her as his cameraman jockeyed for the shot.

"Miss Garrik!" The fist in her heart tightened. "Your mentor, John Lloyd Talbot of Liberty Records, was tonight arrested on a variety of charges, one of which was intent to distribute a controlled substance, namely *cocaine,*" Trendau gave the word an amusing twist designed to draw chuckles from his hip young audience. "Talbot has also been accused of trying to bribe certain members of the Golden Disc Academy. In other words, Mr. Talbot *allegedly*"—the way he pronounced the word there was nothing alleged about it—"conspired to extort the awards you supposedly won tonight. Do you have any comment?"

Gustave pushed forward. "Ronnie is feeling ill. She doesn't know any—"

But Anthony Trendau elbowed Jade out of the way while one of his crew blocked Zach Curtis. He punched the microphone at Ronnie's chin, missing by eighths of an inch.

"A statement, Miss Garrik!"

"Please," said Ronnie. "Please leave me alone."

"Will you voluntarily return the Goldies allegedly procured for you, Miss Garrik?"

She heard Zach roar as he pushed through toward her. He knocked over one of the cameramen who, feet tangled in coaxial cable, fell backward. As he dropped, one flailing hand caught the delicate bodice of her gown, tearing it open. She tried to cover her bared breasts, but it was all she could do to keep the gown from falling below her waist.

Ronnie stood in the glare of lights, exposed, wanting to scream. All she could manage was a pitiful, angry sob.

"Perfect!" Anthony Trendau grinned from ear to ear. "That was absolutely perfect, boys. Wrap it up."

She was sleeping lightly when he turned into the narrow, unmarked road and passed between two stone gates. He saw her eyelids spasm, her lips quivering in a dream, and tried not to imagine what images disturbed her.

He turned his attention to the long, winding road, which was as beautiful and serene as he remembered, with the big wisteria trees arching over, green with spring buds. Patterns of light and shadow rippled over the pewtered lacquer of the coupe, mirroring the morning sky.

Ronnie woke as he slowed to a stop and set the brake.

"Where are we?"

"Buckhill," he said. "Pennsylvania."

Ronnie tried to squeeze the sleep from her eyes, the bitterness from her tongue. Lolling her head on the cushioned backrest, she caught sight of a brick walkway, verdant topiary hedges, and a stately brick mansion with numerous black shutters.

"Who belongs to this place?" she asked. It was an estate, obviously, but a world apart from the glacially modern Aubade. The discordant dream was already melting from her immediate memory, soothed away by the harmony of landscape.

"Once upon a time it belonged to the DuPonts," said Jade as he pushed open his door and began to stretch his legs. "Now it belongs to two very dear friends of mine."

The proprietors presently appeared through an opening in the dense green hedges. Both of the men were so meticulously groomed as to defy age, but Ronnie guessed they were in their mid-forties. She also guessed, rightly, that they were lovers, had been for many years, and that Daniel, who was wearing jodhpurs and was evidently about to go riding, had once been interested in Jade.

Jonathan, whose neatly trimmed moustache was so blond it

was nearly transparent, managed to kiss her hand without affectation.

"An honor, Miss Garrik." His eyes slid to Jade. "Danny has seen to rooms in the west wing. A light breakfast will be brought in whenever you're ready. I'm assuming you're both absolutely exhausted and have instructed the grounds crew not to fire up any of their dreadful gasoline engines." He smiled, and Ronnie understood his exaggerated courtliness was meant to amuse. "After you've had a nice nap we'll sit down to a proper meal and get absolutely hammered, shall we?"

"I think," whispered Ronnie, as Jade took her arm and led her up the walk toward the mansion, "that this is what the doctor ordered."

For three days she passed into an eerie but elegant limbo. Sleep came long after daybreak. In the afternoon the maid entered on crepe soles and gently adjusted the blinds, allowing the light to make a gradual false dawn across the parquet floors of the spacious white room.

Ronnie lay entwined in satin sheets, stupefied by dreams and bottle-green pills.

In her mind the pills were like encapsuled repetitions of the videotape she had played and replayed that first day at Buckhill. The main salon of their suite overlooked an ivied courtyard and formal garden. After gazing blearily at the scene for a few moments Ronnie had drawn the blinds and muted the interior lights. Jade was on the phone as she poured herself another cognac and took it into the bath, where a steaming Jacuzzi had been drawn for her. She tried to luxuriate in the hot swirling waters, but her thoughts were jagged and ugly. It was only by an effort of will that she refrained from smashing her empty goblet on the tiled floor.

In idle nervousness, and not really wanting to overhear Jade's conversation, she had explored the medicine cabinets. There behind a sampling of designer perfumes she discovered a fist-sized bottle of green gelatin capsules.

Take one as needed for periodic anxiety.

Ronnie took two. They were just beginning to take effect some twenty minutes later when she noticed the Betamax machine. Jade had been reviewing something on it when she exited the bath. Feigning casualness, he tried to steer her away.

"No, darling. Let's get you off to bed." Something in his expression made it necessary to see what was on the machine.

"I'll sleep later," she said. It was hard to keep the petulance from her voice. She began to float in a room tinted bottle green. "Please, I want to see."

By then she had read the label on the cassette and it was essential that she know the truth, even what little truth was likely to be gained from such a dubious source.

With hands that seemed oddly still she pressed a sequence of buttons and the Sony screen began to glow. Jade sighed. He sat beside her on a couch, tapping an unlit cigarette against the back of his hand. On the tube Anthony Trendau was looking directly into the camera.

"Tonight the WABZ Star Watch team went to the lavish corridors of the Sherry Netherland hotel to sneak a peek at recording artist Ronnie Garrik, who earlier this evening was awarded an unprecedented three top Golden Disc Awards."

The backdrop dissolved to the Grand Ballroom. Ronnie stiffened as she saw herself moving through the maze of tables. With spotlights slicing though the airy vault of the upper balconies, the ballroom retained a sense of space and grandeur despite the slightly grainy video reproduction and Trendau's chatty monologue. The tape moved quickly through highlights of the ceremony. As Ronnie watched she seemed to be floating an inch or two above the sofa, observing an event distantly removed in time.

Had it really happened, or had it been fabricated for the late night news? But Anthony Trendau made reality abundantly clear.

". . . whose arrest followed a year-long, deep cover investigation by a Special Vice Squad empowered by Albert DiGaza, the New York City Prosecutor, to uncover drug trafficking in the entertainment industry. Director and producer Steffen Von Ranke, arraigned on similar charges today in Los Angeles, has

accused Talbot of attempting to fix the Golden Disc nominations
by bribing several unnamed members of the academy. Large scale
repercussions are expected in the world of pop music, which
hasn't been rocked by a scandal of this magnitude since the Payola
imbroglio of the late fifties . . ."

Ronnie knew all that and was about to drift off, lulled by the
flickering images and Trendau's carefully modulated voice, when
the scene suddenly switched to a handheld camera. And there it
was again—the elevator besieged by reporters, the urgent posi-
tioning of the cameras and lights. Her own face, blurred and
distorted.

The chaotic sequence of Zach shoving the photographer and
of her sheer gown being torn away, one breast sadly exposed, was
repeated in cruel stop-action.

"*Jesus Christ,*" Jade was saying beside her, his voice tight.
"How did that little prick sneak this by the censors?"

But it wasn't the brief nakedness that bothered her now. It
was the venal expression she saw on her face, so perfectly magnified by the screen. It was a face she hardly recognized. Spoiled,
possessive, lips twisted in shrill denial. Even the cobalt blue eyes
were flat and mean.

"Hey," said Jade softly, brushing tears from her cheek. "Hey
there."

"Hey yourself," she said. She moved into his arms. "Oh,
Jade," she said, watching over his shoulder. "What happened to
me?"

3

Albert DiGaza was a law and order man. He'd made himself the most visible prosecutor the city had seen in more than a decade, and he no longer bothered denying mayoral ambitions. DiGaza was out to slay dragons, particularly the opiated dragons of the drug subculture, which he blamed for much of the incidental crime in the city. His office had been instrumental in the recent purge of Central Park, no longer a haven for junkies. Following a suggestion from his PR staff, he had lately been coming down hard on the glitterati. Busting a celebrity for drug trafficking splashed much larger in the media than rounding up a hundred destitute heroin addicts, and DiGaza was intrigued with a new plan that would make his name a permanent feature on the six o'clock news.

John Lloyd Talbot figured prominently in the plan, and DiGaza was gazing impassively at him while his assistant and a liaison to the precinct drug unit, Lieutenant Metcalf, tried to rattle the recording mogul.

"Come on, Talbot," said the young assistant prosecutor, removing his wire-rimmed glasses and polishing them on the cuff of his shirt, "cut the crap. This isn't Watergate. Nobody is watching you on the tube. So wise up and drop all this 'moral crisis' shit."

Lieutenant Metcalf smirked. The idea of John Lloyd Talbot suffering a self-professed moral crisis was amusing. After months of deep background he thought he knew his man intimately, and morality had never even blipped on his personality profile. Style and charm, perhaps. But not morals.

"I admit I've made a dreadful mistake," said Talbot stiffly. "But I fail to see why I should compound it by doing what you ask. Especially without benefit of attorney."

Pending arraignment, he had come in at DiGaza's request, as much out of curiosity as a desire to appear amenable. Now it was apparent that he should have consulted Berenson, his attorney. He was being set up for something larger than he had bargained for.

"He made a dreadful mistake," mimicked the lieutenant, caricaturing Talbot's Back Bay drawl. "And now he wants his mommy."

John Lloyd blinked, nonplussed. He was attempting to comport himself like a gentleman and it was getting him nothing but snide remarks. He stood up, adjusting the crease in his gabardine trousers. "I can't deal with this man," he said to DiGaza, who was, after all, Yale. "He has an animus I find intolerable."

"What'd he say?" Lieutenant Metcalf rubbed the pate of his bald head, frowning at the assistant, who seemed to be amused.

"Okay, John," said DiGaza, speaking for the first time. It was evident that he had decided to take control of the interview. He nodded at his subordinates. "You boys go grab a coffee. Mr. Talbot and I are going to have a little chat."

He waited until the door was pulled shut and then stared levelly at Talbot, who smiled tentatively, determined to keep his temper with a man who was reputedly cunning and pitiless. DiGaza leaned back in his chair, pursing his lips thoughtfully.

"I'm going to lay my cards on the table, John." His tone was reasonable enough, and Talbot tried to make himself relax. "By this time next year I'll be running for office. As a man of certain political talents, you'll understand my position. This is between the two of us. I asked you to leave Berenson out because you may want to keep this quiet. Very quiet."

John Lloyd nodded, waiting. He distrusted DiGaza's immense confidence, and watched warily as the prosecutor sat up and adjusted the rep tie he wore without fail.

"You're a guy got himself in the wrong place at the wrong

time, John. Two years ago you could have beat this with one hand tied behind your back—provided the other was reaching for your wallet. But two years ago I wasn't in this office and let me make it abundantly clear that no one, not even J. Willis Berenson himself, is going to make a deal with me on this." He paused and stabbed a forefinger in the air. "*I* make the deal on this."

Without bothering to ask, a courtesy he usually extended automatically, Talbot took a Cuban cigar from the case in his pocket and fired it up, never once letting his eyes leave DiGaza's.

"We have enough evidence," he thumped the stack of papers on his desk, "to convince even the dumbest jury you're guilty as hell. And once the verdict comes down I'm going to push with everything I've got for maximum. In your case ten years. Maybe your pal Berenson can whittle that down to five, but not a day less, I assure you. So with good behavior you'll be out of Attica in thirty months or so."

Talbot puffed hard, pulling a red glow up the cigar, intensely curious to know what DiGaza was selling him.

"My public relations boys are working out our position now," said the prosecutor affably. "In essence this office will be assuring the public that the rich and famous can no longer buy their way out. That celebrities who traffic in drugs will be treated no better than the poorest black junkie."

Through a haze of blue smoke they both smiled at each other, unwilling to drop the mask.

"The alternative?" asked Talbot finally.

"A victim," said DiGaza, lingering over the word. "I need a victim. Convince me it shouldn't be you and I guarantee a suspended sentence. You'll never spend a day in jail."

The icy ball John Lloyd Talbot had been trying to will away from the pit of his stomach would not melt. He feared imprisonment as another might fear a long, lingering death. He squinted at the green shaded light over DiGaza's desk.

After a while he began to name names.

4

Mr. Brownell resisted the temptation to pinch himself. It would be unseemly for a person of his distinction to do so—and moreover, if it was a dream he didn't care to waken. Not just yet.

"You understand that an estate of this, ah, *type,* is virtually unique, as it were." As he spoke he made one of his careful gestures. Brownell fancied he looked like an Eastern banker, and modified his whole person to that illusion. "A type, shall we say, not immediately disposable. Which is not to imply that the sum you quoted is not equitable." He hardly dared calculate his commission, fearing that greed would show through his thin smile. "No, sir, it is just. Very just. Considering your extensive, ah, *renovations.*"

Kyle observed the agent with bemusement, noting the emphasis on "renovations" rather than the more accurate "fortifications." No doubt he'd been briefed on Hersch's obsession with security and was attempting to acknowledge that without offending a potential client.

A waste of effort. Kyle didn't like Brownell—the man's lifelong toadying to the rich had made him predictably snobbish, a characteristic Kyle loathed above all others. He was, however, prepared to do business with him. Brownell represented the best of the Big Sur agencies, and Kyle's sudden decision to part with Aubade had to be made operational immediately.

"The appraisal report is in my study," he said pleasantly. "This way, please."

The real estate agent smiled weakly and followed him

236

through the vast airy rooms of the estate, casting furtive glances at the manifestations of his unexpected good fortune.

In the study Kyle poured two cups of coffee from an insulated beaker. Brownell leafed through the appraisal. Kyle watched his expression solidify as he examined the subtotals. "Ah, yes," he said. He affected a neat, quick smile and sipped the coffee in little gulps. "All in order. This makes my job that much easier, of course. I'm thinking along the lines of certain, ah, Arabian possibilities. Or perhaps, well, a conference center? Room enough, yes. And of course the existing security provisions lend themselves to—"

"I don't care who buys Aubade, Mr. Brownell."

The agent nodded, returned the saucer adroitly to the tray. "Mmmm. No, of course not, sir. I understand perfectly. Might I ask why you choose to divest at this time?"

"No," said Kyle, not unpleasantly. "You may not."

"Mmmm," said Brownell, his mind clicking like an abacus. "Mmmmm."

Later he thought that divest was not a bad word for what he had in mind. Not a bad word at all.

The decision had been sudden and irrevocable and, he could now plainly see, long overdue. He'd made himself a prisoner of his own obsessions for seven years, and that cycle, like the cycle of his recent depression, had come to an end.

The first glimmer had come to him the night he watched her float across the video screen. The high cheekbones, the full, sensual lips, glistening unreally in the camera lights. Even in the depths of severe depression he recognized the stirrings of desire. An impulse that became, as he watched her, a desire to share himself with her, not only physically, but completely. He was astute enough to realize why she'd kept a distance between them, why she had been so abruptly cruel when he went to visit her in Boston. In that way Ronnie knew him better than he knew himself, he could see that now. He was a man who'd cut himself off from all risk, tried to buy immortality for Louise, and withdrawn from the real world of love and death, pain and pleasure.

Seven years. The number was like an omen from the Kabbala texts his late father had labored over, searching for the mystical answers to the riddle of existence. Kyle had little use for superstition, and yet he seized upon that number as a lever to move himself.

He could not have Ronnie as he was, therefore he must change.

When it came to him, sitting there in the dark, staring morosely at her reflected image on the Advent screen, it was as if his heart turned over and began beating with a new, stronger rhythm.

Change.

Sister word to *chance,* the very thing from which he'd run, and now an idea began to arrive in huge fragments, as if previously scored and perfected in his subconscious: an opera in the grand tradition, yet something utterly new.

His hands gripped the armrests as it flooded into him. He could actually hear the chorus of voices rising through the proscenium of the Met (for that was where he imagined it being staged) rising in triumphant stages, and with them a single, new voice, the voice around which the entire production would be written.

The ideas whirled in a collage of imagery and sound. Once, just once, he had taken LSD, a small square of blotter paper from the Sandoz laboratory. When the drug was peaking, coursing through his brain with electric images, it was not unlike the rush of images he was receiving now, totally undrugged, as sober as the day he was born.

Inspiration. He wanted to laugh, to howl at the word, for he had never understood it before, had never, in his professional career, come close to this feeling.

The images on the Advent became intertwined with his rush of thoughts. Once more the camera dollied in on Ronnie. He saw her rise from the table, heard the cacophony of cheers. The camera cut to a close-up of Jade Gustave, whose eyes were unusually bright. Kyle had always gotten on well with Gustave and he realized, sitting there in his darkened study, that he, too, should have braved the mob, that he belonged there with her.

The announcer was saying, "One very special person . . ."

In the simplest way that summed up what had happened to him, what was still happening to him, and as he rushed to his desk to hurriedly scrawl down the fragments of his idea, which would depend on a mezzosoprano with a unique, extended range, he could see her in his mind's eye and he could hear again the whisper in his head, the whisper of love in a slight, West Texas drawl.

Kyle worked through the night, bringing the songs to life, healing himself anew.

"No, Daddy. I'm not afraid at all. Mr. Nippy lives there and he can teach me everything I need."

"Who?" Kyle stared at his daughter. Her face was framed by a mop of taffy hair that was still baby fine. She was just eight, yet already it seemed she had a private life of her own, a life he did not know.

"Mr. Nippy. Mr. Ellingsworth says he's the *best.*" Louise gave best the same intonation her father did, knowing it would make him laugh. It dawned on him that she was referring to Leopold Niplowski, Rubinstein's famous discovery who was now the grand master of classical technique.

"Did Ellingsworth tell you that?" he asked.

"But I made him tell me, Daddy." Kyle saw the excitement shining in her eyes, and he knew it was not only himself he'd kept prisoner in Aubade. His reflex irritation at her piano teacher vanished. After all, she was a Stavrogin and had her mother's iron will—as well as the Hersch tenacity of purpose. She had the potential to be a great pianist, he'd known that for a long time, and he could no longer deny her the chance. He had wanted to keep her from the stifling world of prodigy; now he saw that he had stifled her in his own way, precisely as he'd stifled himself.

Louise had never known anything but Aubade, and it was

astonishing to Kyle that she was so willing, almost eager, to give it up. She was clearly excited by the idea of going to school with other children, of "making best friends," and he experienced a brief resurgence of dread when he considered how unwittingly he had deprived her of so many of the small pleasures of childhood.

"What's it like, Daddy? Is it like in 'Kojak'?"

"No," he said. He tried to imagine what Manhattan would look like through a child's eyes. "Well, maybe a *little* bit like 'Kojak,' but New York is really much more—"

"That's where you and Mommy lived, isn't it?" She gripped his wrist unconsciously. It took a great deal of courage for her to mention the mother she had never known, and who was a living part of her imagination precisely because her father so rarely spoke of her. "And that's where Ronnie lives now, isn't it?"

Kyle sighed. He fought down a lump in his throat, felt the breath wheezing out of him. Louise's perceptions were expanding at lightning speed right in front of him, and although he thought of it joyfully, he wasn't sure how to proceed. He was going to have to get to know her all over again.

"Yes, honey," he began. "You mother and I lived there. And you were born there, too. . . ."

He took her small hands in his and told her the story of a life he had once longed to forget.

5

The ache eased perceptibly when at last she had a destination. The act of going there, of going *anywhere,* was a form of sedation nearly as effective as the bottle-green pills. The 280SL, equipped with the newest in fidelity expanders, pulsed with a deep funk version of Stevie Wonder's "Sir Duke." Ronnie rolled her head from side to side, imagining the singer bobbing over his keyboards.

It was a giddy sensation, being on the road again. Fleeting images of a convertible cruise to Juarez with a handsome, dangerous boy, of endless miles in a white Chevy van, of the diesel throb of a southern touring bus, came and went, flickering with Stevie's indelible beat. Better times, or so they now seemed. Eyes lidded, immersed in the music, she let the downs wash over her like the filtered dreamlight of emerald glasses.

Jonathan and Daniel had been perfect hosts, but the ethereal distance they maintained made Ronnie feel as if she were cased under glass. Under different circumstances she might have welcomed the opportunity to live as they did; to ride from the stables, to volley on the grass courts with Jon or the elegant, sloe-eyed Danny. But as it was she had barely enough energy to wade in the fired-tile pool under the discreet but watchful eyes of the ubiquitous staff of house servants, at least one of whom was never more than a murmur away.

"Will madame take tea?"

"Madame will take a Remy." Her fingers poised on the stem of the dark glasses, hiding her bloodshot eyes. "And a side of soda."

"Immediately, madame."

And so it was. Muddled on pills, she sipped cognac, thinking Jade would find a visible means of intoxification more acceptable than the barbiturates she hid from him. Chivas and reds had, after all, put an end to Kenny, somewhere there in the dim past.

Never happen to me, she thought, never happen with Remy and greens.

Jade Gustave, reserved by nature, seemed more so at Buckhill. This troubled her, though she tried not to let on. He and his two wealthy friends were like three charming brothers of ambiguous and perhaps incestual sexuality. Time was when her curiosity, if not her ardor, would have been aroused. But at the estate, floating in a pool of disjointed thoughts as she sipped her brandy, she did not care. That theirs was a world to which she would never be privy failed even slightly to rile her.

Once, crossing the terrace in the early evening, when the greenies seemed to have endowed her with an extraordinary equilibrium, she stumbled and fell. Ronnie thought no one had noticed, but Jade was there by her side, helping her up.

"Ronnie," his voice was low as he guided her into the cool interior, "are you okay?"

"No," she said. "I don't feel right."

"You've got to lay off the booze, darling. Do you want a doctor?"

They were sitting knee to knee in the deep cushions of a velveteen divan. Jade waved away a butler, who retreated as if pulled by string on a base of wheels. The thought of being probed and questioned by a doctor, who would surely reveal the secret of her pills, tightened the knot in her chest. She shook her head violently.

"What *do* you want?" he asked. "Can I help?"

The answer came effortlessly, as if it had been hovering just beyond words for the last three days.

"I want," she said. "To go home."

An hour later the Mercedes was packed. Jonathan saw them off; nothing in his manner acknowledged the haste with which they were leaving.

"It has been a pleasure and an honor," he told her, bending to brush her cheek. Crossing to the driver's side he murmured something to Jade, clasped him about the shoulders, then stood to one side as the engine started.

Minutes later they were rolling down 81, heading south into Virginia. The slow southern heat began to thaw the icy center of her mind. They worked themselves into the rhythm of the road, and after a while the old intimacy returned; Jade and Ronnie against the world.

Jade, reflecting on his own tainted past, remembered the ugly incident that had forced his voluntary exile to Europe, an incident similarly engineered by John Lloyd Talbot. He decided to share it with Ronnie. When he slowly eased the stereo volume down Ronnie turned to him as if she thought he was going to scold her for her sullen behavior at Buckhill.

Taking his eyes from the road for a moment, he kissed her full on the lips and felt them tremble beneath his. A lump formed in his throat, but he bore down. It was essential he maintain control for her sake.

"Ronnie, look at me." Her tear-burned eyes blinked, trying to focus. "You earned those awards, darling. John Lloyd didn't *need* to bribe anyone, Ronnie. You were a shoo-in from the beginning. The damn fool has been trying to fix horse races since he was in knee pants and he was in the habit, that's all."

"I hate him," she said, taking a deep, shuddering breath. "Oh, he made me look like such a fool, Jade. I felt like I was back in high school being made fun of because I didn't know what was coming down."

Jade straightened the coupe into the right-hand lane.

"Look," he said, "it's a waste of time hating John Lloyd. Believe me, I know." He paused, trying to clarify his thoughts before going on. "Forget about Talbot, Ronnie, and remember one very important fact. No matter what happens, and I can't promise it won't be rough for a while, they can't take away your voice. They can't take away who you are and what you did."

Ronnie covered her face, hating herself for blubbering yet again, but the tears came of themselves.

"The worst of it is how badly it gets blown out of proportion," he continued. "Hell, you should have been around in the month of September 1959, when those vultures started tearing *me* apart. I thought I was going to disintegrate, or turn into a pillar of salt, or maybe just have an old-fashioned heart attack. I felt so terribly dirty, you know? And that was the same old John Lloyd Talbot."

Jade remembered a small detail suddenly. He cracked a grin and slapped one hand against the dash.

"Hell, *that* was a Mercedes coupe, too, now that I think of it. The wheel of fortune goes round and round, do you agree? Ronnie? Just say yes because it pleases me, darling."

"Yes," she managed.

"Right. Well, time passes. Two years later I had a nice little cottage in Sainte Max—I still do, for that matter. Pretty boys on the beach, and pretty girls, too," he laughed, filing away a memory he was not about to share with anyone. "Once I visited an opium den in Marseilles. I saw Picasso eating snails in Fernado's. Oh, I wouldn't trade those two years away for anything. Then, wouldn't you know, our friend Mr. Talbot had the nerve to ring me up and offer me a job with Liberty. And a good thing he did, or I'd never have had the thrill of finding you. Of seeing you make it, darling."

"I'm not so sure I have."

"What? Come *on*, Ronnie. This is just an interlude. Three, four months tops and this whole Goldie thing will blow over. Like it never happened."

But he could see she wasn't buying it. Jade realized that what was killing Ronnie was not so much losing the Goldies as being publicly embarrassed. Part of her was still fighting a battle begun in adolescence; being humiliated by Anthony Trendau and the other media hawks was a terrible loss of self-esteem.

A cruiser passed, sirens bleating. It jolted her into momentary sobriety.

"I guess I'm being stupid," she said. "I mean, what am I worried about? I've still got lots of money, right?"

"Lots," he said. "Lots and lots. I saw your quarterly return.

And for that matter I very much doubt this will affect *Shooting Star.* If anything it will boost retail sales."

"So I'm almost as rich as those guys at Buckhill?"

"Almost," he agreed. "Believe me, money is the least of your worries."

He laughed at the absurdity of John Lloyd Talbot trying to amass more money when his fortune was already sufficient to last a lifetime. Ronnie, watching his profile, saw his grass-court tan creased by a smile, and glimpsed his true age. It made her love him all the more, made him more valuable to her than any Goldie could have been.

He was still laughing. It began to build inside her, fluttering like wings until she, too, was laughing, rocking back and forth. Finally she was able to find the words she wanted.

"Baby," she said. "This is going to make you laugh harder, maybe. But tonight you sleep with me."

Gustave looked at her curiously, the smile subsiding. Her head was thrown back submissively. Her throat curved up, soft and inviting, as her dark mane of hair undulated in the warm air.

"Okay," he said gravely. "You're on."

They crossed the brown Mississippi at Memphis and were heading west on 40, toward Little Rock, when another siren overtook them on a deserted stretch of the Saint Francis National Forest. This time the flashing lights did not pass and Jade, frowning, pulled over.

In the twilight the forest stirred sluggishly, branches ruffling in the hot breeze. They waited silently as a burly Arkansas trooper unfolded himself from his cruiser and plodded toward them. He got down on one knee, level with the low-slung sports car.

"License and registration, please," he drawled cordially. He studiously avoided looking at Ronnie, who immediately suspected she had been recognized.

"You're Mr. Gustave?"

"Yes," said Jade. "What's the trouble?"

"No trouble, suh. But we have an APB on this vehicle. Y'all

follow me into Little Rock, Mr. Gustave."

"I suppose I have to?" he asked wearily. They had been on the road for twelve hours and he was stiff with fatigue.

"Yes, suh," said the trooper, tipping his hat. "You do."

It was dark when they got to the Little Rock barracks. An agent from the Federal Drug Enforcement Administration was waiting for them. He was a slender man with silver-rimmed spectacles and a paperhanger's mustache. He was so exceedingly polite he terrified Ronnie. As he explained the problem the barracks began to fill with state troopers pretending they had business there. Several of them eyed Ronnie boldly.

"We have a bench warrant issued in New York," said the agent to Jade. "Ordinarily you would be booked here, released on bond sometime tomorrow, and then either fight or waive extradition at a hearing sometime next week."

"The alternative?" Jade's voice was tight, but his anger seemed to be directed elsewhere. "And what are the charges, by the way?"

"The alternative, if you agree, is that you accompany me on the next commercial flight to New York. You'll be booked and released there on personal recognizance and have access to your own attorney. As to the charges . . ."

"Well?"

"Conspiracy." The agent cleared his throat, as if not quite comfortable with the word. "You've been named as a conspirator and material witness to the procurement and dispersal of a controlled drug."

"That damned cocaine of Talbot's?"

"Yes."

"Who named me?"

The agent, rather than reply, smiled tentatively at Ronnie, implying the arrest was all in a day's work, nothing personal.

"Who?" insisted Jade.

"That's not for me to say, Mr. Gustave. All I'm empowered to do is convey you to New York if you so choose, or oversee your arraignment here in Little Rock, if you insist."

"Jade, this is crazy!" Her husky voice broke. "These people are crazy!"

"No," he said. "But I was crazy not to expect it."

"But you didn't *do* anything."

"No. But I know who did, and that is what this is all about."

The agent nodded solemnly. It was then that Ronnie realized Jade was actually going to be taken from her in Little Rock, Arkansas, five hundred miles from home. One of the troopers offered to take her to the airport, but the thought of being confined in a compartment full of inquisitive fellow passengers terrified her.

She wanted the anonymity of the road, and she wanted Jade Gustave beside her, as he had always been.

"I'm sorry, Ronnie," he said. "Give me a rain check on our date?"

"Will you be okay?" She embraced him as he sat at a gray metal desk, waiting for the paper work to be processed.

"I'll be fine," he said. "It's you I'm worried about. You sure you want to drive alone?"

"If I can't have you, yes."

"Look, darling. Maybe you better get while the getting's good. Somebody's sure to tip the papers, sooner or later."

Ronnie caressed his thick mop of silvery hair, unmindful of the lascivious stares of the file clerk or the nonplussed government agent.

"You've got your rain check," she whispered. "In spades."

"Darling, good luck," he said. "And be nice to the coupe."

Ronnie left by the side door, ignoring the dozen or so troopers idly waiting there, and went out into the night. But, as Jade had warned, someone had tipped the UPI stringer, who was snapping a plate into an old Graflex just as Ronnie came out. The bulb exploded, leaving two silver spots in front of her eyes.

"Hey!" The reporter was a young woman dressed in chic jump suit more suitable to Manhattan than Arkansas. "Hey, Ronnie Garrik!"

She jammed another bulb into the flash and tried to cut

Ronnie off at the car by blocking the driver's side door.

"Hey, Ronnie, I mean Miss Garrik." The reporter was bug-eyed at the prospect of filing a hot item, and obviously not an experienced interviewer of celebrities. "I mean, what happened in there? Do you have a statement?"

She got off one more shot before Ronnie yanked open the door. The reporter, tottering on sharp-heeled boots, tried to brace herself in the open window. The Graflex thumped from her shoulder strap.

"Ronnie, please! Do you have a statement?"

Ronnie got the keys in on the third try. Much to her surprise, for she had never driven the coupe, it started immediately. She pried the reporter's fingers from the window jamb.

"This is my statement," she said. "Are you listening? Are you ready?"

The reporter dropped the camera and flipped open a steno pad.

"Fuck you," said Ronnie Garrik. "Fuck *everybody.*"

At four in the morning a dusty brown cab with Oklahoma plates tentatively approached a neighborhood on the outskirts of Lubbock, Texas. The thin wash of headlights dipped to and fro, then slowed to a crawl. Finally the cab turned into the driveway of a one-story farmhouse. In the pool of yellow light a dilapidated porch seemed to leap out of the night.

The driver got out, spat on the ground, and stretched. Then he tapped the back window. A few minutes later it rolled down.

"You awake?" asked the driver. "Saw the name on the mail-box. This the right place?"

He sounded reproachful, as if he expected the family of Ronnie Garrik to inhabit a much more lavish homestead. Ronnie didn't bother answering. After another minute or two she emerged from the cab. Her pants were twisted around her legs, evidence of fitful sleep, and her blouse was wrinkled and buttoned up wrong. She stood in the yard, staring at the porch, at the glider still there with the upholstery coming undone. The sight of that ruined glider made her want to cry.

"Lady," said the driver. "That was some long ride."

"Yeah." She took a roll of bills out of her purse and counted into his open palm. "Five hundred. And don't forget a hundred of that is to forget you drove me here. Don't go calling any newspapers. Please?"

"Sure, Ronnie," said the driver. "I can tell my pals, can't I?"

"Tell 'em whatever you like. But no papers. No television."

"Right. How about that little car? You want me to get it towed away or something?"

Jade's 280SL was now embracing a telephone pole in Clinton, Oklahoma. How she had managed to do that without suffering a scratch was something that would never be clear to her. She'd fallen asleep and woken up on the grass beside the steaming wreck.

"Leave it be," she said. "I'm going to pretend it didn't happen for a while."

"Anything you say." They stood in the driveway. The house was dark. "Can I come in for a drink or something?"

"No," she said. "You can't come in for a drink or something."

The driver, who hadn't expected her to go along with it, got back into his idling cab. It didn't matter. By the time he cleared the driveway he was already perfecting the lies he would tell his pals in Clinton, Oklahoma.

The door opened at her touch, but the house was empty.

"Jack?" she whispered hoarsely. "Daddy?"

Her father's chair was where it always had been. As she crossed to it the back of her neck tingled, spooked by memories. The only new thing in the sitting room was the stereo system she'd shipped back home to Jack. A pair of Lansings big enough to shake glass from the windows crouched like monoliths under the mantle.

The amp lights were on, and there was an album on the turntable. It was a copy of *Shooting Star*, much played from the look of it. She smiled, shaking her head. Hadn't they had enough of that one yet? How could they stand to hear it, now that it had been played to death?

She poured a glass of her father's whiskey, started the turntable, and lay down on the rug between the speakers. She knew the songs by heart and soul. She heard Kenny again, alive and exuberant as he tripped through the beat. And Paul Stokey picking the licks that were engraved in her memory as the Okie brothers filled in with just the right touch. Her own voice, coming boldly through the scratched grooves, was young and unspoiled. Hearing her voice depressed her, but she hadn't the will to get up and turn it off. The whiskey began to work, taking her dizzily down.

Muted daylight filled the room when a face from a dream hovered over her, speaking her name. At first she thought her father had returned in youth, his eyes clear, his face unlined.

"Ronnie," her brother asked, waking her, "is it really you?"

6

"You aren't serious?" she asked, searching his face.

But Jack shook his head, denying her. He was exhausted and his drawl was even slower and more pronounced than usual. "No," he said, "I wouldn't kid about nothin' like this. It happened the night you was on television. I been tryin' to get a holt of you ever since, but . . . ."

Ronnie stared at him, scarcely believing how much her brother had changed in the last few years; physically he was a man, raw-boned and large. "But what happened exactly?" she asked.

"Well, me and him was watching you." Jack shoved his hands in his pockets, his eyes cast down as he spoke. "I wanted to go on up there to New York and see it for real like you asked, Ron, but Daddy wouldn't have none of it. He kind of believed he might be an embarrassment somehow."

"Jack."

"Yeah, well. Anyhow, he got all worked up when they come on with that shit—'scuze me, Sis—about the Goldies bein' faked and all." He eyed the empty bottle of whiskey on the rug where she'd slept. "Fact is he was drinkin' pretty heavy. I thought he just up and passed out, but then he started breathin' kind of funny and I called the ambulance. He ain't woke up since." He paused, his eyes shining. "They say he ain't going to."

"Jack, can we go over there right now?"

"Well, I just got back," he drawled, rubbing a hand across his chin, using a gesture inherited from his father. "But hell yes,

251

I'll take you, Ron. Jes let me splash some cold water on my face."

The clothes she'd left behind were still hanging in her bedroom closet. She was surprised to discover that her once favorite flower-print sundress still fit, more or less. Wearing it, the intervening years seemed less substantial.

As they made small talk on the drive downtown she kept marveling at her new discovery: a grown brother, a real *person* now. She wondered what he must think of her. For years she had been a voice on the telephone, a gift in the mail. Was she real to him? Did he remember climbing up on the barrel to spy on her; the time she dyed her hair?

Little questions to fend off the larger one waiting at the hospital.

The dark glasses and the cheap sundress worked for a little while, as Ronnie and her brother hurried anonymously through the lime green halls, but when Jack gave his name at the Intensive Care desk the nurse looked at Ronnie and squeaked, "Oh! It's you!" before issuing passes. Throughout the duration of their visit a constant stream of interns and nurses casually ambled by for a look. One or two asked for autographs and were rebuffed by Jack.

But Ronnie wasn't aware of the invasion of privacy, or the stir she was creating. She hadn't known what to expect, had been buoyed by the hope that her brother was exaggerating the seriousness of her father's condition. In fact he had understated it. But for the name affixed to the cardiac monitor she wouldn't have recognized him. Larry Garrik's face had already taken on the pallor of death. His lidded eyes were deep set and still and the blue oxygen tube taped to his nostrils whistled in a cruel parody of breath. His jaw and mouth hung limp, revealing the tobacco-stained teeth of an old man.

Ronnie kissed his forehead. She put her lips to his ear and whispered, but he remained as unresponsive as an inanimate object.

"He's gone, isn't he, Jack?"

The sense of loss was so suddenly numbing that the tears

dried in her eyes. A doctor who looked absurdly young took her aside. He explained, in careful layman's terms, the devastation of cerebral hemorrhage.

"Your father has a strong heart," he said gently, "but the brain wave is flat."

"You mean he's already dead, don't you?" she asked, her voice as flat as the feeble electrical impulse he'd just described.

"That's not for us to say, Miss Garrik. Right now we still have a heartbeat, however faint."

"How long?" she asked, watching the barely discernible worm of light on the cardiac monitor.

The doctor shrugged with the special gesture common to his profession.

"Not long," he said, "not long at all."

Jack took care of the arrangements. His stoic presence was a comfort, and as Ronnie backslid into downers and sipping whiskey, it was as if he were the elder of the two. He didn't admonish the drinking, or suspect the pills, but she knew he disapproved of her sluggish behavior.

"Jack, honey," she told him when the numbness made conversation possible again. "This isn't really me. It's just so much happened all at once."

"That's awright, Sis. You just lean on me here awhile."

They tried to keep the ceremony private, but by the time the motorcade left the chapel it was jammed with cars and pickup trucks, many driven by people who had never known Larry Garrik. Jack didn't mind—he said his father would have admired a big send-off—but the quiet mob of strangers at the cemetery frightened Ronnie. At any moment she expected Anthony Trendau to come barging through and shove a microphone at her, demanding she atone for her father's death.

The dust sent up by the motorcade was suspended over the Methodist burying ground, unstirred by the motionless air. Before getting out of the limousine, the cool, darkened interior of which was infinitely preferable to the sun-drenched cemetery, Ronnie opened her purse and counted the pills remaining in her stash. Seven. Enough to get her through.

"Come on, Sis," said Jack, helping her from the limo. "Let's get this over and done."

She turned away from the myriad cameras. None of these people had given a damn for Larry Garrik when he lived, except to pester him about his daughter's indiscretions, and now they continued to use him. Ronnie felt an ugliness welling like bile and fought to keep it down. What they wanted was a scene. She was determined not to give them one.

Ronnie was staring off into space, aching for it to be over, when she saw the woman in the straw sunbonnet. She was a dark woman, partially obscured by the crowd on the opposite side of the grave, but a section of her face was visible beneath the old-fashioned bonnet. Big eyes, piercing blue, and the high cheek-bone signal of Native American blood.

Ronnie tried to get Jack's attention, but he had his chin tucked down, his hands folded in prayer as the casket was being lowered. The minister was murmuring and heat rose from the open earth.

"Jack," she hissed when the last flower had been strewn, "see that woman over there?"

But the ranks had closed and the straw bonnet was gone. Ronnie was about to admit to hallucination when suddenly it was visible again, moving rapidly away. She left Jack conferring with the minister and began to follow it.

The greenies were full upon her, slowing time down and blurring the faces of those who moved toward her, calling her by name. Her feet were enmeshed in taffy. It was a great effort to pull free and run over the trampled grass, her ears ringing with dull, sonorous chimes. She fought through the hands that reached, tendrillike, as she was buffeted by pleas for her signature. Tombstone by tombstone she moved, ignoring strangers who hawked invented memories of growing up with Ronnie G., the Shooting Star.

"Later," she whispered, "later, please," as she followed the tantalizing bonnet that moved like a butterfly just beyond reach. The whiskey and greenies mingled, making the air the consistency of warm honey, as slowly she gained on the slim figure in the wrap-around skirt that brushed the grass as it swayed away.

The words rose up Ronnie's throat, ticking like bubbles as they spilled from her lips.

"Mae Ann!" she cried. "Momma, it's me!"

The straw brim tilted, turning toward her, but in that dark face there was not a glimmer of recognition. The blue eyes were not of Ronnie's blood and never had been. Moreover, in her imagined recognition Ronnie had neglected to account for time. The woman under the bonnet was at least twenty years younger than Mae Ann would have been.

The woman smiled tentatively, speaking with a lilting Spanish accent. Ronnie turned and ran, calling out for her brother as the mob closed in.

She was okay until Jade called. At the sound of his voice Ronnie's glassy green shell began to crack.

"Oh, baby." The tears staunched at the funeral began to flow freely. "Can you come right away?"

There was a hollow silence on the line, and then the distant whine of a jet engine.

"Ronnie," he said at last, "I'm afraid that's impossible. I'm leaving, darling. I'm going back to Sainte Max. For good this time."

"I don't get it." Her tongue was thick, cleaving to the roof of her mouth. "I mean why?"

"I'll write you a long letter and explain everything, darling. But basically I'm getting out. They tell me I can beat this thing, but it means two years or so of pretrial hearings, appeals, etcetera etcetera. In other words, my life is in hock to a bunch of lawyers." Ronnie listened, gripping the phone with trembling hands. "So," he continued, trying to make light of it, "I'm taking an early retirement. Going on the lam, as Mr. Bogart once said. I mean Roman Polanski makes a perfectly good life for himself without setting foot in the U.S. of A., why not Jade Gustave?"

"But baby, I *need* you. There gotta be five hundred reporters outside the door right now."

Actually, most of the crowd was comprised of curiosity seekers, but Ronnie was fixated on the media and the blank eyes of the cameras that seemed, in her stupor, to be sucking out her soul, shot by shot. Jack, to appease her, had gone into the city to see about hiring security guards. Through a slat in the drawn blind she could see the sheriff's cruiser and the one deputy who was managing, by sheer bravado, to keep the swelling mob on the opposite side of the driveway.

"Jade?" she asked. "Are you coming, baby?"

There was another awkward silence on the line. The sound of his breath was so distinct he might have been there in the room with her.

"Ronnie, I'm sorry. I'm sorry about your dad and I'm sorry about those damn Goldies, but there's nothing I can do about it."

He paused and she could hear his fingers drumming the receiver. "You're a hell of a lot stronger than you think, Ronnie. Damn it, you're a heck of a lot tougher than *I* am, when it comes right down to it. Listen, darling," he said, forcing levity into his tone, "I must be off before I start sounding like a Dale Carnegie pitchman. My flight is boarding, Ronnie. Tell me you wish me well?"

She did as he asked. Then she took the four remaining capsules and washed them down with a slug of whiskey directly from the bottle. After a while she felt the renewed stirrings of chemical well-being. If only there was a way to keep that delicate balance, neither rising nor falling, neither insensible nor trembling with raw nerve endings.

That was Kenny's mistake, she told herself, he didn't find the balance point. She returned to her father's chair, cradling the bottle in her lap, convinced she had discovered a basic truth. The downs softened her memory of the sullen, spoiled face looming from countless television screens. They erased the frozen curse the UPI stringer had captured just before Ronnie drove off to ruin

Jade's perfect little car. They enveloped the clawing mob scene at the cemetery in a dreamlike haze so dense her father's death lost meaning.

Nothing mattered. Nothing at all.

She heard the squeak of wood and saw the window moving upward, but at first it did not register. With uncaring, glassy eyes she saw the black camera appear on the windowsill. A pale hand adjusted the stiletto lens. The motorized advance began to click off shot after shot of Ronnie Garrik posed insensibly on a ratty leather chair, a demolished whiskey bottle propped between her legs, looking more like a white trash slattern than the season's hottest ride to pop stardom.

It was only after the photographer exhausted his film that she was able to summon enough energy to slam the window shut. The rattle of glass brought her to full consciousness. A rush of adrenaline made her acutely aware of what had just happened and how it would be made to look on the network news and in next week's *People* magazine.

An idea formed and congealed at once as she staggered into her brother's room and lifted one of his shotguns from the rack.

The floor tilted like the deck of a slowly heaving ship, but she was determined to remain standing until her plan was carried out. She cracked the chamber and with meticulous, stoned patience slipped a shell into the breech.

"Slime," she said, repeating the word because it pleased her. "They're all slime."

Ronnie was breathing heavily through her nose, her pupils contracted to pinpoints when she kicked open the porch door and stood swaying in the harsh sunlight.

Someone in the driveway spotted her.

"Rrrroonneeeeeee!"

The name whipped at her, distorted and enlarged. But she moved forward, pressing into the shout as if it were a hot desert wind, until it was no more than an indistinguishable roaring in her ears.

"Rrrrronnnnnnnn . . ."

She was unable to focus up a single face from what seemed a multitude, but the sun refracting off camera lenses enraged her. She planted both bare feet firmly in the dirt and leveled the shotgun. The thought, clear in her mind, came out jumbled and confused when she spoke.

"Texas! Understand me? Was born here. Mine." But they did not understand. Ronnie sensed that as the blurry mass writhed before her. The deputy sheriff, sidling toward her, stopped dead as the gun jerked in his direction. "My home! I was *born* here. Now get thefugout! GET THE FUCK OUT!"

Ronnie raised the stock to her shoulder and squeezed the trigger, as long ago her father taught her. The explosion of the recoil knocked her backward into the still, black hole of unconsciousness.

7

Zachary Curtis turned left onto Fifty-fifth Street and was mugged by an errant gust of wind. His favorite panama hat somersaulted into the rush of air and landed with a distinct plop! in the gutter. He leaned over the curb and inspected it sadly. Gonzo, he thought, and left it there.

A taxi slowed. The driver rolled down his window and shouted, "Hey man! I dig you, baby!"

Zach assembled his best showtime smile, waved, and walked on. The taxi cruised along at his pace as the driver waved and smiled and shouted.

" 'Astral Jive,' man! That tune got it, know? Slow samba, dig? What I mean, you need bongos, man, I *got* bongos. I'm the Mongo Santamaria of bongos, man, *comprende?*"

For all Zach knew the young driver was a certified genius on the bongos, but he had other rhythms going in his head right then and he kept walking, smiling at the driver but not answering. When he came to the portico of the hotel he waved. The driver tooted his horn goodnaturedly and sped off, wheels smoking. That put a scowl on the pasty face of the St. Regis majordomo, or whatever the hell he was.

"Morning, General," said Zach, tipping an invisible hat.

"Morning, suh," replied the doorman, staring down a nose that would have done justice to an Afghan hound.

Zach entered the lobby with mixed feelings. Once upon a time it had been his refuge in the city. The dazzling, posh interior had a way of intimidating even the most brazen groupies, and it

259

was he who had recommended the place to Ronnie when she elected, rather suddenly as he recalled, to move to Manhattan. Although the old hotel was not guilty of perfidy, it was evidently not the sanctuary he'd imagined it to be.

He hurried passed the concessions, in no mood for the obligatory repartee with the attendants, all of whom knew him by name, and took one of the bronze-sheathed elevators up. A slight sense of claustrophobia rose with him, and he remembered the scuffle at the Sherry that night the whole thing came down. Barely two weeks had passed, but it seemed eons. Strange how life rolled along more or less uneventfully, only to have the conflicts and tragedies of a decade compressed into a few days.

The door opened to his shave-and-a-hair-cut and he was face to face with Kyle Hersch. The two men shook hands solemnly.

"Come in, come in. How have you been, Zachary?"

"I've been better." He turned his hands palm up and tried a real smile. "I've also been worse." He followed Kyle into the main part of the suite, where they found a self-contained bar on a rolling cart. Zach built himself a Glenlivet and tried to mask his incredulity as Hersch, not a drinker by any means, followed suit. "Louise?" He asked, tipping his head toward the piano trills emanating from the adjacent room. Kyle nodded, sipping the scotch.

"Let me ask you this," said Zach. "How in the name of God's dirty white sneakers do you keep up with her?"

Zach considered himself a better than average pianist with a high flash quotient, and he realized Louise was light years beyond him.

"I don't," said Kyle, a little sadly. Then he brightened. "And I don't want to. Niplowski has agreed to take her on."

Zach pushed his dropped jaw back in place, his eyes drawn to the practice room, where Louise was playing Sibelius with professional ease. "Gee whiz," he said, lapsing into the argot of his Mormon childhood. "Niplowski, huh?"

They drank in silence for a few beats, neither of them eager to broach the subject of Zach's visit.

"So how is she?" asked Kyle finally.

"Okay," said Zach. "I think."

"What happened exactly? I only know what I saw on the tube."

Zach followed Kyle to a pair of window seats overlooking Fifth Avenue. The shades had been drawn, but he glimpsed part of the sidewalk, the cars crawling like gleaming beetles in the high-noon traffic.

"Well . . ." he ventured. Zach's relationship to Kyle had never gone beyond cordiality, and it bothered him to proceed on such an intimate level. "I was in Austin for a one-night gig. I get this garbled message from some cat named Jack Garrik. Didn't click until the rumors started flying—you know how roadies are. And then it flashed who Jack was. I called him back myself."

He took a slow sip of the scotch.

"Go on," said Kyle.

"Yeah, well he tells me Ronnie is in a bad way. Messed up on booze. He'd found a bottle of scrip downers in her purse, empty. The brother wasn't there when it all came down, but apparently she got tanked up pretty good and fired a shotgun at a mess of people who followed her home from her daddy's funeral. Lucky for Ronnie she fired high. Maybe that was what she had in mind—she doesn't remember much of it now."

"I see," said Kyle. "I didn't know she was on the stuff."

"I think it was a new thing. I'd swear she was clean the night of the Goldies." He couldn't help staring at the composer. He never thought to see the day when Kyle Hersch, temperant recluse, would be seated opposite him in the dead center of New York City, inhaling straight Scotch. "Anyhow," he continued, "I left the boys in Austin and hightailed it to Lubbock. Poor brother Jack was a wreck. But he has a level head, I'll give him that. After all the trouble Ronnie had, the kid didn't want to make it worse by putting her in the hospital, so he hired a doctor and a couple of nurses to keep an eye on her."

"Coma?"

"Nah. She wasn't *that* high. Just tanked up. When ol' Ronnie came to she had one hell of a headache, let me tell you. She was embarrassed as hell, of course."

"Where is she now?" he asked, trying to make it an idle question. Zach knew better.

"Well, I promised to keep a lid on this, but I don't think she'd mind you knowing, Kyle. Ronnie's up in the Sunveil Wilderness, in a cabin of mine."

"Alone?"

Zach nodded. "She wanted it that way." He cleared his throat, fidgeted. "Years ago we, ah, spent a few days up there together. I've hardly been there since I bought it and figured it was the least I could do to let Ronnie crash there for a while."

"What are her plans?"

"I don't think she has any. I know she wants to be alone, to try and sort things out. She was very quiet about it, really. The poor kid has been through a lot in the last couple of weeks."

Kyle nodded gravely. "That she has," he said.

"You seen John Lloyd?"

"No. Just talked to his mouthpiece, Berenson. They're denying everything, of course."

"I'd like to talk to the motherfucker," said Zach ruthlessly. He tempered his voice, aware of Louise in the next room. "I'd like to start the conversation with a baseball bat for openers, and then move on to heavy artillery."

"He doesn't matter now. What matters is Ronnie."

Zach gazed at him, taken aback by the passion in his voice. He didn't know Hersch beyond the usual professional contacts, the studio work. He thought of him as totally reserved, almost heartless, obsessed with himself—above all, impossible to know intimately. But now Zachary thought he was catching a glimpse of the real Hersch, of the man who had been the wunderkid of Broadway. When the rumor surfaced that Hersch was picking up stakes in California and returning to New York with some kind of immense, unrealized project in mind—a modern opera, no less —Zach dismissed it as utterly impossible. Seeing the evidence of it right before his eyes made him wonder how much of it was due to Ronnie Garrik. He was no psychologist, but even he saw the irony of her deciding to enter seclusion just as Kyle exited.

The composer was looking intently at him, eyes bright and moist, as if trying to suck out Zachary's thoughts. Maybe he did, a little.

"I wanted to be here when she returned," he said. "That's why—" he indicated the luxuriant suite, which Zach knew was just one floor below Ronnie's. "I'm looking for a place near Niplowski's studio, of course, on the West Side. But that may take some time. And for now, well . . ."

He didn't need to finish and Zach waved him off. What sort of reunion had Kyle imagined, he wondered? Certainly it had not included Ronnie's sudden fall from grace, or the flood of publicity generated by Talbot's arrest.

"You know, it's funny," Kyle was saying, "how quick things change."

Just then he heard a patter of light feet and Louise came into the room. Taller than he remembered, and in place of the little girl smile was a look nearly as somber as her father's.

"Hello, Zachary."

"Hi, Louise." Jesus, in a couple of years she was going to be all there, he thought, a full-blown beauty. Hersch would have his hands full trying to rein her back. Eerily, Zach recalled a picture he'd seen of Natalya, and he saw the mother's image like a translucent, beguiling ghost inhabiting the same space as Louise.

The moment was poignant enough so that the scotch worked deep into his bones, warming him. Far below, from the crowded street, a horn honked angrily.

"Daddy," the girl asked gravely, "is Ronnie okay?"

Kyle reached out and swept her into his arms. He looked over her shoulder at Zach, his eyes bright.

"Yes, honey," he said, "Ronnie is going to be fine. Just fine."

It amused her to name the flowers on the mountaintop. The meadow in the clearing was all the world she cared to explore, and it was enough to identify and name the beautiful *Aquilegia canadensis,* the wild columbine.

When Zach suggested the cabin up in the Sunveil she had seized on the idea at once. Jack, for all that he enjoyed seeing his famous sister, raised no objection to her leaving so suddenly. Perhaps the unrelenting presence of the media, steadily building day by day, bothered him more than he was willing to admit.

In any event, Ronnie came and went, a natural phenomenon like a summer storm that was briefly endured, recalled in highlight after it was gone.

For Zach it was an excuse to fly his new Cherokee, as well as a chance to renew his ever-casual relationship with Ronnie. She wasn't particularly responsive and he didn't push. From the Cherokee they transferred to a 4×4 Jeep he kept at the airstrip. After a brief stop for provisions, they took the long washboard road up to Shadow Peak.

The last mile was a steeply elevated foot-path, and Ronnie, weakened by her bout with barbiturates, was almost weeping from exhaustion by the time they got to the meadow of wildflowers.

Zach unslung his shoulder pack and dropped it to the grass.

"Sure you don't want company?" he asked. "I'm a good bedwarmer, honest."

Ronnie was tempted. She liked Zach, but the whole point of the exercise, as she kept reminding herself on the flight over the Rockies, was to go it alone. Left to herself she might be able to find the strength Jade mentioned in that last call before he left. It was the only part of the conversation she clearly remembered, and Ronnie clung to it.

She had to erase the spoiled face that had lately become her own. It was that or return to the twilight limbo of the green bottle.

"Thanks, Zach," she said, hoisting the pack up to test the weight. "But no."

He shrugged cheerfully and left her there in the meadow. As the top of his hat descended over the false horizon of the trail she almost broke and ran after him, for the solitude was instantaneous and unnerving. Even in the relative loneliness of Malibu there had been Didi, hovering over her like a slightly scatterbrained nurse.

Now she was, for the first time, completely on her own.

Zach had left the cabin pretty much as she remembered it, with the exception of installing a large library of cassettes and paperbacks and a gasoline generator to power the stereo. Ronnie smiled; Zach Curtis, transported suddenly to the moon, would find some way to have music there. As to the spinet piano, she wondered how he'd gotten *that* up the steep trail.

The liquor cabinet was well stocked. Ronnie left the latch on. The strongest beverage she intended to let pass her lips was Rocky Mountain spring water. That she drank gallons of, sitting at the edge of the spring, her ankles aching with the intense, liquid cold.

It was then she discovered the wild flowers. In the cabin she found a *Field Guide to Wildflowers* still in wrapper, and carried it back to the meadow, determined to identify every leaf and flower there. It was a pleasant distraction from thoughts she wasn't yet ready to confront.

The days passed easily enough. Whenever her mood plummeted she had only to look out over the wilderness, to the sea of mountains jutting off toward what might have been world's end. High clouds moved in majestic pageants, an animated tapestry of

projected daydreams. Something of the first intimations of seren-
ity came to her there, as they had when she first loved Zachary
Curtis, or thought she did.

But at night it was as if sleep had become her enemy. The
small sounds of night were magnified by nerves until each creak
of a tree limb, each breath of wind became an auditory hallucination.

She kept a fire glowing in the great stone fireplace and kept
well within the rosy circle of light. At dawn she slept fitfully,
unable to prevent the intrusion of unwanted thoughts. In half-
sleep, the cabin walls became an extension of her mind, a screen
upon which nightmare images were projected.

Kenny came to her, crazy and wild and full of life. He
brought with him the endless miles from Tucumcari to Abilene,
the crowded intimacy of Stokey's kidney-shaking van. She saw
him grinning behind his glittering cymbals and thought she heard
him say, "We got the world by the tail, Ron, let's get us a piece!"

Her father stumbled in, as he had once in the darkness,
pressing himself to her. She remembered his rough chin burning
hers, the stench of whiskey and tears, his desolation. "You are
your mother," he seemed to be saying, "you flew the coop . . ."
and it was true and it wasn't. Tossing in her troubled sleep she
dreamt of Didi, once a friend, dismissed in a fit of pointless
jealousy.

When she awoke she lay exhausted, trying to clear the jum-
ble of images from her head, wondering who she was. It was as
if she had no connection to someone named Ronnie Garrik.

9

The theater lay in darkness until a shaft of light expanded from pinpoint to circle. The circle moved from the proscenium to center stage and there it remained. Four figures moved from the unlit orchestra into the light.

One of them smiled. The entrance was melodramatic, perhaps, but it was necessary, at the preliminary stage of the project, to play up the Hersch legend. In the transitory world of theater it was the one thing he had going for him.

In the circle of light four canvas chairs were drawn up around a folding card table. Kyle waited while the others took their seats.

Arthur Cohen, his producer from the old days, was dressed as demurely as ever, right down to the crimson silk bow tie and the matching handkerchief in the breast pocket of his Wall Street blue pinstriped suit. From the fob pocket he extracted his father's gold watch. Consulting it was his most noticeable nervous habit, but the cool metal was reassuring, and the movement consistently accurate, as was its owner.

Lester Jacques, whom Kyle did not know, was obviously nervous. A sheen of sweat was forming on his high forehead. He put his rolled-up sketches on the card table, thought better of it, and took them back into his slender hands.

Eve Rothstein, the costume designer, ignored the house rules and lit up a cigarillo, one of the sixty or so she inhaled in the course of a day. She couldn't take her eyes from Kyle, whom she had known as a very young man. Her memory of Natalya was equally sharp and she had been even more surprised than Arthur

267

Cohen when word got out that Hersch was back.

Kyle sat down. He raised his eyes to the level of the balcony, letting himself adjust to the volume of the theater. He'd had to relinquish the idea of using the Metropolitan because of scheduling conflicts, but the Shubert was an admirable replacement. Yes, it would do nicely, once alterations made room for the full symphony orchestra.

"Lester," he began, "show us what you've got."

Lester Jacques, small-boned and pale, bore a slight resemblance to Joel Grey. He had a similar economy of movement, a sense of restrained energy. Jacques was young, most of his work had been Off Broadway and regional theaters, but he had an original, impetuous style Hersch thought might work.

As he unfurled his sketches, smoothing them, the sight of his finely rendered drawings helped relieve his tension. It was the best he could do, and he knew it.

Arthur Cohen harumphed. Eve Rothstein puffed her black cigarillo, squinting against the smoke, her face a network of fine wrinkles. Kyle shoved his hands in his pockets, looking over the tiny designer's shoulders as he shuffled the pages. Now it was Hersch's turn to feel a tingling of belly nerves, the prelude to excitement.

"I like it," he said finally. Coming from the laconic composer it meant pronounced enthusiasm, although Jacques didn't know that. "When can I see a model?"

"Six days. I'm screening the color chart now, making adjustments to tungsten. A lot will depend on the lights."

"Arthur?" Kyle turned to his old friend.

"Don't ask me yet, Kyle." The producer shrugged. "I'll have to see it up."

The designer, sensing Cohen's resistance, spoke quickly, tripping the words out. "The effect is meant to be operatic, Mr. Cohen. Think of *La Forza del Destino,* or *La Traviata,* or—"

"I've never produced an opera," interrupted Cohen. "Nor have you, to my knowledge, designed one."

"Arthur, don't be a *putz,*" said Eve Rothstein. "Who cares

what he did before? This stuff is gorgeous. Look at the way he's used these columns of light. This is architecture, Arthur, not set design. The costumes, I think, must appear translucent extensions of that light."

This elicited another harumph! from the producer. Hersch smiled. Arthur hadn't changed. Still skeptical of artist's jargon, still critical in the early stages; undoubtedly still enthusiastic and supportive once the thing had actually begun. Cohen had been producing theater on Broadway all his life, as had his father before him.

This time out his initial resistance was hardly surprising. He had never staged anything remotely like what Kyle was proposing.

"Aubade," said Kyle, eyeing the three of them back to their seats, "is not really an opera. We'll be using certain operatic devices, but the music itself owes more to spirituals and southern blues than it does to opera. So let's keep that in mind."

"Got a question," said Arthur. His hands were folded in his lap, his half-moon bifocals down on the bridge of his nose. "Who directs?"

Cohen knew the answer, but wanted Kyle to speak it aloud.

"I direct," he said. "I'll need choreography, of course. I've already spoken to Byron Keane. He's interested."

Eve Rothstein tittered, spit out a little bubble of smoke. "Of course he is. Who wouldn't be?"

Kyle ignored the compliment. He was staring out to where the orchestra would be, trying to imagine the dynamics of sound. It would be lush, he decided, and crisp, if Jacques's scenery worked as a deflector. They'd have to bring in an acoustics expert, no getting around that. There would be the inevitable problems, reassessments, compromises. Incredible preparation.

"The rehearsal halls, Arthur? We need space, lots of it."

"Got it," said the producer. "But it will cost you plenty."

"Who's casting?" asked Eve, feigning idleness. With the Hersch name behind it, fed by the tight theatrical grapevine, they would be swamped.

"Weintraub," said the producer. "He's retained counsel,

Kyle. There may be union troubles. They'll have trouble pegging this one. *Unions.*" Cohen used the word like a curse, and to him it was. He remembered the days when . . . but never mind when. There had been nothing like this way back when, either.

Kyle ordered the lights up. He and Lester Jacques paced off the stage, sizing the set, while Kyle explained, sotto voce, the changes he would require in the design. Cohen, watching, felt a resurgence of the paternal pride he'd taken in Hersch years before. He watched Eve Rothstein feeding off young Lester's visions.

So it begins, he thought. And who knew how it would end? Sold out, if Kyle's magic was still there, a smash. And in this case, though he'd not quite grasped the idea Hersch still had locked in his voluminous compositions, it had a chance of being a classic.

"You're smoking too much," he said to Eve.

"Shut up," she said pleasantly, without looking up. "You worry too much."

"My job. Tell me, Eve, do you think he's changed?"

She put down her pencil, purposely blew smoke toward him, biding a little time before she replied. "Haven't we all, Arthur? You think you haven't, but look in the mirror."

"I'm not talking about the bags under my eyes, Eve."

"Nor am I. I mean the mirror of your soul, you old fuddy-duddy."

Cohen stared at her imperiously, his nostrils tensing at the smoke. "I am not," he insisted, "an old fuddy-duddy. And where did you come up with an antique phrase like that, anyway? I'm simply wondering if he still has it. I can't tell from reading the music, you know. I have to hear it. I have to see it."

Eve was observing Kyle and Lester, who were conversing animatedly in the far corner, pointing to the as yet imaginary shapes of their now mutual idea. "Oh, he has it," she said quietly. "It's the two of us I'm wondering about, Arthur. Are *we* up to it? There will be controversy, false starts, the whole bit. It won't come easy, not this one."

Arthur Cohen chuckled, gazing at her with affection. "So

what's new?" That part of the business he knew best; the troubles that had to be fixed. "One more question, Eve. Is he in love again?"

"Don't be a fool," she said, returning to her sketch pad. "Of course he is."

It was a brisk walk from the theater to Cohen's West Forty-third Street office. A spring breeze freshened the air, and with the heat rising from the pavement and the sun brightening the flat, urban colors, Kyle could not help but think again of that secluded cabin on the mountaintop. What was she thinking, there alone? And yet even such somber thoughts as that could not spoil the excitement of actually starting to make real the idea contained in his two hundred odd pages of score and libretto.

He linked arms with Arthur and Eve and Lester Jacques, knowing they were brimming with questions they had not yet the courage to ask. But it could wait. Time enough.

A. Cohen & Son was on the third floor, no elevator, and Kyle was surprised by the speed with which the sixty-year-old Cohen tripped up the steps.

"You didn't need to shave the first time you came here, Hersch." Arthur pushed open the paneled door, clicked his heels in a mock bow.

It was like being swept into a memory. With the exception of a few additional black framed photographs of Arthur in his standard celebrity greeting pose, nothing had changed. The massive mahogany desk, supposedly shipped over from Vienna. The humidor of Havanas only Arthur knew how to open. The gun metal blue filing cabinets. The old office model Underwood that had belonged to Arthur's first secretary, now Mrs. Naomi Cohen. The coppered umbrella stand with the umbrellas the producer forced you to take on a rainy day and then called up looking for six months later, demanding the return immediately. The secretary was new, of course, but she had the familiar dazed look, and no doubt she was already looking for another job because Arthur was impossible to work for, always had been.

"I'll call for sandwiches," said Arthur. "Forget soup, it's cold by the time it gets here."

Kyle went over scheduling with the two designers while they ate corned beef on rye, drank black coffee, smoked enough cigarettes and cigarillos so that Arthur complained and opened a window—no surprise.

"Bad for the air bags, my children," he said darkly. A few minutes later he surreptitiously removed one of his precious Havanas and set about the complicated business of firing it up.

"Okay, here we are," Kyle was saying. He had the production calendar unfurled on the floor; there wasn't room on the desk. "Ten days from now we see Lester's model, right? Hire another assistant if you think it's warranted. Pay no attention to Arthur rumbling about money, okay? And Eve will have sketches when? Two weeks after that? And Lester, light effects to scale, please."

"What is he building here," interrupted Cohen, peering down from his desk, "a set model or a Fabergé egg?"

"Ignore that man, Lester. Be Fabergé. And after we go over that you'll start on a full scale mock-up. I want to see how it moves, if the depth is right."

"Kyle, please." Cohen sounded genuinely disturbed. "The expense. We'll have to lease more space for a mock-up."

"So lease it."

Eve Rothstein observed these interactions bemusedly. Cohen was going to have his hands full keeping the cost of this one down. She was no accountant, but at a rough guess *Aubade* would be right up there, perhaps the most expensive and lavishly staged musical ever. She knew it was her chance to make a life statement by contributing costume designs that were as lyrical and expressive as Hersch's orchestration was sure to be.

"In ninety days we begin casting. First dancers, then chorus. If the final transcriptions are ready, and I guess they'd better be, I'll begin rehearsing the orchestra. Key parts—kettle drums, harps, synthesizer. Then we'll cast the soloists. You'll be building the set by mid-July, Lester. It will have to be done in parts and assembled later. Eve will have her designs thrashed out, and we'll start to tech the lights."

"Soloists," said Cohen, punctuating with the blunt end of the Havana. "Who you got in mind?"

Kyle looked up from the calendar. "Depends. I'm trying for Tucker, or Leontyne Price if she's free."

"Free," muttered Arthur Cohen, "is a word I like. But it does not apply to those two . . . What about the big star, this 'Voice' you got in the script which I still don't understand much of."

"TBA," said Kyle, avoiding Arthur's eyes.

"A surprise," said Cohen enigmatically, "that is *not.*"

When the two designers were gone, bearing the first of their many checks, the producer took Hersch aside. "Okay, you had your fun today. Now let's talk private." He glanced reproachfully at his hopelessly overworked secretary and closed the door, diminishing the racket of the frantic typewriter. "Kyle, dear boy, you got me worried."

"If it's the money, Arthur—"

"Of course it's the money. What else? Listen to me, this is nuts. Nobody finances his own show in this town. Is not done, *capisce?* And for you it is most certainly not necessary. Know how many calls I got wanting in? All because of this rumor Hersch is back with something big. They want in, Kyle!" The Havana jabbed the air as Arthur grinned, delighted at the idea. "They're calling on me, which is how it should be but mostly it isn't."

"Arthur, please don't let's worry about the money thing. I'm a very wealthy man."

"So *stay* wealthy." He placed the cigar reverently in a cut-glass ashtray. "Look. Kyle. I know you got worries about your friend who's got troubles. I'll say no more on that score. Not my business. But the show *is* my business." He put up a hand, palm out, dipping his chin as he peered up over the bifocals. "I know, you don't like calling it a 'show' because that makes it common, but what else can I call it when I've been in the business so long? Show, schmo, whatever—it's the investment I'm talking. I add it up this way and that way, Kyle, and it keeps coming up the same, give or take a few hundred thou. Four, almost five million before the doors open. So you're wealthy? I believe it, but why risk all of it? Makes no sense with the angels I got begging to let them in, they don't care what it is so long as it's Hersch, Hersch, Hersch."

Kyle was pacing the office. The question of outside investors was crucial, and he'd given it a lot of thought.

"I want to call the shots, Arthur, all of them. No compromises with a block of financiers, no waiting for the attorneys to litigate approval. No angels this time. My money and my way, final."

"It's a terrible risk," said Cohen, taking up the cigar once more. "Terrible. For a guy who don't gamble, what a chance you take."

"Exactly," said Kyle, his eyes sparkling. "That is it exactly."

10

She had been on the mountain for exactly twenty-eight days when someone spoke her name. At first she thought it was an echo from her imagination, or from the mountain itself.

"Ronnie?" said a figure dark against the sunlit doorway. "May I come in?"

The figure came tentatively into the cabin and she moved toward him. Her voice, untested for weeks, sounded strangely detached as she asked, "Kyle? Is that you?" Her limbs were stiff with surprise, but that did not prevent her from embracing him.

An embrace from which she withdrew immediately.

"How did you know?" she asked. "Did Zach—"

"Don't be angry, Ronnie. I had to see you."

"I'm not angry, Kyle. Just surprised. This is a long way from Big Sur."

He laughed. A much more natural and relaxed Kyle Hersch carefully placed a thick manila file on the mantle over the stone fireplace, then turned to her. "I'll explain this later," he said, tapping the file, "but first let me tell you why it's a long way from New York, not Big Sur."

She allowed him to guide her out of the cabin and into the bright meadow.

They talked for hours, until the sky began to darken along the blue-ridged mountains. For the normally reticent Kyle it was an act of willful abrogation, for he was, by his very presence, denying the quiet, withdrawn composer she had first met in the

275

Los Angeles recording studios. He was, he tried to explain, a man who had drawn a veil of mourning over his life after his wife's death. Now he had cast it loose, and he was celebrating that act and wanted Ronnie to share it with him.

It was too sudden an intrusion into her own private world.

"And how is your little girl?" she asked to deflect him. Formerly an integral part of his conversations, he had managed not to mention her thus far.

"Louise is doing great," he said. He told Ronnie about Niplowski and the probability that Louise would, in two years time, debut professionally. "I'm still worried about it," he admitted. "But she doesn't seem the least perturbed, so who am I to interfere?"

They returned to the cabin as twilight settled in. Kyle, circling the mantel like a shark who stalked a particularly desirable fish, began to describe his latest project.

"I brought the manuscript up here because I respect your opinion, musically," he said. "You needn't make a commitment. Just read it."

"Commitment?"

"Well, to be honest there's a part for you," he admitted. "If you want it."

She stared at him, her mood darkening, as if keyed to the fading light. "Kyle, I'd rather be buried alive in a nest of red ants than go back to New York and make myself the target of every snide critic in town. I won't sign up for *that* sideshow. I won't!"

"Fine," he said calmly. "Just read it when you get the chance. That's all I ask."

As she stood there mutely he studied her, committing her to memory, comparing her with the woman he'd taken to Aubade; a laughing, purposely distant woman. Her face was slightly thinner now, the fine facial structure more pronounced. Her thick hair was, for the first time since he'd known her, unstyled, and traced with wisps of sunbleached auburn. Her once perfect hands were engrained with lines of dirt from Zach's hopelessly overgrown garden, but somehow that made her all the more attractive to him.

"Kyle," she said softly. "I've got something to tell you."

He waited expectantly, wondering what it was that could possibly trouble her so.

"I lost it," she said. "I lost the pendant."

"Don't worry about it, darling."

"But I *do,*" she said, close to tears for the first time in two weeks. "I do worry. I don't know what the hell I did with it. It was there and then it wasn't."

Kyle leaned closer and cuffed her gently on the chin, determined to shake her from the mood. "Garrik, listen up. Forget the little stuff, please?"

She nodded. Kyle was right, of course. The pendant wasn't important, anymore than the Goldies were, but it was so terribly hard to let them go, to admit she had lost her way.

"Kyle," she said, so low he leaned even closer, so near to her she could feel the heat of his body. "I think you'd better go now."

"Sure," he said. "Consider me gone."

But there was nothing temporary about his kiss, or the way his hands caressed her supple back through the thin flannel of her blouse. She did not resist; neither, at first, did she respond. Sex had hardly crossed her mind in the last weeks. The pills had stifled her natural drive, the solitude had buried it even deeper. But now the heat returned with a suddenness that made Ronnie feel she had been betrayed by her own body.

She who had been seeking control lost all the ground gained in one long kiss.

She allowed him to carry her to the unmade bed, to ease the denim shorts from her hips, the frayed flannel blouse from her shoulders. She wanted to tell him they must wait, that this was not how it was supposed to happen, but her breath was coming too fast to speak.

"It's been so long," he said, pressing his lips to her breasts. "So long."

She arched under him, pulling him into her.

When the last muscle tremor had shuddered through her thighs she rolled away, hiding her face from his. She felt ugly and dirty, and it wasn't supposed to be that way, not with Kyle.

"Ronnie?" She flinched away as he tried to touch her. "Ronnie, what's wrong?"

"I don't know." She lay curled up, knees against her breasts, face to the pillow. "I'm not ready, Kyle. Not yet. Please go away."

His reply was as gentle as his lovemaking had been. "Ronnie, darling, I didn't expect this to happen anymore than you did. Can't you see it was just—"

"Please." She made her voice as cold as she knew how. "Just forget about me, okay? Go away and forget about me."

He looked at her naked back, memorizing every inch of her, then began to silently dress. Out of the corner of her eyes she saw him tuck in his shirt, pull on his windbreaker.

Before leaving he bent down, gently parted her hair, and put his lips to her ear.

"I can't forget you. No matter what," he said. "I love you, Ronnie."

The cabin was totally dark when she stumbled to the liquor cabinet, kicked up the latch with the palm of her hand, and reached in for a bottle. Any bottle. Naked, she cradled the bottle as carefully as a nursing baby and began to search for a box of matches. Eventually a kerosene lamp glowed to life and her nostrils filled with the acrid smell of it.

She carried the lamp and the bottle over to the couch and put the lamp at her feet. The low circle of flickering light made the shadows jump and quiver.

"Bastard," she said aloud. But it wasn't Kyle who was a bastard, she knew that. She broke the seal on the bottle cap, twisting it off.

What had possessed her to send him away like that? Was it because he had been dominating her thoughts these last few weeks, because showing up in the flesh had spoiled her fantasy of returning to Aubade? Or was it just another example of her talent for ruining anything that had a chance of success?

Ronnie inhaled the alcohol fumes. Her eyes watered. She lifted the bottle to her lips and drank.

I want to get drunk enough to fall off this goddamned mountain, she thought. She opened her throat and let the fiery liquid pour in.

When the bottle was two-thirds empty she dropped it, choking, and crawled from the circle of light. For the second time that evening her body rebelled, and her stomach emptied itself. The spasms continued until there was nothing left to come up and she was gasping, trying to catch her breath.

She crawled back to the couch. Kyle, she thought, could you love me like *this?*

Her sudden impulse to get blackout drunk had passed. She kicked the empty bottle with a bare foot and heard it break. Then she stretched out on the couch and tried to sleep. But anxiety gripped her like a low-grade fever, and because she thought it might distract her from the confusion in her heart, Ronnie got up and took Kyle's manila file from the mantel.

Inside was a manuscript neatly secured with thick rubber bands, and a cassette in a plastic sleeve. Putting the cassette aside for the moment, she opened the manuscript and began to read.

At first she skimmed offhandedly, unable to really focus on the words, on the voluminous stage directions, all rather mysterious to her. Under the listing of principal parts she noticed *The Voice* underlined in red ink. No subtlety there, no question about what part Kyle meant for her.

There were sketches showing the placement of a symphony orchestra and two choirs and a few soaring musical notations in his fine hand, but the manuscript was essentially a story. It slowly dawned on her as she read that *Aubade* was meant to be surrealistic, dreamlike.

Ronnie knew the power of dreams. It was a dream she followed when first she took that lonely bus from Lubbock. And it had been the failure of one that brought her to this cabin in the night.

Anxiety forgotten, she read with increasing interest, recalling the rocking spirituals she'd first sung in the church choir. Kyle's musical was hardly religious, but it evoked the same joy of self-discovery.

She was able to picture it, as the stage became real, the

dream her own. She found herself humming, wondering what it would be like to sing against a full symphony orchestra, or enter into the give and take with two choirs of eighty strong voices.

Choir of angels, he had named one of them. The terminology was strange, and yet it made sense musically as she recognized the transcendence of spirit and song Kyle was daring into existence.

Despite her increasing enthusiasm, Ronnie was perceptive enough to see what Kyle saw, and what Arthur Cohen feared: *Aubade* risked failure. It might, by the sheer weight of ambition, collapse if the production was less than flawless. The line between grandeur and grotesque was a fine one indeed.

Ronnie paced the cabin, the manuscript open in her hands.

How had he known her so well? How was it that Kyle Hersch made animate the song in her heart? It was as if they'd both dipped into the same pool of dreams and emerged as one.

Despite her sense of discovery, she was plagued with doubt. Did she have the stuff for it? She'd been born with the vocal power and volume, but could she evoke the delicate sense of wonder, as the story demanded? Did she, as Kyle obviously did, have the guts to put herself on the line again, maybe to fail?

So obsessed was she with finding out if she still had the talent that she was scarcely aware of her surroundings. She quite forgot she was alone in a cabin in the dark, pacing in the cool mountain air.

The cassette. Suddenly she had to know what was on it. She put it in Zach's deck, flipped on the power switch, and pressed the play button.

An unadorned piano filled the room with the sound of Hersch's overture. The structure was classical, but highly melodic, and Ronnie began to nod to the rhythm. The theme built, carrying her forward, and she was startled to hear a voice singing along.

Her voice.

She stopped, pressed her lips together, and tried to concentrate on what Kyle was doing, but it was useless to resist singing to such a persuasive melody. What the particular lyrics were she did not know, but in her mind's eye—and she smiled to think of him—she saw Mr. Jacobsen of the Methodist choir, baton raised, his kindly eyes on hers.

"With panache," he seemed to be saying, "sopranos sing like bells."

Then he would strike the piano top with the flat of his hand, setting the beat as she sang with a glad heart,

> *Sister Mary had-a but one child*
> *born in Beth-le-hem*

It worked, it melded with Kyle's theme, and once started Ronnie was loathe to stop. She sang with her eyes closed, cradling hands over her naked breasts, her body glowing in the light of the kerosene lamp. She opened up, using her voice to catch the beat and rhythm, letting it carry her, as if on wings, into the choir of invisible angels.

> *Oh Lord, she rocked Him in a wear-ry land*
> *Rocked him in a wear-ry land.*

Epilogue

He knew what he had to do, and the very idea made him feel distinctly ill.

Anthony Trendau put his head in his hands and leaned forward in his seat, trying to ignore the jubilant crowd exiting the Shubert. Smiling faces and laughing voices whirled like visions from a nightmare.

A fact little publicized about his sudden rise in broadcasting was that he had been sober since that awful incident in Los Angeles, when the then unknown Ronnie Garrik had mortified him, the very same incident that had preceded his dismissal from *Rock Steady.* Eighteen months of enforced sobriety for the first time in his adult life. And now he wanted a drink, a desire as strong as anything he had ever experienced. But he was due back at the studio in ninety minutes, where he was expected to review the premiere of *Aubade,* or suffer the consequences.

Trendau took a deep breath and stood up. The old theater was still ringing with applause, at least in his imagination, although the mezzanine was by now two-thirds empty. Already the word would be spreading through the night spots of Manhattan, as those lucky enough to get tickets for the premiere gloated over their good fortune.

Trendau removed his sunglasses, looked balefully at the twin mirrors, and then calmly crushed them underfoot.

It was time for a change.

On stage the last magical set, an almost hallucinatory composition of mirrors and shafts of light, stood like a tribute to Lester

Jacques, who had designed it, to Kyle Hersch, who had inspired it, and to Ronnie Garrik, who made it sing with unmistakable clarity.

He would have to use words very like that when he made his review, and although the idea of praising *her* on network television made his belly tighten and the sweat start to build, he had no choice. The audience reaction had been stupendous, and even Trendau had been moved though he had wanted, with all his will, to loathe the thing. But in this, finally, he could not dissent. The sea of music and ideas Hersch and Garrik had caused to break through the Shubert could not be denied, and if he was fool enough to try it his career would be again destroyed.

Grinding the lenses of his trademark glasses to dust under his heel, he made a decision. And when the theater was finally empty he stood up, squared his shoulders, and moved deliberately toward the backstage rooms, where a celebration was about to take place.

It was time to pay his respect.